MISSING NANCY

Carolyn Lewis

Published by Accent Press Ltd – 2008

ISBN 9781906125073

Printed and bound in the UK

Cover Design by Devil's Kitchen

For Brian

With grateful thanks
to Rob Middlehurst

No one knows I talk to my dead grandmother. It's not the sort of thing you say to people. She always said that she'd keep an eye on me and I prefer that to the way Mum says she's watching me. Even when Mum's reading a book, she says she can still see what I'm doing.

Grandad's not dead and, although I'd told him that we were going on holiday, I wanted Grandma to know too. I thought if they both knew, that would be double the protection. A sort of extra insurance.

I guess Grandma was keeping an eye on us because the holiday started off OK. Mum got the car on the ferry, she didn't get us lost or join the wrong queue or any of those things that can go wrong but I just knew the holiday would be rubbish. For a start we looked different, other cars had roof-racks, they had bikes on proper carriers on the backs of their cars; we had nothing like that, we didn't even have a GB sticker. We didn't have the right camping gear either although Mum had scrounged a Camping Gaz stove and some tatty old saucepans from a neighbour. She had bought new tents, though. They'd been marked down in price because the man said they were last year's stock.

'Even a child could put these up,' the salesman told her. He wasn't looking at me when he said it, he was looking at Mum. She didn't notice, she just stood there twiddling with her hair, sucking at the ends of it.

My brother, he's only a baby, was in his pushchair. He didn't know why we were in that camping showroom listening to the rain thundering down on the corrugated roof. I did, I knew. I knew why we were buying two out-of-season tents. My mother, her name's Nina, she was taking us to France. Taking me and my brother. She was going there to find herself. That's what she said; she kept on saying it too.

'I need to find myself, I'm lost in all this somehow.'

I didn't think she was lost, I could always find her, but she does seem to have lost a lot. First of all my dad left, he left a long time ago when I was four, just a kid really. I'm nearly twelve now. Then there was another bloke, Steven something, but he left her too. Then after him Dan came to stay with us. Daniel, he had long hair and a Volkswagen Beetle. He's the baby's father and it was his idea to call the kid Sebastian.

Mum lost Daniel too. He came back from the pub one Saturday and told Mum he was leaving. He said that she was 'too bogged down with things, useless things'.

I've no idea what he meant by that. I don't think Mum did either but we watched him pack up his boxes of CDs, a bin-liner full of shoes, two old suitcases and a pile of books. Seemed to me that for a bloke who thought things were useless he had more *things* than my mum. The only thing he didn't take was Sebastian: he left him in his pushchair with Mum. She cried for days after Dan left. She'd come downstairs every morning with her face all blotchy and her hair sticking up at the back of her head. Daniel left at the beginning of July and I said I'd stay home from school, to help her, I said. I thought she'd like that.

'No, Jonathan, thanks but you must go to school, you can't stay away. I'll be fine. Honestly. I just need to do some thinking, that's all. Don't worry about me.'

She always patted me on the head when she said that, only now I'm nearly as tall as she is and I don't like being patted.

Mum didn't mention Daniel after that but she started to act in a funny way towards Sebastian. Difficult to explain really, he is only a baby, he can crawl and he can pull himself up and stuff, but she sort of stopped *looking* at him, she didn't see him somehow. She'd change his nappy, she did all that, but when she put him in his high chair to feed him, she'd look over his shoulder, staring at something, then the spoon would miss his mouth, it wouldn't go near him. Things like that. Poor kid, he kept turning round to see what Mum was looking at. He knew she wasn't concentrating, even at eleven months he knew. She just stared, not looking at anything really, just staring beyond Sebastian's head. He got fed up, I could see that, then he'd grab the spoon from her and shove it into his Weetabix or banana or whatever he was eating.

It wasn't long after this, just a couple of weeks, when she started talking about taking a trip, the three of us. She kept on saying that too.

'It's only us now, just the three of us. Just me and my two boys, we don't need anybody else.' She started laughing and then asked the baby where he wanted to go. 'Come on, how about France? We can go anywhere we like, we can fly away.' She held him high up in her arms. He dribbled at her and then she asked me.

'Jon, where do you think we should go? France, what about France? Not just the tourist beaches and the cafés, we could go where the French go, see the real France, eat the real food.'

Don't know why she bothered asking me, she'd made up her mind she wanted to go to France.

'Just the three of us,' she said that all the time. Only it wouldn't just be the three of us, I told Grandma all about it too.

Mum works from home. Before their divorce Dad had built an office in our attic. She has a computer up there and a fax and answering machine but she doesn't have her own web site. I think she should, but she's not interested in all that, she said. Mum works as a freelance editor, she reads lots of manuscripts and there's always masses of brown envelopes arriving for her. Sometimes, when she was fed up with work or it just wasn't going well, she'd collect me from school. She said she needed the walk.

I wish she wouldn't do that, wait for me. Sometimes it was OK, seeing her there, we'd go off and collect Sebastian from his playgroup, that bit was all right but she looked funny.

3

Because she works from home, at home her clothes seem normal. Sitting up in the attic, working at her desk, she wears long floaty skirts in bright colours, red or green. If it was cold she'd wear an ancient pair of Dad's jogging trousers, some he'd left behind. They're enormous on her and sometimes she wears a yellow sweatshirt with them. When she wears those things at home, they were just Mum's clothes, I suppose I got used to them. But, standing outside the school, she looked ... I don't know, *different*. The other mothers sat in their cars, listening to the radio or leaning up against the cars talking; hardly anyone walked to school. All those other mums wore jackets with shiny buttons, their shoes had heels. The last time Mum walked up it was a sunny day and she had a long skirt on, so long it almost touched the pavement; she wore old rubber flip-flops and they made a slapping noise against the soles of her feet as she walked.

Perhaps that's what she meant when she kept saying there was just the three of us now. At home it didn't seem there was any difference but, outside, watching the other mothers and listening to my mother's flip-flops going *slap slap* as we walked home, sometimes then I could feel the difference.

Before we went on holiday I asked Mum if Dad knew we were going to France. 'Does he know, in case he phones or something?' He used to ring every Friday night when I could stay up late. I could talk to him then but they'd had a row, him and Mum, over money and now he hadn't phoned for ages.

'No, I haven't told him.' She was reading the paper and watching Sebastian. He was sitting on the potty and eating a biscuit. Didn't seem very hygienic to me but perhaps Mum thought that, by eating on the loo, Sebastian would get the idea faster, you know, in and out in the same session.

'Don't you think we should tell him, just in case?'

'Mm? Yes, OK, you tell him.' She wasn't listening to me, she had her head bent over the paper. Sebastian had finished, or at least he had finished eating and he grinned at me and wiped the chocolate from his hands onto his hair. Mum sighed and grabbed him, carting him off to the kitchen to clean him

4

up.

This was in the last week of school, just before the holidays started. I always spent part of the school holidays with Dad and I wanted to ring him to see if he had planned anything. Just the two of us, him and me. I suppose I wanted to know if I could still see him. Before I had chance to pick up the phone, Mum came charging back into the living room, her face was bright red.

'Don't tell him about the holiday, don't say a word about going to France. For God's sake don't mention it, not a word. He'll want to know where the money is coming from. I told him I was broke and the back door is warped and needs replacing.' Sebastian was yelling so she ran back into the kitchen.

I knew Dad's number by heart. Didn't need to look it up in the green address book on the table. It was nearly 7 o'clock, he would have been back from work. It rang and rang. I knew he wasn't there but I kept on holding the phone and listening. *Brr ... brr ... brr...* The answer machine clicked on.

'Hello, this is Chris Jones. Sorry I can't take your call right now, if you leave your ...'

I put the phone down, I didn't want to talk to the machine, I wanted to talk to Dad.

'What did he say?' Mum was shouting from the kitchen. I could only just hear her above Sebastian's yells, she was giving him a wash in the sink.

'Nothing, he wasn't there.'

'Did you leave a message?'

'What?' I *could* hear her, I didn't want to talk to her about Dad.

'Did you leave ...? Oh, Sebastian, please, I can't hear a word.'

She came back into the living room with Sebastian under one arm and her skirt soaking wet. She held him out to me. 'I've had enough, put him to bed for me please. Did you leave a message for your dad?'

I took Sebastian and mumbled something, something about his machine not working and I took my baby brother upstairs with me. He'd stopped crying by the time we got to his bedroom. His pyjamas were at the foot of his cot, under a pile of dirty clothes. Mum had been wandering around collecting clothes for washing before we had tea. She must have forgotten this lot and just left it all on Sebastian's cot. I put a clean nappy on him, then put his pyjamas on and tidied up his cot. Well, actually all I did was put his dirty clothes out on the landing and then I straightened up his duvet. He grabbed his favourite toy, an old one of mine, Zebedee from the 'Magic Roundabout' and he lay on his back, watching me.

'Go to sleep, go on, go to sleep.' He smiled and chewed on Zebedee's ear. I left him and closed the door. Mum had turned the television on, I could hear it. She was listening to the news on Channel 4. The sound came up to the landing. I didn't want to go downstairs, I didn't know what I wanted to do. I kicked at the pile of clothes on the landing. There were only a few days left before we went on holiday and it didn't seem right to me that Dad didn't know where we were going. We'd got the passports, we all had new clothes. 'Good old plastic,' Mum said. We had two new tents, neighbours were coming in to check the post and feed the cat and Dad didn't know where I was going.

I picked up the pile of dirty clothes and dropped them, one by one, over the banister. They separated as they fell, T-shirts, shorts, socks, little vests, they dropped down, billowing out like parachutes dropping behind enemy lines and landed all over the stairs. I left them there and went into my bedroom.

It was stuffy in my room so I pushed the window open and leaned out. There was no one in the street, it was very hot, everyone must have been in their back gardens. The neighbours were OK, but they were all a bit old and quiet. None of the other kids in school lived in this street; I messed about on the waste ground at the end of the road sometimes and I told Mum that some of the other boys often play with me there, but they don't.

I could hear yelling, some kids were playing football in a back garden. 'Come *on,* what's the matter with you, go any slower and you'll stop.' Must be the woman over the road, she's got two grandsons. Nerds, they are.

I started to kick the wall by the window. My trainer left a black mark on the wallpaper. I wished Dad was here, or at least at his flat.

'   I looked up at the sky, a skinny cloud moved across the sun. I thought of Grandma. I knew she was watching me, she promised she would. I closed my eyes and I whispered, 'Grandma'.

Don't ask me how I know she's listening, I just do.

I leant out a bit further, I thought it would make it easier for her to hear me. There was still a lot of yelling from the nerdy grandkids.

'Guess what, Grandma? We're going to France. It was Mum's idea, she wants to see the real France she says. Don't know what she means by that, how can it be a pretend France?'

The skinny cloud moved away. 'It'll only be us, Mum, Sebastian and me. Mum says it will be an adventure.' My head felt warm, I knew she heard every word.

'That part's all right, Grandma, and I know you'll be watching out for me but I wanted my dad to know too.'

I didn't say anything else for a while, I waited. I tried to rub out the mark on the wallpaper but I only made it worse. The thing is, with this talking I do, I don't need to hear her, it's. enough for me to know that she's listening.

Suddenly I knew, I knew what I should be doing. If I couldn't tell Dad, I could tell Grandad. 'Thanks, Grandma,' I whispered.

I ran downstairs and collected all the clothes lying on the stairs. Mum was still in the living room. She'd opened a bottle of wine and she held a glass up to her cheek, rolling it on her skin as if she was cooling herself. She'd changed channels and was watching 'Eastenders'. I put all the dirty clothes on top of the washing machine; the sink was full of soapy water, the bubbles small and grey and the water was cold.

'Jon? I thought you'd gone out. It's too warm to be indoors, get some fresh air, find a friend ...' She sipped at her glass and held it on her cheek again.

'Can I ring Grandad? I thought he might know where Dad
is, what do you think? Dad might even *be* with Grandad.
Mum? Can I ring him, Mum?'

'Oh, for God's sake, all this fuss about a holiday. Don't
you trust me? We'll be staying together, Jon, the three of us. I
won't go off and leave you, you won't get lost, we'll be
together the whole time. What on earth are you worrying
about?'

I couldn't tell her. I didn't know what I was worrying
about. I just knew that I'd feel better if someone else knew,
someone like Dad or Grandad. Anyway, it had been
Grandma's idea and I couldn't tell Mum that. I shrugged. I
know she hates it when I do that. She didn't say anything for a
while, she just watched me. I didn't look at her, I couldn't. I
kept my eyes on the telly and waited.

She let out an enormous sigh. 'OK, if that's what you
want, if it'll make you feel better, ring your grandfather.' She
looked at her watch, '7.45, he'll be watering the geraniums or
it might be the fuchsias, but he'll be watering something. Go
on, ring him, anything for a bit of peace and quiet.'

I used the phone in the hall. Mum was still watching the
telly but she had changed her position and she wasn't holding
the wine glass any more.

Brr, brr ...'Frank Jones speaking.'

'Grandad! It's me, Jonathan.'

'Who? Jonathan? Oh, it's you lad. How are you? Is
everything all right? You don't normally ring in the evening. I
was just watering the garden before locking up. Are you all
right?'

'Yes, I'm fine. I'm ringing to ask if you know where Dad
is. I can't get hold of him and I want to tell him ...' Mum
suddenly coughed. 'Well, I just want to talk to him really. I
haven't spoken to him for ages.'

'Is that right? Now, let me see, I seem to remember that he
was off on a course or something. I think I've written it down
somewhere. Hang on a moment, lad, I'll have a look ...'

I could hear Grandad rustling papers; his phone was on the

wall in the kitchen and he had a huge calendar above it. Mum always said he was a sad old man, 'What does he want a calendar for? He does the same things every day.'

'Jonathan?' Grandad's voice was loud and I saw Mum move as she heard his voice.

'Yes, Grandad, do you know where Dad is?'

'Yes, I wrote it down. He's in York and won't be back until late Friday. You could ring him on Saturday, what about that, eh?' Grandad sounded so pleased with himself.

'Great, thanks Grandad. Are you all right?'

'Yes, I'm fine. Right as ninepence. Have you broken up from school yet? Keeping yourself busy, are you, out of trouble?'

'Yes, I'm helping Mum with Sebastian, playing around a bit, usual stuff.'

'Your mother, all right is she?' Grandad's voice was different, as if someone had tipped him upside down.

'Yeah, she's fine, do you want to talk to her?'

'No. No, lad, no need to trouble her. Good to talk to you though. I expect you'll be popping around soon to see me, with the holidays and all. Give me a hand in the garden, always plenty to do.'

'No, Grandad, I can't. Well, not for a while.' I was watching Mum, she'd poured herself another glass of wine. 'Eastenders' was nearly finished and she was listening to the programme and not me.

'Grandad, we're going to France.' I didn't mean to say it, at least I don't think I did, but the words came out anyway.

'France? When? How? Who with? Is that bloke back, the one with the hair, whatsisname? Is he going with you?'

'Daniel, no he left ages ago, I told you that. No, it's just me and Mum and Sebastian. Mum says we all need a holiday. We've bought tents and everything. We're going on the ferry on Saturday.'

'Saturday, but that's, what, *this* Saturday?'

'Yes, this weekend. Grandad …?'

'What? Jonathan, are you all right? Tell me, son, is everything all right?'

Mum was still watching the telly, the soap was almost finished, any minute now the music would start. 'Yes, I'm OK, but I wish my dad knew. I'm glad you know, but I want my dad to know too.'

Grandad didn't say anything for a while. I kept my eyes on Mum, I could hear Grandad wheezing over the phone.

'Could you do with some extra pocket money? Would an extra couple of quid help? I could let you have some spending money, how about that?' Shall I pop it over to you before you go, what do you say?' Grandad's voice had dropped, he was almost whispering. My voice dropped too. The music was starting, 'Eastenders' was finished and Mum was looking through the paper again, checking to see what else was on.

'Yes, thanks, Grandad. That'd be great.'

'Leave it to me, lad. We'll sort this out. Goodnight now, God bless …'

I put the phone down just as Mum looked up from the paper, 'All right, Jon? What did the old man say to you? Does he know where your dad is?'

'York, he said, on a course, be back at the weekend.'

'And that's when we leave. Don't look so miserable, I promise you, we'll have a great time.'

I wasn't miserable. I felt better, the holiday would be all right now. Grandad knew about it even if Dad didn't. *Thanks Grandma.*

FRANK

Frank was awake, he'd been awake since 4 o'clock. The amber numbers on the clock radio were showing 6:54. Without moving his head he could see the top of the bedside unit where the mug with his late-night drink stood, next to his watch and a handful of change. He could hear rain attacking the bedroom window. He slowly shifted. The pain was dormant, it was sleeping although he was wide awake.

Frank was breathing slowly, carefully. He didn't want the pain to start. He spoke softly, 'Stupid old man, too frightened to move ...' The radio blipped into life. 7:00, the newsreader's voice rose and fell, making little impression over the sounds of the rain.

Frank gingerly moved his legs then stopped. He knew the pain was there, he saw it sometimes as a shapeless mass, hiding in a dark cave, waiting for him to walk past.

He concentrated on his breathing, the clock radio showed 7:10. He could hear the sound of the rain gushing down the outside pipe and into the drain. The sound of the rain comforted him, it had been raining the day he showed the house to Nancy, before they got married.

'It's not what I had in mind,' she'd said. 'It's square and it looks like all the others in the road, they're all the same.'

'That's *exactly* why we should have it.' Frank told her. 'It's a solid, well-built house, it's a no-nonsense sort of house.'

Trees lined the short street and, over the years, their roots

11

had pushed up slabs on the pavements. Dusty privet hedging, like a dark green, prickly necklace, outlined every garden and was determinedly pruned by each owner.

It had been Frank parents' house; he'd lived there all his life. After their deaths he initially thought of selling it, buying something new but then he'd met Nancy and it seemed that the sheer *solidity* of the house was something he couldn't walk away from. He wanted to prove to her that they could start their lives together here; it would be a foundation for them, they would grow from this house. Fifty-four years ago.

Nancy grew to love the house, in particular the garden, which was protected by a grey stone wall. She tried softening the walls, planting honeysuckle and wisteria; they grew tendrils over the grey stones. Frank had always loved the symmetry, the squareness, the solid feel of the house, its garden protected from neighbouring eyes. Their son, Christopher, had played in the garden, riding his bike around and around, inside the confines of the walls.

Alone in his bedroom, Frank smiled, remembering the early days with Nancy and Christopher. They had wanted three children. 'Two boys and a girl,' they said to each other after they got married. Christopher arrived and they were delighted but there were no more children. They didn't have tests, Frank couldn't remember talking to their doctor about it. People didn't talk about those things then. They just got on with their lives, made the best of things. They didn't have counselling or *therapy*. None of that malarkey. Frank grunted, no need for other people to be involved, that just led to prying and interfering. Best to make do with what you've got. Just a good marriage between two sensible people. He missed Nancy, he talked to her every day.

He moved his legs slowly. He must get out of bed. Frank inched his way towards the edge, the bed was old and sagged in the middle. Nancy used to complain that it made her back ache. 'We need a new mattress, Frank.'

'Nonsense, plenty of life left in this one. This is a proper mattress, not like the rubbish on the market today.' Frank saw no need to get rid of the bed, Christopher had been born in it, Nancy had died in it. It would see him out too.

So far, so good. Frank stood upright and steadied himself against the bedside table. Gingerly he moved one foot, no pain, not a twinge.

He needed to be in control today, he had to see the lad, to see Jonathan. Another hare-brained scheme of that mother of his, going off to France. *France!* She couldn't find her way to the front door.

In his bathroom, Frank turned on the tap in the wash hand basin, water gushed out and Frank hummed tunelessly as he began shaving.

'*This is the eight o'clock news on Friday 26th July.* After turning the radio on, Frank wrote *Jonathan* in his calendar. The rain had stopped, steam rose from the patio slabs.

Very little had changed in the kitchen since Nancy died. The walls were painted a pale cream and Frank re-painted them every year. Each spring he bought a large can of emulsion in *Buttermilk*, grumbling each time about the price increase. He applied white gloss paint to the windows and skirting boards on one day and on the next he painted the kitchen walls. Frank had moved Nancy's pots of fresh herbs, leaving them outside where they withered and died. The garlic and onion sets that hung on the wall he'd thrown away. But he still ate his meals in the kitchen, just as he and Nancy had done together. Each night, before he went to bed, he placed his cutlery, plates and jar of marmalade on the tray. His breakfast was always the same: two rashers of bacon, a poached egg and two slices of toast with marmalade. Nancy's packets of muesli and All Bran had been thrown out.

Frank spread his morning paper on the table and began to cut into his egg as he scanned the headlines, 'Bloody politicians.' The newsreader ended his report as Frank took the first mouthful of a lightly poached egg.

Frank tugged at the garage door, 'Needs a drop of oil.' One more tug and he opened the doors. As sunlight entered the cool gloom, light bounced off the shiny surfaces of the tools that hung in orderly racks alongside the walls of the garage. Frank ran a hand along the bonnet of his Fiesta and he removed the worn blanket from the car's roof.

He slowly backed the Fiesta out, his head swivelling from side to side as he drove it onto the road. Frank sat outside his house, running his eye over the windows, making certain that each one was closed.

He indicated to an empty road that he was about to pull out then he drove the Fiesta towards the woman who used to be his daughter-in-law.

Bad choice. Christopher had chosen the wrong woman. Frank had told Nancy that straight away, right after Christopher had introduced his latest girlfriend to his parents.

'This is Nina,' he'd said, tucking her hand under his elbow. 'We've just got engaged.'

Frank had shaken the girl's hand, *cold, limp thing* and his eyes had gone straight down to her sandalled feet where her toes, under their coat of dark red nail varnish, twinkled in the sunlight. Christopher and Nina hadn't stayed long that first time, just staying for an uncomfortable hour sitting in the back garden looking at the manicured lawn.

'Mousy thing, covered in freckles,' Frank told Nancy after they'd gone. He remembered Nancy saying something about Nina's hair, 'A cloud of hair, all those red curls. I always believed redheads had pale faces because their hair drains all their colour.'

Waiting at traffic lights, Frank gripped the steering wheel, *you'd have something to say about this mess, wouldn't you Nancy?*

He parked the car a few doors away from Nina's house. He sat there for a while, looking at the paintwork on the houses, at the front gardens.

'Those roses haven't been pruned.' He could see Nina's car, the red Clio parked outside No. 24, wind chimes which hung from the porch roof moved gently in the warm air.

Bloody stupid things. Frank looked at his watch, he hadn't mentioned a time to Jonathan, just told him that he'd pop round. It was almost 3 o'clock as Frank got out of his car and locked it. He walked around the Fiesta, tugging at each door. Walking to No. 24, pushing the chimes away with his hand, he rang the bell.

'I'll get it, I'll get it.' He heard Jonathan's voice, then the door was flung open, 'Grandad, Grandad,' Jonathan flung his arms around his grandfather.

Frank patted his grandson, he was bothered by the exuberance of Jonathan's welcome, his hands rested on Jonathan's shoulders then slowly, gently, he straightened his arms, moving Jonathan away from him.

'There, that's better, I can see you now.' He narrowed his eyes, there seemed to be a suspicion of tears in the lad's eyes, what was that all about?

Frank lightly touched Jonathan's hair, 'You're getting taller all the time, soon be as tall as your dad and me ...' He kept up a stream of bland chatter, the words tumbling from him as he tried to understand the atmosphere in the house, something he could detect but not put a name to. From the back of the house a door slammed and a woman's voice said clearly, 'Bugger it.'

Frank raised an eyebrow, Jonathan spoke quickly, 'Mum, she's trying to get the washing done before we go and the machine's playing up again ... Mum?'

He tugged at Frank's arm, Frank stiffened, resisting the tug then he allowed himself to be pulled in Jonathan's wake towards the back of the house where he could see *her,* his son's ex-wife. Her skirt was bunched up around her knees, a laundry basket in her right hand and Sebastian balanced on her left hip.

'Sod the bloody thing! Jon?' Nina half turned, as if she sensed Jonathan. 'Jon, don't stand there, get some towels, this bloody machine's leaking again, Jon!'

Nina turned, the expression on her face rapidly changing as she caught sight of Frank standing behind Jonathan. With one movement, Frank loosened Jonathan's grip on his arm, then he smoothed down the front of his blazer.

'Frank,' Nina's voice was flat.

Frank inclined his head, 'Nina, you're looking well.' *She looks a right mess. Skirt's not fit for dusters and she's got dirty feet.* He saw Jonathan move close to his mother, his eyes fixed on Nina's face. Jonathan spoke softly, 'I'll clean this up, Mum, you put the kettle on.'

Frank saw the gratitude in Nina's eyes. She spoke quickly, 'Let's move out to the back, shall we? I'm sure you'd like to see the garden, Frank, and I can leave Sebastian to crawl around in the sunshine.'

Frank sat on an old garden chair, the brittle struts on the back dug uncomfortably into his spine. The seat of the chair sagged forcing Frank's knees up so they appeared almost parallel to his shoulders. There were no other chairs in the garden, just a faded rug on the lawn.

'Sit here, Grandad,' Jonathan had said before running back into the kitchen. 'I'll be out in a minute.'

Frank heard the sounds of a door opening, the crackle of paper and subdued conversation coming from the kitchen. Sebastian sat on the rug chewing on a piece of apple. The rug was partially covered by toys, plastic bowls and wooden spoons. The baby regarded Frank with an unblinking stare. *That kid's not natural, staring like that. Suppose that's what happens when you've got a name like Sebastian.* Frank was momentarily ashamed of his harsh thoughts, *Sorry Nancy. Not the kid's fault, I know.* He dreaded the thought of getting up from the dilapidated chair.

'Dear God,' he tutted quietly, looking around the garden. Christopher's efforts had been almost obliterated, there was hardly any sign that he'd re-designed and re-built the entire garden not long after moving in. The rockery was overgrown with white *Snow on the Mountain*, tangles of the rumbustuous plant covered the granite stones hand-picked by Chris.

Someone, presumably Nina, had made a half-hearted attempt to weed the beds. A black bin liner, overflowing with dying leaves of bindweed, nettles and dandelions, was near the edge of the lawn, a mud-encrusted trowel lay alongside. Sebastian saw the direction of Frank's gaze and, dropping the piece of apple, he began to crawl towards the bin-liner.

Frank heard raised voices coming from the kitchen, 'What's *he* doing here? What did you tell him?' Nina's voice, steely and controlled, he couldn't hear Jonathan.

Sebastian had reached the bin-liner and his infant hands began to explore the contents. Frank shook his head, 'Not right, little chap might find anything in there, anything at all.'

He tried to get up and couldn't, the angle of the chair making it impossible for him to stand. Sebastian had found a worm, a pinky-brown muddy worm and he turned his head to stare again at Frank, the worm held aloft like a trophy in his plump hands.

'Christ Almighty, he's going to eat it.' Frank twisted and turned, he couldn't move. 'Useless, bloody useless.'

'Jonathan!' he called out, impatience making his voice angry and sharp. 'Jonathan, what are you doing in there? Look at this little lad, where's your mother?'

Nina came running out of the kitchen and, as Sebastian caught sight of his mother, he waved the worm and laughed. Nina reached him, her long skirt fluttering past Frank, and she picked up the baby.

'What have you got there, little man?' She gently prised his fingers apart and the worm dropped to the ground, wriggling away back to the hidden depths of the bin liner.

Dropping a kiss on Sebastian's head, Nina put him back on the rug. She smiled briefly at Frank, 'No harm done, tea coming up any minute.' She returned to the kitchen.

Frank sat back, the chair savagely pinching his skin. He felt awkward and pathetic, 'Shouldn't have come, bad decision,' he muttered crossly and he wondered how he could get out of the chair, leave money for Jonathan and find out what this trip to France was all about before Nina came back into the garden. He tried again, forcing his arms, using them as a lever. He struggled, beads of perspiration forming on his upper lip.

He was still struggling when Jonathan appeared alongside

the chair. Frank sat back, uncomfortably aware that Jonathan must have seen something of his struggle. Glancing up at his grandson's face, he saw that Jonathan's face was suffused, an ugly red coloured his cheeks.

'Tea, Grandad,' Jonathan said unnecessarily, giving Frank a quick smile.

The silence in the garden was broken only by the harsh gulping sound as Frank tried to drink the scaldingly hot tea. He cleared his throat and sipped again. 'So, Jonathan, what's this all about then, this trip to France? When was this decided?

Frank knew he looked ridiculous, his blazer had bunched up around his ears, his trousers had risen exposing his skinny legs and his highly polished brown shoes seemed far too formal for sitting in a garden.

Nina, coming back into the garden, answered Frank's question. 'It was decided last week, Frank. I'd been thinking about it but thought I'd left it too late. Then I made a few phone calls, found a cancellation, someone else's change of plan meant we could make new ones.'

As she moved towards the tray of tea, the fabric of her skirt brushed up against Frank's exposed leg and he shifted slightly, moving away from the gauze-like touch.

Nina's eyes were on Sebastian, who had grown tired of the apple and was busily splashing at water in a red bowl. Her face softened as she watched bubbles of water drop into the bowl. 'I need a break, Frank. Nothing wrong with that surely?' Her tone was light, almost teasing and Jonathan looked up. He chimed in, 'We've got passports, even Sebastian, and Mum's got new tents for us. France, Grandad, I've never been before, it'll be dead good.'

Frank reached out to touch Jonathan's arm. 'Want to give you some money, lad. Buy yourself something for the trip and you can …' his eyes lifted to meet Nina's, he cleared his throat again, 'you can phone me if there's any problem.'

He watched Jonathan turn his head away from his mother, 'Thanks, Grandad, I'd saved up some, I hadn't spent all my Christmas money …I've been washing cars and I've saved all

18

that …' His voice trailed off.

Nina spoke quietly, 'Go and keep an eye on Sebastian for me, Jon, please.' The last word was like a hiss.

Jonathan glared at his mother and Frank saw the way Nina's head jerked.

Grabbing two biscuits Jonathan slumped his way over to the rug. Sebastian saw the biscuits and put out his dimpled arm. 'No, you can't.' Jonathan shoved both biscuits into his mouth and bit hard on the custard creams. Sebastian began to cry, drumming his legs in temper on the rug.

'Jonathan!'

'Yeah, I know, *take him up to bed.*' He picked up the squirming baby and bundled him in his arms, carrying him past Nina and Frank.

They sat in silence, listening to the baby's angry cries coming from upstairs. Nina was sitting cross-legged on one of the patio slabs and she closed her eyes. Irritated by her silence, Frank rattled his teacup and saucer and was gratified when Nina opened her eyes, 'Shall I make fresh tea, Frank? You must be very hot, why don't you take off your jacket, I'm sure you'll feel more comfortable.'

Frank wanted to go home, away from this awful woman and her neglected children and neglected garden. He was hot, uncomfortable and worried. He recognised though that he *had* to see Jonathan again, just to make certain that the lad understood, understood that he must ring, let Frank know if anything was wrong.'

'Yes, thank you, I'd like another cup of tea.' He couldn't take his coat off, just couldn't do that, he'd have to sit in the stifling heat a bit longer. He didn't meet Nina's eyes, 'Just the one more then I'll be off. I want to mow the lawn and I'm sure you must have plenty to do.'

Nina rose, gathering up the tray and she strode into the kitchen, leaving Frank on his own. He realised that Sebastian's cries were growing softer, soon there was silence. Frank drummed his fingers on the arm of his plastic chair.

Nina re-appeared with the tray and busied herself pouring tea for them both and passing a cup to Frank.

'Let's start again, shall we? Just you and me, it might make it easier to talk without the kids. Well, shall we try?'

Frank shifted, he hated having to sit like this, 'Yes, all right.' He took a deep breath then spoke quickly, 'I do want Jonathan to have some money, I'd like to give him a bit of extra pocket money, he's a good lad.'

Nina inclined her head, 'Thank you, he'll be thrilled. We're all looking forward to the trip, be an adventure for the three of us. The kids have never been abroad before and I like France. Chris and I went there once for ...' her voice trailed off. They'd gone to Paris for their honeymoon.

Frank sipped at his tea, it burnt his lip, 'Where are you going? Got a route planned out?'

Nina pushed her hands through the heavy mass of her hair, 'No, I thought we'd get off the ferry, aim for the nearest camp site I can find and that will be enough for the first day. See how the mood takes us after that.' She smiled brightly at Frank, 'I don't want to be tied down, you know, having to be somewhere at some appointed time. I want us to be free spirits.'

Frank paused, his cup in mid-air, *Dear God.* He sipped at his tea and cleared his throat.

Nina perched on the small wall opposite Frank, her hands cradling her cup of tea, knees slightly apart, she took a deep breath. 'Look, Frank, let me try to tell you how I feel about what we're doing, the trip and what it means to me and, perhaps if you understand that, the need for a break, we won't be fighting each other, tripping over our words. Funny isn't it, I pride myself on being articulate, but I'm struggling here trying to find the right words to explain to you how I feel.'

She straightened up, 'Look, I'm not Chris's wife any more, I'm not half of a couple, I've never really lived on my own before, not properly. Daniel thought I was too *bogged down with things,*' Nina made a face, 'He did me a favour, really he did. He set me free, there are so many things I can do now, I really feel that. I feel positive, a bit scared perhaps, but positive.'

Frank hadn't moved, his head was down and his breathing

was calm. Nina smiled and began to tell him about the idea she'd had. 'You know, Frank, what I'd really like to do is take a course in something, something like aromatherapy, a form of alternative healing perhaps. I deal with words, masses of them on sheets of paper, perhaps I should be dealing with people, I think I'd like that.' Frank could feel Nina's gaze, he listened as she took a deep breath before speaking, 'I know I can do this, I'm sure I can do it part-time which means that I'll be home for the kids as usual. I can combine it with my job, nothing will change for the kids.' She grinned and crossed her fingers. Frank remained silent, his breathing quickened.

Nina kept her eyes on Frank, 'This would be a good time for me to try this, I'm not the same person any more. I need to try something different. It would mean a wonderful opportunity for me and who knows what it could lead to? My job is OK, I like the work and it pays well but I need more, I need stretching. I could find out what I'm really capable of. When Daniel left, I felt as if I'd lost one identity, perhaps it's time to look for another.'

'Identity!' Frank spat the word at her. '*Identity,* you have an identity, you are the mother of these children, isn't that enough? These boys need you at home, not messing about with courses and suchlike. Dear God, Chris must be worried to death about how you're looking after his son. His mother was always home for him, she had her *identity* all right – she was his mother!'

Nina flinched and Frank tried once more to lever himself from the chair. 'Call Jonathan for me, I'll need help to get out of this bloody chair. Never mind holidays, you need some decent chairs.'

Nina stood, her hair moving around her face, 'Frank? Can't you even try to meet me halfway, to try and see my point of view? Won't you try it, if not for my sake, then for Nancy's? She'd have hated the fact that we argue all the time.'

'Leave Nancy out of this, don't talk about her, I don't want you talking about her.' He struggled then sank back down, 'Get Jonathan, I want to go home.'

In silence Nina looked at Frank then, shaking her head, she

called, 'Jonathan?' She moved towards the house, Frank kept his head turned away and they avoided looking at each other until Jonathan almost ran out of the kitchen door. 'Help your grandfather,' Nina said softly before going inside.

Even in his present mood, Frank disguised his discomfort, 'Just a bit stiff, lad, chair is almost as old as me. Give me a hand up will you?' He closed his eyes, biting hard on his lip as Jonathan tugged and pulled his grandfather to a standing position. 'Ooh,' a groan escaped from behind his clenched teeth and Jonathan looked up in alarm.

'Grandad! What's wrong?'

Frank shook his head, he was struggling to control his breathing. 'Nothing, I'm fine. Just walk with me to the car, there's a good lad.' They moved slowly towards the cool interior of the house. Nina had disappeared and the house was silent.

Frank rested his hand on Jonathan's shoulder as they walked from the house. He saw with sad amusement the way Jonathan's pace had slowed. As they reached the Fiesta, Frank patted at the pockets of his blazer He withdrew a white envelope, *Jonathan* written on it in bold letters, and he handed it to his grandson. He watched Jonathan's fingers move over the envelope, testing the number of notes he could feel.

Frank lowered his head, 'Now listen, lad, this is between you and me. No need to let your mother know how much is in there, it's just between us men.' He tapped at the side of his nose, winking as he did so. Jonathan jammed the envelope into the pocket of his jeans.

'Thanks, Grandad, thanks a lot.'

Once again Frank put his hand on Jonathan's shoulders, 'One condition mind. You must ring me. France has got phones, same as us, all over the place and you must ring me. I'll want postcards too, plenty of them so I can put them on my kitchen wall. Money is there for that too, so mind that you send them.

'Yes, course I will, I'll send postcards all the time and I'll ring, I'll ring every day.'

Frank gave a soft laugh, 'Every day? Well, see how your

money lasts but it's not all for phone calls, have a good holiday, enjoy yourself and perhaps, when you come back, you can come over and help me with the garden, perhaps we could have a trip out in the car …'

Suddenly Jonathan lunged at Frank, he wrapped his arms around him, burying his face in Frank's blazer, muffling his voice 'Thanks for the money, and everything.' Frank understood and, putting one arm on the roof of the Fiesta to steady himself, he held Jonathan for a brief second.

'Come on, lad, let me go. That lawn of mine will have grown another five foot if I don't cut it soon.' Unlocking the car door Frank eased himself in and put the keys in the ignition.

'Bye, Grandad, bye.' Jonathan waved until Frank's car had turned the corner, Frank's hand waving from the driver's window.

After driving for a few miles Frank had to stop, to park his car in a lay-by. He pulled out his handkerchief and blew his nose. He could still feel the hug that Jonathan had given him, a warm, steadying hug. He sat for a while watching other cars moving past him, their speed making the Fiesta rock in their wake. *That bloody woman, sorry Nancy, I lost my temper with her. It's the lad, it's not right, you wouldn't put up with that, would you?*

NINA

Sorry, Nancy, I'm sorry. I promised you I'd try really hard to get on with him and for your sake I tried, but I can't, I just can't do it. The moment I heard him clearing his throat, my stomach lurched, you used to say he was sharpening his voice. Talking to him is like playing with a jigsaw – one word out of place and it's all wrong – he explodes. He simply won't listen to another point of view. You'd have known what to say to him, to take the sting out of the situation. But I'm not you.

JONATHAN

'Over there, *there.*' She almost hit the bloke, the one with the clipboard and blue cap; he was waving at us and he wanted us to park in line number seven. She was in a right state, Sebastian was grizzling because we'd been in the car for hours and it was so hot. Then she saw the man and in the end we parked in the right line so that was OK.

There were loads of other cars waiting, we were behind a new Mercedes, even a posh car like that had a GB sticker. I thought that Dover would be different, but there was nothing much to see at all. Not even our ferry to look at. It hadn't arrived when we got there. There were just warehouses, sheds and huge container lorries and rows and rows of cars and caravans. I thought it would be more exciting. I suppose because I've never been abroad before, I wanted it to be like it is on the box, with customs officers and German shepherd dogs sniffing for drugs and stuff. The blokes in the customs kiosk didn't even look up as we passed. Don't know what I wanted to happen but I thought at least they'd *look* at the passports. We just drove through and sat in a queue of cars. There were *masses* of cars.

Sebastian was still grizzling in the back of the car and he got louder. 'Stop it, don't start again.' Mum didn't even turn around when she spoke, she had the car door open and she was fiddling with the controls on the radio. 'We're not even on the damn boat and the reception's gone ... oh, Sebastian, stop it, will you?'

'He's only bored, Mum, he's been sitting there for ages.'

'So, you take him out then.'

'Oh, no, why can't you?' She didn't answer, she just flapped her hands at me and twiddled even more.

Sebastian stopped grizzling as soon as I got the pushchair out of the back of the car. I yanked him out of his car seat. I hate it when people watch me doing this, holding my baby brother, they all think I'm such a good person. Sebastian doesn't help, he just tugs at my hair and laughs. He thinks it's a great game. All the other people in the queue watched and smiled. I strapped him in the pushchair and began to wheel him away from the queues.

'Don't go too far, I don't want to be running up and down these aisles looking for you,' Mum said, I didn't answer, why should I? I walked away from our car.

Everyone seemed to be part of a family, I know we are too but as I pushed my brother up and down the rows of cars, there seemed to be an awful lot of men doing the driving. There were some women drivers but inside most of the cars there was a bloke staring at a large map. There was a lot of stuff inside the cars. I could see boxes of CDs, Game Boys, Walkmans, Ipods, not to mention toys and cameras. Mum said we didn't need any of that stuff. She said I could organise my own packing, 'You're old enough now, Jon.' I put my MP3 player and Walkman and other things I needed all ready on my bed. Dad had given me a new rucksack for my last birthday and I'd piled everything ready to go into it. In the end Mum stopped me packing any of it.

'I'll sort your clothes out, you won't need much, just T-shirts, shorts and swimming trunks, a couple of sweaters. What else can you possibly need? You certainly won't need all this stuff, Jon, we'll be in *France*, the home of good wine and brilliant food. Just think of the scenery, the beaches, the coastline.' She hugged me a lot, every time she mentioned

France.

'It'll be wonderful,' she said it over and over again. 'I can find the real me, I know I can.' I still don't know what she means by that. Bet none of these other people are trying to find themselves. They're going on holiday to have a good time, what's wrong with that?

I could see the top of Mum's head from where I was standing. She put some stuff on her hair last night, to brighten it up a bit, she said. The sun was shining right over our car and her hair looked funny, a really yucky colour, sort of green.

I saw a phone booth at the back of the last row of cars. I wanted to ring Dad, just once more before we went. I'd left a message last night, Mum was finishing our packing, leaving out what we had to wear today, all that sort of stuff and she wasn't taking any notice of me.

Stupid, bloody stupid machine. Made me sound like a right wally. I'd started off OK, 'Hello, Dad, it's me, Jonathan, are you there?' I thought he might be back from York. I thought that if he heard it was me, he'd come to the phone. But he didn't. I started to tell him or at least tell the machine all about school, the project I'm doing. I've got to plan a fountain for a garden. I wanted him to know that. He's an architect, my dad, and I thought he'd want to know all about my fountain. I went on a bit, I must have done, because just as I started telling him about the holiday, the stupid tape ran out. So he still doesn't know.

Mum had taken my mobile phone out of my rucksack but I had enough money for a phone call. Grandad had given me *loads*. In the envelope were euros, squillions of them all wrapped around some coins. When Mum asked me how much he'd given me, I told her I didn't know because I hadn't counted them. I wasn't lying, I only counted them when I got to bed. My holiday money is in my rucksack with my passport, but I've got about £1.50 on me now, enough for a phone call.

I ran to the booth, the pushchair bumping over the ground, jiggling Sebastian up and down. He thought it was a game and started to laugh, his small hands grabbing at the front of the pushchair.

It was stuffy in the kiosk and I jammed the door open with my foot; the pushchair was outside and Sebastian started to whine again. 'Stop it, stop it, I'm not listening. This is *my dad*, not yours – so shut up.' I hissed at him through the open door of the kiosk. A woman walked past and shook her head at me. Stupid cow. I began to push coins in: 20p, 10p, 5p, and I pressed all the buttons for Dad's number: 0117 9752765. It was engaged! He was home! He was there at last. Yesss! I punched the air. Sebastian stopped whining and laughed at me and his fist went up in the air just like mine. I pressed the re-dial button.

Dad lived in a flat in Clifton with a balcony outside his living room with pots of flowers and things on it. He used to ask Mum about the garden at home, how many times had she cut the lawn and did she feed it properly? He'd landscaped all our garden, he had pictures of it on his bedroom wall.

Mum laughed when I'd told her that. 'Sad, he's so sad,' she'd said.

The phone was ringing, it was ringing this time. I knew where it was in my dad's flat, next to his bed. Oh please don't let it be the answer machine again.

'Hello?'

Dad! I pushed the button.

'Dad, hi, it's me. It's Jonathan. Guess what? I'm at Dover, we're going to France for our holiday.' I didn't mean to tell him like that but the words came out all in a rush.

'Jon? Hello, son, I was going to ring you today, been away on a course. *Where* did you say you were? Dover? What the hell are you doing there?'

'We're going to France, now, today. We're waiting for the ferry. Me and Mum and Sebastian.' I could hear the sound of Dad breathing, he didn't speak for ages. The tiny screen on the booth showed £1.15. 'Dad? Are you still there?'

'Yes, sorry. I … what do you mean you're off to France now? Who's going with you?'

£1.05. 'I *told* you. Mum, me and Sebastian. Mum's in the car, waiting in the queue for our ferry. Just the three of us are going.' That's what Mum kept saying, now I'd started it. 'We're going to stay at camp sites. Mum's got new tents and …'

'Whose idea was this? Camping? When, Jon, when was this decided?'

£1.00

Dad was almost shouting. 'Where are you staying? I can't believe this. Did she, did your mother decide all this because I was away?'

I kept watching the little screen, only 90 pence left now. 'No, Dad, we didn't know you were away, you didn't tell anyone, only Grandad.' Dad didn't say anything and I kept looking at the screen watching as the numbers changed.

'This is so *stupid*. What am I supposed to do now? What am I supposed to say?'

I looked through the glass of the phone booth. Sebastian was really crying now, his face was bright red and his hair was all sweaty. I could see people pointing and then I saw two women walking towards him. Sebastian saw them coming and he put his head right back. I knew when he did that he was building up for a screaming fit.

'Dad, listen, I've got to go.' I didn't tell him the real reason. 'Mum's calling me, I've got to get into the car.'

'Jon! Wait a minute, let me speak to her. Oh, this is bloody ridiculous. You just can't ring up and say you're off to France, this is crazy.'

50 pence left.

'I'll ring you from France, I've got to go now.' I don't know what made me say the next words, not sure what I felt. Perhaps I was sorry that we were going away and Dad didn't know, he couldn't come with us. Perhaps I just said it to make me feel better and I thought it might make Dad feel better too. 'I love you, Dad.'

30 pence.

'I love you too, Jon. Ring me when you get to France, don't forget now.'

I put the phone down and then I punched the money button. A 20 pence piece fell down the chute.

Outside the phone booth I put my hands on the pushchair, one of the women had already caught hold of it and was jiggling it up and down, trying to make Sebastian stop crying. Her big tits were jiggling up and down too.

'Are you his brother?' She pushed her face right up to mine. She was so close I could see dark hairs on her upper lip.

'What if I am?'

'Because this little fellow needs a drink and a nap, that's what.' She jabbed a finger into my shoulder as she spoke.

'Mind your own business.' I grabbed the pushchair from her and began to run, past the two women and away from all the other faces watching me from their cars. I hoped Grandma wasn't watching too.

Sebastian had stopped screaming and only hiccupped as I pushed him down the rows of cars looking for Mum's red Clio. She was standing by the side of the car fanning herself with a map.

'There you are. What's the matter with Sebastian?'

'He's tired and hot.' I was angry with her, angry because she'd made me take Sebastian when she knew he was tired and I was angry because until I'd told him Dad didn't know where we were going. I put Sebastian back into his car seat where he closed his eyes and fell asleep.

'You might as well get into the car, too, I don't think it will be long now.' Mum said. 'The ferry is over there, that one is ours, I think.' She waved her hand and I saw it. The whole time Mum said anything about the ferry, I'd been thinking of a boat with just a few cars on it, like the one Dad and I went on in Cornwall last year. This one wasn't like that, this one was huge. *P & O Stena* printed in blue letters on the side, everything else was painted white. I could see people on the top, they looked tiny.

'Here we go,' Mum said, starting up the car. 'France, here we come.' I couldn't say anything, my stomach felt sort of funny, sort of *buzzy* inside as Mum drove the car towards a big ramp where more men in blue overalls were waving their arms about and pointing to a lane right in the middle of the lower deck. Every time a car came up the ramp, it made a big noise, a *thump* noise. Mum stopped the Clio and then we had to squeeze past all the cars.

'We can't stay here,' she was yelling, 'we're going up those stairs, this deck is just for cars. I'll get Sebastian, you get the bags. Stay with me, don't get lost.'

Sebastian didn't wake up, even with all that racket, his head flopped against Mum's shoulder and we climbed millions of stairs to the upper decks. People were already queuing at the duty-free shops and there were kids playing on the fruit machines.

Mum grabbed my arm, 'Aim for the restaurant, Jon. We'll have a decent lunch today, push the boat out.' She laughed, then I had another hug but I didn't mind that one so much. Sebastian really had been tired, he slept all through lunch. Mum ordered wine for herself and Coke for me and we both chose fish.

'Cheers, Jon. Here's to our holiday.' Mum sat back in her chair, Sebastian was still asleep, curled up in the chair next to her. The restaurant was quite posh, pink napkins on the table and Mum's half bottle of wine in a silver bucket. 'I've got a good feeling about this, Jon, this holiday. I think it will do us all good.' She'd finished the first glass of wine very quickly and the waiter poured more into her glass. I pretended I hadn't noticed, but she'd seen me watching her. 'Don't worry, I'm only having two glasses, that's all.'

Our table was right by the window. I asked Mum if they were called portholes but she said she didn't think so. When I'd finished eating, I wanted to go and explore the boat but Mum wanted to talk.

'When did we last have a holiday, Jon? When was the last time we had a break?'

I'd gone to Cornwall with Dad last year and, just before Sebastian was born, Mum went to the Lake District with Daniel. I started to tell her, to remind her of where Dad and I went, but she'd gone all dreamy on me.

'No, no, I'm talking about a real change, a change of country, different views on life, different cultures. I've been

31

feeling very trapped you know.' Oh, God, she was really off this time and I must have started fidgeting because her voice changed.

'Go on, I can see I'm boring you. Go, explore the boat but just remember where the car is if you get lost.' She looked out towards the sea and stroked Sebastian's head.

Before he left, Daniel had brought home the DVD of *Titanic* and now I wanted to go on the top deck and stand where Leonardo di Caprio stood. It was brilliant up there, on the top deck, I could really feel the ferry moving. We must have been travelling dead fast, I couldn't see any land, just miles and miles of sea with white, choppy waves. *Can you see me, Grandma?* She'd never been abroad, not once and I thought that if I talked to her all the time, she'd see France with me.

I couldn't put my arms out like Leonardo di Caprio did, there was a girl sitting close by and I didn't want her to see me. She didn't seem to be with anyone, I couldn't see any parents but there were little kids running around. They were getting on my nerves a bit, but this girl didn't seem to notice. I walked past her really slowly, I didn't look at her though, I kept my head turned around. I stood right at the front, watching the waves. She'd moved, the girl had moved and she was standing next to me, she was wriggling around in her clothes. She had a blue top on and it didn't reach over her stomach. There was something glinting in her belly-button, a stud or something. She saw me looking at it and she breathed in, sucking her stomach in, the stud moved.

I kept on watching the waves, I stood like that for ages and then the girl said something.

'What?'

She giggled and she kept staring at me. I didn't know what else to do so I moved away and went back down the stairs towards the restaurant. Mum was still there, she was the only one left. Sebastian had woken up and she was giving him something out of a jar.

'Hi, where've you been – and who's your friend?'

I didn't know what she meant until I turned around. The

girl had followed me, she was standing right behind me, just standing there with a stupid look on her face. Mum smiled at her, 'Hello, what's your name?'

'Zoe, what's *his* name?' Her head jerked towards me and Mum grabbed my arm.

'Say hello, Jonathan, Zoe won't bite you.' My face was all hot and I felt such a pillock. I sat back in the seat and stared through the window. I didn't want the girl Zoe to see my face all red. Mum was laughing again and shovelling goo into Sebastian's mouth. 'Not sure if I can afford hormones for your brother,' she whispered to him. I glared at her but it didn't make a blind bit of difference. She lifted her head and spoke to the girl, 'My son's name is Jonathan and we're going on a camping trip around France.'

Will all those passengers with cars please make their way to the car decks.

'Mum?'

'Yes, I heard it.' She finished the last spoonful of goo for Sebastian and smiled at Zoe who was still standing by our table. 'Bye, enjoy your holiday.' The girl looked at me, it was as if she was asking me a question only I didn't know what. She shrugged then went out.

Mum seemed to take for ever collecting our bags, picking up newspapers, all sorts of junk. She shoved the bags at me. 'Take these, Jon. I'll have to change Sebastian soon.' I didn't listen to any more, I was so excited, we were in France!

I found our car, it wasn't easy and Mum was running up and down like a headless chicken. We got in with all the usual palaver with Sebastian's seat, putting the bags in again, seat belts on.

'Check the passports, Jon, keep them close.' I put them in my hand and we sat there. We didn't move. I couldn't believe it. The car deck was in darkness, the big doors were shut and some people had turned their engines on so it was pretty noisy. But we sat there, not moving. France was out there, outside those big doors and I couldn't see it. Mum was fiddling with the radio again, she didn't seem to mind that nothing was happening, but I did.

Then the big doors opened; they made a groaning noise, they shuddered as they opened, I could see daylight. One of the blokes in blue overalls waved and the cars began to move. I could hear the *thump* again as each car or lorry moved off the ferry down the ramp and into Calais. Then it was our turn.

France. It looked exactly the same as Dover. Same ugly warehouses and concrete buildings. It was so *boring*. Mum laughed, 'What were you expecting? The road full of French loaves and bottles of wine, smell of garlic in the air? Calais is just a port, same as Dover. This isn't the real France, not this bit. That's what we're going to find, that's where we're heading. Trust me.'

FRANK

Frank sat in the kitchen, the back door was open and a warm, sweet smell of newly cut grass filtered through. He sat bolt upright, hands resting on his knees, gazing out at the stripes on the lawn.

Nancy. Frank could see her in the garden the summer before she died. Her hands with their short nails, covered in soil. She wore old gardening trousers, the colour faded to a pale khaki, pockets bulging with secateurs, a packet of twine, a small trowel. When she was working in the garden she'd run her hands through her hair, pushing it off her face and tucking it behind her ears, splodges of soil spattering her hair and cheeks.

Whatever Frank was doing, he'd keep an eye on her. His garden was his pride, his passion. Weeds were pulled up the minute they rose above the surface, the edges of the flower beds appeared drilled into regimental lines, flowers were chosen for their upright stalks.

'It's like living on a parade ground,' Nancy often complained. 'Flowers are natural, free, their leaves should spread out, petals should shake and fall.' She teased him, calling his flowerbeds, *Sergeant* and *Major.*

Frank smiled, remembering her words and he remembered too her enthusiasm for the trailing clematis she'd planted. 'Look at all the new growth, Frank, look at the shoots, like tiny hands reaching out for the brickwork.' He'd pruned it every autumn, harshly chopping at the delicate plant, tearing at the leaves. 'Bloody thing will take over if I don't cut it right back,' he told Nancy when she saw the shortened skeleton in the ground.

Nancy began growing her plants in brightly glazed pots, she moved them around the garden; she tried out varieties of honeysuckle, climbing roses and, her favourite, a wisteria. It grew at the back of their garden, a mass of blue, shaggy blooms, hiding the grey stonework.

Frank had been staring out at the garden on the day of Nancy's funeral. The house was full of people, family, neighbours and Nancy's friends hovering around his still figure. Nina had moved quietly amongst them, offering cups of tea and plates of sandwiches. She'd tried to make Frank eat something but he ignored her, he ignored everyone. He stared out at the wisteria, eyes narrowing as he looked at the blooms, showering petals like blue confetti in the wind.

When the last of the funeral guests had gone, when Nina and Chris eventually left, Nina's eyes red-rimmed, Chris's face grey, haggard with grief, Frank closed and locked the front door then walked out to his garage and brought out an axe. He marched to the back of the garden, the wind whipping his black tie into his face. Ignoring the tie and the rain that began to fall, Frank hacked at the stem of the wisteria. He raised the axe high, clenching the handle tight, bringing it down, slashing at the foliage, tearing at the blooms and smashing the terracotta pot. The shoes Frank had polished for his wife's funeral were soon hidden under shards of terracotta and mangled blooms. His breathing was harsh and, as he brought the axe down, he chanted, 'She's gone, she's gone.'

From his seat in the kitchen, he could see the back wall, grey stones clearly visible. Clematis and honeysuckle had been removed, the wisteria had died, now there were rows of red geraniums flanked by dark blue lobelia growing in tailored rows at the bottom of the garden.

Frank felt a dull ache at the base of his spine. Like a stain the ache spread out slowly reaching upwards towards his neck.

He closed his eyes. He spoke aloud, talking firmly to the pain.

'No, you'll have to wait. Watering to do first.' He stood slowly, breathing deeply, putting one hand on the table and the other in the small of his back.

Shaking his head he moved out into the garden; spirals of blue smoke from a nearby barbecue hovered in the air. Frank uncoupled the hosepipe and began watering the flowerbeds. The pain was angry, seemingly berating him for his activity, and he shuffled as he directed the stream of water onto hanging baskets, his vegetable plot and the mass of dark red geraniums.

When he finished Frank looked at his watch. 'Almost 8 o'clock, too long, it's taking me too long.' He put the hosepipe away, he checked the garage door tugging hard on the big lock then walked slowly, his head lowered, to the back door. Fine columns of smoke drifted across the fence, *plup* the sound of a cork pulled from a wine bottle, a burst of laughter, Frank ignored it all. Once inside the house and, grunting as he reached down, he locked the kitchen door, pulling at the bolts. His shirt was sticking to his back and he wiped his forehead with the back of his hand. 'That bloody woman's chair has done this, that's what this is all about.'

The phone rang as Frank switched the kettle on. He tried to ignore its ringing. The pain was everywhere, it had crept along his arms reaching his fingers and the backs of his legs, even the worn leather in his shoes seemed to cut into his feet. The shrill ringing infuriated Frank, 'Damn, making me worse, bloody thing, stop it.' He stretched his arm out slowly and picked up the receiver.

'Hello?'

'Dad? Are you all right?' It was Chris, his voice high with anxiety.

'Yes, course I'm all right. What do you want?'

'Where have you been? I've tried ringing a few times. Been out in the garden?'

'Yes, where else would I be this time of night?'

'OK, OK, don't bite my head off. I'm back from my course, you know, York and I was ringing to see if you were

37

all right, that's all.'

Frank closed his eyes, the kettle was sending out clouds of steam, he felt giddy with pain. 'I'm fine, just fine. A bit tired, that's all. Been cutting the lawn, needs doing just about every day, tidying up, a bit of watering …'

'Well I won't keep you.' Frank could hear the hurt in Chris's voice but he couldn't help that, his own pain was all he could think about.

'Wait!' Frank closed his eyes, he must speak to Chris about Jonathan, he must do that.

'Did you speak to Jonathan? Do you know about France?'

'Yes, I spoke to him, he phoned from Dover. Why? What do you know about it?'

'I went over there yesterday, went to see the lad, he phoned me. I wanted to make sure he was all right, give him some money in case of emergencies.'

'She must be off her head camping, she doesn't know the first thing about it. What brought it on, did she say?'

'No, not really. There was some nonsense about wanting to find a new identity or some other rubbish.'

Chris gave a snort, 'Nothing changes. Where are they heading, do you know?'

The pain was gripping Frank's ribcage, his breathing was shallow. 'No.' He forced the word out. 'No, she didn't say. Look, son, I've got to go now, someone at the door. I'll ring you.' Frank brought the phone down with a crash, his hand was clammy, he saw a clear imprint of his fingers on the handset.

He *must* get to bed, only thing for it, rest and try and get rid of the pain. His legs felt heavy, clumsy, and he moved slowly over to the kettle. A warm drink, then bed and he'd be fine. The pain had attacked every part of him and Frank stared resolutely through the kitchen window gripping the sink, his knuckles white with the effort. *Bloody stupid woman.* His thoughts went back to Nina's garden, the chair, the row with Nina, something to do with Jonathan. Jonathan. Something he must do. *What?* He trickled Horlicks into a white mug, slowly pouring boiling water into the powder and stirred. *What was it? Something about this damn fool trip. Shouldn't be out there with that mother of his, anything might happen.* The spoon rattled against the side of the mug, frothy brown liquid bubbled over the rim.

He hated the untidiness of his thoughts, cluttering up his mind. He wanted to sort this out, put everything right before he went to bed, he wouldn't settle until he remembered.

That woman's not fit ... young chap over there ... Frank stopped the frantic activity of his spoon. Passport! That's what he meant to do, he needed to check his passport. He picked up his drink and shuffled out of the kitchen.

Negotiating the stairs took a long time, he tutted angrily as the drink slopped out onto the carpet. He had to stop halfway and, leaning heavily on the banister, he brought his left leg up and stopped. He heard cars driving past, a door closing, voices raised in greeting. Frank gripped the handrail again and hauled himself up; his breathing was harsh, laboured.

Reaching his bedroom he put the mug of rapidly cooling Horlicks on the bedside chest and he pulled at the bottom drawer. The wood was warped and old and, as Frank tugged, perspiration ran into his eyes, stinging and blurring his vision. 'Damn and blast.' He tugged, pulled until the drawer opened to reveal a metal box. Sitting on the edge of the bed, Frank lifted out the box. Wiping his eyes, he lifted the lid. Crammed inside was a mass of receipts held together with an elastic band. Blue covers of Post Office Savings account books and a collection of bank statements and cheque stubs were bundled together and, pushing his hand to the bottom of the pile, his fingers touched the covers of two passports. Bringing them out, Frank squinted at the top one. 'Now, when does this ...?' He relaxed, it was in order, another eighteen months left. 'That's all right then. I might have to go over there, God only knows what that mother of his will get up to.'

He eased himself back on the pillows and, reaching slowly for his drink, he held the mug in both hands and took a sip. The pain was lessening and Frank closed his eyes for a second. He sighed.

He finished his drink and flipped through the pages of his

passport. The pages were crisp, unmarked, no stamp from another country was on any one of them. Frank had never used his passport. He picked up the second one and fingered the pages. Nancy's face, her dark eyes gazed out at him.

She'd been so excited about their passport photos, insisting Frank had a haircut and she'd worn pearl earrings. 'Otherwise we'll look like people on a Wanted poster.' It was Italy she yearned to see. Frank's fingers traced the contours of her face.

'Tuscany, just to see the olive groves, Frank, the vineyards, the heads of those massive sunflowers, bright yellow, laughing at me.' He didn't want to go to Italy, or France or Spain. He simply wanted to spend his holidays with Nancy touring Cornwall. They'd gone there every year, all the time Frank was working, his annual fortnight's holiday. Sansome's Electrical Wholesalers where he worked as stores manager closed down for the last fortnight in July, same time every year.

'What's wrong with Cornwall, you've always liked it.'

Nancy had laughed, 'Yes *always,* we're *always* there. Frank, please, I know every café, every cliff walk, every house. God, I even know when people move out of their homes, I see new curtains! Please, Frank, before we get too old, let's see another country, eat Italian pasta, drink French wine …'

Before we get too old. Nancy didn't get too old. She died the year Frank had finally given in. Frank held Nancy's passport up to his face. *I would have gone, love. I'd have taken you to Tuscany.*

There were sounds of cars moving slowly into the cul-de-sac, doors closing, a muffled greeting, 'Hi, thought you'd never get here.' A smell of barbecued chicken filtered through the open window of Frank's bedroom and, with Nancy's passport resting on his chest, he slept.

JONATHAN

We're trying to find a campsite called *Bel Parc*. Mum's bought masses of camping books, she made notes on all the best ones, there's yellow *Stick-it* notes poking out of the pages. She shoved the books in my lap after we got off the ferry. 'We're looking for the D217, Bel Parc site, you're navigating.'

We seemed to have been driving for hours. It was so flat, miles and miles of fields. And it was hot.

'.... what's your history like?' Mum was saying something.

'Wha?' I sat up and the books and maps fell off my lap.

'Jon! For God's sake, they cost money.'

I leant down to pick them up. 'What did you say?' I pulled the visor down and looked into the little mirror. My face was red and there was a mark on my cheek. I must have fallen asleep with my cheek on the seatbelt.

'I asked what your history is like, in particular your World War Two history.' She spoke slowly, each word taking ages; she spoke to my dad like that sometimes.

'We've only done a little bit, not much at all really.' That's all I needed, a lecture on subjects at school.

'All around these fields are war memorials.' She took her hand off the steering wheel and waved it around. 'Because it's so flat here, it made this whole area vulnerable to invading armies, not just World War Two, battles ancient and modern. There are a lot of cemeteries all over this region.'

They still looked like flat fields to me, dead boring. But then I thought we could have a look at some of the memorials, take photos into school, that might be good. 'Can we see them, not now, on our way back?'

She looked at me quickly, then her eyes went back to the road.

'Yes, OK, we'll do that.' She started humming, her fingers were tapping on the steering wheel. We had to stop not long after that, Sebastian was making a grunting noise, he'd filled his nappy.

This first campsite's OK. It was quite full and I didn't think we'd get in. Mum hadn't booked or anything and the man in the campsite office just said, 'Non, non,' he wouldn't even look up, just stared at his computer screen. Mum got very red in the face and ran back to our car. The man on the desk just shrugged and tapped on his keyboard. When Mum came back she was holding Sebastian, 'Enfant, enfant,' she shouted, holding him up in the air and sort of *waving* him at the man. He stared at her and she glared right back at him. It went very quiet, even Sebastian didn't make a sound.

Then the bloke shrugged and fiddled around on his desk. He squiggled something on a map and said, '87,' his fingers stabbing at the map. Mum plonked Sebastian down on the desk and got out her purse. She kept saying, 'Merci, merci,' to the man. She winked at me.

We got back in the car and drove around looking for pitch 87. The site was full, there were caravans everywhere, kids were running around, some had bikes, there were barbecues all over the place, it was packed.

Pitch 87 was in a squidgy little field, near the toilets, there were just tents there. Mum stopped the car and started to walk about, stretching herself. I wish she wouldn't do that, she marched about as if she was measuring something. She kept looking at me as though she wanted me to say something…what? I didn't know what she wanted. I started to lug the stuff out of the car.

'Just the tents, Jon. We're only here for one night.'

What was the matter with her? I know we're only here for one night, I *know*. Seemed to me that she was talking to the other people in the field, not me. She was talking loudly, using her posh voice, the one she uses on the phone sometimes.

'Just the one night, Jon. This is a staging post for us.' No one took any notice of her. I pulled out the tents. They're dead easy to put up, the man in the camping shop was right. All I had to do was pull them out of their plastic bags and they sort of sprung up. Mum walked around them, 'Are you sure that's all you have to do? Check them again, Jon.'

I tried telling her that they were all right but she kept on saying 'Check them again.'

I fiddled around a bit to keep her happy but I noticed she was turning her head around to see what everyone else had, what camping equipment and stuff. We had the tatty saucepans and a gaz stove and Mum had brought Sebastian's things, drinking mugs and little spoons, but nothing much else. We hadn't got any chairs, we didn't have proper plates or bowls, knives or any of that stuff. Once I'd pulled the sleeping bags out, there wasn't much else left in the car, only our cases. Mum was holding Sebastian, he was tired, his eyes were red and he kept rubbing them. I was hungry but I didn't want to say anything to Mum, she was making me nervous. She just stood still. She was sucking at a chunk of hair, but her eyes weren't really looking at anything. Everyone around us, in all those other pitches, they were eating or playing football or something and there was so much noise it sort of hummed but Mum stood still. She's weird.

Sebastian wriggled, he was trying to get down, then Mum blinked. 'Right, Jon, I'm starving. Let's go and find something to eat.'

The campsite had its own chicken and chip bar and we ate our supper sitting in the front seats of the Clio. 'Not quite what I had in mind for our first night in France,' Mum said.

When we were getting washed and changed for bed, Mum said that Sebastian had to come in with me.

'Why?' I didn't want him.

43

'Because I'd like to be on my own, humour me please, Jon.'

'What for?'

'Jon, for God's sake. I'd just like to have some peace and quiet, do some dreaming, OK?'

She didn't do any dreaming, she couldn't, she didn't sleep. Sebastian was grizzling, whining for hours, he really got on my nerves. I tossed and wriggled so much, my sleeping bag got all tangled up. I'd had enough and, as I pulled his sleeping bag, trying to get it through the opening of my tent so I could shove him into Mum's, I heard her crying.

I was stuck between the two tents: Sebastian grizzling and whining in mine and Mum sobbing in the other. Felt creepy, I was in a field in France, everyone else was quiet except for my mum and baby brother and I'm stuck in the middle. I won't tell Grandad about Mum crying, but I bet Grandma knows.

'Grandad, Grandad! It's me, Jonathan. I'm in France, we've had breakfast, what's the time there? It's 10 o'clock here. We had French bread and cheese, the butter tastes peculiar. Mum had croissants but I don't like them. We're off soon, back on the road; I'm the navigator. Mum says I'm really good. Are you OK?'

Grandad's voice sounded funny, sort of faint, I couldn't hear what he said.

'What? I can't hear you.'

He coughed a bit, 'Where are you, lad? What's the weather like?'

'We're in a campsite outside Calais. Mum's not that keen on it, it's full of English people. It's quite sunny here, it's OK. Mum wants us to pack up quickly and move on but I told her I wanted to ring you.'

'Good lad.' I could tell he was pleased with that, his voice got a bit louder.

'So, lad, the trip on the ferry was OK? And the roads, your mum managed the driving?'

'Yes, she did OK. I navigated, Grandad. Found the auto-

44

route, the D217. Oh, and, Grandad, we passed some of the war cemeteries. Mum says we can stop on the way back so I can take photos.'

'That'll be good, a bit of history for you. Dunkirk and all that, eh?' His voice was weak again, he seemed to be whispering.

'Yes, anyway I'd better go. Mum's not that good with the tents, she'll be looking for me. I'll ring you tomorrow, let you know where we are, OK, Grandad, OK?'

'Yes, fine. Good lad.'

'Au revoir, that's French.'

'I know, bye, Jonathan.' And the line went dead.

When I got back to Mum, she was sitting in the car, knees apart, changing Sebastian's nappy.

'Pass me the Pampers please, Jon' She pretended to bite his tummy, he was squealing and pulling at her hair. I hadn't told her about last night, about her crying, that I heard her, but I could see purply smudges under her eyes. She pulled Sebastian up and he tried to yank on the steering wheel. 'OK, ready to go, I think.'

I stacked all our bits and pieces into the car and sat in the front. Mum strapped Sebastian into his seat then she dropped the maps and the books with their *stick it* notes into my lap.

'Where are we going now?'

'Camp Maison Laffitte, we can stay a couple of nights here. I'd like to see Paris.'

Paris. All I know about Paris is that it's near Euro Disney.

'Isn't Euro Disney there?'

'Mm? Yes, it's close by.'

'Oh, Mum, can we go? I've always wanted to go there, you know I have.'

She didn't say anything for a while.

'Mum?'

'Oh, I don't know. I thought we'd spend a few nights at this next site, look at the Eiffel Tower, perhaps a trip on the Seine. What do you think? That sounds all right, doesn't it?'

Well, yes, it did. But not as good as Euro Disney. I stared

out of the window for a bit.

'Dad said I could go, he said he'd take me.'

We didn't speak for ages after that, the auto-routes are really boring, cars whizzing by, horns blaring, all sorts of noise outside the car but dead quiet inside. Mum fiddled around with the radio, she's always doing that but all she got this time was a load of crackling and jumbled-up French.

'All right, all right. Stop your sulking. I can't be doing with sulking. You win. Euro Disney it is. But we'll do a deal. Paris one day, Euro Disney another day – OK?'

'OK, thanks, Mum.'

She shoved a tape in and we sang along to Tina Turner.

'Grandad! Wait a minute, bonjour, Grandad. It's me again, Jonathan. Guess what? We're going to Euro Disney.'

'Whoa, not so fast. Where? Where did you say you were going? Disney, where's that?'

'Just outside Paris, we're staying at this campsite, Maison something. It's dead good. We went to the Eiffel Tower today, almost up to the top. We could see all of Paris. I took loads of photos.'

'Paris, your grandmother wanted to go there. So, tell me lad, are you coping all right with the food, the language and suchlike?'

'It's brilliant, really good. We've got a book with French words and stuff and the food's smashing. I've had mussels in garlic. Mum let me have some wine last night. Paris was OK, quite good really but Euro Disney, Grandad! I can't wait.'

'Euro Disney, they tell me that it's a big funfair, a circus. Costs a fortune too, doesn't it? Waste of money, what's that mother of yours up to, eh? You'd be better off staying put, seeing a bit more of Paris if you ask me. Museums, things like that would be better for you.'

I didn't want to hear any more, didn't want him to spoil things for me. So I stopped him. I just said, 'Dad promised he'd take me, but he hasn't kept his promise.'

He couldn't say anything to that, he couldn't, it was true.

He coughed a bit, 'Well I expect he's busy and it costs a

46

lot, so I understand; surprised your mother can afford it.'

'Well she can and we're going! Don't know when I can ring again, Grandad. Might not be for a few days. Bye.'

I didn't feel mean until later.

FRANK

When Frank opened his eyes, he thought at first he'd left the light on. His bedroom was bright, the sun streaming in through the windows reflecting on the glass top of the kidney-shaped dressing table. The silver trinket box he'd bought Nancy for her fiftieth birthday twinkled.

He tried to sit up but pain caught at his ribs, holding him.

'Must have fallen asleep, damn, didn't draw the curtains.'

The muted throb of a milk float, bottles tinkling in their crates, told Frank that it was about 6 o'clock. It hurt too much to turn his head, to look at the clock radio.

'Got to get up, no good lying here, won't do.'

He tried again, biting hard on this top lip.

'Leave it a bit, try later, that's best.'

The top half of the window was open, the curtains rippled, birdsong filtered through. Frank closed his eyes.

In the summer Nancy had always been the first to wake up, slipping out of bed and padding quietly downstairs to put the kettle on. After taking tea up to Frank, she'd wander through the garden peering at the roses, checking on the progress of the various pots and tubs of flowers. She usually had a crust or two of bread which she'd crumble and scatter as she walked on the lawn, the hem of her dressing gown soaking up the dew. By the time Frank reached the kitchen, Nancy was sitting at the breakfast table, her hands cradling a fresh cup of coffee, the back door wide open and rashers of bacon under the grill.

Nancy had moved through their home like a wave, lapping against the kitchen or the dining room. Papers fell to the floor as she moved from room to room. She dislodged books, plates. She wasn't a careless woman, she walked on the balls of her feet, moving lightly, rapidly, talking to Frank about things she wanted to do.

'I meant to ring Jill,' her voice would reach Frank, moving past him, her skirts fluttering. Frank often wandered through the house, retrieving coffee mugs, teaspoons, Nancy's reading glasses and library books from odd corners.

With his eyes tight shut, darkness in his head, Frank saw Nancy framed in the doorway, light falling on her coffee-coloured curls, ribbons of silvery grey glinting in the sun. 'Knew there was something I wanted to tell you, Frank.' He'd always loved her quick, soft speech, her slight stammer, the emphasis she placed on her words. She searched for the right word, eyes narrowing, 'No, not that, not *nuisance,* it was more of an *interruption*, that's what Jill told me.' The exultant smile when she found the word she wanted.

He felt tears creeping through his eyelids. 'Damn and blast this bloody pain. I won't have it, I won't.'

Frank took a deep breath and inched his way towards the edge of the bed. Not daring to breath, keeping the pain back that way, he lowered his feet to the floor. The two passports were lying on the carpet. Frank nudged them to one side with his left foot. He straightened up, balancing himself by holding on to the wooden headboard. He breathed out. *Did it.*

The pain was travelling along his body like signals on a railway responding to a switch. *Click.* It splintered along his arm, travelled down his legs and, all the time, a deep throbbing pain in the base of his spine.

'Christ Almighty, this is a bugger.'

He shuffled off to the bathroom, pain or no pain, he wasn't prepared to go without a wash and a shave. It took a long time, the whole tortuous business.

'Cup of tea, that's what's needed, no good giving in to

this, just a blasted nuisance. Got too much to do.'

The veins on his forearms bulged with his efforts at getting down the stairs. Each step, bringing his left foot down to join the right foot then a chance to take a deep breath before attempting the next one. Fourteen stairs, Frank knew each creaking tread, a stain on the carpet where Nancy had spilt coffee, the mark hadn't shifted.

Tightening his grip on the banister, he reached another step. *Godalmighty.*

Frank sat at the kitchen table, watching the sun chase shadows across the walls. The radio was on, a subdued voice in the background. Frank shifted uneasily, *shouldn't be sitting here.* There was so much for him to do. He hadn't got the Sunday papers, he always walked to the newsagents on the corner, he had to do that but he couldn't walk across the *floor* today. *Damn nuisance.* Breakfast had been a slice of toast and no butter on that. Wrists hurt too much, everything hurt. He didn't know how long he'd been sitting here. He'd left his watch upstairs on the side of the wash-hand basin. He strained to hear what the newsreader was saying, was that 8 o'clock or was it later than that?

The phone rang making Frank jump, causing him to flinch.

'Now what? Who on earth is that? I'll have to answer, damn this.'

Frank's agitation and his inability to move intensified with each ring. He tried to rise from the chair, the movement causing the table to jolt, slops of tea puddled out. Frank watched the brown liquid run down the table legs, settling in a pool on the kitchen floor.

'Damn phone,' it rang on and on.

Frank was bothered. He'd asked Jonathan to ring him, insisted in fact, and when he did, he could barely talk to his grandson. From what Frank had heard, it sounded as if he was having a good time, 'Early days yet,' Frank muttered as he shuffled back to his chair. He bent down to wipe up the pools of cold tea and took another deep breath.

The doorbell rang.

'God! Who's that? Can't a man have a bit of peace and quiet in his own home?' He sat still. *Go away, I don't want anything, or anybody.*

The doorbell rang again. Frank turned to face the window, ignoring the noise.

The letterbox clattered, then Chris spoke. 'Are you there? Dad?'

Frank stifled a groan, then Chris spoke again. 'Dad? Are you in there?'

Dear God, I'll have to answer the bloody door.

He stood up again, sweat bubbled on his brow. 'I'm coming, hold on. I'm coming.'

Moving slowly he made his way to the front door and, as he reached it, the letterbox opened up and he saw Chris's eyes and dark brown eyebrows framed there.

'Dad? You OK?'

Without answering, Frank stooped low, unlocking the heavy bottom lock, the chain rattled as he tugged at it and finally he was able to open the front door.

Chris grinned at his father, 'Fort bloody Knox this house. You worry me, what would happen to you if there was a fire?' Chris closed the door and walked ahead of Frank into the kitchen. Frank moved slowly, his eyes on Chris. With his back to his father, Chris filled the kettle and looked out into the garden.

'Looks really good out here, Dad. Geraniums are impressive this year.'

Frank kept his eyes on Chris's head as he inched his way into the kitchen.

'Mm, yes, they are.' He reached his chair as Chris turned to face him.

Chris's eyes swept over Frank. 'I'm on my way to the supermarket, fridge is empty and thought I'd pop in, you sounded a bit off last night. Just wanted to make sure you're all right, see if you need anything. Thought you could tell me more about Jonathan, about France, all this daft nonsense of

Nina's.'

Frank didn't want to talk about France, about Nina and her sudden dash, he didn't have the energy to cope with Chris's hurt feelings.

Chris turned away as the kettle came to the boil and Frank eased himself down into a chair, briefly closing his eyes.

Setting two mugs down on the table Chris faced his father. 'See, I was only away for a week, one week! She must have been plotting this for ages. And camping! The woman can't cope without hot and cold running hairdryers.'

Chris's voice ran on, Frank was silent, watching the expressions chase across his son's face.

'One minute she's screaming at me for more money. God knows what she does with it all; then the next she's running off to France. What with? My money! I bet that Daniel bloke never pays her *his* son's maintenance. That's down to me, I'm sure!

Frank shifted, easing his spine into the upright of the chair. He moved his head, away from Chris's anger and looked out into the garden. He wanted to be there, sitting out on the lawn, feeling the sun on his back, soothing, calming.

Chris's tirade stopped and he moodily sipped at his tea.

'You're quiet, you OK, Dad? Actually, now I can see you properly, you look a bit pale. Anything wrong?'

'No, nothing. I'm fine.' Frank gazed steadily into Chris's eyes. 'I'm fine.'

Chris put his mug down. 'Well, what do you think about all this holiday stuff? Can't imagine you not having an opinion on it.'

Frank looked at the floor, 'Yes, you're right, I do have an opinion on it. You won't like it though.'

Chris opened his mouth, he began to speak, 'Now look ...'

'No, *you* look, look at what you and that ex-wife of yours are doing to your son. Jonathan. In the middle of your angry speech, you didn't mention his name once.'

Chris's face was directly opposite Frank, their eyes were level. 'I didn't expect you to understand, you've got to see the broader picture here. That's all you want to concentrate on,

Jonathan. Yes, he's important, of course he's important but it's more than that. It's her attitude I want to talk about, she thinks she can bleed me bloody dry.'

Frank shook his head, 'It's not about money, it's about whether she can look after Jonathan and the other kid, over there in France. It's got more to do with Jonathan than money.'

Chris moved unhappily on his chair, his fingers laced around the mug of tea.

'Yes, you're right about Jonathan, of course you're right, he *is* important, he's very important, but the whole time Nina keeps me dangling, not knowing what she's up to, what's going on over there in my house, keeping me out, the whole thing makes it very hard for me to be a father to him, the sort of father I want to be for him.' He shrugged, 'How can I expect you to understand, Dad, you and Mum never went through this, this divorce *crap.'*

Frank looked into his mug of tea. *Now what's he going to say?*

Chris pushed his chair back and crossed one leg. 'You know I was thinking about this the other day and if I had to define my marriage to Nina, I would have to call it a *vague* marriage.'

'Vague? What sort of word is that to describe a marriage?'

'That's how it felt to me, vague, undefined. I thought marriage would be positive, something defined by thick, black lines, reinforcing it, strong images. I always thought of your marriage to Mum like that, contained in those strong lines. That's what I wanted too.'

Frank snorted, 'You're talking like an architect! There are no reinforced lines in a marriage. If there's anything at all, it's elasticity. There's give and take, there's space for you both. You can't stay married behind lines. All that was wrong with your marriage was that you picked the wrong woman, she was a wrong 'un. Simple as that.'

Chris hunched over his tea, keeping his eyes away from Frank's face. 'I never told you this before but I thought Nina, not to look at perhaps, but I thought Nina was like Mum.

Something in her that mirrored Mum's love of life. "Free spirit," isn't that what Mum called her?'

The pain was gnawing at Frank. 'Bloody mess was what she was!'

Chris's head shot up, his eyes dark with anger, 'Your attitude didn't help. You made your feelings quite plain. Nina knew what you thought about her, Christ, *everyone* knew.'

Jesus, not now, I can't deal with this now. 'Look, son, this is not the right time. You're upset about Jonathan and his holiday, why don't we leave it for now? Would you like to look at the garden before you go?'

Chris shook his head. 'That's right, start something up, get it out into the open then ignore what's being said. Before you get rid of me, just remember that I came around to see you, to see if you're all right, if you need anything.'

'No, you bloody didn't! You came here because your nose is out of joint. They've gone on holiday and you knew nothing about it. Neither Jonathan nor his mother knew where you were. You'd gone off on your damn course and hadn't told either of them where you were. Admit it. You'd gone storming off to York because you'd had a row. You didn't even tell Jonathan, using him, keeping him in the dark because you wanted to get at her.'

Chris glared at his father. 'That's not true.'

'No?' Frank returned the glare. 'Are you sure?'

'Course I'm bloody sure. I told you where I was going, didn't I? All she had to do was ask you, but of course you've made that impossible. She can't ask you, you've always made your feelings quite plain as far as Nina is concerned.'

Needles of pain stabbed at Frank's neck and shoulders.

'So now what, you're saying I can't have an opinion?'

'Of course you can, just keep it to yourself.'

'I do, your mother and I felt …'

'Leave Mum out of this, she *liked* Nina, she told me that she thought the world of Nina, their interests were the same …'

Frank's laugh was mirthless, 'What interests? All that wife of yours, all Nina wanted, was to talk about books and suchlike.'

'Well sure as hell Mum couldn't talk to you about books. You've never read a book in your entire life. You've no idea have you?' Chris's face was dark red, his arms folded across his chest as he faced Frank.

Frank sighed, he took another deep breath 'Look, Chris, this has gone far enough. Leave it now, you're upset about Jonathan; I was going to tell you, he phoned today, this morning and he sounds fine. They're in Calais, weather's good and he's enjoying himself. 'Spect he'll ring you too.'

Chris shook his head, 'Don't bloody placate me. Don't shut me up just because you don't want to hear what's being said to you. You never listened to Mum and you don't want to listen to me.'

Frank looked away from the anger in Chris's eyes and shook his head. 'Leave your mother out of this. She'd have hated to hear you and I shouting, don't do this.'

'Do you know what Nina told me, do you know what Mum told Nina before she died? Well, do you?'

Frank put a hand out to touch his son's arm but Chris moved back. 'No! It's about time you knew, knew what you did to Mum.'

Frank lifted his head and his eyes met Chris's. 'Your mother knew I loved her. I don't know what you're talking about, but I do know it's pure poison and she'd have hated to hear you talk like this.'

'Loved her? You smothered her, that's what she told Nina. She said she couldn't breathe properly around you. You controlled her, watched everything she did. Christ, it's about time someone told you. You've never understood what you did, the way you did it. You organised everything, stopped her doing what she wanted to do. You made sure that she did everything your way. She couldn't even enjoy her garden, you robbed her of that too.'

'That's enough, I won't have this, you don't know what you're talking about.' *Sweet Jesus, Nancy?*

'Don't I? Do you deny that you curbed her gardening plans? You moved and cut back everything that she grew, you

55

let her do some things then waited until she'd finished so you could move everything back to where *you* wanted. Well? You can't deny it, can you? You bloody controlled her, it wasn't just the garden, it was every bloody thing.'

'I've had enough, I think you'd better go. This is not the time for this.'

'*When* will the time be right, Dad? Do you think that no one has the right to say these things to you? You damn well smothered her. You robbed her of so many things. Take a look around you, go on, look around, here, in this house.'

Frank's breathing was shallow, his voice weary, 'What the hell are you talking about now?'

Tiny beads of perspiration were on Chris's forehead. Impatiently, he rubbed at them, 'Here in this house, my mother's house. What have you left to show that she even lived here? I can't see her, can't see where she lived. All the things that gave her pleasure, you've destroyed every one of them.' He stood up, resting his hands on the back of the chair.

'I want you to leave now, before any more damage is done.' Frank moved his head away, away from Chris's angry stare.

Chris moved suddenly, his chair toppled. He left it there and stood upright. 'I'm going. Look around you, Dad. Can you see where Mum lived? What have you left in this house to remind any of us of Mum? *Is* there anything left? You must have gone right through every bloody room like a tornado, getting rid of every damn thing that Mum loved. Christ knows there's nothing here now.' He swept past Frank, the front door slammed, the kitchen window rattled.

This is the 10 o'clock news on Sunday the 30th of April.

In the sudden, shocking silence, the newsreader's voice blared out, filling the kitchen, creeping into the corners. It seemed to Frank that his ribs were tightening around him, his breathing was rapid, shallow. *The door, must lock the door.*

He eased himself upright and walked slowly to the front door, stooping down again, he slid the bolts and replaced the chain. He leant against the wall, all he could hear was the murmur of the radio then a sharp explosion of noise as a neighbour started up a lawnmower.

Damn noise, just want some peace.

He walked slowly back to the kitchen where sunlight danced on the white-painted windowsill. It was uncluttered, Frank liked it that way, meant he could see the garden. Nancy had grown herbs, lining up the small clay pots along the windowsill. 'Just smell the basil, it's wonderful. Don't the chives look good?'

After her death, Frank had shifted the pots, he'd put them near the garage away from sunlight. He was eating on his own, what did he want with basil or chives?

He liked neatness, order in the kitchen, knowing where things were. Nancy understood, she knew. *Bloody cheek, doesn't know what the hell he's talking about.*

'Silly bugger, needs a kick up the backside. Bloody good mind to ...' His words exploded, rattled from his mouth. He sat back at the kitchen table. *Don't want the papers now, can't be bothered. How dare he come around here, shouting his mouth off.* Somehow his anger had cushioned the pain.

Frank looked around the kitchen, at the shelves of gleaming saucepans lined up in order of size. The cupboards where he knew which shelf held cans of soup, which one held packets of cereal. The folded tea-towel, a clean one every day, put near the sink waiting to dry up his lunch dishes. He grunted, the orderliness pleased him.

'Didn't have a clue, Chris and that wife of his, they were just playing at marriage, didn't have a clue. Her with her endless books and Chris with, what's that rubbish he said, *lines?* For Christ's sake, they didn't have a clue, either of them.

Frank's gaze stopped when he saw the tin tray stacked neatly by the bread bin. An old metal tray with a picture of waving daffodils. Minute bubbles of rust showed through the faded yellow petals. Nancy had wanted to throw it out.

'For God's sake, Frank, the tray is decrepit. You're only putting things on the kitchen table, it's only a bowl of soup, just put what you want on the table, throw the ugly thing out.'

Frank had been impassive, silently placing cutlery,

condiments, butter dish on the tray, covering up the daffodils. 'Doesn't matter,' he told her solemnly, 'sloppiness leads to all sorts of things.'

He would have soup today for his lunch. Tomato soup. Wednesday's he liked to have a bowl of oxtail, Friday he opened a can of vegetable soup.

Nancy used to tease him. 'What happens, Frank, if you change your mind? What happens if you decided to have cheese on toast on Friday?'

'Don't be daft, I always have soup.'

She'd smiled, moving past him to make herself a salad.

Frank sat in the kitchen watching the sun's oscillating rays on the wall. Outside there were muted sounds of lawnmowers, a car engine starting up. He sighed, 'Should do the watering and I must check those beans.'

The phone rang, Frank jerked and the pain woke up. He glared at the phone, *shut up*. It shrilled again and again. 'Might be Jonathan, oh, hang on, wait a minute.' He struggled to get out of the chair; he was very stiff, he could barely move his legs. 'I'm coming, I'm coming.' He reached the phone 'Hello?'

'Dad, are you OK? You took a long time answering the phone.'

'So that's a problem now, is it?'

'Oh, for God's sake. I didn't want to leave things the way, well, the way they were. Just wanted to know that you were all right.'

'Well you know now!' Frank slammed the phone down, wincing as he did so. He put his head down and closed his eyes, *Sorry, Nancy.* As he straightened up he thought that he might as well open a can of soup although it was far too early for lunch. Wouldn't hurt, just open the can ready. Might as well. He shuffled over to the cupboard and found the tin. His fingers were swollen, the skin red and stretched. He scrabbled about in the cutlery drawer for the can opener. It was old, the handle repaired with neatly bound string. He had a sudden picture of Nancy.

'Frank, for God's sake, they're under a pound to buy.'

'Not the point, nothing wrong with this one.'

It was no use, his fingers wouldn't work, they wouldn't bend. He couldn't get a grip on the can opener. Suddenly he threw it to the floor, *stupid thing.* He opened the fridge door, a small piece of cheese sat on a blue saucer. He picked up the cheese and put it into his mouth.

Look at me now, Nancy. Living like a bloody mouse.

JONATHAN

Mum keeps on at me to take my Wild Bill hat off. She says I look stupid wandering around Paris with it on. Don't care. Euro Disney was brilliant and the Wild Bill show was the best of the lot. Wild Bill wore a coat with a fringe and he jumped on and off his horse. They had real buffalo and everything. The other rides were good too. We had to miss loads of them because of Sebastian. Mum said we couldn't leave him anywhere and he was too small for Space Mountain and the Indiana Jones ride. I said we should have left him at the campsite, plenty of people there to look after him but she glared at me. She said we had to take him on the giant tea-cup ride and she made me sit in that. Sebastian loved it, huge cups spinning around, not as good as the dodgems, though.

Snow White and Mickey Mouse were wandering up and down the streets and millions of pathetic parents were taking pictures of their kids with Mickey Mouse and his white gloves. They were quite good, only I saw Donald Duck hiding behind an ice-cream stand with a fag in his hand.

I wanted to go back again, I told Mum I didn't mind going on my own but she said I was being selfish. *Me!* She said we had to stay another day, just so she could see a bit more of Paris. We walked around for ages, she kept grabbing my hand whenever she saw another church or something. The Eiffel Tower was good though, we went up and got almost to the top. I told Mum I felt it move underneath my feet but she said she

60

didn't want to hear that.

There were loads of French kids up there, jabbering at each other. They stared at me when I asked Mum something. She said it was because I was wearing my Wild Bill hat but it wasn't that. At least I don't think it was. I thought of Grandma the whole time I was up there. Mum said she'd have loved the view. I took pictures in my head and whispered to her what I'd seen.

We went to the Louvre, Mum said that the day I saw the Mona Lisa was a day I'd remember for the rest of my life. Don't know about that, suppose the picture was all right. It had a Perspex screen over it and there were so many people with cameras, every time a flash went off, lights bounced off the screen. I told Mum that it looked as if Mona Lisa was firing back, shooting at everyone who was staring at her. Mum said I'd missed the point.

She got all dreamy again, walking around Paris.

'Can you feel the magic here, Jon? There's something so special about Paris.'

She'd already told me about coming here with Dad, how they'd been on honeymoon. 'We had a trip on the Seine, we walked the streets until two in the morning, we drank our coffee out of tiny cups. Who knows, you might come here on your honeymoon too.'

Yeah right. Still rather be at Euro Disney.

I haven't phoned Grandad yet. Not phoned Dad either. I was really cross with Grandad at first. What'd he expect me to do? Not go to Euro Disney? I kept thinking about him though. He'd told me that Grandma wanted to go to Paris so I bought some postcards and I've sent three to him. One had the Eiffel Tower on, another one had the Mona Lisa and the third one had a big Mickey Mouse face. I sent a card to Dad too; his had a picture of the Seine. Wonder if he remembers his trip with Mum?

Mum still hasn't got the hang of these tents. She keeps telling me to do them. 'Go on, Jon, you can do it so easily.' Course I can, that's because I do it all the time.

She laughs when she sees some of the other people on the site. 'They've brought their whole lives with them. Look, there's television sets everywhere. They've got lounger chairs, clothes lines. That woman over there's got rubber gloves on. Might as well be at home.'

Not sure about that, we're still eating our meals in the car or sitting on the grass outside the tents. Sebastian is a pain, he crawls all over the place. There's nowhere to strap him in inside the tent so Mum and I take it in turns to hold him on our laps when he eats.

Some woman sitting in a caravan had been watching us and she came over and asked if we wanted to borrow her daughter's portable high chair for a while. Couldn't believe it when Mum said no. 'Thank you, no, we're fine. He sits in one of those at home so this is much better for him, really it is.'

The woman looked at Sebastian, his nappy was hanging down to his knees and he was tugging at my arm, trying to grab my plate. I had to eat all my meals like this, holding my plate in the air out of his reach.

'Well, we're just over there if you change your mind.' The woman went back to her caravan. She must have said something to her husband because they both looked over. Mum saw them staring at us.

'God! What's the matter with people? Can't they leave things alone? Got to interfere, got to see everyone else conforming, falling into neat patterns.'

She had to speak loudly, Sebastian was bawling because he couldn't reach my plate. I was so fed up with eating this way. '*Why* can't we have it, the highchair?' I was standing, the only way I could eat. Sebastian was hanging on to my knees, his face was red, his nose snotty.

'Not you, Jon, I thought you'd understand. We're fine, aren't we? Aren't we having a good time?'

'Well, yes we are, France is pretty good but ...'

She didn't want to listen, she'd finished eating and went into the car to get the maps. 'About time we moved from here anyway. We've seen all I wanted to see.' She sat down, tucking her feet under her and opened the maps.

'Ok, let's see.' Her head was tilted to one side and she ran her tongue over her lips. 'We can do this in one day.' She jabbed a finger at the open page. 'See, Jon, the Loire Valley, chateaux, good restaurants; some of these are places that people here,' she jerked her head in the direction of the woman in the caravan, 'would never dream of going. They only want mussels and chips. They'll never see the real France, not like we're going to do.'

I could hardly hear above the sound of Sebastian's yells. I was really fed up. Without speaking to Mum, I pushed Sebastian off my knees and got into the car. I slammed the door and finished eating my supper. It had gone cold, I didn't really it want it any more but I ate it anyway. I didn't look at Mum once, she'll have to put up with Sebastian. He'll crawl over her maps and stuff. Serve her right.

We left the campsite early the next day. Mum's mouth was small and tight as if she'd locked words inside her. She barely spoke to me as we got the tents and stuff into the car. She dropped the maps on my lap and her finger pointed to the next campsite. 'L'Etang de la Breche, we're aiming for the N152.'

That was all she said really, well all she said to me. She kept half turning, talking to Sebastian, telling him where we were going. 'Wait till you see the Loire, it meanders through very pretty countryside. It's sometimes called *The Garden of France*, it's so beautiful.'

Don't know what she was going on about gardens for, she hardly ever touches ours at home. Only when she thought it was looking scruffy or Dad had given her a hard time over the lawn. I ignored her and stared out of the window. Then she started telling Sebastian about the campsite.

'This one's got three swimming pools and all the things that we can possibly need and it's close to the Chateaux. It's where the French themselves go. It's near the mushroom farms and,' she held her breath and, out of the corner of my eye, I saw her look at me very quickly before she let her breath out, 'it's close to the Troglodyte villages.' She stared straight ahead, keeping her eyes on the road.

I forgot I wasn't talking to her. 'What? Trog…?'

'Troglodyte villages carved out of the cliff wall. Houses built high up in the hills.'

'Really? Can people go in, do they allow that? Do people still live in them, does that make them trogs?'

'No, but that's where the word came from.'

I picked the map up, there were pictures of caves. I hadn't seen them before. They were amazing, they looked like normal houses only built up on a cliff-side. They had balconies with flowerpots, French doors, everything.

'Can we really go inside them? I mean are you allowed?'

'Yes, some of the are people's homes, but you can visit the caves, I thought you'd like that.'

We both stared out of the windscreen for a while, then I thought of something.

'Mum, did Dad come here, you know to the Loire, to these caves?'

'No, we didn't get this far and, anyway, your dad couldn't go into the caves could he? He's over six foot.' She laughed then and Sebastian joined in even though he didn't know what we were laughing at.

This L'Etang de la Breche site is pretty good. There's masses of places, they've got a football pitch, a small lake for fishing *and* a track for bikes. Mum says I can hire one and they've even got some local girls to look after babies and small kids. Mum's disappointed again because there seems to be loads of British people staying here as well. That's why she made me put the tents in the furthest pitch. It's miles from anywhere, got to walk for ages to get to the toilets and the shop. She says she doesn't want to hear English, she wants to hear French. Don't know why, she can't understand a word.

I don't mind being here at all, it's really good. I can ride a horse or kick a ball about. There's other lads here, they seem to be all right, about my age. The swimming pools are great, they've got slides and everything. There's a company, *Eurocamp*, you can see their tents dotted all over the place, they're bright green with yellow lettering. They're enormous tents, they'll sleep up to eight people. They've got everything, barbecue, garden furniture, even a hammock.

'People book those months ahead so that means they're committed to staying here for the whole time. Our way is much better, we're independent: we don't like something, we can just take off,' Mum said when I showed her the green tents. That might be right, but at least they've got everything they need.

She says we can do it all on this site and she and I worked out a system. She's booked us in for eight days so she says that on one day we can explore the places she wants to see and the next day we stay on the site so I get to do the things I want to do. Going to the troglodyte caves counts as one of Mum's days, so really I get two days for me then.

It's got everything here: restaurants, ice-cream kiosks. Mum says I'm a Philistine. There's a phone too, I can ring Grandad. I'll ring Dad too, let him know where we are this week.

'Grandad – it's me, Jonathan. We're at the Loire Valley.'

'Hello, lad, where did you say you were?'

'Loire Valley. This site is brilliant. It's got three swimming pools and a field to play football in. I can hire a bike too. Me and one of the other lads, we're off exploring tomorrow. Mum and I have worked out a system: she says I mustn't come all this way just to play football, I've got to see France as well so we went to a Chateau today.'

'That sounds fair to me. So what was it like?'

'OK, I suppose. It had a moat but the water was disgusting. Shouldn't think anyone dared fall in, they'd have got the plague.'

'France is working out well for you then? You're having a good time? And that young chap, is he all right?'

'Sebastian, yeah, he's fine. He doesn't know we're in France, well, that's what Mum says. He's trying to walk and he's just discovered how to take his nappy off. Mum just laughs, he crawls all over the place with nothing on.'

65

'That can't be right, must be hot, he should have something on.'

'That's what some woman told Mum but Mum says he's fine. She covers him up with sun cream all the time. Did you get my cards? Did you put them up in the kitchen?'

'Yes, I got them, I can see them now, on the board.'

'I'll send more, Grandad. We're here for a few more days, then Mum says we can have two days in Brittany – so I can go on the beach.'

'But you're all right, you and your mum? Not got into any trouble?'

'What sort of trouble?'

'I don't know, everything's different over there, the money, the euros, the food.'

'No, we're all right. I told you, France is OK. It's great. Me and Mum have worked out a system. One day for me and one day for Mum so we get to do the things that we both want.'

'Glad to hear it, lad. Smashing talking to you. Keep the postcards coming. They're grand, really grand. Take care now.'

It happened again, the feeling that Grandad was having a go at Mum and he shouldn't do that, he shouldn't ask about money and stuff. It really is all right here. It *really* is.

There's a boy on the site, Gareth, he's with his parents and sister. We sort of stick together when we're not out with parents. We can hire bikes and go off and do stuff. He said he thought Mum was *flaky*. He didn't say it in a mean way. He said it after we'd seen her sitting in the car eating her breakfast. Sebastian was sitting on the grass, tugging at her sandals and waving his spoon when he saw Gareth and me.

'Where's your stuff, you know, tables, chairs, all that. Where do you keep everything?'

Mum heard him and smiled. 'We travel light, don't need much for our holiday, do we Jon? Got everything we could possibly want. Got a car, somewhere to sleep at night, we can eat here, what else do we need?'

I didn't look at Gareth's face as he mumbled 'nothing'. Well, what else could he say?

'Jon, are you doing anything now? Could you take Sebastian with you, just for a little while?'

'Oh, Mum, we're going off on the bikes today, we're taking lunch and everything. Gareth's dad wants to come with us, he's found a hill where you can take the bikes … I *told* you about it last night.'

'OK, OK, keep your hair on.' She waggled her fingers at me and scooped Sebastian up on her lap. He grabbed the steering wheel, pulling on one side.

Gareth and I walked back to his caravan and that's when he said it. 'Your mum's a bit flaky isn't she?'

'She's what?' I didn't know what he meant by that.

'Flaky, you know, like Phoebe in *Friends*. Do you watch that? It's good, I like Rachel best.'

'Yeah, me too, she's all right.' Mum liked it and I sometimes watched it with her. Hadn't really taken much notice of it before.

Gareth's caravan was in another field where most of the bigger caravans were. His Mum and Dad were sitting outside drinking coffee. Alice, Gareth's sister, was there too, lying on a towel and listening to an MP3 player. She's younger than Gareth; she wears blue varnish on her toenails. She stares at me when she thinks I'm not looking. Gareth says she's a total dork. I don't know which is worse, a sister or a baby brother. Gareth's dad was teasing him about how fast he can go on the mountain bikes we'd hired.

'Beat you any day, mate. Lot of stamina in these legs of mine.'

'Yeah, right. You're dead fast downhill! The only thing in your legs is red wine.'

It was nice sitting outside in the sun; that's the other good thing about this holiday, it's hardly rained at all. There's always people sitting around on the campsite, drinking coffee or having a glass of wine, reading their books or wandering about. I thought how Grandma would have loved everything about it.

We'd booked the bikes for 10 o'clock and, just as we were going to collect them, Gareth's mum asked if I'd like to have a barbecue with them that night.

'Ask your mum first, we'll be eating about 8.00. Or, perhaps she'd like to join us? Bring the baby, your brother, I'm sorry, I've forgotten his name.'

'*Muum!* The baby's name's Sebastian.' Alice still had her headphones on, don't know how she heard what her mother was saying, but she went all red after she'd spoken.

Gareth's mum laughed, 'Sorry, Sebastian, of course. He's very welcome too.'

'Thanks, I'll ask her. I'll do it now.'

Gareth said he'd come with me and he ran into the caravan to get his Ipod, he'd been showing off about it before. I told him that I'd probably get one for Christmas. In their awning there's two cases of wine, a big umbrella and they've got their trainers and picnic stuff all pushed to one side. The Hendersons drive a Ford Galaxy, it's dark blue with an enormous roof rack and a rack for their bikes. They've brought their ordinary bikes with them and sometimes they go off for the day together. I hadn't thought of asking Mum if I could bring my bike on holiday. Bet I know what she'd have said if I had asked though.

Gareth let me try his Ipod. It was brilliant. He showed me how it worked, told me all about the music he downloaded, all that stuff. We ran over to Mum.

It was hot and I was sweating when we got to the Clio. Mum was still sitting in the front seat with Sebastian on her lap.

'Look at you, like a tomato about to burst.'

Sebastian put his hands up when he saw me. He's been doing that a lot since we've been on holiday. He wants me to pick him up all the time. I ignored him.

'Mum, Gareth's mum and dad want to know if I can have a barbecue with them tonight.' Gareth nudged me. 'Oh, they've asked you too and you can bring Sebastian.'

'A *barbecue*.'

She said the word as if it was something disgusting but I

ignored that too.

'It's very kind of them but I don't think I can. I'm not really that …well, to be honest, it's a bit difficult with this little fellow.' She bent her head and kissed Sebastian's hair. 'Please thank your mum and dad, Gareth, but I don't think I can make it. What about you, Jon? Do you want to go?'

'Yeah, I do.' My face was really hot and I grabbed Gareth's shoulder and I turned away from Mum. 'See you later.' Gareth and I ran as fast as we could over to the bike hire place. *Flaky.*

It was Mum's day today and she planned for us to go to another chateau. *Chenonceaux.* 'Apparently this is where fireworks were first seen in France.' She said there were places to have picnics in the grounds. We could look at the Troglodyte village on the way back. We needed some shopping too. I'd told her about the Hendersons' crates of wines.

'Bought them in the supermarket, I suppose? Thought we'd have a look at the wine cellars. There were masses of them on the road. We'll get some from there.'

I started to say something about where we're going to put them; they'll have to stay in the Clio, there's no room in the tents. Mum was trying to put Sebastian's nappy on and he was yelling so much she couldn't hear a word.

This is the best site so far. We've been here for five days. I've asked Mum if we can come back next year. I told her Gareth's parents come back each year but she just smiled that stupid smile she often uses. 'I don't think so.'

Can't understand her sometimes.

The barbecue was good. Gareth's dad went around saying we were eating horse-burgers. I drank some of their red wine, it wasn't that bad. Alice had put some glittery stuff on her face and Gareth teased her so she hit him. They got a telling off for that.

I didn't come back to our tents until half-past ten. Mum was sitting in the car. She had the interior light on trying to read her book. The inside of our car is a tip. The light was shining on all the junk. Mum's always shouting at me at home, telling me to tidy up my room and not leave cups and things about. It's not fair, the car's much worse than my room. There's empty crisp packets on the back seat, peppermint wrappers, mashed banana on the window, baby wipes and some squashy apples that we'd brought from home. No one wants to eat them now. I don't understand why Mum can't see this mess. People walking past us, they can see. They can see Mum sitting in the front of her car with her book resting on the steering wheel. She ignores them when they say 'hello', pretends she can't hear.

She hadn't seen me and her hair was sticking up all over the place. She rubs her hands over her head when she's tired or cross. With the light shining on her hair, it looked like those rusty Brillo things she cleans the oven with.

I stood right by the front door and only then did she see me. 'So, you're back. Have a good time?'

'Yeah, Mrs Henderson said would you like to have a drink with them one night, before we go?'

She yawned and closed her book, 'We'll see.'

I thought I should ring Dad before he left for work.

'Dad? It's me, Jonathan.'

'Jon? Hello, mate, what've you been up to?'

'Well, yesterday I hired a mountain bike with Gareth and his dad, that was good and then last night I had a barbecue with them.'

'Did your mother go?'

'No, she stayed here with Sebastian. We're off to another chateau today and Mum says we can see the Trog ... wotsit villages again, and the mushroom farms.'

'Are you enjoying France, Jon?'

'Yeah, I like this site the best; there's masses to do. We've only got another three days here. I've asked Mum if we can come back here next year.'

'Oh, have you?'

There was something different in Dad's voice when he

70

said that. I didn't know what it was but I rushed to say something. 'Yes, Gareth and his parents come here all the time and he's asked me to go and stay with them when we're back home. Mum said she'd think about it.'

There was a pause, it was as if Dad was counting and when he did speak his voice sounded rushed, 'Well, before that perhaps you and I can have a trip together, back to Cornwall, what do you think about that?'

'Suppose so,' I didn't want to talk about Cornwall, not when I was in France.

'Dad? Gareth's got one of those new Nintendos, you know, the DS ...'

'Has he? How many banks has his father robbed?'

'They're not that expensive. Gareth's got the top of the range one and I know that was expensive but they're coming down all the time and you can get one for only £100.' I didn't know if that was true but I thought I'd try anyway.

'Only £100! That's still a lot, Jon.'

'Yeah, right.' I was fed up and I didn't want to say anything else.

'I've got to go now, son, got a meeting first thing. Really good talking to you, take care, talk to you soon.'

What is it with parents?

I suppose the chateau at Chenonceau was OK. Mum stumbles around with her nose in a guide book most of the time and she keeps reading bits out to me and then she gets cross if I don't look at what she's talking about. We had our picnic across the road from the chateau, under some trees where it was cooler. Mum left Sebastian sleeping on the blanket from the car and it was nearly 4 o'clock by the time we left.

We stopped to get bread and fruit and Mum said she liked the look of the village we were in so we strolled up the cobbled streets and we had an ice-cream.

'Boulangerie, Patisserie, don't they sound wonderful. Beats going to Tesco's.' She was all dreamy again.

I thought boulangerie sounded the sort of word that I'd find in the magazines that David Staples has in his sports bag.

He gets them from his brother and he shows them to a gang of us at lunch break. *And* he asked me once if I thought Miss Bowden, our English teacher, ever wore crotch less knickers. *Boo lingerie.*

Mum was holding Sebastian and I was holding a stick of French bread and trying to stop the ice-cream from dribbling all down my arms. I dawdled because it was so hot and I wanted to get back to the site. Gareth and me, we're taking part in a swimming tournament.

'Jon! Come here, look at these prices.' She'd stopped outside an estate agent's window.

'Look at this, how much is that? Look at this one. That's only about £56,000. Look at it, it's wonderful.'

It was a really grotty window, it looked to me as if most of the photos were faded by the sun and their edges had curled up. There was a big spider's web covering the left-hand side of the window.

Sebastian wanted to get down so she jiggled him around a bit more, balancing him on her hip. 'Five more minutes, that's all. Here's another one, this one's got two outbuildings, I could work in one of those, wouldn't take much to convert, be masses of cash left over ...'

She was talking to me, at least I think she was. Her head was swivelling from the estate agent's window then back to me. Then she was grinning like an idiot at Sebastian. Her words sort of bounced off us. She didn't want me to say anything, I could see that.

'Jon! Look at this one, this one is only, what? Oh, stupid Euros, I don't know, about £85,000. Look at the size of it. God, Jon, I could buy two houses for what ours is worth at home.'

I was fed up, almost as fed up as Sebastian, my ice-cream had melted and I was really hot.

'What do we want *two* houses for? Giving one to Dad, are you?'

She looked at me then, really stared at me as if she was trying to see the words I'd just spoken, see what else I was going to say to her.

She closed her eyes, keeping them closed as she spoke. 'No, not your dad. It's just us, remember, the three of us?'

She told me that she was determined that I wouldn't spoil her mood. 'There are other estate agents, Jon and I think it's something we should think about and even if you don't want to think about it, then I do!'

The three of us were sticky and hot when we got back to the campsite and I said I was off to find Gareth.

'Oh no you're not. You can go to the small swimming pool and take Sebastian with you. He's hot too.' Even as Mum spoke to me, she was taking off his T-shirt and shorts. His hair was stuck to his forehead and the back of his head was wet.

'Oh, no, Muum. I look such a dork with Sebastian hanging around me all the time. This is one of *your* days, remember?'

'*Dork?* What sort of word is dork?' She'd pulled Sebastian's T-shirt over his head and, as his head came through the neckband, his eyes were watching me. I didn't want to see his eyes and I didn't want to stay there so I just ran off.

'My fucking word, that's what it is.'

'Jonathan! Come back, Jonathan ...'

Flaky old witch. Flaky old witch.

I had to borrow Gareth's swimming trunks. Mrs Henderson asked me if everything was all right when I said I'd been in a rush and just forgot my trunks. She pulled a pair from their washing line, something else Mum hadn't thought about, she dries all our stuff on the hedge at the back of us.

I beat Gareth in the tournament. He said it was a draw but it wasn't. Alice watched us and she said I'd won. Gareth flicked her with his wet towel. She started yelling at him and then Mrs Henderson came over and told them both to stop showing off.

'Showers for the pair of you and then we're going into the village for something to eat.' She smiled at me, 'What about you, Jon? Would you like to come too?'

I thought about Mum, I thought about sitting in the Clio

73

eating our supper or eating on the grass with Sebastian crawling all over me and I said, 'Yes, please.'

I said that I'd tell Mum and get changed and then I ran off. I ran really fast until I knew they wouldn't be able to see me. I went into the shower block furthest away from Mum and from the Hendersons. I stood under the water for ages. I was there so long my feet looked dead white. They looked as if the water had washed away all my tan, they looked just like the pieces of cod that Grandma used to buy when I was little.

'Fish for your brains, to make you very clever,' she always told me that. I felt a bit uncomfortable thinking about Grandma, she wouldn't have liked me swearing at Mum. I held my face up to the water, *Sorry, Grandma.*

The whole time we were out I didn't think about Mum. Well, I did, but only a couple of times when we were in the restaurant. It was the one in the little village close to the campsite so we walked there. Me and Gareth in the front, then Alice, then Mr and Henderson. There were loads of people from our site in the restaurant. Mrs Henderson kept saying *hello* as different people came in. I don't think Mum would have known any of them.

There was a blackboard outside on the pavement and it had *Plat du Jour* written on it and underneath there were all sorts of things. Mr Henderson said I could have anything I wanted from the blackboard menu. Gareth said he wanted mussels and chips. That's when I thought about Mum and what she'd said. I said I'd like mussels and chips too. Alice went bright red and said she wanted them too.

When we left the restaurant, Mr and Mrs Henderson walked in front of us, they were singing *Satisfaction* and Mr Henderson was trying to dance like Mick Jagger. Mrs Henderson started to laugh and then he stopped and held her hand. Gareth put his finger in his mouth and made sick noises. His mother saw him and said, 'You'll be holding someone's hand before too long.'

Alice smirked and stuck her tongue out at her brother.

When I saw the entrance to the campsite I started to feel

funny. Not sick or anything, just *funny*. I knew Mum would be angry with me because I'd sworn at her. I'd never done that before.

When we reached the path where the Hendersons went towards their caravan I started jabbering about the meal. 'It was really great, I love mussels, never had them before I came here, to France, and now I just love them. Thank you ever so much.'

'Only mussels and chips, Jon, glad you enjoyed them. Goodnight, 'spect we'll see you tomorrow.'

They all walked on up the path and I stood there watching them for a while. I wondered what they'd say if I told them I wanted to go back to their caravan with them. Mrs Henderson turned and saw me; I waved at her. She said something to Mr Henderson and then they both turned to look at me. I started to put my arm up to wave again then I thought I looked stupid so I brought my arm down. I had to move otherwise they'd know something was wrong.

It wasn't late, only half-past ten but I couldn't see anyone in our field, usually there are lots of people outside their tents or trailers, drinking wine or playing cards but there was nobody and it was very quiet.

Mum was sitting on the grass leaning up against the driver's door of the Clio. Her legs were stretched out in front of her, a bottle of wine between her knees and she had a glass of wine in her hand. Her head was back, her eyes were closed. Suddenly I felt very scared.

'Mum?'

She didn't move, she didn't open her eyes or anything.

'Mum? You OK?'

She kept her eyes closed. 'What do you care?'

I started to apologise for swearing but she opened her eyes and looked at me. 'I lost Sebastian tonight. He wandered off and I didn't know where he was. He was gone for hours, anything could have happened to him. And where were you? With your new friends.' She gulped down her wine, the gulp was really loud in the silence.

'Is he all right, what happened?' I didn't recognise my

voice.

She took a deep breath and I had the weirdest feeling, I felt that I wasn't the only one listening to her explanation. It was really odd, it seemed to me that all the other people in the field were listening too, it was as if they were holding their breath, same as me.

She poured herself another glass of wine. 'Muum!'

'Interested now, are you? You couldn't care less before, just ran off and left us.'

I didn't know what to say to her so I walked around her over to the tent. Sebastian was fast asleep, his arms over his head, hands curled up into tiny fists.

'He looks OK, what happened?'

Mum was shaking, the wine was spilling all over her T-shirt. She didn't seem to notice it and I could hear her teeth rattling on the glass as she held it up to her mouth again. She began to cry and, as she told me what happened, she hiccupped. 'He screamed for you, he just wouldn't stop crying. He made himself sick, he cried so much. He couldn't understand why you'd run off. He didn't want me, he wanted you. I tried to take him into the little pool but he didn't want that either. He was screaming so much everyone at the pool was staring at me. It was obvious that they felt I'd been hurting him. Every time I went near him, he screamed.' She shivered again, 'It was awful.' She wiped her nose on the sleeve of her T-shirt.

I sat down next to her, I felt really strange. I didn't know what to do or say to her. Part of me wanted to give her a hug.

She always asks me for a hug when she's upset but right then I think I wanted a hug for *me* not for her. I kept quiet, she was too angry with me.

She took a deep breath and started talking again. 'I brought him back here to the tents and he was a bit quieter. I thought I'd get him something to eat, to take his mind off you. I turned my back for one minute, *one minute*, I was talking to him the whole time.

'Look, Sebastian, a banana, a big one, all for you.' When I turned around, he'd gone. Just disappeared. I can remember

76

thinking he can't have gone far, it's only been a minute. I kept
thinking that, I couldn't see him anywhere, he'd gone.

'But he couldn't have gone, he can't *walk.*' I shouted at
her, I didn't mean to but I didn't understand. How could he
have gone? She started to cry again only this time it was much
quieter and she put her head right down. The lights from the
site were glinting on her hair. She must have been really upset,
her hair was such a mess, chunks of it sticking out all over the
place.

I put my hand out to touch her and she jumped, shifted
away from me as if I'd burnt her or something.

She cleared her throat then started talking again.

'Yes, he *can* walk, that's what happened. You were
exactly the same, one day crawling, and the next walking.
Who knows what was in his head. Looking for you, exploring?
Who knows? All I knew was that he'd gone and gone quickly.
I thought someone had taken him.' She took another mouthful
of wine.

'I started running up and down between the tents, then
over to the caravans, calling his name over and over.' She
gave a funny smile. 'What did I expect him to do? Say, "here I
am, Mummy"? I was frantic. Then that woman, you know the
one, she's always watching us, she said she saw him briefly
between two cars. She came with me but all we found was his
nappy, he'd taken it off again. It felt as if he'd been missing
for hours but it was just a few minutes. The woman called her
husband over and he started to look with us, between tents,
inside them, underneath cars, caravans, we looked
everywhere.' She sighed.

'Where was he?'

She looked at me then, squarely in the face, for the first
time since I'd come back.

'Two hours he'd been lost, that's a long time for a little
boy. Two hours, think about it, Jon.'

I did. All the time I'd been in the restaurant with Gareth
and his parents, eating mussels, drinking coke, Sebastian had
been missing.

Mum's glass was empty again and she splashed more wine

into it.

'D'you know what the woman said, what she asked me? She wanted to know if I thought someone had taken him in. Taken him in? Like he was a stray, like I didn't want him, didn't care about him.'

She started crying all over again and this time when I touched her, she didn't move away, she held my hand.

She shuddered and then she stroked my fingers. 'All the time we were looking, I could hear a dirty great big dog barking. Whatever it was it had an *enormous* bark. The whole time.' She looked at me quickly. 'The woman's husband went to check for me, they thought the same as me, that a dog must have ...'

There were loads of dogs on the site. They all had to be kept on a lead, it was a rule. One bloke near us even walked his Siamese cat around at night on a lead.

Every small road on the campsite had lights, almost as big as street lights and they stayed on all night so I could see Mum's face very clearly. Her tears had formed in two, tiny streams, pouring down each cheek.

'Everyone of them, all of them,' her hand waved spilling the wine, 'they all helped look. We walked all over the site, even down to the main road. They asked me questions all the time, where *you* were, had Sebastian been ill, all sorts of questions. I could see in their eyes that they'd been judging me, wondering what sort of mother I was.'

'Where did you find him?' I took the wine glass from her hand.

'She was right,' her head jerked towards the caravan at the back of us. 'Someone had been keeping an eye on him. Some girl found him near the swings. She stayed there with him for a while hoping I'd turn up I suppose, then she took him back to her parents. They thought that he'd soon be missed and someone would find him. He was fine, they'd given him biscuits and a drink. Didn't want to leave them, he started to cry again when I picked him up. Can you *imagine* how that made me feel?'

She put her head back again up against the Clio's door.

'They all heard you swearing at me, Jon, they all judged *me* by your swearing. Not fair is it? Or is it?'

I didn't know what to say to her, how to answer that question. Suppose I thought that it wasn't fair but I still didn't know what to say. Mum looked down at her lap, at her hand holding mine. 'I don't want to stay here, Jon. I don't like it here any more. I think we should pack up and move on.'

All I could think of was that we'd paid for eight days, we had another three left. 'We've paid though.' The words somehow escaped from my mouth before I knew what I'd said.

She looked at me, her eyes were really dark. Not even any reflection from the overhead lights in them, nothing, just her dark eyes looking into mine.

'Does that matter, Jon?'

When Grandad asked me if we'd got into any trouble, I said no because we hadn't then, but we're in trouble now.

Grandma, you know I didn't mean it. Make her change her mind.

NINA

Sometimes, Nancy, life is so hard without you.

FRANK

A combination of pain and the row with Chris had kept Frank indoors for days. *How many days have I been stuck here, what's today? Thursday?* It must have been Wednesday yesterday, he'd had his bowl of oxtail soup so today could only be Thursday. He'd felt locked in. Not just the house, his body felt restricted, tight, as if it was enclosed in a steel box. He hadn't managed to do anything in the garden, instead he spent his days shuffling between his chair and the kitchen. He'd managed to open a few tins, beans and suchlike. *Won't starve anyroad.* Just as well he had a few cans in the cupboard.

'Fat lot Chris cares.' Even as he said this Frank realised how unfair he was being. Chris was totally unaware of Frank's crippling pain. He'd told no one. Nobody knew because Frank didn't want people poking their noses into his business. *I can handle this, I can cope. Don't need nosy parkers shoving their two-pennyworth in. Just need to take it easy. I'll be fine.*

He'd spent days sitting in one of a pair of winged-back armchairs that stood on either side of the fireplace. A small table held a mug, a plate of digestive biscuits, Frank's reading glasses and a photo album. A notebook and pen lay on the floor.

Ever since Chris had stormed out of the house, Frank held silent arguments with his son, replaying the row, over and over. He'd mentally explained to Chris how he'd felt about Nancy until he realised that he'd been defending himself. He'd

81

never felt the need to do that with Nancy. *You understood me, you'd have known what to say to Chris, to tell him he was wrong.*

A bookcase tucked in the alcove behind Frank's chair held four gardening books, three photo albums and, on the top shelf, in a plain wooden frame, a black and white photograph of Frank and Nancy on their wedding day. Frank in a dark suit and blindingly white shirt sitting close to Nancy. Nancy's face was turned towards him; on her head she wore a delicate arrangement of pale rose-buds almost obliterated by her thick, curly hair. Frank's head was down, he was looking at their entwined hands, his large fingers resting on Nancy's wedding ring. A smaller frame stood behind, it held a photograph of a ten-year-old Chris who stared grave-faced, his chin up as if he was trying to distance himself from the prominent knot of his first tie.

In the other recesses Frank had built two shelves where Nancy had kept houseplants and framed photographs of Jonathan. After Nancy's death the house plants died too and Frank had re-arranged the frames, they now stood in chronological order, each one carefully placed four inches away from its neighbour. A newly born Jonathan, his eyes staring blankly at the photographer was closest to the fireplace; then, as a toddler, his mouth wide open, the shriek caught by the camera as he sat in a toy car. School photos, grey-blue background remaining the same, bore silent testimony to Jonathan's steady growth, his open freckled face, laughing, growing. Both shelves were dusted regularly by Frank, it was a chore he took great care over. When he'd finished dusting, he always placed the frames back carefully, regulating the distance between them.

Nancy had loved the photos, she'd enjoyed the history of each one.

'Remember this one, Frank? When he'd fallen the day before, lost his tooth? Cost you 50 pence that time. And this one? He'd grumbled about having his picture taken, said he'd miss the football match.'

Nancy used to move the frames, shifting them around.

Jonathan's face gazing out at his grandparents from different corners of the living room. Frank liked having the photos near him, he liked the *bank* of them there, where he could see them.

The play was produced in Manchester and the part of Edmund was taken by..

'Bloody rubbish, even Nancy would have agreed with me on that one.'

Frank kept the radio on during the day, if he went out into the garden he made a point of turning it off and switching it on again the moment he returned to the house. On one of his bad pain days he needed the radio, telling himself he should keep abreast of the news, the weather. *Won't know what's what if I don't.* It filled the corners of the house, he felt less alone, less isolated, with a voice in the background.

Nancy had enjoyed listening to the afternoon play. She'd make tea for them both and, in the summer, she'd sit in the garden, a Walkman tucked neatly into her pocket, headphones slightly askew, smiling, nodding or frowning as she listened to the drama.

If Frank was working in the garden, tucked behind the garage, he'd watch her out of the corner of his eye, basking in her understanding, her enjoyment. Even without listening to the play he'd share her indignation if it had been a poor production or a poor tale, in Nancy's opinion, 'not worth the telling'. Without realising that he did so, Frank looked over to the armchair on the other side of the fireplace.

From the small table he lifted the photo album onto his lap. He tucked the arms of his reading glasses carefully behind each ear then ran his hands down the flat of his thighs. He opened up the red mock leather album and settled back into the armchair. The first page held Nancy's carefully written date: *September 1960.*

At first, when Nancy bought the albums, she'd labelled and dated each photograph in her energetic scrawl. The enthusiasm for the photographs had remained but most of the photos were undated.

The first photograph showed Nancy holding a nine-month-old Chris, wide-eyed smile, arms outstretched. Frank remembered the day: Chris had been determined to hold the camera. Nancy had been laughing, the camera picking up the tracery of lines around her eyes. *The year we planted the roses,* Nancy had written underneath the snapshot. Frank had placed them by the back door so she could enjoy their delicate fragrance. She'd loved the floribunda, *Lily Marlene,* 'Closest you'll ever get to her,' she told Frank.

Frank slowly turned the pages *Chris aged 4 years.* Three photos of Chris on his first bike, the stabilisers hadn't lasted long, Frank remembered, although a sticking plaster on one rounded knee might have meant they hadn't lasted long enough. Two photos showing Chris sitting stiff and proud in his school uniform. A Christmas photo, Chris's head just visible under mounds of wrapping paper. Nancy in the right-hand corner of the photograph holding out another present, the lights on the tree looking like blurred stars. Frank flicked through the pages, his eyes rested on a graduation photo of Chris, his fingers curled around an impressive roll of paper. He'd been learning the guitar, one fingernail was long, manicured.

Frank felt soothed by the photographs, his body shifted in the chair, he turned another page. A photo of him sitting in a deckchair on the lawn. He'd always loathed the white plastic furniture, preferring instead to drag out the old-fashioned striped deckchairs each summer. In the photo Frank was sitting in the glare of the sun looking uncomfortable, wearing a blazer, shirt and tie. His eyebrows were huddled together as he frowned at the camera.

Nancy had taken that photo, he remembered her voice, 'Frank, for God's sake, *relax!'* He couldn't remember why he was dressed so smartly, where they were going, he had no idea.

Two new faces in the next photograph and Frank narrowed his eyes.

These are her parents, Nina's mum and dad. The mother had some weird name…

Chris was there too, sitting next to Nina, the pair of them cross-legged on the lawn, Nancy was sitting next to a middle-aged couple, their faces, with their fixed smiles, stared out at Frank.

Frank remembered *that* occasion, oh, God what were their names? He'd never been able to remember them. Nancy called it his selective memory. She'd sighed, 'You only remember the things you want to remember and you don't want to remember Nina's parents' names. Their names are Leonara and James.' She'd tapped him lightly on the shoulder with a teaspoon as she prepared a tray of tea to carry out to the garden. They'd invited Nina and her parents to tea a week or so before the wedding. Frank and Nancy had rowed following that afternoon. He could remember each row they'd ever had.

'Stuck up buggers, the pair of them.' His voice had been sharp. He'd been in the kitchen with Nancy clearing up after tea. Chris and Nina had taken her parents home.

Nancy stood at the sink, the back door was wide open, the rays of the early evening sun gave a golden flush to the walls of the kitchen, picking up the coppery threads in her hair. Her hands were immersed in water, bubbles popping as she washed up the tea things. Frank had already put away the deck chairs and the rug and he'd cleared the garden of any sign that six people had sat out on his lawn.

He'd made the remark as he brought the tray into the kitchen. His head had been turned away, he didn't see the expression on Nancy's face as she threw a soggy tea towel at him. It whipped at his face, startling him, he shouted, 'What the …?' he glared at his wife.

Nancy turned to face Frank, 'Stop it, stop it! You've got no reason to say that about Nina's parents. They're two perfectly nice people who care a lot about their only child, as we do.' Two cherry spots appeared on her cheeks, her eyes were bright, sparkling, whether through temper or unshed tears, Frank wasn't sure.

'They *are* stuck up,' he held his nose between his index finger and thumb. 'You can call me Leo,' he mimicked. 'Silly woman,' he grinned at Nancy.

She looked unsmiling at him. 'Do you know how unfair you're being? How stupid, just because, just because …' she shook her head.

'Come on, Nance, they're not worth having a row about, they're not important,' he put his hand out to touch her, but she stepped back.

'But they *are,* they are important, or they're important to Chris, they'll be his in-laws. Frank, for that reason alone, you should have made more of an effort.'

'*Me?* I like that! I tried, be fair now, Nancy, I did try. Couldn't get past the accent, anyroad, she didn't want to talk to me, she made that perfectly clear, snobby, bloody woman.'

'That's enough, Frank.' Nancy's head snapped back, she seemed to be drawing breath, preparing for an onslaught against him. 'You're not being honest, you don't like Nina and no matter who her parents are or what they said, nothing changes that fact.'

Frank tried to argue, to defend himself, but Nancy had turned away, back to the sink, she clattered the dishes, she made the water sound loud.

Frank's arms ached with the weight of the photo album, the memories in them. He closed the album and rested his head on the back of the chair and closed his eyes.

He'd never liked people visiting. Nancy used to laugh at him, she'd called him a hamster. 'You like living in a cage, Frank, not allowing anyone in.' She'd caught him one day, hiding behind the pantry door when the doorbell rang and he'd been in the house on his own She'd been at the bottom of the garden, picking lettuce for their tea and had walked into the kitchen.

Frank smiled, she'd always know what he'd been doing.

'It could be a long-lost cousin, it could be the man from the football pools, it could be someone needing help.'

'Aye and it could just mean trouble, some nosey-parker wanting to know our business, who needs 'em?'

Nancy just ruffled his hair and walked to the front door.

Sitting there on his own, Frank closed his eyes. He could *see* Nancy, conjure up an image of her, her head on one side, questions in her eyes and on her lips. 'Why do you dislike other people? Why do you always think they'll interfere, spoil things?'

Because he liked things the way they were, he didn't need anyone else in their lives, he'd told her that many times. Nancy had never understood his attitude.

'But you do need people, everyone does. Other people balance our lives, they enrich us. Otherwise, Frank, you'll live in some sort of vacuum and that's not right, well it's not right for me.'

What Frank knew about himself was that he didn't need other people: he had Nancy and he had his son. They were enough, more than enough for him. Now that Nancy was dead, he'd cope, he'd always coped. Just like he coped with his pain, it was purely and simply mind over matter, not allowing it to interfere with his life. Nothing to worry about, just a nuisance, it would go away eventually.

BBC Radio Four, this is the four o'clock news.

Frank shook his head, *This won't do, nearly dropped off, need a cup of tea, about time I had a fresh cup.* The pain gnawed at him, his skin felt clammy, he ran a finger around his neck. *Been sitting too long.*

Gripping the armrests, he gently levered himself up. Collecting the mug, Frank moved slowly to the kitchen. He ran cold water over his wrists before filling the kettle. He gripped the sink with both hands watching the veins in his hands as he flexed his fingers. He busied himself rinsing out his tea mug, wiping it carefully before placing a fresh tea-bag inside. Nancy had hated tea, she always drank coffee, insisting on trying out different varieties. 'Why is it that coffee always smells better than it tastes? Why do you think that is, Frank?' At one time the kitchen shelves were lined with different pots of Kenyan coffee, Arabic, de-caffeinated; she'd wanted to try them all. They'd all gone, Frank had put everything into the dustbin a few days after Nancy's funeral. An old tea caddy stood on its own on the shelf. Frank had never liked the taste of coffee, he found it bitter, sharp. He didn't want the smell in the house any longer, couldn't bear to be reminded of Nancy's fingers linked around her mug, with its curling spirals of steam as she sat frowning over a crossword puzzle in the morning paper.

As the kettle began its shrieking, Frank shut his eyes, squeezing the lids. *Damn and blast you, Chris. She is here, she never left.*

The kettle bubbled, steam began to cloud the window. *Click,* it turned itself off. Frank opened his eyes and poured the boiling water into the waiting mug. He shook his head, the row with Chris had shaken him badly, he'd doubted his own beliefs, his feelings. *I don't need things to remind me, she's here, with me all the time.*

The pain was slowly ebbing and Frank moved around the kitchen, pouring milk into his tea, getting rid of the tea-bag in a pile of potato peelings, apple cores, all lumped together in a carrier bag kept underneath the sink. Shaking his head, as if to dislodge Chris's anger and criticism, Frank opened the back door.

The perfumed air, the honeysuckle, roses, lavender, all the scents that Nancy loved, he could smell each one of them. Holding his mug of tea, Frank took a deep breath.

As he stared out at the garden, Frank recognised, not for the first time, that he'd relied on Nancy to put things right, she restored a sense of balance in his life. He'd had no idea what to expect from married life.

Frank's parents died within three months of each other, his father dying first and Frank had always felt that his mother enjoyed her widowhood. He'd find her in the kitchen, wrapping her arms around herself as if she was giving herself a congratulatory hug on having the good sense not to die first, as if she'd finally outsmarted her husband. A massive stroke killed her and, along with a sizeable legacy, his parents left Frank with a warped idea of what marriage should be like.

His parents, Gordon and Edna, had conducted their lives like characters in a play, learning lines, acting out their roles as a devoted couple in front of others but retreating to separate rooms in their home. Edna was delicate, she used the word all the time: *feeling delicate, delicate stomach, I have a delicate head.* Frank's earliest memory of his father was watching him walking home after he'd closed and locked up the gents' outfitters he owned. Gordon had a car, one of the first in the street, a Lanchester in a respectable blue. It was used only on the weekends, 'Saving it, don't want to wear it out,' Gordon told his son. Frank saw how his father's stance changed, he seemed to deflate as he entered their house. He clearly remembered seeing his father's face peering around the front door, 'How's your mother?'

Edna had been a pale woman, face devoid of colour, fine, nondescript hair, limply curling around her neck. She'd always been tired, dreadfully tired cleaning out the fireplace, washing the kitchen floor. As a young boy one of Frank's chores was to take trays of tea up to his mother. The tea was inevitably weak, an insipid colour that matched Edna's lifeless hair as she lay on the silk eiderdown in the front bedroom of their home. Their house was always silent, eerily so as noise gave Edna a headache. Frank lived under a constant threat from his father, 'Don't start anything, no noise mind, you'll disturb your mother.' One of Frank's recurrent fears, each time he took a tray up to his mother or walked downstairs for his breakfast each day, was stepping on the creaky stair tread. He learnt how to plant his feet away from the noisy tread. It haunted him, the worry that he might forget, he might rush downstairs one day and the noise would give his mother another headache.

'But why didn't your father repair it, he could have stopped the creak. Why didn't *you* do it when you got older?' Nancy asked him years later. Frank looked at her, he shook his head, 'No, I couldn't do that. It represented some sort of proof that they both needed. Proof that I was a caring son. It became part of our lives, a ritual that we all observed.'

Frank's parents were achingly polite to each other; Gordon asking Edna each morning as they came face to face on the landing between their bedrooms, 'How are you today, feeling better?'

'A little, thank you,' Edna's tremulous smile, seemingly never strong enough to reach her eyes. Frank realised years later that his parents rarely made eye contact with each other or with their son. His father spoke to him with his gaze directed just above Frank's ear or to the left of his head. His mother kept her head down; Frank couldn't remember ever seeing Edna laugh, her head back, eyes wide open with any kind of joy. He only saw her eyelids, with their pale blue-grey veins, acting like curtains, hiding her eyes, protecting them from seeing anything that might disturb or frighten her. Edna appeared alarmed at the rate that Frank grew. She'd shake her head in disbelief when his trouser legs flapped high above his ankles.

'Look at you, when are you going to stop growing?' As he grew taller, she'd squeeze past Frank, careful not to touch him. Frank felt it was his fault, his size was something he should be able to control. As puberty approached he was embarrassed by the changes he felt in his body. He avoided looking at his mother's face, keeping his eyes averted. The faint, dark line above his top lip he knew would frighten, or even worse, disgust her and he might be blamed; he thought it was something he'd done wrong.

Nancy had always been fascinated by stories of Frank's early years, she'd never met Gordon or Edna, they'd died six months before she met Frank.

'But why separate rooms? Didn't they like each other? Did your father tiptoe into your mother's room late at night, a rose between his teeth? Come on, Frank, you must have noticed, *heard* something.'

Frank shook his head, 'Don't be daft. They'd always had their own room, three bedrooms, one for each of us, it was always like that. It was never spoken about, it just was. I don't know why you find it so odd.'

'No, Frank, you're wrong. For those days in a suburban street, separate bedrooms was odd. And your mother having to lie down all the time. That's what Victorian women did, they went into a decline. It must have been something to do with sex.' She'd been sitting opposite him, her knees touching his. 'Why did you think you were an only child? Did you ever ask for a brother or a sister? What did they tell you?'

Her voice held a hint of a giggle, they'd been married a short time, Nancy revelling in the intimacy between them. As she stared into his eyes, Frank could see flecks of light, like newly minted coins in her eyes. He'd felt uncomfortable, thinking he detected a voyeuristic emphasis to her questions, as if she needed somehow to compare their sex life with that of his parents. As she asked him, Nancy had run her hand along the length of Frank's leg, slowing the pace when she reached his thigh, her small fist edging closer to his crotch. Frank had shifted in his chair; there were times, he thought, when Nancy was too forward. She'd shocked him initially with her artless, open attitude to her body. Wandering naked around their bedroom, trailing her clothes behind her as she walked to the bathroom. Even in the years before Chris's birth, Frank had kept their bedroom door shut.

'There's no one in the house, Frank, just you and me.' Nancy simply laughed at him.

Frank had a sudden image of his parents: he must have been about twelve years old and he was at home, sitting in the dining room waiting for lunch to be served. His father sat at the head of the table which had been covered by a cream lace tablecloth. Edna's best dinner service had been set out. Frank was sitting close to the door and he could remember the rustling sound of his mother's dress as she moved past him, holding a gravy jug. The only sound had been that of Gordon's carving knife slicing through roast beef. They'd eaten their meal in silence as they'd always done. Something about the scene disturbed him. It had been so clear, so still and, for a split second he'd resented Nancy's question. He'd felt an overwhelming urge to defend his parents against his wife's curiosity.

'Nothing, they told me nothing because I didn't ask. It wasn't my business and if it wasn't mine, it's not yours.' Nancy understood she'd stepped over a boundary and she didn't mention Gordon and Edna for a long time.

Out in his garden, Frank sipped at the tea, the pain had almost gone, thoughts of Nancy had done that, he smiled. An overweight tabby cat appeared on the back wall: it stared at Frank for a moment then began to clean itself, a long, pink tongue glided over an extended leg.

'Bloody thing, bet that's the one that's been digging up my dahlias.'

He tested his right leg, moving it forward and putting his weight behind the movement. Nothing, barely a twinge.

See, best thing for it, ignore it and the pain goes away, works every time. Frank nodded at the cat, he felt so pleased with himself, with his philosophy on the treatment of pain. He decided to leave the cat alone, leave it where it was, enjoying the baked warmth of the stones on the back wall. He drank the rest of his tea placing the empty mug on the kitchen step.

Watched by the cat, Frank moved slowly around his garden: it needed watering, there hadn't been any rain for over a week. The whole time he'd been indoors, the pain locking him up, he'd worried about the garden. The petunias and geraniums, tumbling out of the hanging baskets near the back door, looked slightly limp, but that was all. Frank moved between the rows of runner beans noting the burst of scarlet flower against the rich green leaves. He began to hum as he walked over to the hosepipe.

Frank felt warmed by the late afternoon sun and the easing of the pain. He made little sounds, grunts of pleasure as he sprayed the blooms and placed the sprinkler on the luxuriant green of the lawn.

Peter Jefferies' head appeared over the top of the fencing that marked the boundary between Frank's house and that of the Jefferies. A short man, he had to stand on an old milk crate to peer over the fence.

'Look at his face, Frank,' Nancy used to whisper, 'it looks like those pictures we've seen of the moon, craters everywhere.'

Frank thought she'd been right. His neighbour's face had an unhealthy pallor, grey and badly pock-marked by teenage acne.

Peter grinned at Frank and raised his voice, almost shouting at him although the distance between the two men was only a matter of feet.

'Hard at it, Frank? Never lets up this gardening lark does

it? We thought you'd gone away. Meryl said to me that she thought she hadn't seen you for a day or two. She knocked on the door but, well we didn't like to … Been to your son's have you?'

All the pleasure Frank had felt, the sun on his back, the satisfying smell of wet soil and the relief at being pain-free fell away. He held the hosepipe like a weapon, gripping it with both hands and he half-turned towards Peter Jefferies' perspiring face.

'No,' the word was flat, uninviting.

'But you're all right? Not like you missing the garden in this weather.'

'Yes, I'm all right, thank you.'

Frank watched Peter's mouth opening, closing; his skin was over-heated, sweat bubbling up from the deep pores on his skin. Frank deliberately turned, his action causing the water to splash against the fence.

'Excuse me, I must finish the garden. It's very dry.'

Nosy bugger.

Frank *had* heard Peter's wife knocking on the door, she'd even had the nerve to call him through the letterbox. 'Yoo hoo, Mr Jones, Frank, are you all right?' He'd ignored her. Didn't want her in his home, poking her nose in.

Frank finished watering his garden and, before turning the water off, he aimed the hosepipe at the cat.

You can bugger off and all.

Frank was sitting in the winged armchair, he'd pulled the heavy velvet curtains across the windows, a fine sliver of the setting sun's rays danced through a gap in the middle. Frank watched the filtered light and the dancing dust motes. It was nearly 8 o'clock, people were out in their gardens, a child was crying, he could hear a woman's voice, muted, soothing. It was stuffy in the room, the fish he'd eaten for supper had left a strong smell in the house. The room needed air.

Frank's hands were arranged steeple-like, his fingers tapping non-stop against each other. *Comes to something when a bloke can't get a bit of peace in his own garden.* He cleared his throat, 'I've got a bloody good mind to go around there in the morning and …'

Suddenly he could hear Nancy's voice *And do what, Frank? What would you say to them? They were merely keeping a neighbourly eye, checking to see that you were all right.*

He turned, half expecting her to march through the room, yanking hard at the curtains. *What on earth are you doing with the curtains drawn, it's beautiful out there.*

Frank brought his hands down, placing them on the armrests. 'Not heard from Jonathan either, must be a good few days since he called.' *Must be something wrong, what can you expect with that mother of his.* His fingers began drumming against the cloth of the armchair.

JONATHAN.

We're still here at this L'Etang de la Breche site. We didn't leave after all. When I woke up, the morning after Sebastian had gone missing, there was no sign of Mum. The night before I'd told her that I'd sleep in with Sebastian. I felt mean about him getting lost and I wanted to do something, show Mum that I was sorry. She just shook her head at me and got to her feet and left me sitting by the car.

I was awake for ages. Just lying there in the sleeping bag. Ever since we've been on holiday, every night we've been away, the campsites have been noisy. At first it felt funny, lying there listening to people I didn't know laughing or chatting, just a few feet away from where I was trying to sleep. But I got used to it. That's what was so peculiar about that night. It was dead quiet, I didn't hear a thing. No sound of anyone having a bit of a laugh or opening a bottle of wine, nothing. I didn't even hear anyone walking past my tent going to the loo. It was as if a big heavy blanket had come down, covering everyone up, keeping them quiet.

That's why I found it so hard to sleep, it was the silence. And I was thinking about Sebastian. About what might have happened if that girl hadn't found him. He's such a pain, gets on my nerves most of the time, but when I was lying there, wriggling about trying to sleep, I couldn't stop thinking about what it would be like without him. Somehow, I've got used to having a brother. It's not his fault his poxy father left him and it's not his fault his name is Sebastian. In a way I felt sad that I'd missed seeing him walk for the first time.

I must have dropped off and when I looked at my watch again it was nearly 9 o'clock. Sebastian's always awake hours before that. I got a bit worried and unzipped my tent. There was no sign of Mum or Sebastian anywhere.

Felt a bit scared for a second, I wondered if she'd left me on my own to punish me or something for not being around last night. But the Clio was still there, the empty wine bottle and the glass where Mum had left it. The zip was still done up on the other tent.

I put my head outside, it was already hot. I thought about getting some coffee or something for Mum. She's always saying that she's useless in the morning without coffee. Thought I'd clear up a bit too, there was all sorts of junk lying around next to the car.

I got out of my tent, I'd gone to bed in my shorts and T-shirt last night. Couldn't be bothered about changing or washing or anything. When I looked closer at the car, there were boxes, toys, supermarket bags everywhere.

I started to lug stuff back into the car, tidying up a bit really. It looks so scruffy, all our stuff lying on the grass. I kept getting this weird feeling, like everyone was watching me, to see what I'd do. I thought perhaps they were all hiding in their tents or caravans, waiting to see what I'd get up to. It was quite scary, like I was supposed to pass a test or something before anyone would come out.

When I got the gaz stove going, the woman came over, the woman who'd helped Mum look for Sebastian.

'How's your mother today?' She wasn't smiling at me, suppose she felt I was the world's worst son, swearing and running off.

I started to say something, something about me making coffee for Mum and trying to tidy up. I don't know why I wanted to tell her what I was doing, perhaps I wanted her to know that I wasn't the son from hell. The woman wasn't exactly glaring at me, it's just that she wasn't smiling. A lot of women do that, they either smile at you, making out that they're your friend and they know all the latest music, they're really sad. Or, they frown at you, letting you know that they blame you for the time their car was broken into or they think you knock over old ladies when you're out on your skateboard, or something.

All of a sudden she asked me, 'Do you need milk, anything for your mum?'

'Yes, I was going to get some. I thought she'd like coffee.'

Then she smiled at me.

'We've got milk, I'll bring some over for you. I expect your mum could do with some breakfast, she had a terrible scare last night. She'll need some looking after today.'

There was the rasping sound of a zip being undone and Mum came out of her tent; she had both arms around Sebastian, she didn't let go of him even as she struggled through the tent entrance.

Mum looked awful, really washed out. I've never thought about what people meant when they said that, *washed out.* Her face looked ever so pale, like it'd been left out in the rain although she still had purply smudges under her eyes.

She didn't say anything, she just stood next to me and this woman. Sebastian was wriggling like mad, he wanted me, he put his arms up but Mum wouldn't let go.

'Hello, how are you feeling?' The way the woman was speaking, it was as if Mum had been ill. Her voice was soft, like she didn't want to hurt or startle Mum. When I had chicken pox ages ago, Mum spoke to me the same way.

'OK, thanks,' Mum's voice sounded funny too, really quiet, she had her face close to Sebastian's head. He put his hands up and tugged at her hair. She usually hates that but she just smiled at him.

The woman put a hand out to touch Mum's arm. 'Look, we're all organised over there, pots of coffee, we've got fresh bread, we've even got Kelloggs cornflakes. Don't be messing about with breakfast this morning, come over with me, fresh coffee will do you the world of good.'

I felt sorry for the woman, she was only trying to be kind, but I knew exactly what Mum would say.

Mum lifted her head and spoke so quietly I could hardly hear her. 'Thank you, I'd like that.'

I couldn't believe she said that. I was waiting for her to say something really snotty. I though the minute she heard the words *Kelloggs* and *cornflakes* she'd say no. The other woman smiled and put her hand out 'There wasn't time to introduce ourselves last night, I'm Sally.'

Mum switched Sebastian on to her left hip and shook hands, 'Nina, and this,' she nodded towards me, 'is Jonathan.'

Sally smiled at me and that smile made me feel a whole lot better, made me feel that she didn't blame me for what happened last night. Sebastian was making whinging noises. Mum was holding him really tight, he didn't like it.

It's funny, I hadn't noticed it happening, but while we'd been standing there, people had come out of their tents, they were moving around the campsite. I could smell coffee, someone had a radio on, there were kids kicking a ball about. As we walked towards Sally's caravan a few people waved, I thought they were waving at Sally. I thought everyone hated me so I didn't wave. I followed Mum and poked my tongue out at Sebastian when she wasn't looking.

Sally and her husband had a great caravan, it was almost as big as Gareth's parents'. It had a huge awning on the front and they had one of those bench things out on the grass. Sally's husband was sitting there, reading an English paper.

'This is Eddie,' Sally touched his hand, 'and this is Nina and her boys. We've already met Sebastian, this is Jonathan.' He shook hands with me, he smiled at me too. I was beginning to like them both. Sally disappeared into the caravan.

Eddie patted the bench, 'Sit down and, guess what? It's raining in the UK, or it was yesterday. Now isn't that a shame?' He moved the paper towards Mum, 'Here, take a look.'

Even as she got on the bench Mum wouldn't let go of Sebastian. He stopped whinging when he saw what was on the table. Sally and Eddie had loads of stuff. Jam, honey, even marmalade. I thought Mum would start pulling faces and talking in that stupid voice she uses. But she didn't.

Eddie asked us what we'd like to eat and then he smiled at Sebastian, 'Oh, please help yourselves.' Sally came back with a tray, there was juice, coffee and croissants.

I don't know how it happened, I've thought about it since but, all of a sudden, everything was so normal. Mum was drinking coffee, she and Sebastian were eating croissants, masses of them. She put marmalade on hers and honey for Sebastian. It was what other people did, but not us, well not while we've been on holiday. Sally and her husband were brilliant, they talked about where they'd been, what sites they liked. She was a teacher, English she said. She didn't ask me anything, no stupid questions about the books I was reading or grades or any of that stuff. Wish she taught at my school.

Eddie had been an engineer; he was retired and he told me all about the bridges his company built and then I told him all about my fountain project, the one I was doing at school. He was really interested, I could tell. Best of all, though, was that Mum wasn't doing any of that stupid head-shaking stuff she does whenever people talk to me.

See, that's what I mean. I don't know how it happened but we were all sitting there, drinking coffee and orange juice, we looked the same as everybody else. Mum began talking to Sally, telling her all about her job, the books and then she let Sally take Sebastian. Sally said she'd clean him up, he was a right mess, all covered in honey.

When Sally took Sebastian from Mum, I thought she'd say no or hold on to him or something, but she didn't seem to mind.

'Leave him with me,' Sally said. 'Go off an have a shower if you want to, leave him here he'll be fine.'

I thought the world had stopped. You know when you stop a video, just before you rewind it, the whole picture sort of *wobbles*. Then it gets back to normal again. That's what it was like after Sally had spoken. Like Mum was frozen, she didn't move at all. Sally didn't notice a thing, she was giving Sebastian more bread and Eddie was reading the newspaper. I must have been holding my breath because when Mum did speak, this rushing sound came out of me.

Mum actually smiled, 'Are you sure? I'll only be a few minutes, just time for a shower.'

Sally thought everything was OK, she was looking at Sebastian.

I was looking at Mum. She walked away, she didn't look back once and as she went towards our tents, people were coming up to talk to her, they must have wanted to know about Sebastian. Mum was stopped loads of times, even the bloke with the Siamese cats came up to her. He's such a weirdo. He never goes anywhere, just wanders around the site with these two spiteful-looking cats on the end of leads.

I saw how Mum smiled, I saw how she pointed towards Sebastian, I saw how she gave me a little wave. She's forgiven me. She doesn't know what I've done.

I phoned Dad last night and told him Mum was drunk.

After Mum left me last night I sat on my own for ages. There was no one around, no one at all. And it was so quiet but not a nice sort of quiet. Everyone had their doors shut, their tents closed up. It felt as if they'd turned their backs on me. Even the silence felt angry. I was so fed up. First of all, I was fed up with Mum, fed up with the way she lumbers me with Sebastian all the time.

This is my holiday too. I was fed up with being blamed for everything and *really* fed up that we might have to move from this site. I didn't think it was fair. So I phoned Dad. Stupid thing was that the minute I told him about Mum drinking all that wine and losing Sebastian, I wanted the words to come back into my mouth.

Dad went ballistic. 'What do you mean, she's lost him? Christ, Jon, it's what, 10.30 here, so that's 11.30 there. When did this happen? Where's your mother, what's she doing now? Have you called the police, what do they say?'

All those words came shooting down the phone, I had to hold the handset away from my ear.

'Nothing, we didn't call them, there was no need, he's been found.'

'Is he all right? Poor little sod. How come he got lost?

100

What was your mother doing? Staring out into the middle distance, I suppose.'

I didn't know what he meant by that. 'She was drinking wine and Sebastian wandered off.'

That came out all wrong; I didn't mean it that way. You've have thought I'd put a rocket underneath Dad because he went off again.

'She was *drinking!* What are you saying, she'd had so much to drink she didn't notice a baby wandering off, getting lost? Is that what you're saying, Jon? Is it?'

It wasn't meant to be like this. 'No! It wasn't like that at all. Mum's upset, she was worried, she didn't know where he'd gone. Other people helped her look and …'

'I bet they did. Wouldn't have taken Einstein to work out she's incapable of keeping an eye on a baby. God, what a mess. Are you all right? Were you looking for him too?'

'No, I'd gone for a meal with this boy and his family, I didn't know Sebastian was missing until I got back to the site.'

'Just as well someone else is keeping an eye on you. Your mother obviously can't. Where's she now, your mother, where is she? Sleeping it off I suppose.'

'Yes, she's gone to bed but she's really upset …'

Dad snorted and laughed, only it wasn't a proper laugh. 'I'll bet she is.'

I felt worse than ever, it was going all wrong. 'She *is* tired. Sebastian had been playing up, grizzling all day. It's really hot here and then she thought she'd lost him.'

Dad's voice changed, he sounded bossy and it scared me. 'When are you coming home, Jon? How much longer will you be away?'

'I'm not sure, Mum wants us to leave this site now, she's booked us into somewhere in Brittany, near the beaches.'

'I think you'd better come home, don't you? This is getting dangerous. Get your mother to ring me in the morning. I'll have to sort something out if she won't be reasonable and I can't imagine that she will, she hasn't so far. I might have to come out and collect you. Just make sure she rings me. Now, are you sure you're all right? You're not upset or anything?'

'No, I'm not.' What else could I say? That *he'd* upset me? I didn't want to go home, I was just angry with Mum, now I'd made it a million times worse.

'Jon? I didn't hear you, are you all right?'

'Yeah, yeah, I'm fine. Dad? I don't want to come home, well not yet anyway. Things are OK, I was just a bit upset, that's all.'

'*A bit upset?* Hardly surprising. All right, son, you'd better get off to bed, get some sleep. I'll talk to you tomorrow I expect. Goodnight.'

'Goodnight, Dad.'

After I'd spoken to Dad I went back to the tents. There was no sound from Mum's tent and no one was around and I was so fed up. I got into the Clio and threw out carrier bags, Sebastian's toys, bottles, all sorts of junk. Don't ask me why I did all that. I cleared it up in the morning.

When I looked at Mum this morning, saw the smile on her face, I couldn't tell her what I'd done. She even told Eddie and Sally that we'd stay here for a few more days. What am I going to do about Dad? About the phone calls?

I got up suddenly and mumbled something to Eddie and Sally about having a shower. Sally's head was bent over Sebastian, she was sucking on his fingers. That's so disgusting, he puts his hands everywhere. She mumbled something and I said 'Thanks,' before heading over to our tents. I *had* to ring Dad, only problem was that he'd be at work. Mum had his number, she puts everything in this enormous Filofax, huge thing with notes and bits of paper sticking out of it. It's in her tent, she never lets it out of her sight.

I didn't want to ask her for his number, she'd only tell me not to bother him at work or ask stupid questions about why do I want to ring him now, *what's so important you've got to ring him at work?* All that stuff.

There was no sign of Mum as I got closer to the tents. Gareth was walking towards me and Alice was a little way behind him. She stopped walking when she saw me.

He asked me if I fancied trying horse riding later on.

I looked over towards Alice, 'What about Alice, is she coming?'

Gareth didn't turn around to see Alice, 'No, all she does is moan about the riding hat messing her hair about. She only wanted to come with me because I said I was seeing you. She fancies you, she wants to snog you.'

'Don't be stupid,' I shoved him.

'She does, watch.' He turned to look at Alice who was bending down, pretending to tie the laces on her trainers.

'So where do you want to go tonight with Jon? Somewhere dark, so he doesn't have to look at your face when you snog him?'

'I'm telling Mum you said that,' and she ran off towards the other field, back to her parents.

I felt uncomfortable watching her run, looking at the way her hair bounced up and down on her shoulders. 'You shouldn't have said that to her, you'll get a row from your mum and Dad.'

Gareth shrugged, 'She's been moody for days, expect it's a period or something.'

I felt worse than ever, as if Alice had caught me reading her diary. I didn't want to talk about her any more so I told Gareth that I'd meet him at the stables in an hour. That should give me enough time to shower, get some money and ring Dad. I *must* ring Dad. Then I thought about Grandad, he'd have Dad's number and I hadn't phoned him for a few days.

Just then Mum walked towards me, she was wearing clean clothes and a towel was wrapped around her head.

'Hi, what are your plans for today?' She shook her hair out of the towel and rubbed her hands through it. Her hair was bouncing around her head, it was in tiny curls, like flying red question marks. She looked much better, as if the shower had really washed her, got rid of all her stroppiness, she sparkled. She put her arm around me and gave me a hug, I got a mouthful of wet hair.

She stepped back, she kept her eyes down. 'I would like us to spend time together, Jon, you and me and Sebastian of

103

course. No pressure, just a quiet day here, what do you think?'

'Yeah, OK.' I felt awful, she was trying really hard and I didn't have time. If I didn't make those phone calls quickly, Dad might even turn up. I'd told him what site we were on last week. I mumbled something about having a shower and ran into my tent to get some money. She was waiting outside for me. 'You all right, Jon?' There was a tiny frown above her eyebrows.

'Yeah,' We stood a few feet apart, both keeping our heads down, eyes not really making any contact at all. I felt awful, really mean. For a second I wanted to tell her what I'd done, but I couldn't. She'd think that I didn't trust her, she'd think I was talking about her behind her back. She'd be right too. I really wished I hadn't phoned Dad. When people say things like, *it was the drink talking,* that's what happened to me, only Mum's drink had made me talk like that to Dad. And I got it all wrong. I *must* ring Dad. But I'll talk to Grandad first.

'Grandad! It's me, Jonathan. Hello, how are you?'

Grandad always clears his throat before he speaks to me, it's like he's getting rid of words he doesn't want to use.

'Jonathan? Everything all right? Haven't heard from you for a few days, nothing wrong is there?'

'No! Why would there be? Everything's really good, in fact, Grandad, this is the best holiday I've ever had, it's brilliant.'

He laughed, a false laugh, like he didn't believe me. 'That's good. So, what are you up to today then?'

'I'm going horse riding in a few minutes with my friend Gareth, not sure after that. Are you all right, Grandad?'

'Me?' He coughed, 'Nothing wrong with me, why wouldn't I be all right?'

Mum said once that talking to Grandad was like playing chess: one move from him, then another from her, waiting for checkmate. We were both asking the same questions.

'No reason, I just asked that's all. Grandad, do you have Dad's office number?'

'Why do you want to ring him at his office, what's the

problem?'

'There isn't a problem, I just need to talk to him and his office number is at home, that's all.'

Grandad went on and on about why didn't I ask Mum for the number, he was sure she'd have it then he said something I didn't like at all.

'Although, it wouldn't surprise me if she left all that sort of thing at home, no planning for an emergency, that would be so like her.'

'That's not fair! Mum's done nothing wrong, she got us here, we're having a brilliant time. It was all my fault.'

Fault.

'What fault? Whose fault? What are you talking about, Jonathan?'

'Nothing,' I must have mumbled, Grandad started shouting at me. 'You'd better tell me, you can't leave something like that up in the air.'

'It's nothing, everything's OK. It wasn't Mum's fault, it was mine. Sebastian got lost, that's all.'

'Lost! What do you mean, lost? What was your mother doing, what was she thinking of?'

'I keep telling you, it wasn't Mum's fault, it was mine.'

'How could it have been your fault? You're only a lad. You'd better tell me what happened.'

This was going all wrong again and I didn't have time for it.

'Grandad, please, just let me have Dad's work number.'

'Why? What are you going to ask him to do? Come out to collect you? I knew this would happen, I just knew it. Your mother couldn't take care of two puppies, let alone two boys.'

'Shut up! That's not fair, it's not Mum's fault, it's mine. Give me Dad's number, please.'

There was silence, I couldn't even hear Grandad breathing. It was like he was holding his breath, or rehearsing what to say to me.

When he did speak his voice was cold. 'I don't take kindly to my grandson telling me to *shut up*. Whatever else you're learning over in that country, it's certainly not politeness.'

Another chess move. I need to say one word, to get Grandad to move, to get him to give me Dad's number.

'Sorry.'

'Hmmph, I should think so. Now, let me see, I know I've got his office number somewhere, not sure if I can put my hand on it straightaway. Would it be better if I phoned him for you?'

'No! No, Grandad, thanks all the same, there's nothing wrong. I just need to ask him something, that's all.'

'Righto, if you're sure, wait there a minute ...'

As Grandad moved away from the phone, I heard him muttering to himself, I couldn't catch what he was saying but I guessed it was all grumblings about me. Gareth appeared in front of the phone booth and started pulling faces and tapping at his watch.

'Jon? You still there?'

I had to turn away, Gareth was making me laugh. I didn't want Grandad to think I was laughing at him. 'Yes, still here. Have you got the number?'

He spoke so slowly, each number taking for ever. It was just as well that he did, I didn't have a pen or anything. 7 9 3 4 6 8. I kept saying the number in my head. 793468.

'Thanks, Grandad, we are all right. I'm sorry for ...' 793468.

'That's all right, we won't say any more about it. Expect you'll ring me again soon?'

'Yes, yes I will, I promise.'

I had to ring my dad straight away, otherwise I'd forget the number. I put five fingers up to let Gareth know I'd only be another five minutes. He pulled a face.

I punched in the numbers quickly, I was really worried that I'd forget.

'Good morning, James and Jones Architects ...'

'Hello, can I speak to my dad please, Chris Jones?'

'Jonathan? Is that you? Your dad says you're in France, are you calling from there? Are you having a good time? I expect the weather's better than here, it's raining again, it hasn't stopped ...'

Why is it that the minute someone knows you're in another country, they always talk about the bloody weather? 'Please, can I speak to my dad? I haven't got much money left …'

Stupid woman, she said I couldn't speak to him. 'He's not in the office right now, Jonathan, he's at a site meeting. Not sure when he'll be back, can he ring you?'

'No, I'm in a call box. Will he be in this afternoon?'

She laughed, 'Running out of pocket money are you? My daughter is the same, this week she wanted more money from me for some trainers she's seen. I keep telling her, save up like I have to …'

'Thank you.' I put the phone down.

I watched Gareth pretending to be a horse, galloping around the field, trying to make me laugh. I couldn't laugh. I'd made it worse. That silly cow on the switchboard will tell Dad I phoned. Grandad will tell Dad I phoned. He'll think all sorts of things have happened to us. He'll come over and have another row with Mum, the holiday will be ruined.

'What's the matter, you look really fed up.' Gareth's hair was sticking to his face.

'I *am* fed up. I've been trying to get hold of my dad and he's not there and …'

'Why don't you have your own mobile phone? I've got one, you can use mine if you want to.'

I couldn't be bothered to explain that Mum had left mine at home. Mum has got one but she was worried about the bills ringing from France so she didn't bring it with us. All part of her being a free spirit, at least that's what she said.

'Have mine, ring your dad from my phone, I don't mind.' Gareth was fidgeting about all over the place, he just wanted to get to the horses, not stand about near a phone booth.

'Thanks, but there's no point now, I've forgotten the stupid number and, oh, what's the point?'

FRANK

Frank could hear thunder, it was directly above the house. It growled, a deep, heavy noise. Someone was calling him, they were calling his name. The voice rose above the sound of the thunder. Everything was dark, there must be quite a storm, the windows were rattling. Where was Nancy? Was Nancy calling him? Frank stretched out his arm, his fingers reached out to touch Nancy's head, feel her soft curls. Nothing.

'Dad, are you all right? Dad?'

Chris. That was Chris's voice. Frank opened his eyes, he was sitting in the living room. He wore the clothes he had on yesterday, he must have fallen asleep in the chair. There was no thunder. It was Chris trying to get in. Frank tried to rise from the chair, gripping the arms to lever himself up. He bit back a groan. His spine felt rigid as if concrete had been poured into each vertebrae overnight, setting them in a hard, stiff frame. His legs wouldn't move, he gazed at his feet as if the act of looking at them would force them to change position. His long legs, bent at the knees, feet cushioned in soft slippers stayed in the same place.

'Dad? Are you in there? Are you all right?'

Frank heard footsteps: Chris walking around to the back of the house. The handle of the back door rattled. He heard fingers tapping on the pane of glass in the kitchen window. Frank sat still, he didn't know what to do. He'd never fallen asleep in a chair before. *Damn and blast, what a time for Chris to come. Why isn't he in work? What the hell is he doing here?*

'Dad!'

Chris must be standing on the patio, the handle on the French doors rattled. Frank watched, mesmerized as the handle on the inside of the door caught the fabric of the thick curtain, making it shiver.

For God's sake.

He sat still, his breathing slow and measured. He felt convinced that Chris would hear him breathing. He heard the sound of footsteps moving rapidly around the side of the house, past the kitchen door. There was silence for a few seconds. Frank breathed out.

The doorbell rang. A rattle of the letterbox as Chris's voice entered the house. In Frank's agitated state, it seemed that Chris's voice was everywhere, seeping into each room, bending around corners. Frank looked around him, Chris's voice swirled above, like a cloud of steam, filling every space.

'Dad! Are you in there? Talk to me, are you all right?'

Frank held his breath again. He tried to take small breaths, he was so anxious that Chris might hear him. Might even sense that Frank was sitting there, listening to his son's desperate shouts. There was silence again, Frank exhaled slowly.

The phone rang. The shrill tone startled Frank, made him flinch. It must be Chris, ringing from his mobile.

The phone rang on and on. Frank counted each ring. 10, 11, 12. Frank's breathing quickened. 13, 14, 15. *Christ's sake. Stop the bloody ringing. Stop it.* The shrieking stopped after the 24th ring. Frank closed his eyes and listened. Nothing, no further sound from Chris. He looked down at his crumpled clothes, his shirt was creased, his trousers bunched up around his knees. One sock had worked its way down to his ankle and lay like a pale, brown deflated tyre above his slipper.

'I look like an old tramp. This won't do, won't do at all. Must get up, washed, changed …'

The pain was everywhere, the joints of his fingers buzzed as if tiny wasps were sending painful stings into his skin. A deep throbbing in the base of his spine brought tiny beads of perspiration to Frank's scalp. He inched his legs up, placing his feet carefully on the carpet and began to lever himself up. Taking a deep breath and biting hard on his lip, he slowly stood.

The pain rose with him and he closed his eyes. *Be all right in a minute, just stiff, that's all.* Keeping his eyes closed he breathed deeply. In and out. In and out. *There, that's better.*

The closed curtains irritated him. Everything looked untidy. It would be safer if he kept the curtains closed for a while longer. Chris might be lurking about outside. Best to leave them like that until he'd washed, shaved and tidied himself up. Easier that way, to tell Chris that he'd overslept.

'Didn't hear the alarm, slept like a baby. Glass of whisky last night, must have hit the spot.' Frank whispered the words, rehearsing his tone, practising a smile. Important to get it right, make sure that Chris believed him. Frank gingerly moved his head to look at the clock. 9.10.

'What the hell is Chris doing here at this time? Must be something up, must be a problem. That's it then, got to get a move on.'

Grabbing hold of the chair, Frank shuffled towards the door of the lounge, stopping as he looked towards the hall and the front door. Nothing. No shadow through the glass, no sound of footsteps outside. Frank moved slowly towards the stairs.

Even moving at a snail's pace, his shirt was sticking to his shoulder blades and he could feel damp in the waistband of his trousers. He wiped his forehead with his shirtsleeve. He reached the bottom tread.

The stairs seemed almost upright, like a ladder standing vertically, reaching up towards the landing, his bedroom. Frank bit down hard on his lip and lifted one leg onto the first step. He stood still for a moment, trying to regain control of his breathing and he tugged impatiently at his damp shirt, easing it away from his clammy skin.

'Feel better once I've washed, can't start the day like this. A wash and a shave, soon sort me out. Can't waste time, hanging about in dirty clothes Chris might come back any minute.'

His words soothed him and he bent towards the stairs, willing his body to move, to ignore the pain. Sweat ran down into his eyes, mixing with tears of frustration.

'Come *on.'*

Flashes of red light danced across his eyes and suddenly Frank knew what he had to do.

He began rocking, gently, slowly at first, riding through the wave of pain that accompanied each rocking movement. Back and forth, back and forth. With each movement, he increased his hold on the banister, back and forth, back and forth. He gripped the banister and began to pull himself up. He inched his left hand further up the wooden banister, placing his foot on the stairs.

He glanced at his watch, *Godalmighty, it's gone half-past nine.* He pulled harder and inched his way up the stairs. *Oh, Nancy, look what's happened to me, I'm like a bloody great baby.* Frank made his slow progress up the stairs and into the bathroom.

He wiped the steam away from the mirror. *A good wash, clean clothes, thought so, be right as rain in no time.* The pain was ebbing, easing away from his back and his arms were beginning to feel warm as if they'd been soothed by a healing balm. Frank squared his shoulders, *Nothing wrong with me, just sleeping in that damn chair. That's what all that was about.* He began shaving, whistling softly as the lather frothed up around his chin.

'Dad? Where are you?'

Chris. Frank's hand jerked. How the hell had he got in? Frank paused, his hand halfway to his chin, his razor sending soapy bubbles running down his arm. He cleared his throat and frowned at his reflection.

'I'm up here, son, in the bathroom. I'm having a shave, won't be long.'

'Dad! Thank God. Are you all right? I'm coming up.'

'No! Don't do that, I'll be down in a minute, make yourself useful, put the kettle on.'

As he spoke, Frank watched his reflection, listening for the sound of Chris's footsteps in the house. He stared impassively at the mirror until he heard the sound of Chris moving into the kitchen. Frank was holding his breath, he exhaled as he heard the kettle being switched on. He whistled tunelessly and finished his shave.

'I still don't understand it, Dad. You never have a lie-in. Not for years, I can't remember you staying in bed a minute longer than you had to. The curtains were drawn, no sign of life anywhere. That's why I was so worried. Christ, Dad, I knocked on every window, banged on the bloody door for hours.'

Chris was sitting at the breakfast table. He was dressed in a suit and a pale pink shirt. A navy blue tie hung loosely around his neck and the top buttons of his shirt were undone. Clouds of steam curled from two dark green mugs. Frank kept his gaze still as he spoke the words he'd practised earlier. 'Didn't hear the alarm, slept like a baby. Had a glass of whisky last night, must have hit the spot.' He smiled fleetingly at Chris before asking him how he'd got in. 'I didn't think you had a key.'

Chris sipped at his tea. 'Wasn't sure that I did but when I couldn't get any reply and the curtains were drawn, I was really bothered. I seemed to remember that there was a spare key in my bedside drawer.' He touched his pocket, 'I'll put it on my key ring now, know where it is then in case of emergencies.'

Frank looked at his son before dropping his eyes, 'What do you mean *emergencies?*'

Chris shifted in his chair, 'I don't mean anything by it, just that it might be an idea to keep it on my key instead of in my bedside drawer, that's all.'

Frank looked towards the window, speaking across Chris's shoulder, 'Why aren't you in work anyway? Got a problem?'

Chris put his mug down, 'Yeah, you could say that. Have you heard from Jonathan this week? Do you know what she's done now? Only lost that baby, I mean can you believe it, the woman can't look after herself, let alone two children ...'

Frank sat back, 'Yes, he told me something about that. He didn't think it was much of a problem. Jonathan's all right though, isn't he? Do you know what happened?'

Chris rubbed his eyes, 'Jonathan's all right and I'm not really sure what happened. I had this bizarre call from Jon, he was upset and he told me that his mother had been drinking and that she'd lost that baby, Sebastian. She found him, he's not hurt or anything but I'm bothered by the whole thing.'

Frank looked at Chris, he seemed to be engrossed in the dregs of his tea. Frank coughed, 'I'm sure you are, but that still doesn't tell me why you're here, why you were knocking on my door so early in the morning.'

Chris looked up and met Frank's eyes, 'I wanted to check with you first,' he took a deep breath, 'I thought you might have heard something and depending upon that, I was going to try to get over there. To see her, to see Nina and Jonathan. Only thing is, I'm not 100 per cent sure of where they are. I think I know the name of the site but what I'm not sure about is whether they'll still be there when I arrive.'

Frank drained his mug, 'Want a refill?' Chris nodded and Frank walked over to the kettle. Without turning to face Chris he spoke softly, 'I had a call yesterday from Jonathan, he wanted your office number.'

'Yeah, I know, the girl on the switchboard told me he'd phoned. I was out when he rang and he didn't call back. What did he say to you?'

'Nothing much, just something about wanting your office number.' Frank thought it best not to mention the way Jonathan had spoken to him. Only rile Chris even further. Frank rocked from side to side as he waited for the kettle to boil. A residual dull ache in the base of his spine was the only pain left. He heard the drumming of Chris's fingers on the table. There'd been no contact between father and son since Frank had slammed the phone down following their row last week. The aftermath shimmered like a heat haze between them.

'What do you think, Dad? Do you think I should go over

there, see for myself if Jonathan is OK? Don't know why I feel any responsibility for that baby either, but I do. Poor little sod, he didn't ask for a mother like Nina.'

With the edge of a tea-towel Frank wiped a tiny mark on the window. He frowned, 'If you're asking my opinion, Chris, I'd leave well alone. You'll only antagonise her. Jonathan sounded fine to me, no harm has been done and they're coming home, what? Next week? Leave things alone.' He poured boiling water into the two mugs. *I could murder some bacon.* He didn't want to say that, to talk about how his stomach was grumbling gentle reminders that he'd not eaten since 6.30 yesterday evening. How could he talk about mundane matters like breakfast, about grilled bacon, toast and marmalade, when Chris was sitting there, anguishing over his absent son and divorced wife?

'There,' Frank placed the two mugs on the table. Chris jumped up almost as soon as Frank sat down.

'See, I'm not sure you're right. This whole trip has been a shambles from start to finish. She went off half-cocked. Bet your life there was no planning, no preparation. Doesn't bear thinking about.' He paced up and down, his hands moving as they emphasised a point. 'I mean, there was no proper camping equipment, for all I know they're sleeping in the car! One minute she's moaning about the fact that she hasn't got any money, next thing I know she's off on holiday. She must have bought some equipment though, surely she has, and what the bloody hell with?'

Frank avoided looking at Chris, he kept still, his fingers laced around his mug of tea. He waited for Chris to finish his tirade. Chris stopped, aware of his father's silence. He came slowly back to the table and sat down facing Frank. His voice was softer, 'So, Dad, you don't think I should go over there, like some white knight on a charger.' He gave a rueful grin.

Frank sat back, 'No, I don't know what it will achieve if you go over to France. Jonathan said there was nothing to worry about. He said it to me last night.' Frank silently replayed the conversation with Jonathan. He glanced at Chris, 'All he said to me was that he wanted to ask you something, that's all. He sounded fine.' *Fine if you count telling your grandfather to shut up, that is.*

'Mmm,' Chris stared into the mug. 'Probably going to ask me for some money to be sent over. The switchboard girl said something about him running out.'

'There you are then!' Frank took a deep breath. 'That's it, he wants more money.' He couldn't remember if he'd told Chris that he'd gone over to see Jonathan and had given him an envelope full of euros. He darted a glance at his son. Chris was still frowning at his mug of tea. 'The lad probably wants to apologise for worrying you and he was using the phone call as an excuse to ask you for some more cash.'

Chris looked up, 'Yeah, you're probably right. I suppose I was waiting for something to happen, some disaster, hardly surprising. Still can't believe that she'd do something like this, go off to France on a whim. Thought even Nina would understand that holidays with children need some thinking about, need some sort of forward planning.'

Frank crossed his arms over his chest. 'That's what your mother wanted to do, just go off somewhere in the car, 'deciding when we get there', was how she put it. Frank shook his head at the memory, it had taken him by surprise. Nancy had pleaded with him to jump in the car 'head off somewhere, somewhere new'. He felt Chris's gaze on him.

'Do you wish you'd done that now, gone off somewhere?' Chris's eyes were steady.

Frank shifted in his chair, suddenly uncomfortable. He didn't want to talk about Nancy, not with Chris. Their row, and what Chris had accused him of, still bothered him. He felt defensive, unhappy with what had been said last week. He looked away from Chris's eyes.

'No good crying over spilt milk now, we didn't go and there's nothing to be gained from wishing things, does no good at all.' Frank felt Chris watching him and he deliberately averted his own gaze, looking towards the kitchen window, out to his garden. They sat there quietly, the silence only broken by uncomfortable gulps of hot tea.

Eventually Chris stood up. 'I should be making a move,

told the office that I'd only be out for an hour or two. Had all sorts of crazy ideas bouncing around in my head. I wasn't sure what to do. Stupid notions kept coming into my brain, even started packing a small case and shoved my passport in just in case. Stupid bugger. I can design supermarkets, libraries, give deep concentration to structural form, all that and yet I can't make a decision on this. Actually, you've talked me out of it. I think you're right. I can't do any good charging over there. I'd probably make things a lot worse. I'm glad you're all right though. You really had me worried earlier on. There isn't anything wrong, is there? You would tell me?'

'Nothing wrong with me,' Frank turned to look at Chris. His eyes met those of his son with a steady gaze. 'Strong as an ox, me. Outlive you and Jonathan, I expect.'

Chris shifted, for a second his arms moved as if he wanted to hug Frank, but he didn't. His right arm lightly touched his father's shoulder.

'Sorry to have bothered you with all this, I just wanted another opinion. Someone to say that my worry was all in my head. Thanks for listening, Dad. Don't come to the door, I'll see myself out. Thanks for the tea.'

Frank waited until he heard the front door close before rising from the table. *Be time for lunch soon. This will put me back for the rest of the day.*

He moved smoothly, all sign of the jerky, pain-controlled movements gone. Opening the fridge door he took out two rashers of bacon and began to prepare his breakfast. The familiar pattern of his morning ritual, wiping the table, placing cutlery on the clean surface, the smell of bacon bubbling under the grill, it all acted as a comfort blanket, soothing Frank.

Cutting into his bacon he smiled, *Nancy, love, that lad of ours, he's still wet behind the ears.*

Some awful rubbish on the box. Not much choice between the channels. A programme on detoxification for drug addicts, *kick up the backside that's what they need.* A film about an Egyptian Mummy coming to life, lot of hysterical screaming in that, and game shows on the other channels. Frank's index finger jabbed at the remote control as a succession of faces appeared on the screen.

'Drivel! All of it.'

He was pleasantly tired. After a bad start, the day had gone well. His breakfast had lasted until almost lunchtime. Frank felt quite intrepid. What would Nancy have said about that, his breakfast merging into his lunch? *No soup today, Nancy, my breakfast lasted all day.* After that, he'd walked to the shops to buy a paper and stopped off in the local supermarket for fresh milk and some lamb chops for his tea. He'd watered the garden too. Frank yawned, he'd had peace and quiet this time. No sign of that nosey parker from next door. He'd fed the hanging baskets, the bright red of the trailing geraniums was looking good against the white wall. Frank's eyes felt heavy, he waggled the remote control at the television, turning it off.

He woke to a darkened room. A light flashed, startling him. He struggled to sit up in the chair. *What the hell? Is that Chris?* He realised it was a security light from the house at the back, flashing its beam at a stray cat. It must have been the light that had woken him. It was too dark to see his watch, but it must be late, the sky was inky dark.

'Silly old bugger, can't make a habit of this.' He gripped the arms of the chair and began to rise.

Pain gnawed at him, eating into his spine, running down the backs of his legs, Frank gasped. He eased himself back into the chair. The light flashed again. Frank looked out towards the garden, he hadn't drawn the curtains. Something was different: the light went off, plunging the room into darkness. Frank narrowed his eyes.

There was someone else in the room. A dark shadow was standing by the French door. Frank's eyes took a second to readjust. 'Chris, is that you?' As he stared at the shape, it seemed to Frank that it moved. He spoke loudly, 'Is anyone there? Who are you? What are you doing in my house?'

Silence. Suddenly nervous, Frank cleared his throat. 'What are you doing here?' The shape was bulky, it was difficult to tell if it was a man or a woman. Difficult to tell *what* it was.

117

Frank's mouth was dry, he licked his lips, he could feel his heart thumping. He forced words out, hoping they sounded vigorous, strong. 'Hey! Who are you? What are you doing in my house?'

Nothing, no reply, just silence.

The light flashed on briefly illuminating the living room. There was nothing there, just blurred shapes, shadows from the heavy furniture. *Dear God, I thought there was someone skulking there. Silly old bugger.* It must be late, there was no noise from the street and the houses that flanked the garden were all in darkness, apart from the security light flashing its warning. *Like a lighthouse, what people need those for beats me.*

Frank felt quite light-headed with relief and he tried again to rise from the chair. He couldn't, his legs and arms were rigid. He eased back into the chair.

'Damn and blast, I won't let this happen again, stiff as a board now.'

He shook his head, mocking his earlier nervousness. 'Nothing in this house to frighten me, know every inch, silly old sod.' He ran his hands over the arms of the chair. His father used to sit in this one. Frank put his head back, looking up at the ceiling.

Nancy had wanted to change everything, she wanted new furniture, carpets and curtains. 'It's all so *dark*, there's no light, everything is shrouded in gloom.'

She'd been right too. Frank nodded to himself. Never noticed it before, certainly not whilst Gordon and Edna were alive. But the minute Nancy stepped into the house, the day he brought her here for the first time, Frank saw something in Nancy's face. He saw how the sparkle in her eyes began to dim as she slowly looked around each room. He watched as she pulled curtains back, she opened doors and windows. He saw light filtering through each room; he saw how her shoulders squared up each time she yanked at heavy material, how her head lifted as she opened windows, letting air and sunshine into the tired house.

'Furniture's good though, love.' Frank wanted to defend

118

his parents' choices, he'd never really looked at the chairs and the suite before. It was just his parents' house and their furniture. Now, with the net curtains taken down and the heavy, velvet curtains swept to one side, the sun shone in, illuminating the ornate carving on the legs, the fussy frills on settees, the rich, stifling colours.

'Might have been good once, Frank, but it's tired now, old and tired.'

They had to keep the furniture, Frank's legacy hadn't stretched to everything. Nancy had had part of her own way. She'd re-upholstered the furniture, thrown out the lamp standards with their plum-coloured tasselled shades. She bought new curtains and joyfully she'd attacked the wallpaper. Suddenly, Frank could see her: Nancy dressed in old trousers, one of his shirts tied at her waist and a scarf wrapped around her head, hiding the copper curls. She was up a ladder, splashing paint on the walls. Singing at the top of her voice, splashing pale yellow emulsion, bright drops of sunshine.

Frank's mouth lifted as he remembered how he'd come home from work to find all the doors open, old sheets spread over the furniture and the strains of *Chattanooga Choochoo* filling the living room.

The security light flashed on again giving him enough light to look at the clock. Half-past one. No wonder there was no noise anywhere, everyone else was in bed. Which is where he should be. He tried again to move. No. He couldn't shift from his position.

The light went off again, once more leaving him in darkness. He looked towards the settee alongside the wall. Nancy had gone to classes to learn how to re-upholster their inherited furniture. The material she used then was still as good as new. She'd been so proud of her efforts, she'd bought material from the department store, spending hours with pins in her mouth, kneeling, crawling over the floor as she worked on the pale green cloth, cutting, sewing.

Frank had a sudden image of his mother and father sitting in this room. He'd been about nine years old, wearing short trousers. He could remember the scratchy feeling of the moquette on the backs of his legs. The way his feet dangled over the edge of the settee, not quite reaching the floor. Perhaps he'd been younger? Frank narrowed his eyes at the memory. The three of them had been sitting here, in this lounge. Gordon and Edna and him. They were waiting for something, or was it someone?

Frank ran his hands again over the arms of his chair. His father had been sitting in this chair; then it had been covered in the same moquette as the settee. The chairs were on either side of the fireplace. Gordon in one chair, Edna in the other. They'd been dressed in their *best* clothes. Edna always referred to Gordon's suits as his *best* clothes. Frank too had been wearing a clean white shirt, freshly starched. As if he could still feel the starch in his collar, Frank slowly reached up to his neck, fingering the cloth.

He shook his head. *What was that all about? What were we waiting for?*

No, he couldn't remember. All he could remember of that occasion was the formality of their clothes and the fact that the three of them, mother, father and son were sitting in silence. His father on one side of the fireplace, sitting upright in his favourite chair and his mother sitting on the other side, her hands placed neatly in her lap. Frank had been sitting opposite his parents, dressed in his stiff, white shirt. No one spoke. Edna had reprimanded Frank for wriggling as he tried to ease his legs away from the harsh material of the sofa. 'Keep still, you'll crease your shirt.'

That was all that had been said. Frank couldn't remember anything else about that occasion, just the silence as the three of them waited.

There was silence now, Frank looked around his living room. The room was full of ghosts. Some of his memories were slightly out of focus, images blurred. Gordon, Edna, he couldn't recall their faces any more. Sometimes he forgot the contours of Nancy's face too. He closed his eyes and whistled softly. *Chattanooga Choochoo.*

JONATHAN

We're off, leaving this site and heading towards Brittany. I thought I'd be dead excited, after all there's a beach there and everything. I am in a way but it's been so good here ever since Mum lost Sebastian. Sounds weird when I say it like that but that's exactly how it's been. Mum's been spending time with Eddie and Sally, they've had supper with us and stuff but mostly we go over to them. They've been brilliant. Isn't it funny, never realised it before, but it only takes a few days of doing things for you to think that's how it's always been.

Oh, we've also had supper with Gareth's Mum and Dad., That was last night. It sort of just happened really. They walked over to us checking up on where Gareth was and Mum and I were looking at maps. I told them Gareth was at the swimming pool, he stayed there when I'd gone back to Mum. See, that's been the only problem. Every time I left Mum on her own, I was dead sure that Dad would turn up.

I haven't phoned him or Grandad again. Each time I think about either of them, my mouth goes dry and I can feel my heart thumping. I'd been so rude to Grandad and Dad would still be furious with Mum. He'd blame her for losing Sebastian, for not having proper chairs, for *everything*. That's not fair, it hadn't been her fault. I'd even started to think it'd been my fault, but it wasn't, it was no one's fault.

Whatever I was doing, I kept shooting off to see Mum. All the time I had this weird feeling that if I left Mum on her own

121

for one minute, that's the time when Dad would turn up. And I couldn't have that. I thought that even if Dad did come it would be all right if I was with Mum. Somehow that would make things OK, they wouldn't row. That was the main reason, it *was*. But I was also worried that when Mum knew I'd phoned Dad, she'd say I'd been telling tales. And that's what I'd done. I'd told tales about Mum behind her back. I'd been disloyal. She'd be so angry with me. I didn't want that. I wanted it to stay like it has been for the past few days. It's been really good.

Anyway, that's why I was with Mum and not Gareth when the Hendersons came over. Mr Henderson was holding a carrier bag, it was full of bottles of wine, I could hear the clinking of the glass as he walked.

Mum was talking to me, something about '... no need for an early start although it might be better if we did, it gets so hot later in the day ... oh, hello.'

I still couldn't believe this was the same Mum who'd been all snotty about the Hendersons. She'd been really rude about the fact that they ate mussels and chips and bought their wine from local supermarkets, but, now, she was smiling up at them as if she'd known them all her life.

Mrs Henderson didn't miss a beat, 'Hello.' She's got a really nice smile, it goes all the way up to her eyes, as if they're joining in. Mr Henderson winked at me, Mum didn't notice.

I told Mrs Henderson where Gareth was and Mum sort of patted the ground and said, 'Won't you join us?' Sebastian was asleep in one of the tents and a lot of his toys were on the rug we were sitting on. Mum swept everything to one side and Mr and Mrs Henderson sat down. Mr Henderson pulled a face as the bottles of wine clattered against each other.

'Is that any good?' Mum nodded towards the carrier bag, 'I've not tried any from the local supermarkets.'

'I'm not much of a wine buff but this is pretty good, well we think so.' Mr Henderson looked towards his wife.

She leant over and tugged at one of the bottles, pulling it out of the carrier bag. 'It's gone five, would you like a glass of wine, see what this is like?'

'Yes, I'd like that, thank you. I'll get some glasses. Not sure if Jon told you, he probably didn't, but I'm Nina and Jon you obviously know.'

Mr Henderson knelt forward, putting his hand out 'And I'm David and my wife is Jo,' Then they were all shaking hands, chatting, laughing.

Wine glasses were about the only things Mum had brought along from home and she watched as the wine was poured. The three of them sipped at it, swirling it around in the glasses, nodding away to each other, all of them sitting on Sebastian's old rug. Like some teddy bear's picnic for grown-ups.

'I like this, it's very good,' Mum nodded to me. 'We'll get some of this, Jon, before we go tomorrow, take it home with us.'

I opened my mouth to say something to her, something like *you didn't want anything from the supermarkets, remember?* She gave me a look, I know that look and I kept my mouth shut.

I could hear Sebastian, he was making the funny, chattering noise that he does and I picked him up from his tent. Gareth came looking for his parents, Alice wandered by and before long it became a party. Mum got cheese and bread, Mrs Henderson brought fruit and salad and Mr Henderson collected their barbecue and came back with chicken pieces, stuff like that.

We all sat there in front of the Clio until about 11 o'clock. It was really good and for a while I forgot all about Dad, about what I'd told him. Mum was sitting there, her face a bit pink, could have been the wine or sunburn, doesn't matter really, she was laughing and chatting and having a good time. I didn't want to go to bed, I didn't want the day to end or that part of the holiday to finish.

Mum was a bit quiet in the morning. She was OK-ish but I knew she'd had a lot to drink last night, normally that makes her really stroppy with me. We got our packing done really quickly, I can get our tents down in hardly any time at all now.

Sebastian half-walked, half-crawled over to the bloke with the Siamese cats. Mum watched him, her hand shielding her eyes, I saw the way she smiled.

She was very quiet, she barely spoke apart from something about, 'Hangovers are always worse with cheap wine, expensive wine is kinder to my system.' She grinned when she said it though.

We went over to say goodbye to Eddie and Sally. They'd asked if they could meet us in Brittany, Eddie shook my hand and Sally gave me a hug. Eddie smiled at me, 'Ever had oysters, Jon?'

'No, I don't think I have, have I Mum? Are they like mussels?'

Eddie laughed and Mum agreed a date to meet up with them.

I'd already said goodbye to Gareth and his parents and Mrs Henderson had said they'd like to have a few days by the beach. Gareth grabbed his mother's hand, 'Can we visit Jon and his Mum?'

She said what all parents say when they can't think of anything else to say. 'We'll see.'

Alice had given me a piece of paper when Gareth wasn't looking. Her face was bright red and she shoved the paper into my hand. Before going to bed last night I went to the toilet and I looked at what Alice had written. Her phone number was written in soppy pink biro. Could hardly read it. Thought of telling Gareth, he'd have a good laugh. I shoved it into my pocket. I'll probably tell him when we see him in Brittany.

We got on the road about 10.30 and it was already very hot. Some of the people on the site came over to say goodbye and a man asked if we'd come back to this site. Mum looked at me, 'What do you think, Jon, would you like that?'

For a moment I thought she was being sarcastic and then I realised she was grinning at me, 'Yes please.'

Once we were in the car, Mum gave me all the maps again and she put the windows down so we could get some breeze. I almost said something about Dad's car having air-conditioning but I stopped myself. I didn't want to *think* about Dad, never mind talk about him.

I hadn't realised until we were on the road that Mum hadn't been listening to the radio for days. Normally she sits in the car twiddling and playing about with the control buttons searching for Radio 4 or the World Service, but she hadn't done that for ages.

It doesn't feel as if we've been away for over a fortnight. By the time we leave this next site, we'll have been in France for three weeks. That's another funny thing I've realised too, it seems like we've been away for yonks; we've seen Paris, been to Euro-Disney, we've seen loads of chateaux and the Troglodyte caves, all those places, yet the time has gone so quickly. I started to think about Grandad. I'd told him about Dunkirk, about the war graves and I'd said that we might go back so I could take photos.

'Mum? Remember the war graves? Can we still see some of them on the way back?' I had my arm dangling out of the open window, trying to get some breeze.

I felt Mum looking at me, I didn't see her, I just knew that she was.

'Yeah, of course, if that's what you want. We can stop off on our way back to Calais. You work out the route and we'll go. It would be nice to have some of your own photos to show everyone at school, and your grandfather.'

'Thanks, Mum.'

She didn't speak for a little while and then she took one hand off the steering wheel and touched my leg. 'Jon? Has this been a good holiday for you?'

I turned to look at her, 'It's been the best, it's brilliant.'

'I'm glad, I wanted that for the three of us, it's done me a lot of good.'

I thought for a second we were going to have more of the *just the three of us* routine, but she didn't say it again. I closed my eyes, I wanted to keep things the way they were, not to think about my dad. I felt so uncomfortable.

We were all hot and sticky when we got to the site. The place is called St Cast. It's a small village with a huge beach and the camp site, Le Chatelet, is high up on the cliffs overlooking the sea. The sun was shining on the sea and the waves looked like they had shiny white balloons bouncing along the top of each one. There were a few people on the beach, walking dogs or kicking a ball about. Someone even had surfboard. I could hardly wait to get out of the car, felt like we'd been sitting in it for ages.

Mum turned the car into the car-park and said something about the tickets. 'Everything's in the red wallet, Jon, I think it's in the glove compartment. I pre-booked this site, apparently it's very popular because it's so close to the sea and of course there's …' I couldn't hear anything else she said because I'd seen Dad's car in the car park. Was it Dad's car? I shut my eyes, squeezing them really tight so I couldn't see anything.

Mum hadn't noticed a thing, she found a place to park and leant over to the back seat, next to Sebastian, looking for her bag.

'Jon,' have you found the wallet? I'll need it as proof that we've booked. I thought we could do with a really good pitch, close to the beach for you and not far for us to go with carting Sebastian around. Jon? Whatever's the matter? Are you ill? Why are your eyes closed?'

Slowly I opened my eyes. It *was* Dad's car and now he was standing next to Mum's door. She hadn't seen him, she was smiling at me. 'Twit, what can you see with your eyes shut?'

'Nina,' Dad's voice was low.

For a second, a tiny second, before she moved to face him, Mum's eyes caught mine. It was over, faster than a blink, but she knew, she knew I'd spoken to him, that I'd told him about losing Sebastian. I wanted to kill myself. I definitely didn't want to get out of the car. I wanted to stay there, inside the Clio and close all the windows and doors.

Mum turned to face Dad, she didn't try to get out of the car, she stared up at him through the open door. 'Chris, what are you doing here? When did you arrive, how did …?'

She moved her head as if she was going to look at me but she didn't. I wanted to be anywhere else, anywhere in the world would do.

Dad stepped back, 'I wanted to see how my son was, see if you'd managed to lose *him* this week.'

There were loads of people walking near us. Kids were holding ice-creams, babies were in pushchairs, parents were laughing and talking, no one took a blind bit of notice of us, why would they? We looked normal but I knew, as soon as Mum got out of the car and stood facing Dad, all that was about to change.

She put her hands on her hips and shouted at him. 'How dare you, how bloody *dare* you.'

I saw a woman nudge her husband, he whispered something to her and they grinned. Sebastian knew something was going on, he started to grizzle, he put his arms out towards me.

Dad looked over to me, 'Jon, are you OK? Let me have a look at you.'

'Of course he's OK, he's fine. He's just told me that this has been the best holiday he's ever had. Did you hear that, the best he's *ever* had.'

Oh shit. Why did she have to say that? Dad put his hand out. 'Come on, Jon, get out of the car, let me see for myself.'

'Oh, for God's sake. Jon, get out of the car, prove to your father that I haven't killed or lost you.' She leant back in the seat and tugged at my arm, 'Go on, get out.' Mum didn't look at me.

She put her hand on the glove box, 'While you're proving to your father that I haven't done you any serious damage, I'm going to get us checked in. We can sort this out, *if* anything needs sorting out, later on. Would you keep an eye on Sebastian please.' She was all bossy and abrupt. She moved out of the car and I got out of my side. Dad put his hands up as if he was going to stop her but she ignored him and walked into the Reception office. Even with those horrible flip flops she's always wearing and her hair sticking up worse than ever, she somehow made Dad look stupid.

I felt embarrassed. There were a few moments when Dad flounced, no that's not the right word. He made a noise like a tyre with the air escaping. *Phup.* He looked at me, he raised his eyebrows. I knew what he was trying to do: get me on his side, trying to make me laugh but I didn't. We both stood there, on either side of the car, not sure what to do. In the end Dad walked over to me and gave me a hug.

'Swear you've got taller, Jon. Must be all this sun. You *are* OK though, aren't you?'

'Yeah, I'm fine, honest, Dad, I'm OK. How did you know where we were?'

He dropped his arms to his sides. 'You mentioned this site in one of your phone calls. You were going on about the sites, all sorts of stuff about you and your mum having a day each at all the campsites but this one, I can remember you saying, was for you both. I doodled the name down when you said it. I had to go through all sorts of bits of paper before I found it again.'

I looked at him, he looked, not sure really, but he didn't look like my dad. He's always so clean, so smart. But now he looked as if he'd been run over by a steamroller. Everything about him was crumpled: his trousers were baggy around the knees, his shirt was all wrong it looked fussy and there were huge sweat patches under his arms. Even his face looked as if it needed ironing.

'Dad, there's nothing wrong, we're OK, I'm fine, honestly...'

Mum came out of the Reception area then. She was walking very fast, her bag tucked underneath her arm, she almost marched over to the car. 'Right, Jon, we're pitch number 43, we're in that field,' her hand waved upwards, 'overlooking the beach.' She glanced at Dad, 'I've no idea what you intend to do, but we're going to put our tents up now and settle ourselves in. We're on holiday!'

She got back into the Clio and threw her bag onto the back seat. She ran her hand over Sebastian's knees. I'd never known him to be so quiet. He'd only grizzled a tiny bit just after we'd parked the car, then nothing. It was as if he knew there was something going on.

I looked at Dad for a second and his eyes met mine before they slid away.

'Jon?' Mum was sitting in the car. I opened the passenger door. I hated this, the feeling that they both wanted me to go with them, whatever I did, one of them would think I was doing the wrong thing, one of them would be hurt.

I got into the Clio and didn't look at Dad. Why did I feel as if I'd stabbed him? Because he was here and it was my fault.

Mum didn't talk to me. It only took a few minutes to get to our pitch but it felt like hours. Dad was behind us, I could see his car in the wing mirror following us. The sun was shining on the windscreen so I couldn't see his face.

Mum turned the car onto pitch 43, it was the best pitch of the entire holiday. We were overlooking the sea, the path to get to the beach was behind a small hedge, the toilets and shower block were close by, all the stuff that Mum says we need, but the *sea!* I could smell it. Mum turned the engine off and sat looking at the beach. I wanted to make it right again, like it was before, before Dad came, before I phoned him.

'Oh, wow, Mum. This is the best, this is ace, it's the best site yet.'

She looked at me quickly, 'Well, that was the intention.' She got out of the Clio as Dad stopped his car.

Mum opened up the boot and began pulling the tents and sleeping bags out of the car. She didn't speak to me, her mouth was closed tight as if she'd locked it.

I'd always put the tents up, that was my job and it didn't seem right to me that Mum was doing it now so I got out and began to help her. Dad was standing between the two cars, he was jiggling coins around in his pockets and sort of whistling. No music, only a muddled noise. It all felt so stupid. Mum and I tugging tents from the car, Dad standing around, neither of them talking to the other one. No one took any notice of us but I felt sure that the whole of the campsite must be staring.

Sebastian began making a noise, he'd been so quiet, I'd almost forgotten about him. Dad stepped forward as if he was going to get him out of the car.

Mum didn't move, she just said 'Don't touch him.'

'Oh, for God's sake.' Dad stepped back again and we left Sebastian in his car seat.

I know it was unfair, but Dad, in his crumpled clothes, didn't look as if he belonged with us. I hadn't realised it until now but Mum and I looked like we were on holiday, we were wearing the same stuff as everyone else. Mum was wearing shorts and an old T-shirt and I had my swimming trunks on and my Euro Disney baseball cap. Dad didn't look as if he was on holiday, he looked as if he was going to work. I resented him being there. I resented him for turning up and making Mum stroppy with me again and I really wished he hadn't come.

Mum brought the sleeping bags from the car and I put the tents up. I was proud of the way that we did all that. I can put the tents up so fast now, *bang.* They're up, no messing about. The sleeping bags we just shove in the tents, our gaz stove and other stuff we put between the tents and Mum leaves the boot of the Clio up so we can get what we want when we want it,

I know at first that I did go on a bit to Mum about us not having all the right stuff but I didn't want Dad looking at everything, all our things and thinking that Mum wasn't looking after us properly, because she was.

'Is that it?' Dad's voice was cold and hard.

'What do you mean, "is that it?" What else do we need?'

I knew it, there was going to be a huge fight. Dad was standing near one tent and Mum was putting some of Sebastian's toys in another.

'Well, chairs might be a good thing, you know those things you sit on. Where are your plates? You've got hardly anything here. For God's sake, woman, you've taken two children on holiday with, with, bugger all! Well, that's it, I can't do anything about Sebastian, he's your responsibility, not mine but I'm taking Jon back with me. This is bloody ridiculous. You're nearly 40, this is what kids do on their gap year, taking off without any responsibility. For Christ's sake, when will you start behaving like an adult? When will you bloody grow up?'

130

I was sweating, it was pouring off me. It wasn't only the heat although the sun was blazing hot, it was everything. This was all my fault; I'd phoned Dad when I was angry with Mum and now he was here and the holiday was going pear-shaped.

Mum was really angry too, she'd got Sebastian out of the car and was holding him tightly to her. 'Get lost, Chris. You can't come barnstorming your way over here, throwing your weight around. Nothing is wrong. No one's hurt and before you tell me what you're going to do, perhaps if might be better if you asked Jon what he wants to do. Well? Had you thought of that? No, you bloody well hadn't. That's typical of you.'

Sebastian's eyes were fixed on Mum's face, he put his fingers up to her mouth. I thought he wanted her to stop shouting, stop those horrible words coming from her mouth. I know I did.

Like it always is with Mum and Dad, they kept arguing, saying the same things over and over again. At first, when Dad used to come around to pick me up, to take me to the zoo or cinema or something, they'd make me go out of the room or they'd wait until Dad had brought me home and I'd gone to bed before they started their rows. Then they began rowing when I was there, in the room, stuck in the middle. Even if the argument was about me, they didn't seem to notice that I was there. They'd make me feel like a roundabout, in the middle of traffic, they went round and round, saying the same things, the same old stuff. It was happening again.

But then Dad said, 'It's not a question of me, what did you call it, *barnstorming* over here. Jon phoned *me*, he told me all about you getting drunk and losing the baby. Come on, Nina, even by your standards, that's pretty extreme. Some people lose passports, others lose money on holiday, but you, no you go one better, you lose your sodding baby!'

Mum looked at me then, her eyes were very dark, I didn't know what she was thinking, I had to look away. I'd let her down and I felt awful.

'I gathered Jon spoke to you,' she was speaking in a much softer voice this time. She pushed her face into Sebastian's hair, she does that a lot lately. It never bothered me before but this time, it was as if she was saying to him, 'You won't let me down, I can depend on you.'

'Yes, he did. Late at night when he should have been in bed. What else could he have done? You were out of it, probably drunk out of your brains. This whole thing, this entire trip has been a wild goose chase; you made no proper plan, you waited until I was away …'

Sebastian was looking at me, he seemed to be asking me to stop what was going on, he didn't understand any of it. All I knew was that Mum and Dad were having a row, another one.

Mum's turn now, 'No! No, I bloody didn't. As per usual, you'd gone off without telling anyone.'

All of a sudden I wondered what we looked like to other people. Mum holding Sebastian, Dad shouting at her, Mum shouting back and me, like a wally, somewhere in the middle. People were wandering up and down and I've learnt something on holiday. It's not the French or the Italians who stare if anyone's having a row, it's the Brits who stare. They don't hide the fact either, they just stop whatever they're doing and gawp. Two couples were staring at us, I could see from the plates on their cars that they were British. I turned away, I didn't want to see them, why should I let them see me? But I started to think about what we must look like and I thought that as I'd started all this, well I had, I'd phoned Dad, it probably should be me who tried to stop it.

'Look, Mum, Dad.' They didn't hear me. Sebastian did though, he grinned and held his arms out and I pulled him from Mum. She barely noticed.

I tried again, louder, 'Mum, Dad, this is stupid. It's all my fault, I'm sorry, please, Dad.'

Dad shoved his hands deeper into his pockets. His hair had gone dark with sweat, he was soaking wet, sweat was pouring down his face, running down his neck, soaking his shirt. 'It's not your fault, Jon. You did the only responsible thing you could have done although it …'

Mum opened her mouth to say something but I said quickly to them both, 'Stop it, shut up, the pair of you, please.'

This was getting really weird, earlier I'd been thinking that

Dad was the odd one out, now I felt that I was. Well, me and Sebastian. The balance between kids and adults had shifted. My parents were standing apart from us.

Mum nodded slowly, 'OK, OK, Jon, you're right, this is upsetting for us all. Why don't we try and calm down. Sebastian needs to stretch his legs a bit and I guess we could all do with a drink. How does that sound?'

Dad nodded, I nodded and Mum got Sebastian's rug and his favourite drinking cup out of the boot and I sat him down. Mum found drinks for all of us and in a few moments we looked like a normal family. I turned, the British couples were still staring over at us. Before I sat down on the rug, I bowed, a big, over-the-top sort of bow, just like the one that I'd seen the ring-master do the last time Dad and I went to the circus. Their heads snapped back so fast, I thought they'd broken their necks.

We'd been sitting on Sebastian's rug last night, then it was like a party. Not now, it was painful to listen to them now. All this chat.

Dad: 'So you've had no problems with the car then?'

Mum: 'No, it's been fine.'

Dad: 'Has the weather been this hot all the time?

Mum: 'Pretty much, we've only had one day of rain.'

I mean, pleassse. They were skating around each other. Then Dad asked Mum about her job and she started saying something about how part of the reason behind the holiday was for her to have a re-think. 'The job is fine and I still love doing what I do but I began to think I needed something else, something I can do for people, *with* people.'

I watched Dad's face as Mum spoke. I wanted to warn her, I could see what was happening to Dad. He sat back, leaning on his arms, his eyes fixed on Sebastian's toy telephone. She went rabbiting on, 'It's more to do with missing out on contact with people.'

Dad's eyes moved slowly away from the toy telephone. 'What, so now you're prepared to give up a salaried job for what?'

Mum shook her head, 'No, that's not what I meant, that's not what I said. Listen, I can do both.' She started to tell Dad about some course she'd seen, about how she'd worked out how to cope with childcare arrangements.

Dad sat upright, he crossed his arms.

I knew there was another row coming. I yanked Sebastian up and told Mum I'd get him an ice-cream.

Dad said *no* and Mum said OK at the same time.

'I've come a long way to see you, Jon, don't wander off just when I've got here.'

'Yeah, I know that but it's hot and Sebastian's been sitting down all day, he wants some exercise and so do I.'

'OK, fair enough,' Dad began rustling through his pockets, 'Wait a minute, I'll give you some money, I changed quite a bit.'

''S OK, Grandad gave me loads. Do you want an ice-cream?'

'No.' They both said that at the same time.

I left them to it and took Sebastian with me. I held him by both hands, letting him walk. He kept on pulling his hands away from me though, he thought I should let him walk on his own. The only reason I was doing it was to let Dad see how well he was getting on. Nothing awful had happened to him.

I walked for a bit with Sebastian and I waited until I couldn't see Mum and Dad any more then I picked him up and carried him. All that dawdling about, if I walked at his pace, it would take for ever to get the ice creams.

Just as well that Mum and Dad didn't want any ice-cream, it was so hot that everything just melted. Sebastian was screaming his head off when his ice-cream ran over his fingers. He didn't like that one bit and held his hands out for me to wash them. I took him into the nearest toilet block and lifted him up so I could wash him. He was yelling the whole time.

'Shut up, I can't help it if you don't eat it fast enough, it's hot. Shut up!'

Why do women stare at me when Sebastian's yelling?

There were three of them in the toilets, nudging each other and looking at me. What do they think I was doing? I was only washing his hands, *and* I paid for the ice-cream.

His nose was all snotty when we got back outside the toilet block and I couldn't be bothered to go back inside for some toilet paper to wipe it. I rubbed the sleeve of his T-shirt around his nose. Another woman saw me and tutted. What did she think I should do? Let it run everywhere? Now that is disgusting.

I'd had enough of being a big brother. Mum could have him back. I wanted to go and explore the site. See what they had, there might be surfboards, or bikes, and I wanted to look at the beach. Mum did say that was one of the reasons we were here.

I could see Mum and Dad, they were still sitting on the rug. That might have been a good sign, difficult to tell really. I put Sebastian down so he could walk but when I wanted him to, he wouldn't. That's so typical of the kid. He held his arms up and started whining. So I had to carry him back over to Mum and Dad. Didn't really want Dad to see me doing that, it felt all wrong. I was really uncomfortable with it.

When people say *you could cut the air with a knife,* it's another of those phrases that I hear all the time. Walking back to my parents, getting closer to where they were sitting, was like walking towards a really thick fog or something. It was like the heat haze that Mum and I have seen on the auto-routes. The atmosphere around them simmered somehow. I didn't want to go back to the pair of them, if Sebastian hadn't been hanging around my neck like a sack of spuds, I'd have disappeared, gone exploring on my own. But I needed to offload him on Mum first. So I walked towards them, trying to ignore the horrible feeling inside me.

Mum saw me first and she looked up smiling, her hand shielding the sun from her eyes, 'Jon, you're back.'

Why do parents always say those stupid things? I'm standing right in front of her. *No, I haven't arrived yet.*

'Eaten your ice-cream already?' That's another daft thing

135

they say. Somehow I didn't think this was the time to say something cheeky. *No, I've still got it in my hand.*

She took Sebastian from me and gave him another drink.

Dad cleared his throat, 'Jon, I was explaining to your mother that I thought I might stay on a bit, certainly for the weekend. There's an hotel up the road, they do cheap rooms and there shouldn't be a problem with one for me, for a few days. What do you think?'

I kept my eyes down, I couldn't look at him, I thought he might be able to see what I felt, it might be there, written all over my face.

'Jon? What do you think? We could spend some time together.'

No! 'Yeah, OK, sounds good.' I still couldn't look at him.

He got to his feet. 'I'll make tracks, see if there's a room for me and then I might drive around, check the area out, look at the village. I'll come back and see you later, perhaps we could have supper together, is that OK?'

I didn't look at Dad's face, I looked at Mum's. She was holding Sebastian on her lap, playing with his telephone.

'Can we all go, Mum and Sebastian too?'

They spoke at the same time. Dad said something like, 'Well, I'm not sure ...' and Mum said 'No, I don't think so.'

Dad laughed, one of those laughs that's not a laugh, just a noise that people make when they don't think things are funny. 'He said, 'Perhaps not this time, Jon. What about you and I having supper and a chat on our own. I haven't seen you for weeks. You told me about your project, what is it, something for the garden?'

'It's a fountain.'

'Yes, that's right, a fountain. You can tell me all about that, where you're up to, all that sort of thing.'

I looked at Mum sitting on the rug. Her fingers were dialling the bright colours on Sebastian's telephone. I realised she was dialling our phone number at home.

'Mum hasn't been out for ages.'

She looked up at me, 'Jon, it's OK. I'll be fine. It probably wouldn't be right anyway, Sebastian and I, it just wouldn't be right.'

'I want you to come, please.'

I heard Dad sighing. 'Jon, for God's sake, how old are you? You *can* go out without your mother now.'

I looked at him then. 'I know I can, but I want her to come too.'

They looked at each other and I saw Mum shrug, just a tiny shrug. I knew she'd come.

Dad saw it too, 'Right, if that's what you want. I'll get off, get myself sorted out and I'll be back here, at what? 7 o'clock?' He didn't know what to do next, it was written all over him. He looked at Mum and me and then patted his pockets, looking for his keys. '7 o'clock then?'

I nodded. Mum didn't say anything and Dad just bent slightly and ruffled Sebastian's hair. He'll get to hate that as much as I do when he's older.

Dad walked over to his car, it must have been like an oven inside, he'd left it in the sun.

He started up the engine and drove off, I could hear the gravel popping like tiny bullets under the tyres of his car.

Once Dad had gone I felt better. The atmosphere had gone, the air that was thick enough to cut before, all that had gone and now it was just us again, it was OK. I wanted to say something to Mum, to say I was sorry, to see if we could get back to where we were before, before Dad turned up. I didn't know how to say it, sometimes I've found that once you start apologising, parents seem to want to go all over the problem again, asking stuff like 'Why did you do it? Why don't you think before you open your mouth?'

I just said the first thing that came into my head. 'Mum? Fancy coming to look around the site with me? We could have a walk on the beach, too, look at the surf, what do you think?'

For a second she didn't speak then she looked up at me, 'Sounds good, grab hold of Sebastian while I get up.' She stood and we each grabbed one of Sebastian's hands so he could walk between us.

'I think we could all do with a shower later on, it's been quite a day.' That was all she said as we started off on our trip around the site. That sounded like parent-speak for 'Let's forget about it, wash it away.' Whatever it was, it sounded all right to me.

FRANK.

The rain was running down the windows in wavy lines, blurring the shapes of the geraniums in the hanging baskets making them look larger, blowsy.

'Like a tart's drawers,' Nancy said one summer sitting with him in the kitchen on a wet summer's day.

Frank walked over to the sink, his back and legs had a dull, residual ache. Frank thought of the pain as an old adversary, well-versed in his movements and rituals. He felt that he and the pain were locked in a battle each day. That nagging ache was the pain warning him that it hadn't gone away, it was still there, reminding him. He rinsed out his cup and walked out to the hall to check if the post had arrived.

A bank statement, a gas bill and a folded piece of paper, *Dad* scrawled by a hurried hand.

He squinted at the note, 'Damn and blast, left my glasses upstairs.' He gazed at the piece of the paper, holding it at arm's length, squinting. 'Bugger this, I can't leave it, I'll have to get my glasses after all.'

He took a deep breath and put both hands on the banister, pulling himself onto the first step and he began a slow climb to his bedroom.

Steam curled its way up from his mug as Frank read Chris's note for the third time: *Decided to go to France after all. Seemed to be the only way that I could make certain that*

Jonathan is all right. Will probably stay there over the weekend. Not sure if you've got my mobile no. It's 0770 771847. Tell you everything when I get back, Chris.

Frank shook his head, 'What good will that do? Chasing over there, really puts the cat amongst the pigeons.' He folded the note carefully, dividing the paper up the same way Chris had. He slid the note between the salt and pepper pots. The bank statement and gas bill had also been slotted between the two pots. Frank would go through both of them later, a task that took him some time. Everything had to be meticulously double-checked, then Frank ticked everything if all the items matched up.

The gas bill had been an area of huge problems when Nancy was alive. She used to laugh as Frank knelt down, peering into the cupboard under the stairs, a torch in one hand and a notebook in the other.

'What are you doing? You saw the man read the meter, how can there be a mistake? Why *would* there be a mistake?'

She'd sing *I am a mole and I live in a hole.*

Frank always ignored her, he knew that people made mistakes, mistakes that could cost him money, no point in taking chances. Once, when they'd been out, their meter hadn't been read and the next gas bill had arrived with an E sitting alongside units they'd used.

'Look at this,' Frank waved the bill in front of Nancy. 'I'll give them bloody estimates. Cost us a fortune if we use their figures.'

'So change them, put in what we have used,' Nancy was reading her horoscope, she didn't look up. 'Hardly worth making a song and dance about it.'

Frank sighed, a deep, theatrical sigh. 'You just don't understand do you? Once you start going down that road, all sorts of mistakes happen. No, nothing else for it, I'll have to go into the Gas Board myself.'

Nancy's eyes moved upwards towards Frank. He hadn't seen her looking at him, his eyes were firmly fixed on the gas bill he held in his hands.

'Whatever you say,' she dropped her gaze and turned the

pages of her newspaper.

Frank sat inside his car, listening to the rain drumming on the roof of the garage. The rain had irritated him and he'd thought he'd see if there were any chores he could do in the garage.

Sitting with one leg inside the car and the other resting on the garage floor he remembered his father working in the garage, polishing, tinkering with the old Lanchester on wet Sunday afternoons. He'd allow Frank to sit in the driver's seat, twisting and turning the steering wheel while he checked the levels, bending down low over the engine, wiping his hands on an old cloth.

Whenever he went out with his parents, Frank always sat in the back of the car, his father always insisted on Frank sitting in the back seat, right behind his mother.

'I need all the room you can give me so I can see where I'm going. Do you understand, son?'

Frank always said yes, nodding eagerly, but he hadn't really understood at all. He just loved the feeling that his dad included him in the grown-up business of driving.

Alone in the gloom of the garage, he remembered going on picnics with his parents. Frank shook his head, there weren't many picnics. One he could remember, he must have been about ten years old. And, as he thought about it, it probably was the last one they'd had. He was sure of it. The whole performance must have put his father off for life. Frank kept his head still as the memories tumbled over themselves.

He knew his father had talked of picnics, of a 'run in the car, taking a trip'. He could remember how his mother used to shake her head, pursing her lips against such enthusiasm, 'I'll think about it, let me see how I am in the morning.'

But, one day, they *had* gone on a picnic. Frank had a sudden, clear image of his mother, two pink patches of colour high on her cheeks, her hand pressed against her rib-cage. 'Stop jumping about, Frank, my heart's doing a tap dance as it is.'

He could remember his mother doing a sort of checklist:
1. There mustn't be a cloud in the sky.

141

2. They all had to listen to the weather forecast the night before.

3. They all had to get up early to make preparations.

As a child, Frank thought of *preparations* as a word written in capital letters. Edna always spoke of them in important stress-bearing tones. 'I'll need to have plenty of time for the preparations.'

Frank was never sure what these entailed and why they took so long. His mother shooed him out of the kitchen, 'Out from under my feet, Frank. Do you want this picnic or not? If you do, you'll have to give me room.'

His friends at school went on picnics. They went for day trips, carrying flasks of tea and sandwiches wrapped in grease-proof paper. They took hardboiled eggs and slices of home-made fruit cake. He told his father that his friends often stopped off on the way home to have fish and chips. 'They sit in their cars, eating chips out of newspaper.' Frank thought it sounded the perfect ending to a day trip. He knew where the fish and chip shop was, he even had money of his own to buy some.

Gordon had been on the driveway, shirt sleeves rolled up, an old blue cloth in his hand, wiping down the Lanchester, making it gleam for their day out. He'd paused to listen to Frank's request, 'Best ask your mother, son. See what she has to say.'

He *had* asked, he could remember opening the kitchen door, watching his mother buttering slices of bread, cutting off the marbled fat on cold slices of beef, slicing tomatoes into paper-thin circles, steam rising from her second-best saucepan where three eggs jostled against each other.

'Mum, can we have…?'

She hadn't looked up from her tasks.

He tried again, 'Mum, can we stop off for fish and chips on the way home?'

She'd looked at him then, pushing a stray curl behind her ear. 'Fish and chips, when I've prepared all this? You've got no idea how that sort of thing is cooked and it's probably all stale, *days* old. No, I don't think so. Now, close the door, let

142

me get on.'

There was a lot of toing and froing that day. Frank remembered his father tugging a wicker picnic basket from its resting place in the loft. The dark red travel rug that had to be hung over the washing line and rigorously beaten with a brush. Then the trek back and forth from the house to the car while all manner of equipment was installed in the Lanchester's boot.

Most of all, Frank could still see the fixed, controlled look on his father's face as he carried each item from the house to the waiting car. A separate journey, one for the picnic basket, a cumbersome item with stiff, unwieldy straps. Edna insisted on it being used. 'Put that in first, Gordon, that must go on the bottom of the pile, you do understand that?'

Another trip for the deck-chairs, one each for Gordon and Edna, both to be stacked neatly on the basket then back to the house for the various bags containing woollen jumpers for the three of them. Another trip for the cushions that would be placed behind Edna's aching back, and another trip for the hats, a cotton one for Frank and a wide-brimmed straw hat for Edna. Then the ball, 'In case you and Frank want a game, I won't be able to join you but I can watch.' A cotton bag containing knitting wool and the latest pattern and Edna's library book. Frank remembered his father's steady walk back and forth until everything was at last covered up with the heavy travel rug.

And then, when the car was packed up, when it stood on the driveway, the sun's rays bouncing off the twin headlights, Gordon and Frank were dispatched upstairs to change, 'Wash properly, mind, both of you. Clean shirt and a handkerchief each.'

When, at last, the three of them climbed into the car the guilt that Frank and Gordon had somehow brought all this extra work on Edna's shoulders was reinforced by the stifled groans as she sat in the front seat. 'Well, if you two don't enjoy yourselves today, don't blame me. I've done more than my fair share towards your day out. God knows I have, lot of hard work these trips, you know.'

Frank put all idea of a fish and chip supper to the back of his mind. His mother had gone to so much trouble, she'd worked hard. It would have been so ungrateful, for such an uncaring thought to even enter his head.

When they were on the road, Edna sitting next to Gordon, there was an air of suppressed emotion. Frank, even at his young age, felt it. 'It felt like a lid on a saucepan,' he told Nancy years later. 'Never felt it since, it was just the feeling of something hidden, bubbling away underneath.'

The drive simply to find a place for a picnic was tortured. Edna ordering Gordon to drive more slowly, pushing at his elbow as he drove the car, looking for an unoccupied stretch of road, a place to park. 'Not there! There's no sun, what's the point of coming all this way if we have to sit in gloom?'

Then, when Gordon did find a quiet spot away from other families, away from cows in fields, near a tree where Edna could enjoy sunlight and dappled shade, the unloading of the car began.

That process was as tortuous as the packing. The rug had to be shaken out, flattened with the back of Gordon's hand as he knelt on it, securing the corners with four heavy stones placed according to Edna's commands. Then he moved the chairs from the car.

'He held those chairs like a bullfighter holds the red cloak, moving them to the left, then to the right and waiting to see which way Mum would choose.' Frank told Nancy on the day they had their first picnic together.

The picnic basket was brought out, Gordon tugging and pulling at the thick, leather straps and the red and white checked table cloth was put on the rug. Then, in an almost religious silence, Edna's second-best china tea service was taken and laid out almost covering the table cloth. By then, Edna was sitting in the striped deck-chair directing operations. 'Put that plate in the middle, no, *that one.*' Crisp starched napkins were handed silently to Frank who sat cross-legged on the rug. The sandwiches cut into almost perfect triangles were passed around. Salt and pepper pots nestled in the middle of the cloth. Edna's home-made lemonade poured into glass beakers for the three of them. Frank remembered the jaw-aching ceremony of the whole thing.

Both Frank and Gordon knew that it was a mistake not to praise Edna for their meals. Whether it was sandwiches eaten in a field or a three-course Sunday lunch, noises of pleasure, of appreciation, had to be made. They also knew that the right amount of time had to pass before their praise could be voiced. Like a double act, they waited for a cue from each other. Frank had learnt that, when his father cleared his throat, that was his signal and they each used phrases, chosen to placate and please Edna.

'These are really nice, Mum, not too thick, just right.'

'Mm, Frank's right, love. Beef's very good, cut how I like it.'

Edna preened, sitting upright in the deck-chair as they spoke to her. 'Well, I try hard, you know I do, only the best beef. Takes a long time getting it like that, cut thin with no fat. Picnic for you two means a lot of work for me but as long as you're happy, then it's all been worth it.'

Frank couldn't remember anything else his mother said on these picnics. Only the memory of her sitting in her chair, knitting or reading. He couldn't remember her ever sitting cross-legged on the rug as he did or lying full length like his father, arms crossed behind his head, eyes closed. When he thought of that last picnic he remembered the way his father and he had sat, close together, like courtiers at the foot of a throne.

After that picnic Frank could no longer rely on Gordon's support whenever he asked for a day out. His father muttered, 'I don't think so, son.' Frank stopped asking, merely accepting that picnics like a lot of other things were something other families did.

Sometimes, another boy at school invited him home to have tea and, as he got older, Frank saw the interaction between the members of other families. There was a smoothness, an openness that intrigued and sometimes startled him. He'd come home lulled after one of these visits and then the disparity between the relationships of the family he'd just

145

left and the controlled, invisible tensions in his own family confused him. He'd say something he'd heard one of his friends say to his mother and when Edna didn't react in the same way, he was more bothered than ever. Frank so wanted to recreate the warmth of what he thought was normal family life in his own. He saw how a friend would tease his mother, gently laughing at something she'd said or done. He watched how a mock punch to the head, a friendly tap on the shoulder was nearly always followed by laughter. Then, more than ever, the silences in his own house unnerved him. Other homes had sounds of raised voices, doors slamming, laughter, a radio playing.

Only once did Frank bring someone back from school with him, another lad from his class and it was only after an interrogation from Edna, 'Do we know these people? What does his father do?'

The two boys ate their tea in the dining room with Edna presiding over the tea-pot and her home-made scones. After all this time Frank couldn't remember his friend's name but he could remember hearing the lad gulp down the dry, floury scone in the uncomfortable silence of their dining room.

Frank and his friend escaped after tea and kicked a ball around in the back garden. When Gordon came home from work he rolled his sleeves up and joined in, hurling himself full length on the manicured lawn.

Edna went to bed early that night, 'All that noise, got one of my heads now.' When Frank was a small boy he was never sure what his mother meant by that phrase. Did she have different heads, one with a smiley face, one with a sad face? Where did she keep them, perhaps they were in her wardrobe alongside the hats she wore; the blue one she liked to put on when she went shopping or the one with the pink roses she wore when she went to see her sister.

It didn't take Frank long to learn that it was hardly worth the effort having someone else in his house. The whole performance, the build-up, the tension, it was never worth it. Only a few hours of company before the house reverted to its normal state.

'It was like our house had been zipped up tight.' he told Nancy later on. It had been another part of life with her as his wife that had initially delighted him. Nancy left doors open, radios playing in unoccupied rooms, she laughed and sang nursery rhymes to Christopher. Each room felt different, open, friendly.

'Houses should be open, a closed door to a child sends out all sorts of messages,' she told Frank.

The rain had stopped, there was only the sound of water running down the guttering at the back of the garage. Close by, a dog barked. Frank got out of the car and locked it up again. He whistled as he wiped down the shelves in his garage, moving jamjars of nails and screws, reaching behind them, shaking his head at the film of dust he could see on every surface.

JONATHAN

This place, St Cast, is really good. There's a long road that goes all along the sea-front and you can walk the whole length, looking at the beach. The beach goes on for ages, and the town has got masses of restaurants and little cafés to sit and have ice-cream and coffee and stuff.

'Look, Jon, what do you see?' Mum asked me, 'What can you smell?'

I didn't know what she was on about, there was no smell apart from the sea.

'The *sea*, I can smell the sea and I can see it too!' We were coming back to the campsite after we'd had a long walk.

'Exactly,' she tapped me on the head. 'Got it in one, no burger vans, no fish and chip cafés, not even that many people spoiling the view. Just this glorious beach and unspoilt town. You see, Jon, our seasides in the UK have been swamped by trash, buried in burgers.'

I wasn't sure what she was on about. Dad and me had a pretty good holiday in St Ives last year but it didn't seem the right time to remind her of that. I just mumbled, 'Yeah.' Actually I was dead chuffed she was in such a good mood again. Sebastian was on her shoulders, he was laughing and pulling at her hair and whenever Mum yelled *ow* he laughed even harder.

Mum didn't seem angry or upset either. We walked around the campsite and it was smashing. We both said so and Mum said that it was a shame we weren't going to be able to spend that much time here. She looked at me then and said that we could always come back another year.

The campsite has got two big swimming pools and another smaller one for kids like Sebastian. There were bikes to hire and they also had buses to different village markets and one evening one of the local vineyards would bring loads of wine to taste. Mum said that it sounded good and she might go. There was a big sandy area with different barbecues on it, away from the rest of the campsite.

Mum made me look at all the showers and toilets, all that stuff. They looked OK to me but she said they were superb. A toilet's a toilet but she said it was all to do with standards of cleanliness – yeah right.

It was about 6.10 when we got back to the tents. 'Showers, I think,' Mum said and she went over to get the shampoo and stuff. We keep it all in a big carrier bag in the car. She put Sebastian on the ground and then turned to look at me.

'Jon? I won't refer to this again, I promise, well not in this way but ringing your dad, I understand. What I mean is I understand why you did it. There were mistakes on your part and on mine but as far as I'm concerned it's over and done with, is that OK?'

OK? It was the best news I had that day. I didn't know what to say to her and I had to keep swallowing because I knew I was going to start crying.

Mum knew that too, she knew. She put her arms out, 'How about a hug?'

She held me really tight, her head was almost level with mine. She whispered to me, 'So, are we all right? You and me?'

I still couldn't speak so I just nodded very fast. She gave me another squeeze then said, 'Showers I think for the three of us, I can't remember ever feeling so hot.'

When I took my shorts off to get under the shower, I found the piece of paper that Alice had given me, the one with her telephone number on. I held it in my hand for a second and my fingers started to curl around it, as if I was going to scrunch it up. I didn't need it, I've already got their telephone number, Gareth gave it to me. I looked at the paper for a second, looking at the way she'd written the numbers. I put it under my pile of clean clothes so it wouldn't get wet when I showered.

When I got back Mum was sitting in the front seat of the Clio and putting make-up on. I don't think she's worn any since we've been away, but I wouldn't have noticed even if she had. She was grumbling about the heat melting her favourite lipstick, 'God, my hair's a mess too. Haircuts for both of us I think, Jon, when we get home.'

I didn't want to think about going home, didn't even like hearing her mention it, somehow. I was trying to keep Sebastian quiet and stop him wandering off, he'd only get dirty again. Mum was taking ages and Sebastian was a real pain. She kept parting her hair and sighing, 'Never mind silver threads, I've got enough for a blanket.'

'Muum!'

'What?'

'It's Sebastian, he's hungry, can't you have him now?'

'Just a few more seconds, Jon. Give him an apple or something. But don't let him get dirty.'

Actually I was hungry too. I didn't have a clue about where we were going to eat.

'Mum?'

She was still messing about with her face.

'Mum?'

'Jon! For God's sake, give me a break will you? We're going out to have supper and I'd like to look a bit presentable, whether it's with your dad or Russell Crowe – just understand that I'm doing it for me and I need a bit more time, for me, OK?'

She swung herself out of the car and stood up.

She *did* look OK. Clean skirt and T-shirt, dark red varnish on her toe-nails and for once she wasn't wearing those horrible flip-flops.

'Well?' She put her hands on her hips and smiled at me.

'Not bad, for an old woman.'

'Cheeky beggar, hope your dad brings plenty of money, I'm starving. Come on, hand young bugger-lugs over to me. I'll keep him quiet for a few more minutes.' She got a book out of the car and settled down on the rug to read to Sebastian.

I had a fluttery feeling inside, like the time I was waiting to go on stage at the Christmas concert last year only this time I'm not playing a part. This had more to do with Mum and Dad, thinking about how they'd behave, whether they'd be cagey, nervously polite with each other. Although, thinking about it, I was playing a part. Perhaps we all were, playing happy families.

Mum's always great when she's reading to Sebastian, she makes up all these different voices for him and he looks up at her because he can't work out if it's the same person speaking. Watching them I couldn't help thinking that getting Mum to come to dinner with Dad and me probably wasn't the best idea I'd ever had. I've got used to the fact that my parents are divorced. It's been a long time and I know that they won't get back together, I understand that. I can't even remember when Dad was living at home with us.

When I asked Dad if Mum could come with us, I wasn't being a wimp or being difficult, I *did* feel it would be better if Mum came. She'd hasn't been out much, we've had most of our meals sitting either in the Clio or in front of our tents. I'm not trying to pull the pieces together, it's more to do with this whole thing of being on holiday, seeing people together, laughing, teasing each other, mucking about. I thought about Gareth too and part of me wanted to be able to say to him, 'Yeah my dad's arrived, we're having supper together, the four of us.' It's all that, wanting to be the same as everyone else. But I think I know now that it doesn't have to be with Dad any more, he's not part of us. I only needed him to fill the space.

Dad's car pulled up alongside the Clio. Mum and Sebastian looked up and I saw the way Sebastian closed the book they were reading.

Dad got out and clapped his hands together, 'Right then, are we all ready?'

Mum got up and yanked Sebastian on to her hip, 'Yes, I think so.'

Dad must have showered too, he looked much better than he did before. He had shorts on and a clean polo shirt. He was doing that thing with shorts, that tugging business that a lot of blokes do when they haven't worn shorts since the year before. I don't think I do it, but blokes of my dad's age do. They stand with one leg apart then they tug at the leg of the shorts. It always looked to me like they were settling their private bits, making them comfortable. Suppose Dad will stop doing it before long.

Mum was standing in front of Dad, 'How is your hotel, room OK?'

'Yeah, it's fine. I couldn't believe how cheap it was, but it's hardly surprising what with the pound being so strong ...'

They were off, rabbiting on about the exchange rate and all that stuff. At least it got us into the car without all the fuss we had the last time I had to drive in the same car with my parents.

I can still remember that. It was at Grandma's funeral. Mum hadn't stopped crying for days and Dad thought the three of us should go in one car. Sebastian wasn't born then and Mum was useless, she couldn't see where she was going, she was crying so much.

Dad kept going on about why we should present a united front. 'Showing everyone that we are together for this. That's what Mum would have wanted.' He said that just as *my* mum was getting in the front seat. She was half in, half out and she stopped, just stopped moving.

'You haven't got a clue what Nancy wanted, not you nor Frank, not a bloody clue!' She yelled it at the top of her voice, her face only a few inches away from Dad's. 'You didn't know her, neither of you. You simply didn't know her.'

She got out then, she was crying even harder. Dad had put his arm around her or tried to. She pushed him away. People in the street were watching us, they always do that when there's a wedding or a funeral. Dad hated it, he told Mum she was turning it into a pantomime. She'd ignored him and cried into my hair. I could hear her hiccupping and trying to control her tears when she stopped and told Dad that she and I would go in one car and he could go on his own.

'But you can't do that, that's not right.' Dad wasn't far from tears, I could hear them in his voice. That was all I needed, both parents crying in the street. I hated the pair of them then, really hated them. We hadn't even got to Grandma's funeral and they couldn't behave like adults. They expected me to, I'd had all sorts of lectures on it but my parents couldn't control themselves.

I'd taken a deep breath and told Dad that I'd sit in the front with him and Mum would be better off in the back of his car. I tugged at her arm, it seemed as if all her anger had gone, her arm felt like an old sock, she nodded at me and got into the back of Dad's car. The whole thing was awful.

This time it was much better; by the time I'd picked up my baseball cap, Mum had got into Dad's car and strapped Sebastian in next to her. I sat in the front with Dad.

'OK?' Dad switched the engine on and we drove off.

The restaurant was pretty good. The waiters found us a table at the front so we could see the waves splashing up on the beach and they brought out a high chair for Sebastian. When we were given the menu, one of the waiters tied a big white cloth around Sebastian. It was enormous and he tried blowing his nose in it. Dad laughed. It wasn't that funny but I knew what Dad was doing. People always do that when they don't know what to say: they focus on the kids. They stare at them trying to find things to say. Dad was absolutely classic.

'So, is he walking yet?'

Bad question. Sebastian had started walking and walked away from Mum that time he wandered off and got lost. That's how all this started. Mum smiled and said something about how he was half walking, half crawling, 'Just like Jon was at the same age.'

Dad nodded as the waiter arrived to take our order. They both smiled and thanked him, falling over themselves as they said *thank you* so many times you'd never believe that the waiter *had* to do it, it was his job. Listening to my mum and dad you'd think that this bloke was only there for them, it was the one reason he'd got up that morning. It's sad really and made me realise that it's easier for my parents to talk to other people than it is for them to talk to each other. What a performance!

'What would you like, Jon? Choose something you'd really like, look at the mussels. Would you like those? Nina? What about you? I seem to remember you liked lobster …'

The waiter was staring out towards the beach while all this was going on. Don't suppose he cared at all what we ate but Dad kept apologising about the time we were taking, how there was so much to choose from, all that. Finally we ordered and Mum said she wanted some fish cakes for Sebastian. Dad ordered a bottle of wine but even that didn't come without a fuss.

'A crisp white but I don't think we'll have the house white, let's have something a bit better, what do you recommend?' I asked for Coke. The waiter scribbled everything down and went away, then there was silence.

Dad picked up the salt pot and jiggled it around, spilling the salt on the blue and white checked cloth and Mum fussed with Sebastian, smoothing his hair away from his face. He was beginning to get fed up with that. I knew he would. He pushed her hand away and Dad laughed. I wanted to tell him to stop the stupid laughing, just relax a bit. I looked at him and his eyes moved away from Sebastian and caught mine; he looked relieved as if he was drowning and I'd thrown him a life raft.

'So, Jon, everything all right at school? What's with this project of yours, the fountain? How's that coming along? Anything I can do to help?'

I started to tell him about how far I'd got when the waiter came back with the bottle of wine. I stopped talking, Dad wasn't listening anyway, he was tasting the wine and watching as Mum's glass was filled. I thought he'd say something again but he didn't. He asked Mum when we were going home.

'We've only got four days here, then we head off to Calais. Should get home by early evening on the 26th August,

154

I think.' Mum smiled at me, 'I think Jon would like to stay here for much longer.'

'Well, that's not possible, you know my feelings about children being taken out of school time. They already have almost seven weeks of holiday as it is. He should be back at school on the proper day.'

Mum was giving Sebastian his bottle of juice and she didn't look at Dad as she spoke. 'He *will* be back, we'll have nearly a week to get his stuff ready for the return to school. We'll have plenty of time to get your uniform and books sorted out, won't we, Jon?'

'Yeah, loads of time. Dad? Mum's promised we can stop near Dunkirk on the way back so I can see the war museums, take some photos of them. I thought Grandad might want to see those, what do you think?'

Dad's glass was empty and he reached over to the wine bucket at the side of our table and poured wine into his glass. Mum had barely touched hers. 'Yes, I'm sure he would. He's never been to France.'

Mum looked up, 'He's never been anywhere.'

Dad pulled a face and looked at me again, 'Where did you get your baseball cap? Why don't you wear it the proper way?' He leant forward as if he was going to turn my cap around and I pulled away from him.

'I like wearing it this way, all the kids do. We got it in Euro Disney. I got another hat too, a Western hat. Mum won't let me wear it when we go out. I got that one from the Wild Bill Western show. You should have seen it, Dad. It was amazing, they had buffaloes, real ones and they jumped on and off them …'

Dad wasn't looking at me any more, he was staring at Mum. 'You took Jonathan to Euro Disney? You know that I said I'd take him. Why did you do that? What were you trying to do to me. I hardly see him as it is and now you're taking him to places that I said I'd take him to.'

I heard Mum sigh and, from the corner of my eye, I saw her body slump as if she'd been punctured.

'Look, Chris, this isn't the proper place or time to start.'

'Lobster?' The waiters had arrived at our table, there were three of them and they all had enormous steel dishes of lobster, crab, mussels. It seemed to me that they'd brought just about everything there was on the menu. A boy a bit older than me held a basket of French sticks and he was smirking at me. I felt uncomfortable, he couldn't have heard anything or if he had, would he have understood English?

I've never been so glad to see a meal arrive before. Even I liked the performance this time; the waiters putting plates down, moving dishes around, trying to find room on the table for salad and finger bowls. It was much easier to smile and say *thank you* to the waiters than to listen to Mum and Dad having a go at each other.

Finally the waiters left us alone, 'Bon appetit,' Dad said.

'Doesn't it look wonderful – Jon, what do you think?' Mum's hand crept under the table and she squeezed my knee. 'Yeah, looks great,' I touched her hand to show her that I was doing my bit too.

We all tucked pale pink napkins under our chins. Sebastian laughed when he saw us and tugged at his napkin. He got another hair ruffling session from Mum for that.

'Well, isn't this nice?' Not sure who said it first but both Mum and Dad came up with that one. Honestly it was painful listening to them. Trouble was, I wasn't sure what to do or say myself. When I'm with Dad, the two of us on our own, we get along OK. We don't spend the whole time rabbiting on about things but then I don't do that with Mum either.

There were quite a lot of people in the restaurant. Dad had said that he drove around the town earlier and this one looked as if might be the best one to try. Seemed to me that a lot of other people thought so too. All around us I could hear conversations rising and falling. I remembered watching a programme on the box once about how engineers keep an eye on sound levels when they're making radio or television programmes. They have a special monitor so they can see how the levels rise and fall as people speak. They use things called *faders*, they move them up and down, softening voices or sounds that are too loud or too harsh. It'd be really great if I could have one of those, then each time Mum or Dad started fighting, I could fade them out.

Dad topped up Mum's glass, he was on his third glass of wine. 'I think we should have another bottle, Jon, do you want more Coke?' He'd already signalled to the waiter and I saw Mum's eyebrows move.

Sebastian was halfway through his fish cakes, he was making a disgusting mess as usual and Mum gave him some of her lobster, just bits on the edge of a spoon.

'That's pretty expensive food to be giving a baby,' Dad looked at me as he spoke, as if he wanted me to agree with him, to be on his side. I drank more Coke and looked at my plate.

'Mm, you're right, it *is* expensive. Let me know how much you think he's eaten and I'll pay you for it. In fact, I'll pay for it all.' Two bright red spot had appeared on Mum's cheeks and there were signs of red creeping up on her neck. That always happens when she's angry, I'd never seen them arrive that fast before.

Dad sighed, 'Don't be stupid, I didn't mean anything by it. Although, now I come to think about it, are you sure that you can afford to pay for it? Or would that be my money you'd be using?'

'I've had enough of this,' Mum tugged at her napkin, trying to get it off.

Dad put his hand out to touch Mum's arm, 'I'm sorry, please sit down. That was wrong of me. Have another glass of wine.' Dad emptied the first bottle into Mum's glass and looked around for the waiter. 'Where is he with that bottle?'

For one moment I thought Mum would go; she looked at me and then sat back. I didn't want her to go. For a start the food was really good and if she went then I'd probably have to go with her, give her a hand with Sebastian, but it just seemed to me that for once it wouldn't hurt either of them to sit with me and eat properly. Why can't they do that? Other people can. The waiter came then and Dad filled his glass and gave me another Coke although I don't remember asking for one. *Then* it was all right, there was some chat about the ferry

157

crossing, the price of petrol, more stuff on the exchange rate, price of properties in France. I nearly put my foot in it, though, when I told Dad that Mum had been looking in estate agents' windows. 'Said you thought we could afford one, didn't you Mum?'

She kicked me really hard on my ankle; wouldn't have been so bad if she'd been wearing her flip flops but she had leather sandals on and it hurt. 'Ow.'

'A house, here in France? How on earth would you manage that?'

She shook her head, 'I couldn't, I just couldn't. It was the holiday talking, that's all. I could actually relocate with my job or at least I thought I could. Technology makes my job remarkably moveable. Working from home means just that, I can work from wherever my home is. But the practicality of receiving manuscripts, meeting deadlines and getting work back in time, on the right date.' She shook her head again. 'As I said, it was the holiday talking. The idea didn't last long, it was looking at the house prices meandering around a quaint village like everyone does in this part of the world. We've really loved France, haven't we, Jon?'

'Yeah, it's been great. But you're talking as if the holiday is over and it's not.'

They both laughed then, at the same time. I felt really good, really clever as if I'd done something magical.

There was some more chat then Dad said he'd been to see Grandad. He said that one day he'd gone round to see him and he couldn't get any reply and it had bothered him.

'Curtains drawn, milk bottles on the front step, not like the old man at all. I really was quite bothered, I can tell you. It's the worst scenario for me, him living on his own, stubborn old sod won't talk to his neighbours so, if anything did happen, it might take *days* before anyone knew about it.'

Mum kept her head down when Dad was saying all this, there was hardly anything left on her plate, she was just moving the fork around. 'Was he all right? I presume you did get in to see him?'

'Yes, he was fine, he said he'd overslept. Had a couple of

glasses of whisky the night before and didn't hear his alarm.'

Mum smiled then, 'Only Frank would still have an alarm, nothing to get up early for any more but the alarm still has to go on. I'm glad he's all right, though. Does he know you're over here, in France?'

Dad pulled a face, 'He does now, I left him a note. Actually,' he cleared his throat, 'when I went to see him he thought it would be best if I stayed away. He said that Jon sounded fine in his phone calls and that I ... well, he said that I should stay away, let you get on with your holiday.'

We all looked at our plates then although I think my head went further down than either Mum or Dad. I didn't need reminding that this was my fault, although as things were going, it wasn't working out too badly after all. At least they were talking together. We seemed to be like all the other people in the restaurant now, a normal family. It would have been really great if Gareth and his parents, and Alice too I suppose, could have been there. We'd have looked the same as them.

The waiters came back to clear up the plates and one of them handed Dad another menu.

'Ice-cream, Jon, Nina?'

Mum shook her head, 'Not for me, thank you, but a small portion of ice-cream for Sebastian might be nice. Jon?'

I took the menu from Dad, pointless really as I can't understand much French. I keep telling Mum that it's not the same French that we're taught at school. 'Can I have crepes, with ice-cream and a chocolate sauce?' I had crepes when I was with the Hendersons.

'Might even join you, Jon.' Dad made a big thing of peering into the bottle and waggling it from side to side, checking to see how much was left. He put it back into the wine cooler and didn't order any more. He told the waiter what we wanted and said that he and Mum would have coffee later on. He leant back in his chair and his arm stretched out over the chair next to him.

'You've done well finding this place, Nina. It's got a lot going for it. Can see the appeal for kids, for their parents, even babies are well catered for. What was it, a happy accident? You can't honestly say it was weeks of planning and searching, can you?'

Mum shook her head, 'No, I can't, but a neighbour told me about this village and the campsite and all it took was a phone call to make the booking. Once I decided that we'd come to France, you'd be amazed how many people want to tell you about their favourite places, the best route to take, all that sort of thing. I'd made up my mind that the holiday had to be for the three of us.' She looked at me then. 'We needed a break, certainly Jon and I did. It really wasn't that difficult, I was looking for somewhere where Jon could make new friends, take off and enjoy himself and somewhere where I could see the bits of France I haven't seen before. Not sure if we've managed that totally but there's always another year.'

I looked at her, 'You mean that? We can come again, you said before that …'

'Of *course* we can come again. I'm really thrilled that you feel you want to come again, Jon.' She touched my arm just as the plates of crepes and ice-cream arrived. Sebastian started banging on his highchair with his fists when he saw the dollops of ice-cream.

I was so busy trenching my way through my dessert that I hadn't noticed that Dad was barely eating. Mum was helping Sebastian with his bowl and pinching some of my ice-cream. I was trying to fight her off and I wasn't looking at Dad when he spoke,

What about me?'

Mum and I looked up at the same time. I'm not sure that I understood what he meant: I thought perhaps he meant his own ice-cream.

Mum must have thought so too. 'You've got your own.'

'Not the bloody ice-cream.' He pushed his plate away. 'Another holiday, here in France. Don't I get a say in any future plans concerning Jonathan?'

Mum put her spoon down and looked at him. 'Of course you do, what's the problem? You've heard how much Jon has enjoyed this holiday we've done on the cheap. I always had it

160

in mind that this holiday was a test, a toe in the water affair, see if we could cope with camping and if it worked out, then we could try it again another year, perhaps a bit better organised!' She laughed and looked at me. I grinned, I knew what she meant.

Dad didn't grin, he sat bolt upright and crossed his arms over his chest. 'But what about me? What about any plans I may have for holidays with Jon? He is my son too, or is that something you'd forgotten along with the chairs you didn't bring?'

Mum sighed, 'Oh, Chris, why start this now? Just when things were going so well. As for future holidays with Jon, nothing's decided. As I've said, we took off on the spur of the moment, badly prepared, I admit, but the holiday has been a success, we've both enjoyed it and all I'm saying is ...'

'*All* you're saying is focused around your plans for my son, without any thought as to what my plans might be, what *I'd* like to do for a holiday!'

'That's ridiculous, what on earth are you talking about? You can still have a holiday with Jon. For God's sake, as you've just reminded us, he does have nearly seven weeks holiday in the summer, not to mention Easter and Christmas!' Why can't he have two holidays? One with each of us? What's wrong with that?' Now it was her turn to sit back in her chair, her arms crossed.

I looked around the room, there was a silence, the sound levels had gone down and I knew that everyone else in the restaurant was waiting for the next word.

'There's nothing wrong with that, it's just that, typical of you, you spout forth these half-baked plans of yours without any thought as to what I'd like to do.'

They were glaring at each other so hard their eyes weren't blinking. I wondered which one of them would blink first. It was Mum. 'Tell me what you want to do, go on tell us both.'

Dad moved his head from side to side as if his neck was hurting him and he was loosening up the muscles. 'Well, nothing definite, as you know everything depends on my job, my schedule, what part of the country I'm working in, all that.

But what we need to firm up here, is that my needs *must* be taken into account when you're thinking of swanning off to another country. I must be consulted.'

Mum snorted, a really ugly noise. 'Your *needs!* That's what this is all about, isn't it Chris? Never mind mine or those of your son, just as long as your needs are taken into account first and foremost. Just like your bloody father.'

I was fed up with this, really fed up. I scooped up the rest of my ice-cream, turning away from Sebastian, putting my arm around my plate so he couldn't see me eating. He'd only want some of mine and I didn't want him to have any. It was all right for him, he was only a baby, he didn't have to listen to all this, not in the same way that I did.

Dad made a big production of draining his glass, there can't have been anything in it, but he put his head right back and held the glass up to his mouth. I could see his Adam's apple bobbing up and down, not sure why it did that, he didn't have anything to swallow. He thumped the glass back on the table. 'Leave Dad out of this, he's not here, it's got nothing to do with him.'

Mum wiped Sebastian's mouth, he grabbed at her hands, trying to stop her, he knew that once she did that there would be no more ice-cream and there was no way I was giving him any of mine.

Mum picked up her glass, she at least had some wine left. 'Oh, but you're wrong.'

Dad was fidgeting around in his pockets, looking for his wallet. 'For God's sake, Nina, you've never been able to disguise your hatred of him, leave it alone. He's an old man and he's not here to defend himself so why bring him into it? Just leave it. I don't see any point in continuing this, do you? I'll call for the bill and we can go.'

'I think that's best, we'll split the bill shall we? Or will that be an issue for you, too?' Mum was already on her feet, trying to get Sebastian out of his highchair. He was crying, he didn't want to go, he wanted more ice-cream. For a second or two I wished that I was the same age as him. It would be all right then for me to make a fuss, crying and whining. I was just so fed up with all these crappy conversations between my parents.

Dad was quite red in the face and I worked it out, he must have had about a bottle and a half of wine. Mum hadn't drunk that much, Dad had had most of it. He stood up too quickly and his chair fell back. It made a terrible crashing sound. *That* was a noise a sound engineer would have faded out. The whole restaurant was watching us now.

Dad was furious, furious with Mum but even more furious with himself for making such a noise, causing such a scene.

'Where are those bloody waiters? Hanging about all over you when you're reading the menu, nowhere to be seen when you want to leave. Don't bother with paying half of this, you're probably paying with my money anyway, so what's the point?'

Mum was holding Sebastian in her arms, he was struggling so hard the veins in her hands were twitching with the effort. 'How dare you, how bloody dare you? I earn my own money, I can pay my way and that of my sons.' She looked so angry, for a moment it looked to me that, if Sebastian had been a weapon, she'd have used him to hit Dad. I can't remember ever seeing her so cross. I stood up too, I wanted Dad to know that I was on Mum's side, he shouldn't have said that, it was out of order.

'Whatever, let's just get this over and done with. Let's get out of here. The evening's ruined, can't think why I bothered.' Dad's arms were flapping about like wings on a big bird, he didn't seem to care that the entire restaurant was watching him. I could see the waiters staring too. They were all grouped in the entrance to the kitchen. Amongst them was the boy I'd seen earlier, the smirk on his face had got bigger. I wanted to hit him.

Mum was packing up her bag, jamming Sebastian's bottle and the wipes she uses for him into it. 'I can't think why you bothered either, you've obviously lost the knack of behaving in a civilised fashion. Drinking too much wine is not a good example for Jonathan. You've certainly forgotten how to behave around children.'

'Well, whose fault is that? Even if it is true and I don't accept that it is, whose bloody fault is it?'

One of the waiters had finally arrived with our bill and, before Dad could see the amount Mum grabbed it and started rummaging through her handbag again. She was still holding on to Sebastian and all the junk she'd just put in clattered back on the table, spilling out on to the floor. Bottles, tissues, crumpled baby wipes, a lipstick, the pink vinyl purse we'd bought in Euro Disney, the one with a Mickey Mouse face on it, it all fell out of her handbag. I didn't want anyone else to see this, this mess that was in Mum's handbag. I thought it made her look sad, a bit pathetic. I wanted her to stop it and she made one last dive into the bag and she said loudly 'OK, *my* wallet, *my* credit card, *my* bill.'

Dad leant over the table to take the bill from Mum but she moved back. Dad couldn't stop himself, he fell on to the table, spilling the wine glasses, the salad bowls, pepper pots, bread basket, everything tumbled on to the floor where it lay all tangled up in the contents of Mum's handbag.

I looked around the restaurant, no one was even pretending any more that they weren't watching us. One bloke in the corner was standing up so he could see better. That's what we were, that's what my parents had made us, a comic turn, entertaining people in restaurants. I'd had enough, I ran out of the restaurant.

'Jonathan!'

I walked on the beach for a while, the reflection of the moon shining on the sea made it look as if it was melting, like Cheddar cheese on toast under the grill. How come the surf didn't sound so loud at night? When Mum and I came in the day the surf was really noisy, Mum called it 'thundering'. Didn't sound like that at night, it was quite soft, like big cushions banging up against each other. There was no one else on the beach and I began talking to Grandma, telling her how fed up I was with Mum and Dad, 'I wish you were here, Grandma, they wouldn't behave like this if you were still here.'

Felt like I'd been on the beach for ages, hours and hours. The whole thing in the restaurant seemed as if it had happened weeks ago. It hadn't though. My watch said it had only been about three quarters of an hour. Dad bought the watch for me last year. It's waterproof and when I pushed the buttons on the side, the whole face was illuminated. It showed 10 o'clock. Mum would be worried and I didn't like the thought, not after last time, when she lost Sebastian. I couldn't help it but there was no way I wanted to face either Mum or Dad. Anyway, it was way past Sebastian's bed time. I thought Dad might have been looking for me but I didn't want to see him. I didn't want any more of that, that *performance*.

I walked around near the sand dunes and there was a boy and a girl there. They were doing it, bonking. They didn't hear me, the sand was very soft. His trousers were down around his ankles and his bum was all white. The moon was shining on it as it moved up and down. The girl's legs were wrapped around his waist, they looked just like pearly white scissors. Never seen anyone actually doing it before. David Staples always brings in the porn magazines he finds in his brother's wardrobe, there's masses of photos in them, but that's all I've seen before. Before tonight.

I felt a real berk, I said 'sorry' before I realised what I was doing or saying. The boy looked around, he didn't stop though. I might not have been there at all for all the difference it made to him.

I didn't fancy sleeping on the beach. It might have sounded OK, but I'd much rather be in the sleeping bag. Mum would be worrying too.

I didn't want to see Dad. I didn't want all the rowing, the fighting to start up again. There's no way I could face that. It's just as I thought before. When Mum and me are on our own, we're OK, most of the time we get on fine. When I'm with Dad, that's OK too. We mess about together and go out and it's fine. But when Mum and Dad are together, that's when the problems start, then it goes all wrong.

When I left the beach I had one last look at the couple near the sand dunes. I could just make out the shape of a pale, white bum. Looked like another moon from where I was standing. I hope Grandma wasn't watching.

It didn't take me long to walk to the campsite. They lock the gates at 10.30 each night and I could see Dad's car parked in the car park outside the site. He'd parked his car badly, at an angle, it was taking up space for at least three cars. I did think about the drink driving laws in France, they can't be any different from ours. Served him right if I reported him. I didn't, my French is rubbish.

I could feel sweat starting to roll down between my shoulder blades as I walked towards our tents. There were a few people walking about, carrying wash bags and towels or walking back from the campsite bar. They all seemed perfectly happy, they weren't at all bothered about going back to their tents. I was. I was really worried and, at the same time, I was still angry. Angry with Mum and Dad. I get all this stuff about learning to act like a grown-up, behaving in public, all that. Yet neither of them can manage it.

As I got into the field, I had another view of the beach, of the moon reflected in the sea. I wondered if the boy and girl were still at it or whether they'd finished and got dressed and gone home.

Mum was sitting in the Clio, the driver's door was open and the interior light was shining on her hair. She was holding her head in both hands. She didn't hear me until I put my hand out to touch her shoulder. 'Mum.'

She jerked and put her arms out to hold me. She held me so tight I could barely breath.

'Oh, Jon, thank God. I was so worried, I started to walk about looking for you but then I thought ...' She held me for a little while, I could feel her heart beating, it was faster than mine.

'Jonathan?'

It was Dad's voice and I hadn't seen him. I pulled away from Mum to see where his voice was coming from. He was standing by the trees at the back of our tents. 'Are you all right? Where did you go? What have you been doing all this time?'

Mum still held my hand and she tugged me back towards her but I shook myself free. 'I've been walking on the beach, getting some fresh air. Where's Sebastian, Mum, is he OK?'

'Yes, he's fine, just tired that's all. He's in the tent now, out like a light.'

Dad moved away from the trees, towards the Clio. 'I owe you an apology, Jon. I can't say anything that will put right what happened. There might be some excuse, tiredness, upset, but the bottom line is that I had too much to drink. I said and did some pretty stupid things and I upset you and for that I'm deeply ashamed.'

'Me too, Jon.' Mum stood away from the car and touched my hand.

I couldn't look at either of them.

Dad came a bit closer, 'Jon? How about, if it's OK with your mum, if you and I spent a few hours together tomorrow? Just you and me, we could go on the beach, get a couple of surfboards, what d'you think?'

I felt terribly tired, too tired even to think about this. I wasn't sure either if that's what I wanted to do. It was just so hard, all this *division*. Mum would be on her own on our holiday and that didn't seem fair. I'd be feeling guilty about that if I spent time with Dad. 'I don't know, I'm tired. I don't want to talk about anything right now.' Didn't even care if I sounded rude. Serves them both right.

Mum took a step closer to me and she put an arm around my shoulders. 'Jon, this is OK. Take time out to spend with your dad. If you think about it, you can have tomorrow with your dad as one of your days, and the day after that I'll drag you around a museum or something.' She had her head on one side and, even in the dark, I could see that she was smiling. 'See, nothing's changed really has it? We keep to the same rules, it's still our holiday, nothing can change that.'

Somehow I doubted that things would be the same.

The next day Dad arrived at 10 o'clock. He was really polite to Mum and she did a lot of smiling and saying stuff like, 'The site owners tell me the forecast is good for the rest of the week. Plenty of sun.'

Dad played along with this too, 'Hear that, Jon? Let's hope the wind is OK for the surf.'

It was already very hot and the thought of being in the sea, crashing about in the waves sounded really good. We all waved politely to each other, Mum held Sebastian's arm up so he could wave too.

I thought we'd walk to the beach, it wasn't far but Dad said he wanted to take the car in case we fancied a drive later on. His car is pretty cool, he's got one of the big Saabs. Turbo-charged 2-litre engine. He's always moaning about the fuel consumption on it but I knew he wouldn't change it, not unless he bought a newer model. Sometimes he lets me drive it, only on deserted bits of land. He made me swear never to tell Mum. Why would I tell her? She'd go ballistic.

Because it was early, we were practically the only people on the beach. There were a couple of people walking dogs and a few kids with kites but that was all. Dad had already picked up two surfboards, he'd stashed them in the boot.

'Race you,' Dad pulled his shorts off and threw everything onto the sand.

'You're on,' I pulled my T-shirt over my head and kicked off my trainers and ran down towards the sea.

Dad yelled something but I couldn't hear him I was running so fast. The surfboards were really light, mine didn't slow me down at all. I beat him by *miles*.

I yelled and yelled as the waves hit me, shouting at the top of my voice. It was just like that advert on the telly, only it was me in the surf and not some poxy model, just me. Dad's pretty useless, he kept falling off but he didn't seem to mind; he just swore a bit and waited for the next wave and each one was pretty big. We spent hours in the sea, I know we did, but the time went really quickly. It was just like we'd been in a washing machine, all that water, all that foam, bubbling around us, it washed everything away. It was as if last night, the rows, me walking off, all that hadn't happened. Everything went, leaving no trace, it was just Dad and me and we were having a good time.

Dad thought it might be an idea for us to go off in the car to find somewhere to have lunch. He said he fancied looking at the coastline and he promised we wouldn't be sitting in the car for hours. Sounded OK to me.

'This is the Emerald Coast, all this, as far as you can see. Your mum chose well, didn't she?

We'd only been driving a little while, we had all the windows and the sunshine roof open, I could feel the salt drying on my skin. I'd put my baseball cap on too.

'Yeah, it's been good. The whole holiday.' I didn't look at him, just stared out of the window, feeling the warm breeze on my face.

'It's OK, Jon. I promise I won't start another slanging match, you've got my word. I'm just really pleased that you've enjoyed your holiday. Hope that we can enjoy this day together too, OK?'

'OK by me,' I said.

Dad said that the bloke on the desk at his hotel had recommended a place to eat in Dinan, he said it wasn't too for us to go.

'Nothing fancy but he promised me fresh crab and apparently we can see the fishermen with their catches coming up from the beach from where this restaurant is, how does that sound?'

I told him it sounded fine and I thought too that I might be able to buy something for Grandad, to take back from holiday. Something he could put in his kitchen. I asked Dad if he had any ideas.

'Don't know really, Jon. He's not easy to buy for, but what about a print of some place that you've seen and liked? He could put it up in the kitchen and every time he looked at it, he'll know that you had a good time there. Needn't cost a lot of money.'

We didn't say much after that, just looked at the coastline

and listened to Dad's CDs. He likes Van Morrison and Eric Clapton, really different from Mum's taste.

The restaurant was OK, it didn't look up to much at all when we parked the car and I didn't think it was the sort of place that he would go into. It was just odd tables and chairs set out on the pavement. Right by where Dad wanted to sit, the gutter was running with water, at least I think it was water but Dad said it was the place and I'd know what he meant when the food arrived.

There was none of the fuss that we had last night, we both ordered crab and it came on two huge platters. There was sea-weed on the platters, *sea-weed!* Dad laughed when he saw my face, 'You don't eat the sea-weed, Jon, just the crab. This place is famous for its crab.'

I kept quiet when he ordered a beer for himself, it would only have stirred up last night all over again. I asked for a Coke. Dad had been right too, in front of the pavement was the beach and lorries were driving past us and, sitting in the back of these lorries, were fishermen, they waved when they saw me with the crab.

The crab was OK I suppose. It was a lot of work to get the meat out. The waiters gave us these tiny silver things that looked like screwdrivers and Dad said I had to pick at the crab until I got the meat out.

All the time we were there, I could hear French being spoken all around us, every table was full. Seemed to me that the whole place was full of French families. Waiters kept walking back and forth with baskets of French bread and big jugs of wine, they were talking to the other people the whole time.

Dad saw me looking and bent forward. 'This is where the French come to eat, the bloke in the hotel told me. This is not for tourists, this is where the French bring their families.'

I smiled at him but I felt a bit sad. 'That's what Mum's been on about the whole time. She called it "the real France".'

Look, I thought the crab was good and I enjoyed it and everything but it wasn't like a *proper* meal, with chips and carrots and stuff. I asked Dad if I could have some ice-cream when I finished.

'You're a Philistine, Jon,' but he asked the waiter to bring a dish of *glace*. He laughed when he saw my face. 'Don't be too impressed, that's about as good as my French gets.'

Dad didn't want any ice-cream, he asked for coffee. Those tiny cups, the coffee looks like black treacle to me, I don't know how he drinks it.

We sat there looking out over the beach, most of the fishermen had gone but there were lots of lobster and crab pots scattered about all over the sand. The tide had gone out and the beach looked huge, there was no one on it. Dad said it wasn't a beach for sunbathing. The families behind us were still chattering on, shouting at each other all the time, trying to make themselves heard. It sounded like what Grandma used to say to me, *trying to get a word in sideways.* It wasn't just Mum, Grandma would have liked it too.

Dad asked me what I was thinking about and I told him that I thought Grandma would have loved France, 'The beaches, the food.'

'Yeah, you're right, she would. She wanted to see France and Italy, tour Switzerland, she dreamt about travelling.' Dad looked out towards the sea, 'Even a channel crossing would have meant the world to her.'

'Was it Grandad's fault, that she didn't travel? Did he stop her?'

'Not sure that *fault* is the right word, Jon. Your grandad never understood what other people saw in travel. It's too easy to say that he *stopped* her. Your grandma probably could have gone on her own and I know your mum would have gone with her. It's more to do with the fact that your grandad never thought of other countries. I suppose you could even say, he didn't see the *point* of them. He can only think in terms of the UK, although, like a lot of older people, he sees his country changing too and it's changing at a rate he can't keep up with any more.'

I looked around at the beach, the bubbling waves, the noise of the restaurant around us, 'Don't suppose he'd have liked this too much, Dad.'

Dad laughed, 'Guess no, your grandad likes the proper order of things, restaurants with matching tables and chairs, quiet noise in the background and what he'd call 'normal' food. Steak and kidney pie, roast potatoes, mustard on the side of his plate …'

'… and oxtail soup to start.' I said quickly.

Dad laughed again, 'You're right. He'd take one look at this place and say it's like this because it's French! He'd see the chairs that don't match, the stains on the table-cloth and no proper menu. The very thing, the almost ramshackle quality of this place makes it special, gives it charm. But for someone like your grandad, these are the things that he'd focus on, he'd grumble about. He'd say the English wouldn't run a restaurant like this. It's a shame because sometimes letting go of what you've always done can bring amazing things into your life. Takes courage though and I don't know that your grandad *can* change now. He likes things the way they are, keeping things static, unchanged, makes him feel safe. We really shouldn't laugh, he's living on his own and he's coping very well. He misses your grandma a lot.'

'I do too,' I looked down, the ice-cream had left a sticky pattern over the plate. I traced it with my fingers.

'I know you do, Jon, she was a lovely lady. I miss her, think about her every day.' Dad looked out towards the sea, his eyes squinting against the sun. 'Right, perhaps we could have a walk along this beach before we head back, what d'you think?'

'Yeah, OK.'

Dad and I walked through the little town and I bought a print for Grandad of where we'd had lunch. I bought one for Mum too. I'll give it to her when we get home. Not sure if it's the right thing to do, after all she didn't come with us. Anyway, if she doesn't want it, I'll put it in my bedroom. On the drive back, we talked a bit about school; Dad said he'd come over and look at my fountain project when we got home and I told him things about some of my tests and stuff about some of the other boys. Nothing heavy.

When we got back Mum was sitting with Sebastian on the rug again. He had a pair of old pants on and a weird sunhat Mum makes him wear. It makes him look like something out of the Foreign Legion.

Mum had a pile of books on her lap, she must have been doing some work. 'Hello you two. Had a good day?'

'Brilliant! We had crab for lunch and I had to eat it with these funny fork things and before that we went surf riding. I got the best waves, Dad's useless.'

She smiled, easing the books away from her lap. 'Sebastian and I walked to the beach earlier on and I thought I could see you. It looked good fun.' She lifted her head as if she was including Dad in what she had to say.

Dad stood near me, he had his hands in his pockets, I could hear coins rattling.

Mum got to her feet, 'I was going to get a drink and Sebastian needs a nap, do you want a drink?'

I don't know how they manage it but Mum avoided looking at Dad and he said yes without looking at her. All that effort.

'I'll get the drinks,' I almost ran to the coolbox to get the cans, otherwise I knew Mum would make me put Sebastian in the tent for his nap and that meant putting a nappy on him.

Dad squatted down on the rug as Mum picked up all her books; she was hanging on to Sebastian with the other arm.

'Won't be a second,' she said as I gave Dad a cold can.

I couldn't think of anything to say once Mum had gone, Dad was running his fingers around the side of the can.

'Thanks, Dad, I had a really good time.' I said it quietly, I didn't want Mum to hear, I didn't want her to feel hurt.

He smiled at me and pulled my baseball cap off. I tried to get it back and we had a sort of mock fight, but I got it back from him.

'Why do you wear it back to front?'

How does he expect me to answer that one? 'Because all the kids do, it's how you wear them, that's all.'

I could hear Mum in the background nattering on to

Sebastian, she keeps up some story whenever she puts him to bed. She's made up this thing about a family of camels and they've all got silly names. I could hear giggling. Dad sighed and lay back on the rug with his hands behind his head.

'It's good here, Jon, shame I've got to go back by Monday. I can see why you and your mum like it so much.'

'Do you have to go back, Dad? Can't you stay for a few more days, we're only here for a little while anyway then we've got to get back too. Dad, can't you stay?'

He closed his eyes as if he was thinking about what I'd said, as if it was something that he could do. I watched his face trying to work out what he'd say.

'Jon, I can't, believe me, son, I'd love to. There's a job waiting for me, I've taken too long over it as it is. Some supermarket plan; local residents want all sorts of changes. God, if I never see another supermarket that'll be fine with me. I'm sorry but maybe you and I can come here, or at least somewhere in France another year.'

I hoped Mum hadn't heard him, I didn't want to start another row but she was still in the tent with Sebastian.

'That's OK, perhaps we can do something at home before I go back to school. I've promised Grandad too that I'll give him a hand in the garden.'

Dad made another lunge at me and we started arm-wrestling, still trying to be as silent as we could because of Sebastian. Sometimes I wish time was a piece of elastic and when things are OK and I'm having a good time, I could stretch it, make it last longer. But it never works out, nothing stays the same.

Mum came out and she sat on one of the corners of the rug. She didn't seem to mind Dad lying on it, but she sat well away from him. She winked at me.

'Got much work on, Nina? I saw you had brought some books with you out here. Are you busy?' For the first time since we'd come back, Dad looked at Mum.

Mum took a few seconds to answer but she lifted her head too and looked at him. 'Enough I suppose. Various deadlines when I get back. If I bring work out with me it eases my conscience a bit.' She laughed, a light, tinny sort of laugh.

'You mentioned something about a course, "working with people" you said.' Dad was pleating a bit of the rug with his fingers.

'Mm, yes I did. I've felt for some time that although I still like my job, I like pretty much all of it, I do miss people. Contact, talking to people face to face. I've given it a lot of thought whilst I've been away, part of the reason for the holiday too I suppose. I've thought about reflexology, aromatherapy, that sort of thing. Not sure if I could handle anything too New Agey but I do like the thought of trying to help in some way. One course that does appeal a lot is working with disturbed children. Something along the lines of healing through writing and reading. It's only a vague idea. I'm pretty sure that I'd have to do a counselling course first. See,' Mum straightened her back, 'although that part isn't clear, I *am* sure that I need something else. My work is fine,' I hoped Dad hadn't noticed it but Mum was speaking very carefully just then, 'nothing wrong with it, it pays well and I'm good at it but for some time I've felt that it just wasn't enough.'

She stopped, it was as if she was waiting for Dad's approval. I realised I was holding my breath.

Dad was still playing with the rug. 'I came out before with all guns blazing, didn't I? Sorry, Nina, I didn't give you a chance. Your ideas sound good, let me know if I can help with, well with anything really.'

Mum flashed a look at me, her eyes widened. 'Thanks, Chris, I'll let you know what I decide on and whether or not I need any help.'

Wow! They were talking properly, no arguments, no fights, nothing.

Dad started to shift about, it looked to me as if he was getting ready to go back to the hotel. I didn't want him to go, I thought it was so good with the two of them chatting like normal human beings. To stop him I said the first thing that came into my head.

'Mum? Before, Dad and me, we were talking about Grandma, about how much she'd have liked where we were today, that place we had lunch. She'd have liked France, wouldn't she?'

Mum nodded,' She'd have loved every square inch I'm sure.' She looked towards Dad then, 'You know I'd spoken to Nancy about this plan of mine. I'd only got a vaguely formed idea, half-formed, nothing concrete but she listened to me so carefully. That was one of her qualities, wasn't it? That's what made her so special, she always listened. She never mocked, she had a way of listening, putting her head on one side, do you remember how she did that? She'd stay perfectly still until whatever it was you were saying was said. Whenever I finished talking to her I felt energised – if she thought I could do it – then I could.'

Dad was watching Mum's face the whole time she was talking. He nodded, 'I know you miss her, it's not the same thing talking to Frank either.'

'No! I tried to tell him about how I felt about this course. Stupid really, I should have left it alone. Some instinctive need in me to have to his approval. Waste of time that was.'

Dad smiled then, a smile for both Mum and me, 'He begrudged the time you spent with Mum. Certainly when she was so ill, you must have known that.'

Mum snorted. 'Are you kidding? He kept barging in whenever we were talking, he was so *rude*.' He'd look over me, sort of skating over my head somehow. *Are you all right, Nance? She's not tiring you, is she?* She! I was sitting there right in front of him. Unbelievable.'

Dad looked at his hands, 'He's paying the price now. He must miss her although you wouldn't know it. The house is so empty without her. All her things, her books, her plants, all gone. It's not the same without her. I told him too, we had a huge row about it the other day.' He looked again at Mum and me. 'Making a habit of fighting, aren't I? Must be more like him than I thought.'

'No, you're not.' Mum spoke softly and Dad laughed.

There was a silence, not one of those when everyone is staring around, trying to think of something to say. I *hate* those. Mum always charges in trying to fill every space with words. No, this was a good silence. Perhaps we were all thinking of Grandma, I know I was.

Dad spoke first, 'I think part of Dad getting rid of all Mum's stuff was something to do with guilt. He hadn't come to terms with the seriousness of her illness. He hated her being ill, just hated it. I know he tried to jolly her along, telling her that the reason she was so tired was that she'd been overdoing it in the garden or she'd spent too long ironing or whatever. He simply couldn't face losing her, couldn't come to terms with her dying.

Mum looked at Dad, 'You know how she was with him, keeping uncomfortable things away from him, that was one of the reasons she took so long before she got help. She kept a lot of stuff to herself. I was angry, really angry. I so wanted her to be all right, to live. She was quite placid, quite accepting of what was happening. I was crying and being a complete idiot one day, no sodding use to anyone. Only thinking of how I'd feel without her to help me, to listen to me. I so wanted her to try different treatments, alternative therapies. Everything Frank hated. He hated the thought of him not being in control. She said it wasn't Frank's fault, she said it was hers, she'd make the decision to leave things alone. But you can't tell me that Frank's attitude wasn't behind her thinking. She knew he wouldn't cope with illness, chemotherapy, whatever it was she had to handle, she knew.'

Mum was staring into space, her voice was hard, words like pebbles. I hadn't heard half of this stuff before, it seemed to me that they'd both forgotten I was there. I hated the talk about Grandma but in some peculiar way, I couldn't move. I couldn't leave that rug. I had to know what else they'd say, what else would come out.

Dad's voice sounded all choked up, 'Don't be too hard on him, Nina. I'm sure part of him understands what he did, what happened. He misses her dreadfully I do know that, but in his own way.'

Mum was on the edge of tears, I could hear them in her voice, 'We *all* miss her. I can't help it though, Chris, I still think that if she'd sorted things out earlier, she'd still be alive.

But she didn't and she's dead and I blame Frank. I'll always blame him. Can't help it, I just do.' She was staring over my head, looking towards the sea. I could see the tears in her eyes, waiting to fall.

Dad sat up, 'Nina, you've got to stop this. It's not fair, it's not right. I didn't realise you still felt this way. Oh, I knew how you felt about Mum. You had a really special bond but you can't keep on with this destructive attitude towards Dad. Their relationship was complex, sure it was, but whose isn't? Let it go, Nina, you can't bring her back, let it go.'

Mum scrambled to her feet, she wrapped hear arms around herself and stood right in front of Dad. Tears were pouring down her face as she looked at him. 'You don't get it, do you? The whole time we've been away, Jon and me and Sebastian, I've been thinking about my life, about the boys, about you, about Nancy, *especially* Nancy. You've no idea how much I miss her. She was everything I'd ever want to be. Sounds weird now but there's not a day goes by without your mum waltzing into my head. She's with me all the time, whatever I do, whatever I think, she's there with me. You know what my mum was like, couldn't talk to her about anything, but I was able to borrow your mum. She was the next best thing. Nancy was a fighter. She took everything life threw at her, grabbed everything with both hands just to see if she could handle it. She was like a big, glossy boat charging through waves, parting the sea, making her way through.'

Dad got to his feet and he put an arm out as if he was going to touch Mum, comfort her I suppose, but she stepped back slightly and shook her head.

'Hear me out, Chris. I've thought about this the whole time we've been away. God, it was one of the reasons *why* I came away.'

Dad shrugged and looked at me for a second but he stepped back and Mum moved towards the edge of the rug and kept on staring at the sea. I thought she looked like Boadicea in our school play. For some reason I felt a bit nervous but I wasn't going to miss a word of this.

Mum took a deep breath, 'Nancy told me all about her

marriage, all about her life with Frank, right from the early days when you were growing up. She told me how he grumbled like mad about his own childhood, *hated* it, Nancy said but initially was unable to change when it came to bringing you up. At first, she'd been able to tease him, make him laugh at himself, see how ridiculous he was being and things were good for a while, but after you'd grown up, she said he reverted again, gradually becoming stolid, unchanging, rigid in everything he did. *Boring* was the word she'd used.'

Dad started saying something about me then, 'This is not anything that Jonathan should hear, this isn't fair on him, you're talking about his grandfather after all.'

Mum closed her eyes, 'Jonathan is old enough to know.'

'Know what?' Dad stood opposite Mum.

Tears were streaming down Mum's face again, her arms were straight down at her sides. 'I'm going to break a promise I made to your mum and I'm sorry, sorry, Nancy, forgive me.' She put her head up and looked right into Dad's eyes.

'Before her illness, before she developed cancer, your mum was going to leave Frank.'

Dad laughed, I couldn't believe he'd done that. I could hardly breathe with what I was hearing and Dad *laughed.*

'Codswallop, bollocks. Don't be so bloody melodramatic. That's my mother you're talking about. I'd have known, she'd have told me. She was up to her eyeballs in drugs, she was in a lot of pain towards the end ...'

Mum held her head up, 'You're not listening to me, I said *before* she got cancer. Months before her illness was diagnosed she was planning to leave Frank.'

Dad's mouth opened and then he shut it again.

Mum spoke softly. 'She was desperately unhappy. She said she thought she was living in a tomb, she said her life was desiccated. She knew what Frank was going to say, to do, before he did. She said that people stopped phoning her, ringing the doorbell because Frank was so rude to everyone. She had to make excuses to see her friends, telling him she was shopping or something ...'

Dad frowned, 'Well, that's Dad, he's never been any

different. But leave him? Mum leave him? I can't believe it. I mean where would she have gone, how would she have lived? She had no money of her own.'

Mum pulled a face, 'No she didn't, only the housekeeping that Frank doled out once a week.'

Dad sounded impatient, 'Well there you go, she might have said something in the heat of the moment, we all do that, but she'd never have left him. Sorry, Nina, I don't buy into any of this.'

'Why would I lie? What would be the point?' Mum wiped the tears away. 'She talked about leaving for a long time, even before their Golden Wedding anniversary. Do you know what she asked for when I talked to her about an anniversary gift. She smiled when she said it but she asked me if I'd pay for a divorce.'

Dad's face was red and he spluttered, 'No, she didn't, she asked me if I'd pay for a holiday.'

Mum's hands were on her hips, 'Yes, that's right but you didn't, did you? And why not? Because Frank said he'd rather have a new lawnmower!'

'If she wanted to leave him and I'm not saying that I believe you, but if she wanted to go, why didn't she say anything to me?' Dad sounded hurt.

Mum closed her eyes, 'Because she said you wouldn't have understood, she said you were so like your father.'

Dad's mouth opened wide and then he started walking around the rug, 'No, I'm not. This is all ludicrous. My mother was an intelligent woman, she must have known that at her age she couldn't have walked out of a marriage, she'd nowhere to go for a start. She couldn't have made a fresh start, none of it makes sense.'

'She was going to move in with me and Jonathan.' Mum spoke softly.

'What? With you?' Don't be daft.' Dad stopped his pacing.

'Yes, with me. We had it all worked out.'

Dad stared at her, 'With you? Living with you?'

Mum's voice was hard. '*Yes*, with me, hard to believe is

180

it?'

Dad shook his head, 'This just gets more and more bizarre. Why on earth would she leave my dad and stay with you? She wouldn't have done it, she'd have known it would cause the most appalling row.'

Mum gave a tiny smile, 'That's right, as far as Frank's concerned, living with me would be living with the enemy, he would have had a hard time coping with that, wouldn't he?'

Dad stopped his pacing, 'You're making this up, this crap, I don't believe a word of it. I'd have known, I would, I would have sensed how unhappy she was.'

Mum looked at him, 'Would you? Frank didn't notice, why would you?'

'I don't believe any of it and I can't understand why you're saying all this now.' Dad was sweating.

Mum shook her head, her curls were swinging so fast they looked as if they were trying to catch up with her head. 'I'm not making any of it up, none of it! She just wanted to have some freedom, something away from Frank.'

A car was coming down the gravel road towards us and, out of the corner of my eye, it registered with me that it was dark blue. I didn't want to shift from where I was sitting. I knew that if either of them realised that I was still there, listening to all that was going on, they'd make me move and I'd miss all of this.

'Oh, this is bloody ridiculous. My mother embarking on some Thelma and Louise adventure with you. Ludicrous, bloody ludicrous.' Dad's voice was loud.

The blue car had parked alongside the Clio. It was the Galaxy, the Henderson's car. The windows were open and Mr Henderson shouted 'Hello, guess who?' In the back I could see Gareth and Alice, they were waving at me.

Dad heard them arrive and he turned as the Hendersons were getting out of their car.

'Oh, welcome to the party. Please forgive me, I'm not staying. We've been trying to act like a normal family today, talking, discussing things but, as usual, my ex-wife is talking out of the crack of her arse!'

I hoped Grandma hadn't heard that.

NINA

I'm sorry, Nancy. Please forgive me.

FRANK

Frank knew exactly how long he'd been lying on the floor: 4 hours and 35 minutes. The time was 9.35, he could see the numbers on the clock radio. He'd fallen at 5 a.m. when he'd got up to go to the toilet. He'd managed to get out of bed all right, he'd managed that but, when his feet stretched out for his slippers, he crashed to the floor. He'd always kept a pale, green rug by the side of the bed, a habit left over from when his parents lived in the house.

'Serves no purpose, you'll trip over that thing one day,' Nancy often told him. She used to hang the rug over the banister whenever she cleaned the bedroom. It became a silent battle between them each week. Nancy flinging the rug over the rails on top of the stairs, the avocado green fringe fluttering as she stalked past it. Frank always replaced the rug before he got into bed. They never spoke to each other about the contest of the rug.

He'd tripped over something, he was sure of it, it was difficult to tell as he lay spread-eagled on the floor, unable to move, the rug underneath him.

He was badly frightened. He could stretch his arms out, he'd strained to touch the side of the bed with one hand and the door with the other. His fingertips made contact with the pleats of the valance and, on the other side, he could just feel the smoothness of the gloss paint on the bottom of the door but that was all he could manage. Frank's blue-and-white striped pyjama top was bunched up underneath him and, to his distress and shame, he'd wet himself. The pain of a full bladder had simply been too much. He'd closed his eyes as he felt warm liquid seeping around the waist of his pyjamas, soaking the backs of his legs before the rug absorbed his urine.

For God's sake, bloody peed myself.

The pain was in control, it held him, rigidly encasing him as if he was in a straitjacket. He'd tried inching forward, moving his buttocks slightly and he'd thought he'd made some progress, but he wasn't sure. He remembered watching some programme about spinal injuries and tried to wiggle his toes; he thought the programme said that, if he could do that, his back was all right. He could feel his toes move, he was sure he could, but he couldn't lift his head to see them.

Sunshine flared against the windows, a breeze shook the drawn curtains; the bedroom was bathed in a soft, apricot light. Frank had a strong sense of the day starting, leaving him behind. He was desperate to get up, to rid himself of the nuisance that the pain was causing him. He moaned and tried to shift, pulling himself away from the rug. The phone rang. Frank closed his eyes. 'Dear God, I can't stay here for ever.'

The phone rang on, the noise seemingly filling the house with its sharp tone.

For Christ's sake stop it. I can't answer the bloody thing.

When the phone eventually stopped, Frank realised that he'd been holding his breath. In the accentuated silence he exhaled. He hated the coarseness of his situation, *lying in my own piss. Like a baby, wetting myself. Come on, man, what would Nancy say, what would she do?*

He closed his eyes, willing himself to ignore the dampness he was lying in and he tried to conjure up Nancy's face. He squeezed his lids tight, shutting out all light from the room. *Nancy?* Frank moaned, all he could see was a shape, movement of curls on a head, but the face was blank.

He spoke aloud, 'I'm in a right mess, Nancy love. I'm that ashamed of myself. I couldn't help it, really I couldn't but Christ, love, I could do with your help right now.'

He remembered something she'd told him about a

185

relaxation tape Nina had bought for her. Something to do with breathing techniques and, all of a sudden, Frank could see Nancy's face, her earnest expression as she explained to him about the right way to breathe.

'Coming from the bottom of your lungs. Most of us breathe wrongly, Frank. It's shallow, we don't put our lungs to proper use.'

He'd laughed at her, 'Come on, love, breathing is what we all do, we don't need lessons in it.'

Nancy had persisted. 'But we do, it's not just about using our lungs properly. If you breathe in the right way, it'll help in moments of stress, pain, think about the breathing techniques we heard about for childbirth. It makes sense, Frank, at least listen to the tape. Listen with me, we could put it on the stereo system.'

She'd put it on straight away, then stood in the middle of their living room, her head cocked to one side, a serious expression on her face as she listened to the soft tones of the instructor extolling the principles of *Breathing Therapy.*

'See, Frank, it makes perfect sense, deep breathing to take your mind off pain and stress. Concentrate on the breathing and the pain eases.'

He'd sniggered at her. 'Codswallop. And another thing, there's a name for any bloke who sounds like that.' He'd left the room to prune the roses.

After that Nancy played the tape when he wasn't in the house. Frank remembered throwing it out after the funeral. It might originally have been Nina's, he wasn't sure, but he hadn't the patience or stamina to ask if it had been hers. Either way, it ended up in the black bin bags ready to be taken to the charity shop.

Lying there Frank kept his eyes squeezed shut and fought hard to remember anything at all from the tape he'd laughed at. Nothing. He couldn't remember one word but he did know that the voice had a slow, dreamy quality. Frank tried to slow his breathing down and took a deep breath, holding it for a few seconds, then he slowly exhaled. Again. In and out, in and out. Nancy's face was still with him, he wanted her to know that he was trying, he had been listening. In and out. In and out.

He kept on breathing deeply for a few minutes, focusing on Nancy's face, his eyes were still closed. *See love, I was listening.* He was breathing in through his nose and out from his mouth. It seemed to Frank that the pain ebbed, just slightly, with each deep breath. The phone rang again.

'Bugger it.' He stopped his deep breathing. 'You've made it worse, shut up damn you, shut up!'

Frank's breathing grew shallow, the pain took hold again. He felt cold, damp pyjamas and the soiled rug chilled him. Tears formed, trickling down his face. The phone rang on and on.

JONATHAN

I couldn't move. I didn't want to look at Gareth and I *definitely* didn't want to say a word to Alice. My head wouldn't turn towards them, all I could see were Dad's shoulders. They seemed really big, square. He looked so angry, he was furious and for one tiny second I really thought he'd hit Mum. But he didn't. He walked away. He just grunted at me and then stomped off. It looked as if his temper was making his legs work. It didn't seem the time to tell him either that he was walking in the wrong direction. His car was in the big car park, behind us.

Mum had a peculiar look on her face. She was looking at the Hendersons but not really *seeing* them. Mrs Henderson moved over to Mum and spoke softly to her, 'Are you all right? Is this a really bad time, would you like us to go away?'

Mum gave her a quick smile, 'No, of course not. I'm sorry you had to hear that. No matter how hard I try, Jon's father and I always end up fighting.'

I watched Mrs Henderson's face; she glanced very quickly at her husband. It was as if she was asking permission to say what she said. 'Men! Drive you mad, can't live with them, can't live without them.'

Mum smiled but the smile didn't reach her eyes. She put her hand out towards me and touched me on the shoulder. 'Jon, do you fancy an ice-cream with Gareth and his dad?'

I shook my head, my mouth opened to say *no* and Mum's

fingers squeezed my shoulder. I stared at her, she looked so pale and her eyes were asking me something. I looked at her for a moment without speaking.

'Come with us, Jon, your mum'll be fine.' Mr Henderson smiled at me and Gareth was giving me the thumbs up sign.

I couldn't stop looking at Mum. It didn't seem right that I was going off to have an ice-cream and leaving her. She must have known what I was thinking, she nodded, 'Go on, Jon, I'll be all right, I promise.'

Mrs Henderson moved closer to Mum, 'I'll keep an eye on her, Jon.'

We drove back into town, past the shop where Dad hired the surfboards this morning, past the restaurant where I'd stormed off last night. I could see where Mum and I had walked yesterday. It wouldn't surprise me if, in years to come, this whole town is named after us, or perhaps they'll declare a special Bank Holiday. It will be like Mother's Day only they'll have to call it *The Jones Day* or even *National Jonathan's Day* and the whole town will line up along the street and they'll have someone dressed up to look like me, then everyone will stare at him and laugh.

Mr Henderson stopped the car outside an ice-cream parlour and then, even before he'd turned the engine off, Alice spoke, 'Dad? Can I have one of those double-chocolate ones, you know the ones in the big glass dish?'

Mr Henderson turned to look at her, 'Well that's a surprise. You haven't had one of those since … yesterday. Jon, what about you? Would you rather have a cone or something, take a walk along the beach with it?

The three of them were looking at me. My stomach was hurting, it felt as if a tight band was around it. I wasn't hungry. Not even for an ice-cream.

Gareth nudged me. 'We'll have a cone each, Dad.'

Mr Henderson was unbuckling his seatbelt. 'OK, how about if Alice and I sit in here with an ice-cream and a cup of coffee and you and Jonathan take a walk along the beach, how does that sound?'

'Sounds good, thank you.' Gareth and I got out of the car and Mr Henderson and Alice went into the ice-cream parlour. I felt so embarrassed. I couldn't look at Gareth so I stared out at the beach, watching the waves.

Gareth coughed, 'You OK?'

'Yeah, fine.' We didn't say another word until Mr Henderson came back with two cones, the ice-cream already dribbling down over his fingers. Alice was sitting at a table inside. She saw me looking at her and she turned her head away.

'Thanks, Dad.'

'Thanks, Mr Henderson.'

I didn't know what to do next. Gareth was avoiding my eyes and I didn't want to talk. I really didn't want to talk about the row. I didn't know if he'd heard anything, he must have done though, everyone on the planet must have heard. I'd never heard Dad say that sort of thing before, that 'crack of her arse' thing. Those words and Mum somehow didn't go together. There were words that I kept totally separate from her. Even if I thought about them, they didn't get mixed up with the words I used for her. I hated the fact that Dad had said that, it was as if he was attacking Mum.

I couldn't look at Gareth in case I'd know by his expression that he'd heard it. If I didn't look at him, then I wouldn't know, would I?'

Neither Gareth nor I knew what to do next. Mr Henderson had gone back in to sit next to Alice. I saw her dipping one of those long spoons into her ice-cream. But, almost at the same time and without speaking to each other, Gareth and I started to walk towards the beach. I'd no idea what time it was. It seemed ages since Dad and I had had lunch, it felt to me as if that belonged to another day. I looked at my watch, it was 6.30. Didn't mean a thing, it could have been any time of the day. It just didn't feel like any time, morning, supper time, no time at all.

When we got to the beach it was almost deserted and our ice-creams were nearly all gone. I'd dribbled some down my T-shirt and my hands were sticky. There was a woman walking near the dunes and I thought of the couple I'd seen last night, the ones who were doing it near the spot she was walking. I wanted to tell Gareth all about them, all about the boy's bare bum. Bet Gareth's never seen anyone doing it before. But, in some way, I thought we needed to get this bit over with first, the bit about the row, about what he'd heard, about the fact that my family wasn't a bit like his. We needed to get that out of the way first *then* I could tell him about the couple shagging on the beach.

'My hands are covered in ice-cream, I'm going to wash them off in the sea,' I nudged Gareth as I spoke and I ran as fast as I could towards the waves.

I heard him behind me, I could hear his feet pounding on the sand, but he couldn't catch up with me. Somehow that made me feel a bit better. We both kicked off our trainers and waded in, splashing our hands and faces with seawater. I made a fist with my hands and hit the waves. Water came up in an arc, soaking Gareth. He yelled and brought his arm down hitting a wave.

Seawater poured over me, drenching my hair, face and T-shirt. I kicked out trying to splash him again but I missed my footing and I fell. As I went under I could hear Gareth laughing.

I told him all about it. We walked up the beach and back down again both of us soaking wet. I told him all about the way Mum and Dad fought all the time. I told him what it was like when I was on my own with either of them. I told him about ringing Dad after Sebastian had gone missing, how I'd screwed things up by doing that. I told him about Grandma but I didn't mention that I talked to her all the time, I thought that there were some things I should keep to myself. Then I told him what Mum had said, about Grandma wanting to live with us.

Gareth didn't say anything for ages and I began to think that I'd embarrassed him.

He looked at the sand, he didn't look at me when he spoke, 'My parents row too, you know.' He jabbed at the sand with his foot. 'They say some horrible things to each other too, they think I can't hear them, but I can.'

Seemed to me that he was searching for stuff to say to me, almost as if he was competing with what I'd told him.

He still didn't look at me, 'My mum likes your mum, she thinks she's very brave. She says she likes what she's doing, coping with work and your brother, all that stuff.'

I thought about that for a while, I liked hearing him say it. 'Yeah, she's OK, my mum. Stupid thing is, my dad's OK too, they're just not OK together any more.'

We'd come almost to the place where we'd started, close to the ice-cream parlour, and I could see Alice jumping up and down waving her hands around. Gareth had seen her too. 'If my Mum and Dad ever split up, I wonder who'd have her.' He looked at me quickly then, 'Bet you wish you could see her more often.'

I punched him, 'Shut up, she's your sister. What do you want me to say?'

He threw a punch at me, 'She's got itchy knickers for you.'

Gareth! Jon! Alice was jumping up and down calling us.

'Come on, I'll have to go back and see how Mum is.' I looked at my watch, it was almost half-past eight. 'We've been gone for hours.' I still hadn't told Gareth about the bonking on the beach.

Driving back to the campsite was totally different. Gareth's dad had a go at us about our damp clothes and Alice said Gareth would get a row from his mother. Somehow I didn't think Mum would be cross with me.

Just before we drove into the campsite I sneaked a look at the car park. There was no sign of Dad's car. He must have gone back to the hotel. Suddenly I felt sorry for him. Whatever he thought of Mum's announcement, he was on his own. He had no one to talk it over with. That didn't seem fair.

Mum and Mrs Henderson were sitting on our rug. Sebastian was doing his half crawling, half walking thing around the edges. Mum had a glass of wine in her hand and she was sitting quite close to Gareth's mum. She looked all right, even her hair wasn't such a mess.

'Hi, are you OK?' She looked at me and held her hand out.

'Yeah, I'm fine.' I felt a bit embarrassed about holding her hand with Gareth and Alice there as well. But it wasn't just that, it was more to do with the fact that Dad had shouted at her, shouted at her in front of me. I touched her fingers lightly and felt her squeeze my hand.

'Guess what, Jon? Gareth's mum and dad have booked in at the next site. They came looking for us to see if we'd like to have a meal with them or something before we head back home.'

I looked over at Gareth, 'You didn't say.'

'You didn't give me a chance.'

I knew, though, even without Mum saying a word about it that we'd be leaving France in a day or two. I just knew.

It wasn't the same as before but we had quite a good evening. Sebastian was the only one who wanted something to eat, but he's always hungry, greedy pig.

Mr and Mrs Henderson were all chatty and cheerful and there was a lot of rolling of eyes between Gareth and his Dad. Alice was sucking at the ends of her hair and not saying that much at all. She did ask me what music I liked though; she said she liked Girls Aloud and Britney Spears. I've never seen the point of that sort of music. I like Stevie Wonder and all the early Tamla Motown stuff. Mum's got masses of Tamla records and she lets me play them up in my room. She goes on and on about the different ones and tells me all the time to be careful. 'Can't get hold of these any more.' When I tried to tell Alice that the bands she liked only played copies of the old stuff, she didn't know what I was on about. Don't see much of a future for her and me if she doesn't even know who Stevie Wonder is.

Every now and then I'd start thinking about Dad. Mum and I were sitting here having a good time and he was on his own.

193

*   *   *

The next day when I woke up, I could hear Mum talking to Sebastian; she was speaking in her camel voice, telling him the story of how Camilla and Cameron the camels got married.

'... and when Camilla saw Cameron standing there at the altar, she galloped down the aisle, her veil flying over her hump. Cameron had to put a leg out to stop her falling. Camilla thought he'd never looked so handsome with 100 pink carnations tied around his ears.'

Sebastian didn't understand a word of these stories, he just loved hearing Mum's silly voice. I could hear him giggling as Mum told him all about page-boys and bridesmaids dressed in pink cotton 'with their hooves polished and shining as they all walked down the aisle behind Camilla and Cameron Camel.'

Last night Sebastian had been overtired, it was Alice's fault. She wanted to play with him all the time, holding his hands and walking him over to the swings.

'Are you coming too, Jon?' She went on and on. She didn't seem to understand that I'm with him all day – watching my baby brother on a swing is hardly going to be exciting now is it?

All the time Mum had been trying hard to be cheerful. She drank a lot of wine, although it didn't make her stupid like it usually does. It was about 10.30 when the Hendersons left. Mum said she'd have Sebastian in with her.

I couldn't go to sleep for ages, I kept thinking about what it would have been like if Grandma had lived with us. What would Grandad have thought about that, all that sort of stuff.

Mum's silly voice woke me up, talking about a camel wedding. Bet she slept, she must have done otherwise she wouldn't be spouting all that rubbish about camels.

I poked my head out of the tent flap. Mum and Sebastian were sitting together on the rug. His eyes were fixed on Mum's face as she went on talking in her silly voice '... all the guests threw pink rice and pink confetti all over Camilla and Cameron.'

Oh God Why doesn't she shut up?

194

'Muum!' she didn't stop and Sebastian's eyes remained fixed on hers.

'... and Camilla thought she'd never been so happy. Cameron trotted behind her a they all made their way to the Camel Camp for coffee and cake.'

I got out of my tent and Sebastian leant over to pull at Mum's mouth. He wanted more of the story and I was dead grateful that it had stopped.

Mum looked up at me, 'There's fresh bread in the car, Jon. I also bought croissants. Took a walk to the bakery first thing this morning. I needed to clear my head a bit. Quite a day yesterday, wasn't it?'

Quite a day?

'Suppose it was,' I had to shout as Sebastian was yelling at Mum. He was trying to say something. I thought it sounded like *camel* but his words all sound the same to me. Mum kissed his cheek and plonked him down next to me. 'Enough young man, I'm all camelled out.'

I wasn't hungry but I picked up a peach from the back of the car and half sat in the open boot to eat it. Mum was giving Sebastian something to drink to take his mind off the camels and their stupid wedding.

There were just a few seconds when nobody said anything. Sebastian was guzzling and Mum was concentrating on him. She doesn't normally do that, she just lets him get on with it but today, she had her head down so I couldn't see her face.

She cleared her throat and my stomach did a sort of lurch.

'Jon? It might be better if we didn't discuss what happened yesterday, what I said to your dad. I was very wrong, really out of order. I should never have blurted all that stuff out. I won't go over why I did it, why I said it, there's no point but …'

'Was it true?' I didn't want to hear anything else. I only wanted to know if it was the truth.

She kept her head down and stroked Sebastian's hair. 'What your grandmother told me was in confidence. I broke that confidence and I'm bitterly ashamed of myself.'

'Was it true?'

I didn't mean to shout at her, I really didn't. Sebastian looked up at me, dribbles of apple juice running down his chin, onto his T-shirt. His eyes flicked from mine back to Mum's.

'Yes, everything I said was the truth.' She kept her head down and I could hardly hear her.

'Grandma wanted to come and live with us, not live with Grandad?'

'Please, Jon. Your grandma was very unhappy, had been for a long time and it was something she'd thought about very hard. In the end nothing came of it, your grandma developed cancer and, well, you know the rest. The thing that distresses me is that I broke a confidence, a promise I'd made to her.'

As Mum was talking, she was waving her hands about, she always does that. Dad used to say that if she sat on her hands she couldn't speak, and her voice was rising, she shook her head. She did all those things when she's telling Sebastian those stupid camel stories. He couldn't understand it, you could tell. He thought she was telling more stories to him but she wasn't using her *camel* voice. I wanted to push him away, to say to him that this was something she was talking to *me* about.

I didn't understand half of what Mum was saying, stuff about broken promises, static lives, what a terrible strain on Grandma, when Mum looked away suddenly. She wasn't talking to either Sebastian or me, she just stared out into space. 'She simply couldn't bear to continue living the life she had, life with Frank was simply unbearable.'

'Unbearable, why?' I knew Grandad was a miserable old sod, Dad said it all the time, but, living with him was unbearable?

Mum looked at me then and it seemed as if she suddenly remembered that I was still there, that I was listening to all this.

'Forget I said that, I didn't mean anything by it.'

'Yes you did, what did you mean, why was living with Grandad so unbearable?'

Mum closed her eyes for a second and then she looked at

me. 'Your grandad had been an only child, his parents were difficult, they didn't know how to cope with him when he was growing up and, as he grew older, Nancy felt that he was smothering her, destroying what was left in her life.' She closed her eyes as if she was stopping herself from saying any more.

Now it was *my* turn for the story line. My only consolation was that she wasn't using a funny camel voice to tell me stories.

'Mum!' I wanted to shake her, to let her know that I was almost twelve, I could take all this family stuff, I wasn't a kid like Sebastian.

'That's enough, Jon. I've betrayed a confidence and, in doing so, I've hurt your father. Now, until I've had a chance to talk to your dad, to apologise and make him understand that he mustn't say anything to your grandad, I really don't want to talk about this any more, is that understood?'

I licked the juice from my hand, the peach had been one of those enormous French ones, it had dribbled everywhere.

'Jon? Do you understand?'

'Yeah, I suppose so.'

'Good, when you're a bit older, I'll explain things to you but, right now, I need to talk this things through with your dad, OK?'

'Yeah.'

I'm going to ring Grandad though.

I'd arranged to meet Gareth later on and Mum also wanted us to have lunch at St Malo. She wanted to do some exploring, she said. 'We haven't even seen St Michel yet, Jon. Be back by 12 at the latest. It's my day remember.

She was trying to make everything normal, to put things back into place and I had a lot of hugs and ruffling of my hair. I went along with it but the whole time I was working out when I could ring Grandad, what phone kiosk I could use. Which one was furthest away from Mum, where she couldn't see me. There was one by the site entrance and when I told Mum I was going to have a shower, I legged it over there instead. I didn't know what I was going to say to Grandad, I wasn't going to tell him what Mum had said, it was nothing to do with that, I just wanted to hear his voice. In some funny way, I thought that if I acted as if everything was all right, that nothing had changed, that whatever Mum had said didn't make any difference. I just felt that I had to let him know that I was on his side without letting him know why.

The beach looked good, there was a whole line of surfers dressed in black wetsuits, bobbing about in the sea. Even from where I was standing, the waves looked huge. I could hear them thudding as they hit the sand. Perhaps Gareth and I could go in before we left. I didn't want to think about going home but I couldn't help feeling that we might not have much more time in France.

The kiosk was disgusting! Someone had been smoking those smelly Gauloises fags, I had to keep the door open with my foot when I dialled Grandad's number.

It rang on and on. I knew that it was Thursday, the day he collects his pension. He refuses to have it paid into his bank, something about banks and their charges and I've walked with him to the Post Office a few times. He leaves the house at 9.15 and he's home again by 10.15. Every week, the same thing. He should have been at home but there was no reply. I heard the phone ringing and the funny thing is that when I hear the phone I can *see* it in Grandad's kitchen. I'll have to try later, after my shower.

Gareth was waiting for me when I came out. He grumbled a bit when I told him I had to be back with Mum by 12 o'clock. 'That gives us no time to do anything.'

I'd already thought of that and said that we could go surfing when I came back or even hire mountain bikes. I told him too that I wanted to ring Grandad and he pulled a face but walked over to the kiosk with me.

I started to tell him about the couple I'd seen on the beach the other day. 'You should have seen them, she was screaming and moaning, "Oh, God, oh God." She said it all the time. They were both starkers, I saw his dick, it was huge! The bloke got dead stroppy with me, started shouting in French.'

Nothing like that happened but I didn't want Gareth to know that the couple hardly noticed I was there. Truth was I'd been a bit disappointed. I thought bonking would have been better than that, but I didn't let on to Gareth.

We didn't look at each other when I was telling him all this but, out of the corner of my eye, I saw his head jerk towards me as if he was making his mind up about something. We walked towards the kiosk but it had someone in it. I slowed down a bit.

Gareth nudged me, 'That's nothing, I've seen Mum and Dad at it.'

'That's not the same thing at all,' I told him.

'Yes it is, it was last Christmas and they let me and Alice stay up late to watch a film. They'd both had loads to drink and Mum said she was tired out. Nan and Gramps had been over and she'd been cooking for ages. Well, anyway, the film was crappy so I went to bed too. It was only about twenty minutes after they'd gone and I could hear all this moaning and groaning coming from their bedroom.'

I didn't want to listen, I didn't want to hear what he had to say about his parents. I kept my eyes on the kiosk, waiting until I could go in.

'... and I saw Dad's bare bum pumping up and down, Mum's hands were on the headboard and she ...'

I liked Mr and Mrs Henderson, they'd been really kind to Mum and me. This was like watching them on the toilet. It felt to me as if Gareth was only saying all this because he thought he was in competition with me. It made me feel uncomfortable. Felt guilty too, I'd started this. I kept my eyes focused on the kiosk and concentrated on getting through to Grandad.

'... and the whole time they didn't know I was there.'

The door of the kiosk opened and I started to run towards it.

'Jon! Wait!' It was Dad's voice and I turned. He was waving at me, 'Stop, I've got to talk to you. It's about your grandad, he's had an accident, he's in hospital.'

FRANK.

It was quiet in the ward, only three beds were occupied. Frank could hear laughter coming from the television in the Day Room. Most of the patients must be in there he thought. *All right for them, they can move. Can't be as bad as me.* After looking around, Frank settled back on the stiff sheets and closed his eyes. If the staff thought he was resting, they might leave him alone. He needed some time to himself, to sort out what had happened to him. The sheer weight of events would take some sifting through. Frank sighed, first of all there was that business of that woman next door. Meryl. He'd heard her yelling through his letter-box, screeching at the top of her voice. 'Mr Jones? Are you all right? Yoo hoo.'

Frank's lips moved. 'Bugger all I could do, I couldn't move. Silly bitch.'

His thoughts moved uncomfortably over the next section of his recollection. The phone kept on ringing and ringing and then he'd heard a thumping on his back door. Frank shook his head, 'God knows what they've done to that door. Paint'll be ruined, need a new lock. Cost a bit too I expect.'

After that he remembered hearing feet pounding up his stairs and then, from his position on the rug, he'd seen the shocked, white faces of his neighbours, Meryl and Peter Jefferies. Frank squeezed his eyes shut, clenching his jaw. Those people, they'd seen him helpless, lying in that state.

The next bit wasn't so bad; there had been all sorts of

noise, feet running up and down stairs, voices from the kitchen, he felt the warmth of a blanket being wrapped around him, no mention had been made of the wet pyjamas. And then he remembered the ambulance. He'd heard it, the siren wailing from streets away. As he lay on his bedroom floor, Frank remembered feeling that it was all wrong, that it shouldn't be coming for him, it seemed far too dramatic. He had tried to tell Mrs Jefferies, Meryl, that it wasn't necessary. She'd calmed him and urged him to drink sweet tea she'd made. Frank smiled then, Peter Jefferies had been sharp with his wife, 'For God's sake, woman. How many times have you seen *Casualty?* You can't give him anything, nothing at all.'

The next part was blurred, the whole business of the ambulance men, or *paramedics*, that's what was written on their uniforms, that part wasn't very clear. Either through pain or embarrassment at being taken out of his own house on a stretcher, Frank had only a hazy recollection of that. The ride in the ambulance was brief, that woman, Meryl, came with him and insisted on holding his hand. Frank hadn't wanted the paramedic bloke to think she was part of his family, part of *him,* but she'd insisted.

Her husband stayed behind in Frank's house to secure the back door. Frank nodded again, he'd approved of that, perhaps the bloke wasn't such a bad sort after all.

Frank hated hospitals, the smell, the colour of the walls, the squeak of the nurses' shoes on the shiny floors, everything brought Nancy's illness rushing back. He'd felt sweat breaking out when they'd put him in a cubicle and he was abrupt, rude to the young nurse who'd tried to help him out of the wet pyjamas, washing him with soft, cool hands.

'I can do this, I'm not dead or daft yet.' He felt ashamed by his outburst, young lass was only trying to help, she was doing her job. It was the humiliation he hated, not her.

Meryl Jefferies had been waiting outside the cubicle; the whole time he could hear her chatting away to nurses and doctors, getting in their way, making out that they were best friends, really good neighbours. He couldn't wait to put everyone straight about *that.*

As soon as the nurse had left him with a hospital gown and instructions to keep still, Frank had barked at Meryl Jefferies, 'No good in waiting around, might as well go home now, I'm fine.'

The woman must have had the hide of a rhinoceros, she'd smiled at him and patted his arm again. ''S OK, Mr Jones, Frank, I've told them that I'll wait until you've been seen, then I'll go home and pick up your things, shaving stuff, that sort of thing. Then I'll come back and bring your stuff in. I though you might want me to ring up your son, let him know what's happened to you.'

'No!' Frank had been bothered by the thought. He didn't want Chris to know, that would lead to all sorts of things, he wasn't sure what exactly but it seemed to him to mean problems and he didn't know what all this, this hospital lark, would lead to.

'I mean, thanks and all that, but Chris is away anyway, not sure when he'll be back. I'll be out of here soon, right as rain, and it wouldn't be proper to bother Chris, now would it? I might not even be staying in.'

She'd gone after that, Frank had heard her shrill voice getting fainter as she talked her way all the way through the Accident and Emergency unit.

He must have dozed off because all he could remember after that was hearing the sound as the cubicle curtains were pushed aside and a young doctor smiled down at him. Frank *did* remember the purply greyish shadow under the young woman's eyes. Her brown eyes, devoid of make-up, looked intently into his face.

'Mr Jones? How are you feeling, still in pain?'

She kept her hand on his wrist and her eyes dropped to her watch as she checked his pulse.

Frank struggled to sit up but relaxed back on the pillows. 'A bit, not much, couple of aspirins will do, then I'll be out of here. Don't want to waste your time, doctor. You're all busy people.'

She'd smiled, Frank remembered thinking that she looked about the same age as Jonathan and she'd scribbled something on a chart.

'Before we think about sending you home, we'll have an X-ray, see what damage you may or may not have done, *then* we'll talk about an aspirin, that's the deal, OK?'

The deal. He only saw her once more after that, when she produced the X-ray and, using her finger, pointed out to him the fracture on his left hip. 'Can you see, Mr Jones, it's a clean break; but we'll need to keep you in and the orthopaedic surgeon will have to talk to you. I suspect you'll need an operation for this.'

Frank hadn't taken in much of what she'd said. His eyes were drawn to the shadowy outline of his hips pinned up on the wall of the cubicle. It seemed obscene, he felt it was wrong that the image of his spine, hip sockets and his legs spread out, was being peered at, discussed by strangers and by a girl at that. He'd felt an urge to rip it down, hide it from strangers' eyes. He didn't want anyone looking at it, at him. He closed his eyes, shutting out the image and the face of the young doctor.

'Mr Jones? I'm going to give you an injection, to help with the pain.' Frank nodded and whispered his thanks. She left him alone and, after a short time, Frank was wheeled along to the men's surgical ward.

He didn't think much of the other patients. They were nearly all bare-chested, some of the blokes had tattoos and none of them seemed to possess a decent pair of pyjamas, they wore shorts or, even worse, those baggy tracksuit bottoms, nothing on their feet either. Two men wandered over to Frank's bed after the nurses had finished with the temperature and blood pressure performance but Frank resolutely kept his eyes shut. He didn't want to talk to anybody yet, the whole business had wearied and frightened him. He needed to get his head clear, get the day's events sorted out, and he'd need to work out what this meant, this operation lark. Another burst of laughter from the television lounge exploded into the ward but Frank had fallen asleep.

When he woke it was to find an Asian doctor peering at the

notes at the foot of his bed and a young nurse holding Frank's wrist. She winked at him and then her eyes flicked back to the silver watch pinned on the pocket of her uniform. For a second, Frank's eyes were fixed on her pale blue uniform and, at the watch resting almost horizontally on her enormous breasts.

'Everything's back to normal,' she smiled at him, eyes twinkling. Frank felt momentarily ashamed.

'Mr Jones? Are you feeling better, did the injection work?' The Asian doctor was speaking to him, there was a badge pinned on his coat but, without his glasses, Frank couldn't see, couldn't tell what this man's name was. But surely he wasn't the surgeon, this chap was years younger than Chris. His mouth felt dry and Frank ran his tongue around his lips. Without a word the nurse put a hand under his head and brought a glass of water to his mouth.

'Thank you,' he was grateful, not only for the water, but for the few seconds it gave him. Frank swallowed and turned to look at the doctor.

'Yes, thank you, Dr...?'

'Raskovsky, Ian Raskovsky.' The young doctor smiled when he said his name and Frank couldn't think of a thing to say.

'Russian father, Indian mother.'

'Oh, OK, right.' Frank swallowed again. He cleared his throat. 'Can you tell me what will happen doctor? Has it been discussed, do you know? There was some mention of an operation, surely that's not necessary. It would he most inconvenient for me, I live on my own you see.'

'Inconvenient or not, Mr Jones, you do need surgery. You've had a nasty fall and our job now is to put matters right. You're scheduled for an operation tomorrow.' He checked again on his notes, 'We've put you down for 10 o'clock. Perfectly straightforward, quite routine these days. How old are you?' He squinted again at the charts.

'I'm 79, I'll be 80 next April.' Frank told him, shifting his shoulders slightly as he spoke. 'Keep myself fit, eat properly, all that.' He wanted the doctor to know that the accident was just that, an accident. He knew how to look after himself: daily walks, fresh air, never smoked, he knew all about that sort of thing, Nancy had made certain of that.

As if Dr Raskovsky had read Frank's mind he asked if Frank had been widowed. 'Your wife, when did she die? Is there anyone you could get in to help you?'

Frank shifted again, moving his head against the pillow. 'No! I'm on my own. My wife died almost five years ago. Lived on my own ever since. Cope very well too.'

Frank missed the sudden glance between the nurse and the doctor.

'I'm sure you do, Mr Jones, and not to worry now, let's get the operation over with and see how you get on. I'll see you in the morning.' He gripped Frank's hand and moved on to the patient in the opposite bed.

Frank could feel the expression on his face beginning to stiffen, like quick-drying cement. *Of course I can cope, always have, always will.* He felt a pounding in his chest and he put his hand up to his rib cage. The pounding felt violent, he pressed his hand down hard. He was suddenly frightened that someone, the nurse or the doctor, would look over and see it. He took a deep breath, willing the pounding to slow down. His heartbeat settled. Quite suddenly he felt very hungry.

'Yoo hoo, Mr Jones. It's me back again, how are you feeling?'

Oh Christ, that bloody woman.

Her heels clacked their way over to him. He smelt her perfume coming towards him, like a thick cloud.

'Well you look better, I must say.' Meryl Jefferies leant down over the bed and, for one dreadful second, Frank thought she was going to kiss him and he shrunk back into the bed.

'Now, let me tell you what happened and what I've done so in that way I won't miss anything out, head like a sieve my Peter says.' She had a dreadful laugh, it reminded Frank of the noise the starting handle made on his father's Lanchester. *Aatch Aatch.*

Some of the other patients were beginning to wander back into the ward and Frank didn't want them to think that this woman, this Meryl, was in any way connected to him. She'd brought in one carrier bag with his pyjamas, wash bag some clean underwear and slippers and another one which held his dressing gown and two books. She propped a bottle of Lucozade on the bedside locker and busied herself putting Frank's clothes on the shelves inside. She kept up a running commentary as she moved around the bed. 'So, my Peter says to tell you that the door is fine, he's secured it and he says he'll keep popping over to make certain everything's OK.'

Frank mumbled words of thanks but Meryl didn't stop her monologue. 'Then, as I was upstairs getting things ready for you, I must say too, Mr Jones, that your bedroom, your wardrobe and everything, is a real credit to you. So neat and tidy, puts me to shame.'

Frank closed his eyes at the thought of this woman going through drawers and shelves in his bedroom. He opened them again as she said something about 'your son coming back'.

'What? What did you say? Chris, Chris is coming back?' Frank barked the words at her, his tone was sharp and two patients opposite glanced up from the crossword they'd spent all day working on.

'Yes, that's right. When I told him all about what had happened.'

'But I'll be all right, I told you not to tell him.'

'Mr Jones, he's your son, he was worried about you, he couldn't get you on the phone … I was there when he rang, that's all. He does have a right to know.' Meryl's tone was placatory and she glanced over at the two patients.

'Worried about his son finding out, doesn't want to be a nuisance he says, but the poor lad's got a right to know abut his father, hasn't he?'

The two men nodded then they dropped their gaze to the crossword.

Frank was furious. 'Don't discuss my business with strangers, don't do that!'

Meryl smiled, patting at his hand, Frank rudely shook his arm away.

Meryl leant closer, the smell of her perfume intensified

and Frank's eyes began to water. 'Come on, I know you don't mean it, you've had a terrible day. I told your son, Chris isn't it? I told him you were being looked after and me and Peter will do all we can to help.' She sat back, a smile on her face which infuriated Frank.

'That's not the point! I told you there was no need to tell him. Only lead to all sorts of bother. I can look after myself, always have, always will.' Frank crossed his arms across his chest and turned his head away.

She sat down, pulling the chair closer to the bed, she dropped her voice. 'Look, Frank, I can call you Frank, can't I?' Frank didn't move. Meryl smiled, ignoring his rudeness. 'Your son was bothered, he was really shocked when I told him what had happened to you. He said he never thought of you being ill, "always in control," that's what he said to me. That's true, isn't it, Frank? Although, actually, when you think about it, that's what saved you, might even have saved your life.'

Frank's head snapped around to look at Meryl. 'What on earth are you talking about?'

She gave him a coy smile, 'Well, as I told your Chris, if you hadn't been so precise in everything you do, Peter and me, we'd never have known that you were lying on the bedroom floor.'

Frank looked at her, 'I don't understand, what are you talking about?'

'Your curtains! You pull your curtains across early every morning, something I noticed about you straight away. When your curtains were still drawn at nearly 10 o'clock, I knew there was something wrong, I just knew it.' She sat back in the chair, a triumphant smile on her face.

Frank felt bothered by what she'd said. This woman keeping tabs on him, her and her husband checking up on his habits, talking about him? The thought confused him. He shook his head, 'What else did Chris say to you?'

Meryl leant back, pleased that she finally had his attention.

'He said to tell you to do as you're told and he'll be with you as soon as he possibly can. I told him we'd keep an eye on you, after all, what are neighbours for?'

Frank couldn't reply, he didn't know what to say to that. He had to content himself with a noise, a disgruntled *humph.*

Along with the two carrier bags, Meryl had also brought in a plate and, before removing the tin foil that covered it, she winked at Frank, 'I know what hospital food is like from when I was in with my hysterectomy, dreadful stuff they feed you so I've brought you in some cold chicken.'

The chicken looked appetising, crisp shiny glaze on a plump breast, white meat, his favourite. Frank's mouth ran with saliva and he swallowed, his hand reaching out for the plate. One of the patients sitting opposite spoke loudly to Meryl when he saw Frank's hand touching the plate of chicken. 'Oi, love, best check with the sister that the old man can eat. He's down for his op in the morning isn't he? You know what hospitals are like, they wouldn't let *me* eat.' His voice dropped and he spoke softly to the man sitting on the bed.

Meryl withdrew the plate, her eyes widened, 'Oh, I forgot. Leave it on the top here, Frank, and I'll go and check if you're allowed to eat.'

Frank sat back on the pillow and listened to the *clack, clack* of Meryl Jefferies' heels as she went off in search of a nurse, her piercing voice stabbing at his skull. 'Yoo hoo, hello, nurse?'

Oh Christ Almighty.

JONATHAN

See, I knew it. Holiday's over. Ruined. Mum says I'm being unfair. She keeps on about the good parts, 'Concentrate on the best parts, Jon.' She says that all the time. But I can't. I keep thinking that if Dad hadn't turned up, none of this would have happened. We wouldn't be going home early. We'd got another two whole days left, days that we paid for, now they'll be wasted.

After Dad told me about Grandad, how he'd broken his hip and he's in hospital, Dad said that he'd have to go home to see what he could do. That's what he said, to see what *he* could do. Nothing about Mum or me going with him. Doesn't sound right now when I say this but I thought that was all that was needed. If Dad went back, he could see Grandad in hospital, visit him, do all that stuff that people do. That would be enough. What's wrong with that? That's why I couldn't understand why Mum and I had to go back home too. What for? Grandad doesn't *like* Mum!

After he told me, Dad went charging off to tell Mum. Gareth was still with me and he looked at me the way people do when they don't know what to say to you. It's like they're watching your face to see what you'll do first. If I was really upset then I'm sure Gareth would have said something to cheer me up. But I looked at him and shrugged, 'Oh well, suppose that's why he wasn't answering his phone.' As soon as I said it though I felt dead mean.

I mock-punched Gareth and, just as I was saying something about perhaps we should check if they had any bikes left for us to hire, all of a sudden I had this weird feeling, a sort of *nagging* in the back of my head about Mum.

Gareth was already heading off towards the bike centre when I grabbed his arm. 'Sorry about this, but I think I should check with Mum first.'

'Oh, you're kidding. You said you didn't have to go back until 12.' He pulled a face, I could tell he was getting seriously pissed off with me.

'Yeah, I know. It's just that I'd feel better if we did – five minutes tops – OK?'

'S'pose so.' He was narked though. He thinks I'm sad, all this business about checking with Mum, I know he does, but I just felt it was something I should do. He didn't say another word to me as we walked back.

Even in the short time since Dad had told Mum, she'd started to drag stuff from our tents, pulling sleeping bags out, putting our things into cardboard boxes. Dad was standing under a tree, a mobile phone in one hand and timetable in the other. I couldn't see any sign of Sebastian anywhere, perhaps Mum was going to leave him here – I wish.

'Mum? What are you doing?'

She didn't even look up at me, just kept on stacking things into boxes.

'We're packing up, Jon. After what your dad has just told me, I don't think we have any option but to head on home. Give me a hand will you?'

'Why?'

She looked up, 'Why what?'

'Why are we going home, we've got at least another two days left.'

She turned to look at Dad before she spoke to me. 'You're asking me why we're going home. Let me tell you why …' her voice got louder, 'because your grandfather has had a serious accident and is in *hospital!*' Her voice was really loud and Dad looked up. She touched Gareth's arm, 'It might be better if you joined your mum and dad, Gareth. Jon will be pretty busy for a while.'

Gareth's eyes flickered over to mine. I looked up to the sky, to show him I was fed up.

'OK, shall I come back later?'

I said *yes* and Mum said *no*.

Mum sighed, pulling a face, 'Tell you what, Gareth, what about if Jon and I come over later on to see you and your mum and dad. We can sort something out about meeting up at home, that sort of thing. Would that be OK?'

He'd have moaned if I'd said that to him but he mumbled something about seeing us later then scuffed his trainers on the grass and went off.

I was so fed up. Mum had already moved over to the car and I stood by the door. I didn't say anything for a while, just watched as she pulled out our tickets and passports from the glove compartment. Seeing her with the passports in our folder made it worse. I knew then she wouldn't change her mind, not with those in her hand.

But I tried anyway.

'Mum? Why do we have to go? Dad's going, he can see Grandad in hospital. We've only got two more days left anyway. Two days! What difference would two days make?'

I'd forgotten that Dad was close by. I hadn't seen him move across until I felt his hand on my shoulder.

'Do you want to repeat those words to me, Jon? Say them to my face? Go on, tell me why you'd rather spend two days on holiday, feeding your face with ice-cream, lying about on a beach, cavorting with your friends, than see your grandfather. Go on, Jon, explain to me, I'm interested.'

Mum wasn't going to help me out, she'd got into the car, sitting in the driver's seat, her head bent low over her lap.

'I'm waiting, Jon. Explain to me why you don't want to go home and see your grandfather who's had the most dreadful accident, may not walk again, may have to go into residential care, lose his independence, his dignity. The old man who gave you money so you could have a good time on holiday. Tell me, Jon, why none of that is important to you, bloody tell

211

me!'

Almost every time Dad said a word, he pushed his finger into my shoulder. It hurt and I rubbed my skin. 'I don't know.'

'What?'

'I don't know.' If Dad could shout at me, I could shout back. 'I don't fucking know.'

He hit me.

All I could think of was that I was glad Gareth had already gone. It would have been a million times worse if he'd seen my dad giving me a wallop. I turned, I wasn't going to stay there, why should I? But Mum put her arm out and grabbed my hand.

'That's enough – Jon, apologise to your dad.' She tugged at my hand and I mumbled sorry, but I wasn't. Mum kept hold of my hand. Her grip was really tight. 'I don't want to hear you using that word again. I'm not stupid enough to think that you don't use it, but don't ever use it around me again. Chris, you're taking your concern out on Jon, it's not his fault, it's not anyone's fault. Let's calm down and try to get ourselves organised. We need to think this through calmly, decide all sorts of things. Apart from anything else, we've got a lot of driving to do.'

She got out of the car and with a lot of shaking her head and rolling her eyes, she made Dad go back to the trees where he'd been standing earlier. She put her arms around me and walked to the other side of the Clio.

I'm turning into a girl, I must be, stupid tears were running down all over my face. Mum seeing them is bad enough but I didn't want Dad knowing that he made me cry. Mum didn't say anything, nothing about the tears or why I was crying. She gave me a handkerchief and kept her arm around me. She talked normally to me too, totally ignoring the act that I was hiccupping and sniffing like a baby. Actually, that's what she was talking about, Sebastian.

'There's a lot to be said for being his age, don't you think? Decisions are made for him, he has nothing to worry about except when he has his next meal. You and I have got to do the work, all he does is crawl about getting in the way.'

'Where is he?' My voice sounded as if I had a cold.

Mum must have thought I was feeling better, she gave me a hug. 'He's with the Kids' Camp patrol, they were organising something, bouncy castle or something. I asked if he could tag along with them. I gave the patrol leader some money, bingo! He's off my hands for an hour or two.'

She still had her arm around my shoulders and we stayed where we were by the car for a few minutes. 'Do you believe in sixth sense, Jon?'

She didn't want me to answer, I knew that. She was looking at the trees, at the patch of sand where Dad was standing. He was talking into his mobile again and, when he saw us looking towards him, he turned his head away.

Mum looked at me instead. 'When I woke up this morning, I had the most peculiar feeling, it was somehow connected to your grandfather but I could hear Nancy's voice. I couldn't make out what she was saying, it was like a soft noise in the background ...' She shook her head, 'That's all I need, hearing voices.' She smiled, 'Your poor grandad, God, he'll hate being in hospital. He's such a stubborn old goat, he'll be driving them all mad, telling everyone he can cope, that he'll be all right, demanding to go home and complaining like hell about the food. Doesn't bear thinking about, does it?'

'No,' I shook my head. 'It'll be sad for him though because he'll be remembering when Grandma was in there. He hasn't been anywhere near a hospital since then has he?'

Mum pulled me closer to her, 'No, he hasn't and he blames the hospital for her death. He swore blind that she'd have lived longer if they hadn't interfered. All nonsense of course but he ...' she dropped her arm, moving away from me. 'Anyway, nattering on isn't going to help your grandad or us right now. We've got to start packing.'

So that's what we did. Dad parked the Saab next to the Clio and we packed everything up and shoved it all in both cars. That was the only funny thing about the whole time we were packing: we had masses more to take back home than we came out with. Mum had bought loads of wine, we had cases of it.

There were carrier bags full of clothes she'd bought from the local supermarkets. Dad pulled a face when he saw what was inside one bag. 'Why on earth are you buying this sort of crap? It's cheap and ...'

'That's why I bought it.' She grabbed the bag from him and shoved it in the Clio's boot. I realised then that Mum would have said something about the clothes before the holiday, why she'd bought them, some excuse to give Dad. She didn't this time, she just walked past him without another word.

She'd also bought pictures of each place we'd visited; she said she was going to hang them in our hall so we could see them each time we came into the house or went up the stairs. As I put them on the floor of the boot, I remembered the print I'd bought Grandad when Dad and I went out. Mum was right, Grandad'll go mad in hospital, he'll be really worried about his house. I knew then I'd been spiteful and mean and I made a sort of promise, a private one to Grandad. Once he's better, I'll do more to help him and I'll put the picture up for him, wherever he wants it to go.

The whole time we'd been packing up, people from the campsite were walking past, no one took any notice of us at all. It's been like that the whole time, people moving out, people arriving. I really wished we were arriving and not leaving.

Dad was leaning up against the Saab and I stood at the back of the Clio and we both watched Mum as she walked off to get Sebastian. Dad and I hadn't spoken to each other since he hit me. I started to jab at the ground with my trainer, making a hole in the sandy earth.

'Don't suppose there's any point in asking you which car you want to sit in for the drive home, is there?'

I couldn't look at him, I shrugged.

'Jon?'

'What?'

For the first time since Sebastian was born, I'd have given anything to have seen him, to see Mum bringing him back towards me. Just so I wouldn't have to talk to Dad.

Dad moved slowly from the Saab and inched towards me. Just then I heard Gareth's voice calling my name. I moved so fast, almost running towards Gareth. He must have thought I was mad, I made such a fuss over him being there. 'Hey, Gareth, how're you doing?'

'Oh, OK, pretty much the same as I was half an hour ago.'

I thumped him, couldn't think of anything else to do, but I was grinning like an idiot.

Gareth was holding an envelope, *Nina* was written on the front of it and he was looking around. 'Where's your mum?'

'She's getting Sebastian, we're all packed up ready to go.'

'Aw no, already?'

He looked really disappointed and I felt uncomfortable. Dad was still hovering and I wanted him to move away. Even better I wanted him not to have turned up in the first place. Thinking about it, if he'd behaved like a proper dad he'd have known that my phone call to him, the night Sebastian went missing, was nothing serious. I was just stroppy, that's all, no big deal. That's what most dads would have known, but he's not a proper dad any more, I mean is he? He's like an uncle who turns up every now and then. He doesn't have a clue about me, what moods I have or anything.

I deliberately turned my back on Dad and faced Gareth. I didn't want Dad getting any nearer to Gareth, he was *my* friend, not Dad's.

Dad moved closer, I could see his shadow and then he spoke. 'Jon, I think we're going to have to leave pretty soon.' He was looking at Gareth so I got even closer to him. I didn't care that I was being rude, I really didn't.

Gareth kept his eyes on the envelope and then shoved it into my hand. 'Well,' his eyes met mine for a second, then he lowered them again, 'give this to your mum, OK?'

'OK.' Both of us looked at the ground for a while, neither of us saying a word but we shuffled our feet around. We even coughed at the same time.

'Hi, Gareth, again.' It was Mum holding Sebastian; he was filthy, covered in paint and sand. I felt peculiar, glad Mum had turned up, even holding Sebastian I was glad to see her. But

215

sad too because I knew that, once she'd arrived, we'd be leaving very soon. I really didn't want to go home.

Gareth turned towards Mum, he was pleased to see her too, I could see the relief in his eyes. He grabbed the envelope out of my hand and held it out to her. 'It's from Mum, she says to say *good luck* and have a safe trip home.'

Mum swapped Sebastian from one hip to the other and took the envelope. 'I was hoping we could call in on your mum and dad on our way out of here.' For the first time since she'd come back, Mum glanced towards Dad. In the second it took Mum to look from Dad's face and back again to Gareth, she'd made up her mind. 'Yeah, we will call in, I'll keep this but we'll stop by on our way out, OK? I know we'll be seeing more of you, Gareth. Jon would like that, I know. Perhaps you could come and stay with us sometime?'

Gareth mumbled, 'Thanks Mrs Jones, that'd be great.'

Mum jiggled Sebastian about a bit, he's such a great big lump. 'Thinking about it, we've got room for your sister too, do you think she'd like to come and stay?'

Again, there was a tiny movement of her eyes towards Dad, she was smiling too. I knew what she was doing, getting her message over to him. *See, I'm good with kids, they like me. I'm a good person.*

Without even realising that I'd done it, I stepped even closer to Gareth, keeping Dad out of the circle.

Gareth looked at me, 'I don't know about Alice, I'd have to ask her.'

Mum tapped Gareth on the arm, 'She'll come if she knows she can sleep next door to Jon.'

'Muum!'

She grinned at me, jerking her head, 'Go on, have ten minutes, you two. We can't go anywhere until I've cleaned up bugger-lugs. I don't even want him in the same car as me in this state, never mind being on a long journey with him.'

Mum moved off towards the showers and I pulled Gareth away, leaving Dad on his own. We ran from the two cars. We didn't say a word, we just legged it as fast as we could until we came to the path leading to the beach. The sea looked dead good, there were surfers and even from where we were standing, we could hear their yells as they came in on a good wave.

'I really don't want to go home.' I didn't think I'd spoken aloud.

Gareth nudged me, 'You can come back here, we both can.'

'Yeah, course we can.' I knew it, I was turning into a girl, I felt like crying again. If Gareth noticed he didn't say anything. He started talking about his school, about some boy who'd got excluded. I was listening, well sort of, but I kept looking at the beach the whole time. It was like my eyes were a camera and, if I looked at the waves long enough, then I could always keep the picture in my head. I blinked a few times, locking the pictures in.

'Jon? Come on, we're ready to go.'

It was Mum's voice, I was so glad it wasn't Dad. I didn't want him to say it was time to go.

I don't know how it happened. I really don't know, but I had to sit with Dad on the journey home. Perhaps he'd had a word with Mum when I was with Gareth but when I got back to the cars, Mum was in the Clio and Sebastian was already in his seat. Dad was holding the door of the Saab open for me. I ignored him at first and moved over to the Clio but Mum shook her head and she switched the Clio's engine on.

Gareth came in the car with me and Dad so we could take him back to his parents' caravan. Mum and Sebastian drove behind us.

No one spoke a word. That's not true, Dad kept talking, all this stupid stuff about blokes needing to be on their own, away from nattering women. Gareth and I ignored him.

It didn't take long to say goodbye to the Hendersons. I wanted it to last longer. Seemed to me that once we'd done that it really was the end of the holiday. It was as if we were closing the door on the whole trip. Goodbye holiday, back to normal.

Dad stayed in the car while we were with Gareth's parents.

217

Mum and I didn't mention him, not once. We said how smashing it had been meeting them and we all made promises to keep in touch. Alice put her hand out as if she wanted to touch me but Gareth pulled my arm and Alice missed and her arm fell back; she pretended she was scratching her leg. I actually felt sorry for her. Then all the goodbyes were over and Mum and I got back into the cars to go home. Mum said she'd go first, 'Setting the pace,' she told Dad.

Just as I got into the Saab Dad asked me if I needed to go to the toilet, like I was a kid or something. I told him I didn't, that I was OK. I wished I hadn't said it because pretty soon I did need to go. I was uncomfortable. I stared out of the window for ages, hoping he wouldn't notice me jiggling up and down. But he did.

'Do you want to stop, Jon? You look very uncomfortable, do you want to go to the toilet now?'

'Me? No. Why?'

'Oh, for God's sake, how long are you going to keep this up? If you don't want to bloody go, I do!' He lifted his foot up for a second then pushed it down on the accelerator pedal really hard.

In a second we'd overtaken Mum's car. I could see her mouth opening wide as we drove past. I tried to mouth the word *toilet* at her but I don't think she understood.

Dad drove like a mad thing, just like the French drivers, overtaking, out of one lane into another, then back out again. The other drivers blew their horns at us. Dad ignored all the noise, all he did was put one finger up to the other drivers. We came to a layby sign, one with toilets in, so Dad drove into that; the tyres squealed as he yanked the brakes on.

'Go on, get out, toilets are over there.'

'I can see, I'm not blind, where's Mum?'

The Clio pulled up next to us and Mum got out of the car. She was frowning, 'What's the matter? Are you OK, Jon?'

Dad got out of the car, 'Yeah, he's fine, just doing the best job in the world of winding me up. He'll live, I might not.' He stormed off.

I got out of the car and Mum grabbed at my T-shirt. 'Ease

up, Jon, we've got a long drive ahead of us. Your Dad's worried about Grandad, go easy on him, OK?'

'What about me? I'm worried too.' I didn't want a row with Mum, it wasn't her fault. I was so fed up. I didn't want to go home, I wanted to stay in France. I left her and walked over to the toilets.

They were those disgusting hole in the floor jobs. In the mood I was in, that was all I needed. The first time I used one, it took me ages to work out which way you're supposed to stand. What's the matter with the French? Why can't they have the same toilets as us? What's all this Common Market stuff about if the French won't have normal toilets?

Dad and Mum were talking when I got back to the cars. Dad's face was a blotchy red, his hair was sticking to his forehead. When I looked inside the Clio, I could see Sebastian, he had a red face too but he was fast asleep. I wished I was his age, he doesn't have to put up with parents.

'OK?' Dad didn't look at me, he just opened the door of the Saab.

I looked at Mum. 'Let me come in the car with you, you need me to read the maps, please?'

She shook her head. 'No, go with your dad, you must.'

'Why?'

'Just do it, Jon, I don't need you to read the maps on the way home. I'll follow your dad from now on. Go on, get in the car, he's waiting for you.'

He was, he'd turned the engine on and he was revving it up, like some middle-aged boy racer. Pathetic. I couldn't even slam the Saab's door to make me feel better. It sort of *sucked* itself shut.

We didn't speak for ages. We drove quite fast most of the time and every now and then, he'd have to slow down a bit so that Mum could catch up. The Clio's a good car, Mum likes it, but the engine's only small; not as fast as the Saab.

I turned around and watched Mum, she had the sunshine roof open and her hair was flying about. I could see her mouth opening and closing. She must have been singing along to her

CDs.

Suddenly I remembered Dunkirk, how I wanted to take photos. I'd have to speak to Dad. It was important, I wanted to take pictures for Grandad, I wanted to do that for him. I had a big, jumbled-up mass of thoughts in my head and I could see Grandad in hospital. I had an image of him lying in a hospital bed. He was wearing blue pyjamas and I was sitting on the edge of the bed and I was showing him my photos. He was smiling at me. No one else was there, just me and Grandad. But first I needed to get to Dunkirk.

'Can we, are you going to Dunkirk?'

'What?'

'Are we going to Dunkirk? I promised Grandad I'd take photos of the war memorials for him.'

'So you're thinking about him now, are you?'

'I think of him a lot, not just when you say I should.'

Dad slowed the car right down. Mum wasn't far behind, I could see her face, her mouth was wide open, she was singing along to something. Bet it was Tina Turner, she always plays *Simply the Best* when she's driving.

Dad turned to look at me, I pretended I hadn't noticed and I kept staring out of the window.

'Jon?'

'Yes?'

'Come on, son, give this a rest, you've made your point. I'm sorry, really sorry your holiday has been cut short but it's only by two days and you do know that you can come back sometime. Right now we all need to give Grandad our support and help. I'm sorry too that I've upset you. That's the last thing in the world I wanted to do Now, can we at least talk properly, without me feeling that you're on one side of a barbed wire fence and I'm on the other?'

'Alright.' I still didn't turn to look at him, though.

He coughed. 'I hadn't forgotten about Dunkirk, this road takes us there. We're going to have to stop for something to eat and I dare say your mum will want to sort Sebastian out with a nappy or something.'

Dad let out a huge sigh, it sounded as if he'd been holding

220

his breath for ages. The air from his lungs somehow filled the car and I felt really uncomfortable. I didn't know what to do or say to him. I kept staring out of the window, it seemed to be the safest thing to do.

'Jon? Come on, son, give me a break. How about … what music do you want, you choose.'

'Stevie Wonder.'

'Don't think I've got any.'

'Tina Turner.'

'Nor her, your mum likes her, not me.'

'Beatles.'

'Oh, for Christ's sake. You know I don't have any of those, you bloody know that.'

Without turning my head I could see his hands on the steering wheel. His knuckles were white. Seeing them like that made me feel better. Serves him right. He coughed again. 'OK, you choose. Go and have a look in the CD box, under your seat.'

I waited a few seconds, counting in my head, *one, two three, four, five* … before I reached for the box. I looked at his hands again. I could see the knobbly white bones of his knuckles under the skin.

Mum keeps all her CDs in the glove box. I'm never sure what CD I've picked up in Mum's car, not one of them's ever in the right case. Every CD in Dad's box had been properly stored. He had loads of them: Van Morrison, Eric Clapton, Sting. *Boring.*

'Anything you fancy?' He cleared his throat again.

'No, not really.'

'OK then, my choice.' He took one hand from the steering wheel and took out a CD.

'This'll do, Van Morrison, it's new.'

He shoved the CD in and leant back in his seat, he stretched his arms out on the steering wheel like rally drivers do. He looked in both mirrors again, checking to see where Mum was, I suppose.

'So, Jon, first time in France and I know you've enjoyed yourself. What's been the best bit? The food, the beaches,

Euro Disney?' His eyes flicked over to me when he said that.

'Dunno, Euro Disney was OK, pretty good really. It's all been good. Meeting Gareth was good too.'

Dad tapped his fingers on the wheel. 'How were you with the language? You do French at school, did you get much chance to practice any?'

'No, we haven't done that much and anyway they all talk too fast. I couldn't understand what they were saying half the time, well, all the time really.'

'You should have tried a bit harder, Jon. Languages are important, the ability to speak to other people, it's essential.'

Yeah right. My dad has a hard enough time talking to me and I'm his son.

For a while we drove in silence. We both tapped in time to the music. Suited me but then Dad started giving me these glances out of the corner of his eye. His arms flexed again. 'I really miss not being around you, Jon.'

Oh God. What was I supposed to say to that?

'Coming over here on the ferry I seemed to be the only bloke on his own. Everywhere I looked there were families, hundreds of them. Kids yelling, fighting, talking all the time. Every other word on that ferry was *Dad.*' He half turned towards me, checking to see if I was listening, I suppose. Not that I had any choice.

He coughed again, 'I kept looking at lads about your age, thinking about what you might have been up to in France. That's such a hard part of this, Jon, the not knowing what you're doing. I don't just mean here, in France, I mean every day. When you wake up each morning, I don't know what you've got planned for the day. I don't know what your life is like any more, do you know how that feels?'

What started this off?

I began squirming around in my seat. I was uncomfortable again. I didn't want to go to the toilet this time, I just didn't want to hear any more of this boring stuff. But he didn't stop.

'There was a family of four. Mum and Dad and two girls. They might have been twins, they certainly looked the same age, but what do I know?' He looked over again but I couldn't, I just couldn't turn my head to look at him. This was dead embarrassing.

Dad's voice was soft, 'The mother and father were drinking, they seemed to be doing a lot of drinking. And these two girls just sat there. They had cans of Coke in front of them and plenty of crisps and chocolate. The parents were shrieking at something they were watching on a big television screen. They couldn't take their eyes off it. Then, one of the girls asked her father something, I couldn't catch what she said. Her father didn't look up, didn't take his eyes from the screen, he nodded. That was all he did. Just nodded at her.'

So?

'I had to leave that table, Jon. I couldn't stay there and watch that family. Do you know why?'

I shook my head. *Who cares?*

'I had to go because I was worried that, if I'd stayed there, I'd shout something at those parents. They weren't taking a blind bit of notice of their kids, couldn't have cared less about them. These two girls were bored out of their brains, sitting there on a ferry going across to France for their holidays and their parents couldn't take their eyes from a TV screen. I wanted to yell, to shout at them that they were missing out on their daughters' lives, *wasting* them. A part of their lives that they can never get back, criminal.' Dad shook his head. 'I expect they'd have thought I was barking mad, completely off the wall. Might even have thought I was some sort of freak, a pervert even. But all around me on that ferry there were families, kids yelling at their parents, couples arguing and these two girls sitting drinking Coke and I wasn't a part of any of it.'

So? Whose fault is that?

Dad was still shaking his head. I realised then that he really didn't expect me to say anything, he only wanted to say this stuff out aloud.

'Do you know what that makes me, Jon?'

I shook my head.

'Part-time, that's what I am. A part-time dad. Not even

that.' He thumped the steering wheel. 'For me, it's like watching a film, seeing things happen on a wide screen, knowing that I can't share it or, if I do, it's only for a short while. But, just like watching a film, I go home on my own again.'

I turned to look at Mum. She saw me looking and waved.

I didn't know what to say to Dad. I didn't know what he wanted me to say.

He cleared his throat again. *Oh God, he's off again.*

'You must think I'm behaving like someone out of the Ark.' He paused as if he expected me to say something but I kept my mouth shut. He started up again, 'Some of the clothes that young girls wear, the ones on the ferry. What happened to T-shirts? When did it become all right for young girls to walk about showing their belly buttons? When did that happen?' He looked at me quickly then his eyes snapped back to the road.

He'd really lost me. 'They're all right, all the girls wear them. You must have seen some on the site. They're just T-shirts.'

'Not what I'd call T-shirts.' He shook his head.

There was silence for a while then he started up again. 'Do you still read *The Lion, the Witch and the Wardrobe?* Have you still got all those books?'

'Yeah, somewhere. Haven't read them for ages. They're all right but they're for kids.'

'*Kids?* What does that make you? Suppose you're reading Harry Potter.'

'Yeah, what's wrong with that – they're great books.'

'I'm sure they are, I wouldn't know.'

We didn't say anything for ages after that, just listened to Van Morrison. Every now and then I caught sight of Mum's face behind us. Her curls were flying all over the place. I thought that next time we stopped, I'd go and sit with her. We could sing to Stevie Wonder or Tina Turner.

FRANK

The light in the ward was grey, mottled shadows moved sluggishly on the emulsioned walls. Frank had no idea what time it was. He'd barely slept, his eyes felt gritty and his mouth was dry. It was very hot, not one window open anywhere; the air in the ward was stale, clammy.

In the bed opposite Frank, a middle-aged man lay on his back, his mouth wide open. In the dim light of the ward Frank could see a puddle of moisture on the man's chest where dribble had collected. Every six seconds, a guttural snore erupted from his mouth. Frank knew how many seconds, he'd been counting them throughout the night.

There were noises from the other beds too, a mumbled word, a cough, muted background sounds. Another snore and Frank turned his head towards the jug of water on his bedside unit. His bed was close to the window and the streetlights shone on the water, giving it an amber colour. *Wish that was whisky. That's what I could do with now. Two small glasses, that's all I'd need. Shut out the bloody racket for a start.*

He couldn't reach the water and he fell listlessly back on the pillows. His pyjamas were damp with sweat. *Glad I'm not paying the bills, like a bloody hothouse in here.*

He closed his eyes. *What the hell am I doing in here? Should be home, damn nuisance, the whole thing, a damn nuisance.*

A saucer of light from a desk lamp at the entrance to the

ward gave a greenish tinge to the blonde head of the night sister. She'd been reading notes, writing reports for most of the time although twice during the night, she'd checked on each bed. Frank had felt the pressure of her warm fingers on his wrist. Each time she'd arrived at the side of his bed, Frank tried to engage her in conversation. 'Where are you from then? Got any children?'

Each time she'd smiled, shaking her head, her eyes locked on her watch. 'Try to get some sleep, Mr Jones.' She said it each time before leaving him, moving on to the next patient.

A harsh cough caused Frank to look over towards the far end of the ward. A young man lay on his side, one arm dangling, fingers almost touching the floor. Cards had been arranged on every surface around his bed, some were folded over the top of his metal headboard. A silver balloon moved in the warm air.

Frank's bed was the only one without cards and flowers. Everybody else had a selection of limp-headed roses or carnations displayed in a variety of vases and containers. Their perfume added to the muggy air of the ward. He shifted, trying to find a cool place on the tangled sheets. He felt very alone. Everyone in the ward belonged somewhere, to someone. They all had wives, families, children. They were all part of units, he wasn't. What was he? Isolated. Not since the time immediately after Nancy's death had Frank felt so lonely.

Following Nancy's funeral, when everyone had left him and gone home, Frank had sat in his kitchen looking aimlessly at the remnants of sandwiches, the jumble of used napkins and smeared glasses. He'd come back into the kitchen after his demolition of the wisteria, the funeral guests avoiding his eyes, making no mention of what he'd done, what they'd seen.

Frank had sat with his knees apart, splodges of rusty-coloured mud covered his knees and his white shirt was creased and stained. It had been dark outside, there was a full moon glittering on the garden, giving a metallic brightness to the inside of the house.

His kitchen didn't seem to belong to him any more, there were strange smells in the house, a mixture of cigarette smoke, perfume and moth-balled clothes. Nina had wanted to clear up but he didn't want her there. He hadn't wanted anyone there.

With a recognition that what he was about to do should be unseen by anyone else, Frank had walked to the back door and locked it. Then he'd moved calmly to the front door and slammed each bolt home, sliding the chain across, securing it. He'd then gone back into the kitchen and picked up one of the tumblers. Sniffing first at the glass, Frank poured himself a large measure of whisky. Cradling the glass in both hands, he moved steadily to the living room.

The condolence cards were everywhere, lined up along the mantelpiece, the bookcases, the windowsills. The silvery, harsh light of the moon shone on the cards, highlighting their message: *In Sympathy, With Deep Sorrow, In Our Thoughts.* There were so many cards, the sheer volume of them somehow managed to give the room an air of festivity, of happiness.

With a grunt, Frank settled into an armchair and sipped at his drink, his eyes on the cards. People he'd not known, had never met before had sent cards. His house had been full of strangers, they all knew Nancy but hardly anyone had known him.

He'd taken another sip of whisky then, leaving the chair, he swept the cards off the mantelpiece. He ran the back of his hand along the bookcases, the windowsill, scattering the cards to the floor. Leaving them where they fell, Frank returned to the kitchen and brought the bottle of whisky into the living room.

The sight of the scattered card brought sudden tears and impatiently he brushed them away.

'No one knew her like I knew her, no one.' He flopped heavily into the armchair and refilled the tumbler, drinking from it even before he'd replaced the bottle. The whisky burnt his throat, making him cough. 'What bloody use are cards? What good are they? What do I want with cards?'

He stared balefully at the muddle of cards lying on the floor and in the empty grate. Moving suddenly, the whisky spilling over his fingers, Frank got to his feet and kicked out at the cards, scattering them even more. 'Useless to me, bloody useless.'

Reaching over to the mantelpiece, Frank's fingers scrabbled at the back of a framed photograph of Chris, taken at his graduation. The jerky movement of Frank's hand dislodged the photo and it fell to the floor, the glass shattering as it hit the marble tiles of the fireplace.

'Damn and blast.' Frank had found the matches he'd been looking for and, bending down, he struck a light and put the flame to the cards. With one hand gripping the mantelpiece, Frank watched as the orange tongue of the flame licked at the heap of cards in the fireplace. He took a deep breath and, moving towards the windows, he picked up all the other cards that were lying on the carpet. Holding the remainder, Frank fed each one to the growing flames. He watched as the small fire slowly destroyed the ornate silver and gold lettering on every card. Tiny, burnt particles of paper floated around the room. He moved back to his chair and sipped again from the tumbler.

'Bloody good riddance.'

He had no memory of how long he'd sat there, watching as the flames ate all the cards. He drank steadily as the fire grew smaller until all that was left was a pile of jagged grey fragments in the grate.

The phone rang a few times and someone knocked on the door but Frank ignored everything; his gaze was fixed on the fireplace. His cheeks were wet, tears ran unchecked into the fabric of his shirt.

'It's all gone now, Nancy love,' he whispered. 'You and me, finished. Dust to dust, that's what he said, ashes to ashes. It's true, there's nothing left, nothing for me.'

Frank pushed his head back on the pillow. His memory of that night embarrassed him; he tried to avoid thinking about it, skirting around his behaviour, his drunkenness. Somehow, over the years it had become swallowed up in the distress of Nancy's funeral. Like a disused room, Frank had closed the memory.

He longed to be home, lying in the big double bed with his

clock radio close by and the pictures of Nancy on his bedside table. Things that were his, giving him some sort of anchor, some substance, he didn't want to be part of hospital life, he wanted to be back in his own life. Frank felt as if he was being swallowed, absorbed by the warmth of the ward, the noise from the sleeping patients. He closed his eyes.

When he opened them again, the light was different, sunshine was flooding into the ward. He could smell bacon and Frank struggled to sit up.

'Back with us, Mr Jones? How are you feeling, got any pain this morning?'

'Course I've got pain. Bloody stupid question. Got a broken hip haven't I?'

A nurse was standing by Frank's pillows; he hated the thought that she must have seen him sleeping, she must have seen his slack, open mouth. He felt vulnerable, pathetic.

Avoiding her eyes he ran a hand around his jaw. 'I need a shave, don't want to start the day without one. I'll need water, how do I get water?' He nodded towards his locker, 'Expect everything I need is in there.'

'Not to worry, I can do that for you. I'm going to give you a good wash anyway. We need to get you into a hospital gown for your operation.'

The clattering of the stainless steel food trolley brought the smell of bacon closer and Frank swallowed. He jerked his head towards an auxiliary nurse who was taking a tray to the young man in the end bed. 'I could do with some of that, smells good.' His mouth flickered in a grudging smile, he was sorry he'd been so rude to the nurse, the young lass was only doing her job.

'I'm sure you would like some, Mr Jones, but I'm afraid there's nothing for you until after your operation.' She reached up and began tugging at the curtains around the bed, pulling them together until Frank felt he was in a strange tent, one with garish red butterflies covering the canvas. 'What, nothing? Not even a cup of tea?'

'No, you're first on this morning's list. Now, lie back and

I'll give you a good wash. Make you feel better, I'm sure.'

'But that can't be right! I'm parched, mouth feels like the bottom of a budgie's cage. A cup of tea can't hurt surely.' In his indignation Frank hadn't realised what the nurse was doing. Her slim fingers were undoing the buttons on his pyjama jacket and she began easing it away from his shoulders. He put his hand on hers. 'Now what? What do you think you're doing?'

'I told you, I'm going to give you a wash before we put the gown on you. You can't have an operation in your pyjamas, the surgeon wouldn't like that at all.'

Frank's fingers were still holding hers. He tightened his grip. 'I'll have you know, young woman, that I'm almost eighty years old and not about to have any young lass taking my clothes off, thank you very much!'

Frank saw a tiny flicker of exasperation in the nurse's eyes before she tugged her hand free and she stepped back from the bed.

When she spoke, it was in a slow, controlled voice. Frank felt that the words she used had been spoken many times before, they had an easy, placatory sound. 'Now, Mr Jones, I'm a nurse and this is my job, I'm paid to do this. We need to get you out of your pyjamas and into the hospital gown. It's what the surgeon asks for and that's what I must do. Please believe me, I get no pleasure out of doing this, it's just my job. Now, shall we start again?'

Her fingers were tapping on her elbow and once again Frank saw exasperation in her eyes. He felt old and stupid. He cleared his throat. 'Can't a man do this? Surely there must be someone, some man, who could help me?'

Frank looked away from the expression in the nurse's eyes.

'We are short-staffed as it is, Mr Jones. We don't have any male nurses at all on this ward and only three male orderlies on the whole of the floor. Mr Jones, please!'

Frank's mouth was very dry and he ran his tongue around his lips. He closed his eyes. 'All right, seems I don't have any choice in the matter.'

With his eyes still shut Frank missed the mouthed *silly old bugger* from the nurse as she leant over him and tugged at his pyjama jacket. In silence she eased Frank's pyjama bottoms away from him, gently rolling him to one side so she could wash him. Efficiently, deftly, she ran a flannel down the length of his legs, patting at his loose flesh. He felt the warm, damp flannel moving over his feet. When she'd patted him dry, she shaved him. Frank's arm moved upwards in a silent protest but he let it fall back on the bed. As the razor was dragged over the grey stubble on his chin, Frank opened his eyes and stared at one of the butterflies that covered the curtains around his bed. It bore no resemblance to any butterfly that Frank had ever seen: it had a chunky body, its wings were a carroty red and, on every foot, it was wearing what looked like a heavy, industrial boot. From beyond the closed curtains, Frank could hear voices but all he could see were the boot-wearing butterflies and all he could feel was the razor being dragged across his skin.

He closed his eyes once more as the flannel moved over his face and, when the nurse moved away to pick up a towel, Frank opened his mouth. 'So, this operation, pretty big one I understand. How long will it take? Two hours, three hours, what?'

'Nothing for you to worry about. Mr Armstrong is doing your operation. He does them all the time. You won't know or feel a thing. You'll be back on the ward before you know it.'

Frank chewed on the inside of his lip. Again she was using well-used words, words that had been tested a million times. But she wasn't talking to an idiot or some frightened child. He wanted to know. He lifted his head from the pillow. 'I'm not worried, what's the point of being worried? I merely want to know how long this operation will take, how many hours?'

As he spoke she held out the operating gown and, like an obedient child, he slipped his arms through the wide sleeves and bent his head forward as she tied the straps behind him. Still without speaking, she clipped a plastic identity bracelet around his right wrist, checking the details quietly as she looked at the notes pinned to the foot of Frank's bed.

When she'd satisfied herself that all was in order, the nurse turned away from him and began pulling at the curtains, tucking them behind the bed. 'Hip operations are what Mr Armstrong does best. He operates on hips every day, you've got nothing to …'

Frank interrupted. 'Yes, you've already said that. If you can't tell me surely someone else can. All I want to know is how long this operation will take, that's all I'm asking!'

Suddenly the nurse grabbed the bowl she'd been using, water slopped over her shoes. Anger flared in her eyes as she bent forward whispering to Frank, 'Mr Armstrong has been known to replace a hip in 45 minutes. I can't tell you anything else, it all depends what he finds when he opens you up.'

She turned, her rubber-soled shoes squeaking in protest. 'You're down for 8.45, I expect you'll be given a pre-med soon, something to calm you, I think you need it.' She moved away, walking quickly towards the open door of the ward.

Frank could feel his heart thumping underneath the stiff cotton of his gown. *Open me up? What, like a can of soup?*

A radio was playing, he could hear the hum of conversation; some of the other patients were sitting in chairs alongside their beds eating breakfast. A few waved a fork or a spoon in greeting as they caught Frank's gaze but he turned away and lay back on the pillows. His fingers tugged at the sheet he was lying on. *Nancy love, I could do with seeing your face right now.*

His stomach made a low, grumbling sound. He thought that the nurse might just as well have left the curtains up around him, he felt so isolated, so alone. An enormous wave of questions pounded inside his head.

What are they going to do?
How long will I be kept here?
Will I be able to move after the operation?
Will I be able to walk again?
What about my house, my garden?

The smell of the bacon was driving him mad. He swallowed hard looking away from the breakfast trays on the other beds. He was very hungry, he'd been able to eat some of the chicken that Meryl Jefferies had brought in last night. She'd talked the whole time he'd been eating, her jabbering had put him off and he'd felt at a disadvantage, half-lying, half-sitting trying to eat a plate of cold chicken. He'd swallowed the tender chicken breast quickly, gulping down chunks of it in the hope that she'd go, she'd leave him alone. When she did eventually leave the ward, she'd taken the plate and the remainder of the chicken with her. She could have left him some, she needn't have taken it all. He could have eaten some of it this morning, no one would know, no one would notice. *Bloody woman.*

'Mr Jones?'

Frank jerked, he hadn't seen the stocky, white-coated man arrive; he stood at the side of Frank's bed, both hands holding an X-ray.

'Who are you?' Frank heard the belligerence in his voice and did nothing to hide it. 'Are you the surgeon? Are you Dr Armstrong, because if you are I've got some questions to ask you *and* I'd like some answers before you start cutting me up.'

'Yes, I'm the Consultant Orthopaedic surgeon, *Mr* Armstrong.' There was a gentle emphasis on the *Mr* which Frank ignored.

The surgeon waited a few seconds then, realising Frank wasn't going to speak, went on, 'I thought I'd come and see you, Mr Jones, to discuss what we'll be doing this morning and hopefully put your mind at ease.'

Frank crossed his arms around his chest. 'I should think so. I've been told nothing. Only that I'm to have a hip operation. I wouldn't let people into my house without seeing their credentials, why should I agree to an operation without knowing what's what?'

'Quite right too.' Mr Armstrong gravely nodded. He was almost bald and the harsh overhead lights in the ward shone greasily on his scalp. Half-moon glasses perched dangerously low on his nose and his tiny eyes, like brown buttons, gazed sympathetically at Frank.

Frank felt slightly mollified; at least this bloke was taking him seriously. He cleared his throat, 'First of all I want to

233

know exactly what you're going to do and how long will it take and when can I go home? I'm a widower you see and I want to be back in my own house in my own bed as soon as possible.'

Mr Armstrong held the X-ray up and, pushing his glasses further up towards the bridge of his nose, he jabbed at the image that Frank had seen the night before. 'Can you see, Mr Jones, can you see the break?'

There it was again, that unseemly picture of his hips and legs. 'Yes, yes, I can see it, saw it last night. But what are you going to do? Can it be fixed?'

Mr Armstrong lowered his arm, the X-ray wobbled, making a peculiar sound. For a second, Frank was reminded of the noise that Rolf Harris made on the record that Nancy used to play for Chris. He had a sudden image of the two of them dancing together in the living room. With a tiny shake of his head, he listened to what Mr Armstrong was saying.

'OK, Mr Jones, would it be all right if I called you …' his eyes flickered to the side of the X-ray, 'Frank?'

Frank nodded.

'Well, Frank, the X-rays show that you've fractured your right hip and I can put that right. What they also show is that you've got pretty advanced osteoarthritis. You must have been in a lot of pain even before your fall, am I right?'

Frank looked away from Mr Armstrong's gaze and once again he nodded.

The surgeon lowered his voice, his tone was softer, 'My experience also tells me that your mobility wouldn't have been that good either and what is also apparent from your X-rays is that you've also got osteoporosis. I'm arranging to have further tests done, scans, more X-rays taken of your spine in the thoracic, lumbar and cervical areas. If the osteoporosis is in your spine, and I would guess that it is, we'll need to think of ways of treating you. It's potentially a very serious condition for someone your age.'

Frank shook his head, 'Yes, all right, never mind about all that, when can I go home? When can I get out of here and back to normal?'

Mr Armstrong put a hand up to his face, his fingers moved across his eyes, brushing over the lids as if he'd walked into a spider's web. 'Mr Jones, I think you should prepare yourself for a stay of about a week, possibly ten days.'

'Ten days, impossible!'

Mr Armstrong ignored Frank's outburst and he perched on the side of the bed. He gave a brief smile, 'I suppose, Frank, it might be fair to say that the fall you had was a good thing.'

Frank turned his head to one side and he glared at the surgeon in silence.

Mr Armstrong gave a brief smile, 'The damage caused to your hip joint by the arthritis was, *is,* pretty severe. Arthritis is relentless and, in your case, the cartilage which lines the ball and socket-shaped bones that make up the hip joint, has just about worn away. What you're left with now is a situation where bone is rubbing against bone.'

Frank shifted in the bed. 'Yes, yes, I know all about arthritis, *everyone* knows that but what are you going to do? I want to go home.'

Mr Armstrong glanced at his watch and moved off the bed. 'Hip replacement is one of the most reliable operations in orthopaedics and I've been doing hips for a long time. I'll replace the natural worn out part of your hip, it's called the femoral head, with an artificial one. I don't think it would achieve anything if I went into greater detail but be assured, Frank, that once it's all over, you'll feel a lot better. No more pain, you'll be able to get about much easier, it'll give you a new lease of life.' He patted at Frank's hand.

'Well, that's all very well, but I'm not staying here for ten days.'

The surgeon put his head on one side as he looked at Frank. 'The length of time you stay in hospital depends on a lot of things. I'll know more after the operation and after the physiotherapists have seen you. Either way, you'll need help when you go home. Do you live on your own, do you have stairs to get to bed?'

Frank felt an almost overwhelming urge to grab the surgeon's hand, pinning him down, keeping him at his bedside. 'Yes, I live on my own and yes I've got stairs and my bedroom is where everybody else's is, up the bloody stairs!'

Mr Armstrong lifted the X-ray in the air and waved it like a flag before walking away. 'Try not to worry, we'll sort something out. See you later, Frank.'

Frank watched as Mr Armstrong walked briskly towards the open doors. He saw him stop to speak to a sister and he saw both the surgeon and the nurse look towards his bed. Frank felt a sudden prickling in his eyes, *too bloody hot in here by half. Making my eyes water. Oh God, Nancy, I don't know how I'm going to cope with all this.*

It was still early, not yet 8 o'clock. Frank didn't know what to do. He hadn't got anything to read and even if someone did bring him a newspaper, he wasn't sure if he'd got his glasses. He'd always hated wasting time. Time was like money, not to be squandered or wasted. He believed every hour was important, needing to be filled, spent properly. He plucked unhappily at the tangled sheet underneath him. His eyes closed.

'Mr Jones?'

They'd done it again! Someone else had crept up on him, startling him. A man, about 35 years old, tall and dark-haired stood next to his bed. Frank noticed a stain on his dark blue tie.

'What? Who are you?' Frank barked, hiding his anxiety.

The dark-haired man held out his hand 'David Leigh, Mr Jones. I'm the anaesthetist, I'll be putting your to sleep for your operation.'

Like some knackered old dog.

Frank ignored the outstretched hand. 'What do you want?' he asked rudely.

'I've brought you your pre-med. These are just mild tranquillisers.'

'*Tranquillisers?* Don't want any of that sort of thing, thank you very much.'

'Well I can't force you, Mr Jones, but I would strongly recommend that you take them. There really is no point in you being anxious before your operation. These will merely make

236

you feel a bit calmer, that's all.'

'Drugged, you mean.'

'Not at all, they are only meant as a temporary measure, they will alleviate any anxiety you may be feeling.'

Snotty-nosed little twerp's talking to me as if I was ga-ga.

'Well, I don't want them, take them away.' Frank turned his head away and closed his eyes again.

He heard a soft sigh from the young anaesthetist, then a light rattling sound. 'I've put them on your locker, just in case you change your mind.'

'Suit yourself.' Frank opened one eye and he saw David Leigh stop on his way out of the ward to talk to the sister. Once again, both faces turned towards Frank's bed. He closed his eyes.

He heard a rattle as the curtains were pulled around his bed, he must have been dozing, his mouth felt very dry.

'Mr Jones, we're taking you down to theatre now. We just need to check your details.' The sister picked up his wrist and read out his name and date of birth to a younger nurse.

'Have you signed the consent form, Mr Jones?'

'What form?'

'Your consent to the operation, have you signed it yet?'

'What happens if I don't?'

'The operation cannot go ahead if the consent form isn't signed.'

Frank had a sudden picture of him scrambling out of bed, running past the other patients who waved and cheered him on as he sprinted down the corridors. He shook his head, he'd need clothes for that and he'd no idea where his were and, anyway, he couldn't walk.

'OK, give me a pen, I'll sign your form.'

With a degree of ceremony the consent form was produced from the thin folder lying on Frank's locker and a pen handed to him. Without his glasses Frank squinted at the dotted line underneath the Sister's outstretched finger. He scrawled his name. 'There.'

The sides of the bed were brought up with a clatter and

one of the nurses bent down to release the brake. The butterflies wobbled as the curtains were pulled back and Frank's bed was pushed towards the open door of the ward.

'Good luck, mate. Sweet dreams.'

'Be all over before you know it.'

'We'll keep a drink waiting for you.'

The voices of the other patients rose up on either side of the ward as Frank was wheeled towards the corridor. He felt like an explorer leaving safe shores. He realised, just in time, that his right arm was beginning to rise in an attempt to wave at the others. He brought it back down and instead he nodded graciously at the patients.

In the corridor heading towards the lift Frank lay quite still and watched as the overhead lights merged as he was wheeled towards the lift.

One of the nurses stabbed at the control panel and a lift appeared almost immediately. As his bed was pushed into the lift, Frank could feel the pounding of his heart again. He swallowed as the doors of the lift closed.

JONATHAN

Was I glad to see the sign for Dunkirk? It had been such a long drive, it took ages. We'd stopped a few times, mostly for Mum and Sebastian. She'd flash the Clio's lights at Dad and he'd pull in at the next lay-by. Each time I got out I asked Mum if I could sit with her, but every time she said the same thing, 'It's best that you stay with your dad.'

I don't know why, she couldn't manage it.

Dad was really getting on my nerves, he kept saying all sorts of weird stuff to me, about how great things would be once we'd got home. 'There's so much to catch up on, so much we can do together, Jon.'

He was full of it. He made me feel like a parcel that had been sitting on a shelf for ages and he'd only just got around to opening it.

'You're a young man now, soon have all the girls after you. Hah! You already have one, though, don't you? I saw the way that Gareth's sister was looking at you. Pretty little thing, what was her name?'

'Alice.' I didn't feel like talking to Dad about her. Not sure why really, except that she was part of my holiday, the good part, and I still felt that Dad had spoilt things for Mum and me.

Before too long he was off again, 'You're almost the same height as your mother now, soon be up to my height. What are you now, Jon 5'4", 5'5"?'

'5'5", well almost.'

239

He laughed and hit the steering wheel when I said that. Haven't got a clue why, it wasn't supposed to be funny. He was trying really hard, trying to make me feel that he was a good dad. It'll take more than that.

It had started to rain by the time we got to Dunkirk which somehow seemed right to me. The holiday was ending and what with the rain and the boring flat fields all around us, I thought we might as well be at home already. If it hadn't been for Grandad and the promise I made him, I wouldn't even have got out of the car, well, I don't think I would. But I did and I looked at the long, sandy beaches and tried to imagine what it must have been like. Dad got out of the car too and just then Mum arrived and we all looked at the beach. I thought it would look different somehow but it didn't. It just looked like any other beach to me. Dad put his hand on my shoulder.

'Over half a million British and Allied troops rescued, hard to imagine, isn't it?'

'Mmm.' My camera was covered in sand and I pretended that I was cleaning it up with both hands so I could shrug Dad's hand away. He knew what I was doing and started to say something to me but I walked away from him. All of a sudden it seemed really important that I took the best photos I could to show Grandad. I wanted him to see these beaches, to see where I'd been so I could prove to him that I had been thinking of him all the time. Then I thought that if I took loads of pictures, somehow it might prove something to Grandad and he'd like me again.

I left Mum and Dad and walked all over the beach taking photos. I moved towards the sea and Mum called me. 'Enough, Jon. You've got more than enough now. I thought you were going to take some of the Memorials, pictures of the war graves to show your grandad?'

Dad barked at her, 'We haven't got time for that now, I want to try and get the earlier ferry.' He was sitting on a bench, he was holding an enormous umbrella. It must have been something from his office, a bright red thing with the letters *P & J* dotted all over it like flakes of dandruff.

Mum looked a bit bothered, 'Surely we've got a bit more time?'

'No,' As Dad stood up, he poked himself in the eye with a broken spoke in the umbrella and he glared at Mum as if it was her fault. 'There isn't any time left. If we leave now we'll be first in the queue for the next ferry. Your grandad will never know, Jon. Just take a picture of that graveyard over there.' He pointed to the church behind us, 'He'll never know the difference.'

'But *I* will, I'll know the difference.' I really hated Dad then. I was glad he'd bashed himself in the eye.

'Don't be silly. I bet you didn't even give Dunkirk a thought until your mum mentioned it to you, did you? Trust me, Jon, your grandad is never likely to come over here, he won't know. Just tell him they're photos of war graves and that you weren't allowed to take any more, that'll be enough for him, there's no need for him to know anything else.'

Dad shrugged then as he looked over towards Mum. It was that shrug and the look he gave Mum. It did my head in, it really did. I lost it then, really lost it and I started shouting at Dad.

'Why can't Grandad have proper pictures of the graves? Why can't he have the real thing? I can't tell him that those graves are the proper Dunkirk graves when they're not. Why can't he be told the truth? He deserves the truth.'

I ran off again. I could hear Mum shouting my name, calling me back. But I didn't. I just ran, only I couldn't run that fast as the sand was too soft and my trainers kept sinking.

One of the problems with parents is that they totally forget you're one person, they want you to be all sorts of people, all at the same time. They want you to do well at school, they want you to be kind to brothers or sisters, to be polite to older people, especially grandparents; stand up for yourself if bullies have a go and be a helpful son around the house. I can't be all those people, I'm just one, me. And the worst thing of all, the hardest thing of all, is trying not to take sides when parents split up. I do try, I try to be a good son for Mum, caring and helpful but I also try to be a good son for Dad, stand on my own two feet, be a man. I can't do it any more, why should I? Dad's not a good son, he's just a shit.

By now both Mum and Dad were yelling my name. I could hear them: *Jon, Jon.* They were making such a row that dogs at the far side of the beach began to bark then seagulls started to scream. It sounded to me as if the whole world was calling my name.

Go away, leave me alone.

FRANK

Leave me alone. For God's sake, can't a man get a bit of peace and quiet?

'Mr Jones? Frank, can you hear me?'

Bugger off.

Frank didn't know who was calling his name. 'Hello, Frank, can you hear me?' It was Nancy, he could feel her hand on his arm, what *was* she doing? Something was being prodded into his ear. He shook his head, trying to dislodge it. A woman's voice spoke softly, 'Keep still, Frank, it won't take a second.'

What won't take a second? Nancy, stop it. Leave me alone.

There she was. Nancy was there, he could see her. Her reading glasses were hanging from a string around her neck, grey smudges were under her eyes. What was she wearing? New blouse? Frank struggled to sit up but then he felt a hand on his shoulder and another hand supporting his head. 'Keep still, Frank, just keep still.'

He had a terrible taste in his mouth and when he tried to run his tongue around his lips, his tongue stuck to the roof of his mouth. Nancy had disappeared. A sudden, sharp pain in his right thigh, something rubbing at his leg. 'Get off, leave me alone. I'm tired.'

A cool hand touched his forehead, his eyelids felt very heavy. 'Lie still, Frank. You'll feel better in a minute.'

Nancy?

243

There she was, that's better, he could see her. She was walking into the living room, she wore blue trousers and her feet were bare. In her outstretched hands she held a pile of brochures. She held them carefully as if she'd been bringing something precious, fragile to him. There was something about her face, an air of excitement she was trying to contain.

'Frank? Look at these, I collected them today, look Frank.' She perched on the arm of his chair. It had been a Saturday afternoon in January, Frank had switched the lamp on, the one on the coffee table, so he could read the paper. He'd been irritated when Nancy pushed the pages of newsprint to the floor. She opened the first brochure, putting it down on his lap. 'Look, Frank, what do you think? Isn't it the most beautiful place you've ever seen?'

He grudgingly looked at the open page, at the red-tiled houses, the sun glinting on the aquamarine ocean, the mass of dusty red geraniums growing from window boxes.

'What am I looking at? Where is this?' He didn't bother to mask the tetchiness in his voice.

Nancy sighed, he knew that sigh well. 'Frank, don't. Don't spoil it for me. Just look, look at the flowers, look at the colour of that sea. Have you ever seen anything like it?' Her fingers traced the outline of the roofs.

'Where is *this*?' He'd pushed her hand away and prodded a finger at the open page.

'France, Menton, it's a small village behind Cannes.'

'These colours aren't natural, well-known fact, they touch the red up, flowers don't look like this. Colour's not normal.' He tried to close the pages but Nancy stopped him.

'All I ask is that you look at these brochures, take a look at the views, think about what it would be like to sit on one of these balconies, drinking a glass of wine in the evening, looking at that view. Take a look, Frank, please. What have you got to lose?'

Frank had shifted in his chair, he didn't want to look at the brochures, he wanted to get back to his paper. 'Nancy, love, every year you get these brochures and every year you make me look at them.' He laughed, grabbing hold of her hand.

'You know we can't go, not this year, perhaps next year.'

Nancy brushed him off and she stood and the brochures fell to the floor. 'Why not this year? Why not? Can you give me one reason why we can't go? Go on, Frank, give me one reason.'

She stood on the crumpled pages of his newspaper and Frank bent to retrieve them. Nancy didn't budge, she stood feet apart, the red varnish on her toenails shining in the light from the lamp, hands on her hips as she glared at him, repeating, 'One reason, Frank, just one.'

Frank let out a deep, theatrical sigh. 'Oh, for God's sake. What do you want me to say to you? What do you want to hear?' Nancy didn't move, her eyes were fixed on Frank's face. He took another sigh, a sigh of resignation. 'Right, you asked for reasons, I'll give you reasons: they're exactly the same as last year: we're too old, neither of us speak any other language, not French, not Italian, not Spanish. We've never been before, we don't know if we can eat the food, we won't know what's what and what about the garden? Be reasonable, love, how can I leave the bloody garden?'

He was angry, all this shouting, all this anger. It wasn't nice but why did he have to go through this every year? Why wouldn't she listen? Why was she never satisfied? He softened his voice, 'Who will look after the garden, eh? Who will come in and water it properly, do the weeding, check on the tomatoes, feed the beans and those hanging baskets of yours don't water themselves you know. I can't leave them to just anyone, now can I?'

'Why not?' Nancy hadn't moved, she stood firmly on Frank's newspaper.

'What are you talking about? *Why not?* What d'you mean? You know I can't leave the garden to just anyone.'

'Why can't you leave the garden? What will it matter for one year?'

Frank was shocked. 'Leave the garden? Are you mad? We eat the beans I grow, the tomatoes, the potatoes and you like the flowers. I can't leave the garden, you don't know what you're talking about. What about the lawn? It will burn, get parched, needs a lot of looking after does that lawn.'

'Sod the lawn, sod the beans, sod the tomatoes and sod you!' Nancy deliberately dragged her foot over the newspaper, tearing great chunks of paper with her toes. She almost ran out of the room then Frank heard her footsteps thumping up the stairs. The door of their bedroom slammed shut.

She stayed up there for hours. Frank walked to the foot of the stairs a few times, his hand on the banister, head cocked, listening for any sound. But there was nothing. Frank felt very uncomfortable, Nancy could make silence seem very loud.

Just before six o'clock, he walked once again to the foot of the stairs and called up, his voice firm with a confidence he didn't feel. 'Nance? What do you fancy for tea? We've got a nice piece of fish in the fridge, do you fancy that?'

She came downstairs then, she'd brushed her hair and she'd put on an old pair of weatherbeaten slippers. Her eyes sparkled as if she'd washed them, rinsing them off with fresh rainwater.

A few months after that Nancy told him about her lump. It was in April on a Wednesday morning. She'd been out early, almost before Frank had finished his breakfast. 'Just a few errands, want to catch the early bus.' She bent to kiss the top of his head before leaving. He grunted in response, not looking up from his newspaper.

He hadn't heard her come back. He'd been working in his greenhouse, preparing trays of petunias, geraniums and fuchsia for the borders. It was too early to plant them out, he was always very careful about the risk of frost. He was scathing about anyone who filled tubs and hanging baskets with bedding plants before the end of May. 'Why take the risk? People always rush these things, not worth it.' He'd said it to Nancy as she stood in the doorway. She was still wearing her coat and she held her handbag across her chest as if it was warming her, holding her.

Frank held up two petunia seedlings, shaking their thin, spindly roots. 'See these, love? *Surfinia*, thought I'd give them a go, just the one basket though, that way if they're no good, we'll only have spoilt one ...'

'Shut up, Frank.'

He looked at her, noticing for the first time how pale she was. 'What, what did you say? What's the matter, are you ill?'

'Yes, you could say that.' Her eyes glittered, 'Do you know where I went this morning?'

'No, not really. A few errands you said, I thought shopping…'

'No, not shopping. I went to see Dr Griffiths for the results of some tests I had last week.'

'Tests, what tests? What are you talking about? He gently put the petunias down and, as if by command, his fingers pressed the fragile roots into the compost.

'Tests for cancer, Frank. I had a mammogram; you see I found a lump and Dr Griffiths thought I should have the test to see what the lump was. The results are through, he told me today, it's cancer. I've got breast cancer.'

Whenever Frank thought of that day, he could smell the yeasty damp smell of compost and the gritty feel of it under his fingernails. Cancer, his wife had cancer and he thought of compost.

Frank stared at her, he saw then that she was wearing her new skirt, the one she'd bought when she went shopping with Nina the week before. In silence he watched as Nancy's hand reached up to touch one of her earrings. She was wearing the blue pearls she'd worn when Chris and Nina were married. Nina.

'Does she know, does Nina know? Have you told her, before me?' He watched as tears spilled from Nancy' s eyes as she wordlessly nodded.

'She knew before me?' Frank couldn't stop the words, this wasn't what he wanted to say but he couldn't find any way to stem the flow of words. 'You told *her* before you told me, your husband. You kept me in the dark but let her in on your secret.' He made no attempt to stop Nancy as she ran, putting a hand across her mouth, back towards the house.

It seemed important to Frank that before he did anything else he finished the job he'd been working on when Nancy broke her news. He had a strange burning feeling in his chest and his throat hurt each time he swallowed as he put the remainder of the tiny seedlings into their pots and baskets. He tidied up his tools, carefully wiping down the bench he'd been working on and returned to the house.

When he went looking for Nancy he found her in their bedroom; she was lying on the bed, her head turned towards the wall, a crumpled handkerchief in her hand. When the bed moved as Frank sat beside her, she lifted her arms up and Frank held her, rocking her back and forth as she cried.

Frank always thought that the huge task of battling Nancy's cancer became a business. The whole thing was a business. There were consultations with specialists, surgeons, radiographers. Frank and Nancy held meetings with Nina and Chris, the four of them sitting over a table. Nancy's illness had temporarily reunited Chris and Nina, Nina coming from her house, Chris from his flat, to talk over how they'd cope, how they'd help Nancy, help her recover. Chris bought books on combating cancer, he pored over his computer screen, searching the web for cures, for pain relief, for any help he could find. Frank welcomed the help that was offered to Nancy and, for her sake, he was civil to Nina. He tolerated the fact that she made endless cups of tea in his kitchen bringing with her boxes of herbal and fruit tea. He watched her climb up and down stairs to collect something for Nancy; he'd listen behind the bedroom door when Nina sat with Nancy, he could hear their soft giggles, smell the oils Nina used to soothe Nancy's skin. He hated the fact that she was doing those things for Nancy, helping her, leaving him outside the special friendship they had.

The cancer spread, like a savage weed it grew, choking the life out of Nancy. Frank made an appointment to see her specialist, going on his own. He sat opposite the consultant, noting again the number of framed certificates on the wall, the array of letters after the surgeon's name. Frank wore his best suit, a freshly ironed shirt and his face was raw from a brutal shave when he begged the surgeon to 'do something, there must be something you can do'. He practised what he wanted to say in the car driving to the appointment, speaking the words aloud, going over them again and again, his fingers flexing on the steering wheel. He sat on the other side of the polished desk, telling the sympathetic consultant what a good woman Nancy was, what she meant to him, what she meant to her son. Frank said that he knew the hospital was doing all it could, 'But you're a professional man, an educated man, you'll find a way, I know you will.'

The consultant's name was Atkins, Frederick Atkins and he'd gazed at Frank sitting nervously on the edge of his seat.

'Mr Jones, we're doing all we can, we're trying everything in our power, using all our skills. I know your wife is a good woman, but I'm afraid, right now, all we can do is to make her comfortable, reduce her pain.'

When Frank left Mr Atkins's office, he walked slowly, steadily to the car, then he sat in the car park watching as people walked to and from the doors of the hospital. He saw a number of ambulances stop, he saw how gentle the paramedics were with their patients; he saw people in wheelchairs, children in pushchairs and he saw delivery vans bringing supplies. He sat in his car, tears running unchecked down his cheeks.

Frank moved his head up to touch the front of his shirt, it still felt damp. 'Keep still, Mr Jones, keep your arms by your sides, don't move.'

'Got to change my shirt.'

'No, no, keep still, Frank. It's all over, the operation went very well. Lie still, we'll take you back to the ward soon.'

Ward? What operation? What's she talking about, she must mean Nancy.

'Nancy? Are you all right, love?'

'Sshh, lie still, take a few deep breaths, that's it, that's better.'

Frank heard a rattling noise and he opened his eyes. The sides of his bed were being let down and something was squeezing his arm, it hurt. 'Welcome back, Frank. How are you feeling?'

Frank stared at the nurse who was removing a blood

pressure cuff from his right arm. His throat felt sore and his mouth was very dry.

'Don't know what I feel, need a drink, mouth's dry.' His lips were sticking together.

'We'll see how you get on with a sip of water.'

Frank slowly raised his head, a thin man dressed in a tracksuit raised a hand in greeting as he caught Frank's eye. 'All right, mate? How are you feeling?'

Frank grunted, then lowered his head. The butterflies began moving as the curtain shook around the bed. A dark haired nurse bent low at his side, 'Just checking your urine, Mr Jones.'

Frank had no idea what she was talking about; he felt a slight tugging and he looked at the butterflies. *Bloody stupid things to have in a men's ward. What are we, children?*

He felt very tired.

JONATHAN

I had to go back to them and I knew when I walked towards them that they'd had words. Had words. What a stupid expression. Sounds as if the words were something you could buy or could order for a meal. *I've had words for tea.* In my parents' case it means that one says one word then the other hurls it right back as if the words were the wrong size, they didn't fit.

They'd decided something, that was obvious. Mum was being cheerful and bright and Dad had a sort of stiff smile on his face.

'Jon? Are you OK?' Mum put her hand up to touch my head but I jerked away. She ignored that. 'Listen, how about if we take photos at St Omer, I've looked through my guide books again and there are a lot of war graves around there.'

I stared at the ground. Mum's feet were only a few inches away from mine. She didn't have any shoes on and my feet in my old trainers looked huge compared to hers.

'Jon? How about it, your dad says we have time.'

I still couldn't say anything but I looked towards Dad. He was staring at me and he'd put the umbrella down. I hadn't noticed but it had stopped raining.

Mum touched me again, 'Come on, Jon, give me a break, please?'

I felt mean then because she looked really tired, so I tried to smile. I didn't feel like it but she did look tired. She had

251

these tiny lines around her eyes, I never think of my mum getting older, she's my mum, she's always looked the same. But, even before Daniel left us, she had those tiny lines. I hadn't noticed them the whole time we were on holiday but they were back again. They made me feel funny, I didn't want them to be there. It felt as if they'd wandered over to her face, as if they were trespassing, they had no right to be there. I couldn't say that to Mum, she'd think I was barking.

I mumbled something about being hungry, 'Could we have something to eat, too?'

She gave me a quick smile, 'Yeah, we can do that. Not sure about how much time we've got left but we should have something. Our last meal in France.'

I nodded, there didn't seem to be anything else to say and we walked over to the cars. Dad was sitting astride a bench; there was a red mark by his right eyebrow, must have been where the umbrella poked him. He saw me looking at it and he put his hand up to rub it.

Mum started to change Sebastian's nappy and, when he started to yell she told Dad that she and I wanted something to eat. Sebastian was fighting with Mum, he was trying hard to stand up; each time Mum moved to get a fresh nappy, he struggled with her, shouting at the top of his voice the whole time.

'Give me a hand please, Jon.' Mum was holding Sebastian down with both hands. She turned her head towards me. Before I could do anything, Dad had got up from the bench and he knelt down, one hand holding Sebastian still, the other hand tickling him. Sebastian didn't laugh but I wanted to. Dad was making all these stupid faces, talking in a silly voice and Sebastian's eyes were getting bigger and bigger. But he didn't laugh, not once. Mum didn't say anything, she just got on with changing Sebastian's nappy.

Dad looked up at me, 'See, Jon, he's not like you, you loved being tickled. Couldn't get enough of it, you were always asking me to tickle you.'

Yeah, right.

He pushed his face right down until his nose was almost

touching Sebastian's. Sebastian hit him. It must have hurt too because when he lifted his head up I could see another red mark, this time over the left eye. He had a matching pair. Sebastian laughed then. Dad didn't but I could see Mum's face, she was biting her lip and trying hard not to laugh. Dad didn't say another word, he held both Sebastian's arms down while Mum changed him. Sebastian was watching me, I grinned at him.

We made the earlier ferry. Dad was pleased. We had just enough time for a stop at the war memorials. I took pictures and I also got some postcards for Grandad. It was all a bit rushed but at least I took them. And we managed to find somewhere to eat. That was OK too. Mum and Dad were still being polite to each other and to me. Dad said that I could have anything I wanted from the menu. So I ordered mussels, Mum did too. 'Don't suppose we'll be eating these for some time,' she said.

I behaved, I really did. We talked about Grandad, how we hoped he'd be OK, what we could do to help and then Mum said, 'Should he move in with us? With Jon and me and Sebastian?' I looked at her face when she said that and she looked right at me. 'He could stay, we could put a bed in the front room. I'm home most of the time, it might work.'

Dad leant forward and touched Mum's hand, just a tiny touch. She let it stay there for a second before she pulled her hand away.

'Well, it's a lovely thought, Nina, it really is. But a house with a baby, he'll need lots of quiet, I expect. He'd get that at my flat but I couldn't take the time off work and I'm sure that a flat on the fourth floor wouldn't be at all suitable. But either way, we're ahead of ourselves somewhat. We don't know what condition he'll be in, what the operation will have done for him. We'll have to keep these things up in the air for the moment.'

'I can look after Grandad, I can take time off school. I can get homework and stuff sent to me.' Both Mum and Dad shook their heads when I said that.

'No, Jon, we can't have that and your grandad wouldn't want it either.' Dad shook his head. 'It's best that we don't jump the gun here either. We'll know more when we get to the hospital. Each time I've phoned they say he's doing fine, the operation went well and he's recovering.'

After the meal we drove to Calais: me and Dad in the Saab and Mum tucking in behind us in the Clio. Dad seemed better after we'd eaten, or perhaps it was me. Anyway we didn't have any more of the conversations about what life was like for him: why he thought the rest of the world was awful and he was OK. Fine by me.

Calais was just as boring on the return trip as it was coming in and as we were driving the car up the ramps into the ferry, Dad muttering something about the exhaust system, suddenly I felt different. The minute Dad and I got out of the car waiting for Mum to park behind us, I just knew, that's it, holiday over. Even above the noise of the engines, I could hear British voices. All around us, kids yelling for their parents, parents yelling for their kids, I swear everyone on that ferry spoke English. We'd left the French behind. I started to say something to Dad then I thought I'd better keep quiet just in case he started banging on about what rotten parents most people were and why some kids show their belly buttons. I really couldn't face hearing all that again.

We scrambled up the stairs, Mum carried Sebastian who was fast asleep. Dad and I found a table and we all sat down. It had been a rush getting this ferry, there were an awful lot of people on board. Kids were jostling and arguing near the slot machines; there was a queue forming by the Duty Free shop then Dad went off to see if he could find a newspaper, 'one that's only a day old'.

Mum sat back in her chair, tucking Sebastian's head under her chin. She sighed and closed her eyes. She didn't say anything, she just sat there. For a second I thought she'd fallen asleep, she was so still.

Not sure if this makes sense but just then, looking at her with her eyes closed, with her hair sort of *crackling* around her face, I knew everything would be all right. Whatever state Grandad was in, whatever we had to do to cope with getting him better, Mum would do it. She'd got us to France, we'd had a brilliant time, her rule of one day for her, one day for me, worked and I just knew that Mum would always be able to cope. I wanted to tell her that, to let her know that I thought she was great, she was the best mum but then it seemed like a naff thing to do, not enough of a reason to disturb her, so I didn't. I just sat there, listening to the noise around us and watching the other people on the ferry. That's when I knew Grandma was around. She'd smoothed things, 'ironing out the creases' she used to call it.

Dad came back with a load of papers under his arm and a tray of coffee. He nudged me just before the papers fell onto Mum's lap. She opened her eyes, Sebastian did too and he started to whine. Dad suddenly got all domestic and he began fussing about with the tray, putting a cup of coffee in front of Mum. Sebastian wanted something to drink and he made a grab for the cup.

Dad frowned, 'Jon, take Sebastian for a walk or something. Give your mother a break, son, so she can read the papers in peace.' He shoved his hand in his pocket and brought out a handful of change. 'Here, buy some Coke or fruit juice or whatever you think Sebastian needs and get something for you too, OK?'

I opened my mouth to say something but I saw Mum shaking her head at me.

Dad pushed the money at me, 'Leave your mother alone, Jon. She needs some peace and quiet, a few minutes to catch up with the news, that's all.'

'Go on, Jon, just for a little while.' Mum smiled at me.

I took all the money Dad had in his hand, I took the lot: pound coins, 50 pence pieces, everything. I grabbed hold of Sebastian, he was wriggling about all over the place and the minute I held him, he put his hand on my face.

'See, he'd rather be with you. Go on, Jon, be a good lad. Just give us half an hour, please?' Dad had already settled back with the paper. For one second I wanted to push my fist through it, tear a great hole in the front page. But I didn't. I wrapped one arm around Sebastian and went off to get some Cokes or something. I'd only gone a few steps when I looked back at Mum and Dad. Both of them had their legs crossed, newspapers held high. All that crap Dad had said about not wanting to miss out on childhood, spending time with the kids, he's just the same as everyone else. Getting rid of us when it suited him. I hoisted Sebastian higher on my hip and when he yelled I told him to shut up.

When I got back to the table Dad had gone to the Duty Free shop and when the loudspeakers began talking about *foot passengers* and *those with cars* he rushed back to our table with his hands full of carrier bags. He'd bought whisky for Grandad, some gin for himself he said and then he shoved one bag at Mum and one into my hands.

'Chris, what's this?' Mum pushed her hand into the bag, 'Chanel 19, thank you. It's my favourite, that's very kind of you.'

I looked inside the bag he'd given me: there were some CDs and a baseball cap with *P & O Ferry* written on the peak. 'Thanks, Dad, the CDs look great.' They weren't, Britney Spears and Miss Dynamite. Crap, but I thought I'd be able to swap them at school.

He had one more bag, there were stuffed toys inside. I could see a pair of bright orange ears sticking out and he gave that bag to Mum. 'This one's for Sebastian. I'm sure he's got all the toys he needs but these looked about right for him.'

Mum looked at Dad for a second as if she wanted to say something to him but all she said quietly was, 'Thank you, I'm sure he'll love them.'

Everyone around us was moving to the stairs leading to the cars. Seemed to me that there were millions of people, all clutching bottles of duty-free booze and armfuls of newspapers and assorted bags. For a second I remembered what I was feeling when I was with Gareth. That feeling of being different and of wanting to be the same as everyone else. Well, right now, we looked the same as everyone else: Mum and Dad and two kids.

I wondered if Dad had remembered the rambling conversation he'd had with me about him being on the outside, not being part of anything any more. Well he wasn't on the outside now. He was doing his good shepherd bit, walking behind Mum, picking up the various bags and telling me to keep close and keep an eye on Sebastian. 'We don't want to lose either of you in this crush.' Why does he care all of a sudden?

Funny thing though, when we got to the cars, both Dad and I got Sebastian and Mum sorted out in the Clio. Dad strapped Sebastian in, telling Mum that the 'design on these car seats hasn't changed much'. Then, without thinking about it, I got into the Saab with Dad. Dad turned the engine on and he adjusted the rear-view mirror. I could see him looking at Mum.

'Well, that's your holiday over son, back to reality. Wonder how your grandad's getting on? I'm going to try and see him tonight, that is if we're not too late getting back. Depends on the roads, traffic, that sort of thing.' He kept his eyes on the mirror, watching Mum.

'Can I come with you, if you get into the hospital to see Grandad? Dad, can I?'

Dad's eyes remained fixed on the mirror. 'Yes, course you can; let's see what time we get home. The hospital might not want to let us in if it's too late.'

Suddenly he opened the car door and walked back towards Mum. I turned, I could see him bending down; I saw Mum slide her window down then Dad moved forward to say something. Mum looked towards me, then I saw her nodding.

Just then the big ferry doors opened and, as if on some signal, all the drivers began to rev up their engines. The noise was deafening, someone was trying to make an announcement over the loudspeaker but it was useless. No one could have heard a thing. Dad flung himself back into the car. 'Well, that's OK, you can come with me to the hospital. Your mum says she'll have to go straight home, she'll need to get Sebastian to bed straight away but you can stay with me after

257

we've been to the hospital. Is that all right with you?'

'Yeah, OK.'

I must have fallen asleep in the car, I don't remember much about the journey back at all. It seemed to me as if we'd only just got in the car after leaving the ferry when Dad was prodding me. 'We're here, Jon, at the hospital. Wait in the car until I find out if we can go in.'

'No, I want to come with you. I'll find the ward with you.' I still felt half-asleep but I undid my seat-belt. Dad had parked the car at the big car park at the back of the hospital. I hadn't been anywhere near the place since Grandma died and it seemed really weird to be back again only this time for Grandad.

Just before Dad switched the engine off, I looked at the clock on the dashboard, it was 10.55. 'Will they let us in? It's almost 11 o'clock.'

Dad shrugged, 'Don't know but we'll try. They know we've been away, actually it might help that you're here with me.' He raised an eyebrow, 'Who knows?'

There were only about ten other cars in the carpark. It must have been raining, they were all shiny wet under the big lights that illuminated every corner. We walked towards the hospital entrance without speaking and, as some bloke walked through the double doors, he held one open for us and we went inside.

It was so quiet, there wasn't a sound anywhere, only a buzzing coming from the fluorescent tubes in the high ceilings. There was no one in sight and certainly no one near the Reception desk. Dad pointed to a sigh that said *Orthopaedic Ward* and he tugged at my sleeve. Somehow the silence had affected us both. I didn't want to speak, I thought I'd get into trouble for disturbing someone. Dad must have felt the same way too. We began walking towards the ward.

We must have walked miles and miles. We didn't see a soul, not one person. It didn't seem right either. We could have been anyone, we might have been burglars or murderers. There were CCTV cameras all around but even I could see dust and cobwebs, like a grey blanket, behind each one.

Dad looked really serious as we walked. I wondered if he was remembering the times we'd walked through this hospital when Grandma was here. He must have been thinking of her, I know I was.

We passed other wards, they all had their doors closed. I could see nurses through the glass panels in the doors; one or two looked up as we walked by but no one came out no one stopped us to ask what we were doing.

Then we found the ward: *Male Orthopaedic Ward* and Dad put his hand on my arm, 'Just wait here a moment, Jon. I need to find out if it's OK to go in to see your grandad.'

He pushed open the swing doors and then I watched him walk over to a nurse. The nurse pointed to something then Dad looked over towards a bed at the end of the ward. I stood on tip-toe, squinting through the glass panel. It must have been Grandad they were looking at. All I could make out was a mound under the bedclothes.

Then Dad came out, 'Come on, they say we can see him for a minute. He's sleeping but the nurse said that he's been dozing on and off all day. I promised we wouldn't be long, only a minute or so, she said he's very tired.'

We walked towards the end bed. There weren't that many lights on. One was on the desk where the nurse was sitting and another one in the middle of the ward; some bloke was sitting up in bed reading. There was also one over Grandad's bed.

There was hardly any noise coming from the other patients. My trainers were making a squeaking noise and the nurse looked up as I walked near her. 'Sorry,' I whispered and she gave me a half-smile.

As we got closer to Grandad's bed, one of the other men in the ward farted and I snorted. The whole thing, being in the hospital, visiting Grandad so late at night was making me nervous but Dad gave me a look, a *keep quiet* sort of look. 'Sorry,' I said again then we both stopped as we got to Grandad's bed. The sheets were pulled up almost to his chin and his face looked so different. I wanted to say to Dad that this old man couldn't possibly be Grandad this was a *really* old man. We'd only been away a few weeks; he looked as if we'd been away for years and he'd grown very old while we'd been away.

There were tubes and drips and bits of metal all over him. I kept looking at his face, he was so white. It looked as if the tubes and drips and things were taking something out of him, draining his blood, his life away. He didn't look like my grandad any more.

Dad moved over to the other side of the bed and he picked up Grandad's hand; I could see tears in Dad's eyes. I'd only ever seen him cry once before, when Grandma died. It frightened me, seeing his tears.

He sniffed, a really loud sniff then he perched on the edge of the bed, still holding Grandad's hand. 'Oh, Dad, I'm so sorry this has happened and I'm really sorry I was away. But we're all back now and everything will be all right. I promise you. We're all going to look after you. You've got my word on that. See, Jon's here too. Everything will be OK now.'

Dad was stroking Grandad's hand and he kept on saying, 'Everything will be OK, you'll see, everything will be fine now.' I didn't know what to do. I was scared to move in case I knocked something, pulled one of those tubes out of Grandad.

'Talk to your grandad, Jon. Let him hear your voice. He'll hear you, I'm sure of it.'

'But I don't know what to say and anyway he can't hear me.' I thought Dad had been watching too many of those hospital programmes on TV.

'Tell him anything, tell him about Franc.'

I coughed, trying to think of something but I couldn't, I just couldn't think of a single word to say.

'What, you went all the way to France and you've got nothing to say to me?'

It was Grandad! He opened one eye, the one nearest to me and he was trying to smile. His voice was really croaky and soft and I had to bend down really close so I could hear him. 'Hello, lad.'

I was so pleased that he'd spoken, I tried to give him a hug. He sort of moaned and then I was so scared that I'd hurt him I shot straight back up again.

Dad was blowing his nose, a really disgusting noise that must have woken most of the patients up. 'Dad, how are you feeling? Did we wake you? Are you in any pain? What have the doctors told you?'

Grandad opened both eyes and looked at Dad. 'Which one of those would you like me to answer first?'

It seemed to me that Dad was trying to rip his handkerchief in two, he was pulling and tugging at it so much. 'Sorry, sorry, I've been worried, we *all* have. We've driven all the way from France today.'

'Is that right?' Grandad was looking at me as he spoke and I could have sworn that he winked at me, 'All the way from France, eh?'

I nodded at him, the voice sounded like Grandad's voice but I couldn't get used to hearing his voice coming from such an old face. His neck and face were just a total mass of deep lines. They hadn't been there before, where had they come from?

The nurse came up to Dad and whispered something to him. Dad nodded the whole time she was speaking. 'Yes, sure, we'll be off now,' he said to her.

'But we've only just got here,' I blurted out, looking at Grandad.

He closed his eyes and gave a really deep sigh. 'I know, lad, but I'm very tired and it is late.'

The nurse was still standing there, like a sentry, keeping watch over her patient. 'Come on, please,' she said.

I put my hand out to touch Grandad's arm. 'I'll be in tomorrow I promise and I'll tell you all about France, about Disneyland, about the food, everything. I promise.'

I think he heard me, I hope so. It was difficult to tell really because he had closed his eyes again. Dad leant over and kissed Grandad's forehead. I'd never seen him do that before. 'Good night,' he whispered. 'See you tomorrow.'

We both tiptoed out of the ward. I looked towards the bed where the bloke had farted but he was fast asleep. We mouthed *thank you* to the nurse and went out of the ward and back into that deserted corridor.

Back in the car, Dad was talking. I don't think he wanted me to say anything, he just talked about what he had to do in his office; when he could come back into the hospital. 'The site meeting isn't until 2.30. I could come first thing in the morning. I'll need to check the house, bet that's the first thing the old man will ask me about. Check the post, check the locks, oh, and the garden.'

'Can I come with you, when you go to Grandad's house? Can I come?'

I think Dad had forgotten I was sitting next to him. 'What? Oh, yes I suppose so. Won't your mum want some help, you know, sorting stuff out after the holiday?'

'Well, yes, but she'll understand if I spend some time with Grandad, she'll know that's important. She'll want me to help him.'

Dad drummed his fingers on the steering wheel. 'Oh, OK if it's all right with your mum, you can come in with me in the morning. I'll drop you back home before I go on to the site meeting.'

I must have dozed off because when I looked again we'd pulled up outside Dad's flat. His flat is OK but to get to the front door you've got to climb up a metal staircase on the outside of the building. He kept telling me to be quiet and I was trying very hard not to let the suitcases bang on the sides of the staircase. Dad said 'Sshh,' all the time and I kept whispering that I was being quiet. It seemed like we were climbing up to the moon, I thought we'd never get there.

At last we made it, we were both breathing really hard when we got to the front door. There was a lot of mail lying on Dad's door mat and he kicked it to one side as we struggled through with the suitcases.

I've got my own room in Dad's flat, shelves, wardrobe and everything. Dad built the bed himself. When he first showed me what he'd done, how he'd built a bunk-bed type of thing with a desk where the bottom bunk should be, I felt mean and upset at the same time. Difficult to explain but I felt mean because it was much better than the bed I've got at home with Mum, and upset because I had to leave it here with Dad.

There's always something a bit weird about coming in to my room when I'm with Dad. Nothing ever gets moved around or messed up. Dad keeps everything the same each time I stay with him. Weeks sometimes go by when I don't stay overnight but each time the room looks as if I've just stepped outside to get something, a book or something to eat. It's always the same, like the room is waiting for me to come back in.

Dad said how tired he was, 'I'm really bushed, Jon. You know where everything is, not sure if there's anything in the fridge worth drinking ...'

I told him I didn't want anything and went into my room. I tugged my T-shirt and shorts off and went up the ladder to my bed. Dad yelled goodnight from his room. I closed my eyes. A car went past. I could hear the sound of its diesel engine. Dad always moans about the taxis up and down his road; he says the people around him go out more than he does. Taxis crawl up and down the road, looking for numbers on the flats. 'They never ring my doorbell,' he says. The sound of the engine grew fainter and fainter until I couldn't hear it any more.

FRANK

The night nurse bent over, her head at Frank's waist as she tugged at the tube by the side of his bed.

'What are you doing down there, saying your prayers?'

She gave a practised laugh. 'Just checking your urine is flowing properly, that's all.'

From the corner of his eye, Frank saw a dark blue plastic clip in her hair, keeping the nursing cap in place. He wanted her to stop, to stand upright, it wasn't right that she was bent down like that, checking on his pee. He squirmed, it wasn't decent. His mouth was so dry he couldn't even imagine forming any words to tell her to stop.

She stood up and looked at him. 'Do you think we can try you with a sip of water?'

She gently supported his head and Frank took a few sips of tepid water. His tongue pushed the water into every crevice and then ran around his mouth. 'Thank you, what time is it?'

'About 4 o'clock. Are you in any pain?'

'No, I'm all right, thank you.'

'Don't be brave, Mr Jones. We can control your pain but we can only do that if you tell us you'd like some help. Now, are you sure?'

'No, love, thank you, I'm fine. Just sleepy, that's all. Stupid really, I've done nothing but lie here all the time.' His eyes felt heavy again. The nurse touched his arm. 'We don't want you to do anything but lie still, get some rest.' She wrote

264

something on his chart then moved away.

Frank settled back into the pillows. The rest of the ward was sleeping, just the occasional cough was all he could hear. He thought of Chris and Jonathan, seeing their faces, seeing the worry and distress in Chris's eye.

Never could hide his feelings, just like his mother, like reading a book. He grunted softly. *Fancy them coming all the way from France. No need for them to have done that. Not going to die, just had an accident, could have happened to anyone.*

There was a call button on the bedclothes, Frank could feel its round shape under his right hand. 'Call if you need anything,' that's what the nurse had said when Frank returned from the operating theatre. That's what he'd said to Nancy when she came out of hospital, the last time.

'We can control her pain, district nurses will help with that. There's no need for the pain to become unbearable, it can be controlled.' That's what they all told him. Dr Griffiths, Mr Atkins, they kept on talking about *controlling* the pain. As if it was a beast that needed caging, taming. 'Don't allow it to get out of control, Frank, we can increase the dosage, there's no need for Nancy to suffer …'

'Call me, let me know if you need anything, anything at all. I won't be far away.' He'd sat on the edge of their bed, unwilling to leave her side. During all the weeks he'd nursed her at home, he'd felt an invisible cord tugging at him, keeping him close to her. For a few weeks he slept in the same bed, watching as she slept, then, as her pain grew, and she couldn't tolerate anything near her skin, Frank moved into Chris's old room. He'd lie still, his hands crossed over his chest, listening until her breathing slowed right down, easing into a measured rhythm and only then could he sleep.

'Take a break, Frank. I'll take over,' Nina urged him. 'Just get some fresh air, go for a walk, it'll do you good.'

He did go out a few times but each time he walked away from the house, he felt uneasy, uncomfortable as if the coat he was wearing was too heavy. Just a short walk to the newsagents made Frank breathless with guilt, anxiety and the dreadful fear that Nancy would ask for him or even that she'd die and he wouldn't be there.

He'd rush back, not even bothering to take his coat off as he climbed the stairs to their bedroom and then he'd hover outside the door, listening, holding his breath until he heard Nancy's voice.

He began to hate hearing Nina's soft tones behind the door as she sat with Nancy, reading to her or simply telling her something that she'd done or Jonathan had said.

Frank was jealous of the gifts that Nina brought: simple, fresh gifts to comfort Nancy. 'Look, Frank, Nina brought me this bottle of lavender water. She brought these freesias, don't they smell wonderful? Look at the nightdress Nina brought, such a delicate shade of blue.'

Away from Nancy his manner had been abrupt, rude towards Nina. 'You're tiring her, all this talk, all this reading. She needs her rest, she's too polite to say so but you're making her very tired.'

Nina had flinched, 'I don't mean to, Frank. I only want to help her, to see if there's anything I can do to make her feel better.'

'Better! How will bottles of cheap cologne and nightdresses do that?'

He'd stand in the corner of the kitchen watching as Nina laid a tray of tea. Sometimes, in the centre, Nina put a single rose in a tiny vase and then he'd spit the words out. 'You're doing this for yourself, making yourself feel better so you can tell all and sundry what a good person you are. Well I'm not fooled, your performance doesn't work on me.'

Nina moved past him carrying the tray in her outstretched arms. 'I'm sorry you feel that way, Frank. Nancy means an awful lot to me. I simply want to help her.'

He'd followed her to the stairs and, in a low voice, told her that she must never, ever touch Nancy's medication. 'You can waste your time with fancy cups of tea and nightdresses if it makes you feel better but you're not touching her pills. I'm the only one to touch them, do you understand?'

Nina nodded and she climbed the stairs to sit with Nancy.

Frank had control of the morphine, he'd promised the doctors that he'd keep Nancy's pain under control so it wouldn't get out of hand, it wouldn't overwhelm her. They trusted him, Nancy trusted him. But the pain had got out of control, it had been impossible to tame.

Chris moved in and out of the house, coming in at odd hours when he had a few hours between jobs, between meetings. Frank noticed as, each time he went upstairs, Chris took a deep breath before running up the stairs. 'She's looking better don't you think, Dad? Her colour's much improved and she's talking of putting more honeysuckle in next summer.' Sitting together in the kitchen, Frank wanted to catch hold of Chris's words, feel them in his hands, to make them come true.

He'd woken up in the early hours of a September morning not sure at first what had disturbed his sleep. A cat was calling, its cry grating and harsh. Frank listened for a while, no more cries, the cat must have left the garden. Everything was quiet. As he stretched, pushing his feet to the bottom of Chris's old single bed, Frank realised he could hear nothing from Nancy. He lay still, his breathing was shallow. He eased himself out of the narrow bed. The door to their bedroom was ajar and he stood on the landing his eyes straining in the half light, his heart pounding. When he saw Nancy, Frank swallowed and held his breath. Nancy was lying on her back, arms flat to her sides, her head turned towards the door as if she was waiting for him.

Frank opened his eyes to see Nina standing by the side of his bed. She held Sebastian, balancing him on her hip and she held a bunch of dahlias in the other hand.

'What are you doing here?' He hadn't meant to say that, to be so rude, but he felt thoroughly bewildered. For a second he'd forgotten he was in hospital, he'd forgotten that he'd had a fall, an operation and seeing Nina confused him.

'I've come to see you, Frank, see how you are and if you need anything.' She smiled at him, 'They tell me that the operation went well.'

'Why did they tell you that? Not even told me yet.'

Frank watched as the expression on Nina's face changed. As if she'd been standing under a shower, the hesitant smile that had lifted up the corners of her mouth disappeared and the lights in her eyes drained away. She hoisted Sebastian up and she stepped back from Frank's bed. 'I asked the nurse, she said that you'd had a comfortable night and that the surgeon will be in later to see you.' She lowered her eyes, her lips grazing Sebastian's head.

'Hmm, the night wasn't that comfortable, people won't leave you alone. I'd rather be back home, in my own bed.'

'I'm sure you would, but it's better to be here, let the professionals care for you until you're feeling much better.' Nina placed the dahlias on the bedside unit. 'I thought you'd like these, Frank. You always said you liked dahlias.'

'It's too hot in here, petals will drop, make a right mess. These nurses have enough to do without clearing up …' He saw an ugly blotch, like a stain from spilled red wine creep across Nina's neck.

'Oh, yes, I didn't think..' Her hand moved towards the flowers.

'Leave them there,' Frank sighed.

Nina pulled her hand back quickly as if the petals had given her an electric shock and she perched on the edge of the dull green vinyl chair that was pushed up close to Frank's bed. She held Sebastian firmly on her lap. He was quiet and very still, his eyes fixed on Frank.

'So, how did the accident…?'

'The holiday, what was that like…?'

'Sorry, sorry, Frank, you go first.' Nina's arms were clasped around Sebastian as if she was shielding behind him.

'Well, I just wanted to ask about the holiday, you know, was it all right? Did you have a good time? Didn't get a chance to ask Jonathan last night, lad was only here for a minute. Didn't get to ask anything, nothing at all.'

A smile crept back onto Nina's face, the lines around her eyes crinkled as she answered him. 'Oh, it was wonderful. Just the best holiday we could have wished for. We saw some wonderful places, the weather was perfect, everyone we met was friendly and kind. Jonathan made new friends and well,' she shrugged, eyes twinkling as she looked at Frank. 'It was perfect, Frank, a really good holiday.'

'Good, that's good. I'm glad you enjoyed yourselves, you and the lad. That's good.'

'We all had a superb time. Jonathan is desperate to go back, he really loved France.' Nina held Frank's gaze for a second. 'He took lots of photos of all sorts of places. He kept saying that he was taking them for you.'

Frank grunted softly, he nodded. They sat in silence for a while then Nina put one hand on the bedclothes. 'What happened, Frank? How did you fall? How bad was it?'

He cleared his throat. 'A lot of fuss, if you ask me. I tripped, that's all. Could have happened to anyone. Tripped over that rug, the one by the bed. Could have happened to anybody.'

Nina nodded, 'Yes I'm sure you're right. Was it the pale green rug?'

Frank looked away before nodding. 'They told me I broke my hip. Operation was to mend it. I'll soon be up and about. Back to normal.'

Nina swallowed, a nervous tic caused the skin around her left eye to flicker 'You'll need some help, Frank. These things take time to heal. We'll have to listen to what the doctor says, the nurse mentioned something about recuperation and not getting up the stairs for a while.' She swallowed again. 'Chris and I wondered about putting a bed downstairs for you, not in your house, Frank, in mine. You might want to consider moving in with me, me and Jonathan, for a while.'

As Frank's mouth opened to respond, Nina became aware of someone standing behind her. She heard a low cough and, turning, she saw a man holding an X-ray. 'Hello?' he smiled questioningly at her.

Still holding Sebastian, Nina stood, one arm outstretched.

'Hello, I'm Nina Jones, Frank's daughter-in-law.'

'*Ex*-daughter-in- law,' Frank muttered.

Both Nina and Mr Armstrong ignored Frank's rudeness.

269

Mr Armstrong walked to the foot of Frank's bed. He held the X-ray plate up to the light, his stubby forefinger again jabbing at the image of Frank's hip.

'See what we've managed to do, Frank?'

There it was again, that obscene image, his legs apart, outstretched, his bones. Nina's eyes remained fixed on the X-ray.

'Yes, yes, you can put it down now.' Frank wanted to snatch the image away. He hated the fact that Nina had seen it, seen his hips, his legs. She might even have seen his private parts, everything else was on display. Nina stepped closer to Mr Armstrong, her eyes on the X-ray. Sebastian held his hands out, his fingers flailing.

Christ Almighty, the whole bloody world and his wife want to look.

'Shouldn't you be going now? Won't that baby of yours want a sleep or a feed or something?' Frank barked at Nina, and again she ignored his rudeness.

'Can you show us what you've done, Mr Armstrong?' She smiled at him.

'Yes of course.' He glanced at Frank. 'Expect you'll want to know too, Frank.'

'Course I do, my bones, aren't they?'

'Quite.' Mr Armstrong put the X-ray on the bed and folded his arms. 'First of all we dislocated the hip joint, that's to say the ball of the thigh bone is slipped out from the socket of the pelvis. The natural ball end of the bone is removed. We then remove a thin layer of bone. Then the artificial socket is inserted. We used bone cement in your case, Frank.'

'Cement? What inside me?'

Mr Armstrong smiled, 'Yes, not your garden cement, this is like a type of grout. We use this to fix a special plastic socket into the bone of the pelvis. We've also replaced the worn femoral head.' His finger moved towards the X-ray, 'And then the upper end of the thigh bone is shaped to conform to the stem of the artificial ball.'

Dear God, I'm held together with cement.

'And it was successful, the operation went well?' Nina's

head swung from Mr Armstrong back to Frank.

The surgeon nodded, 'It went very well, that's why we take a second set of X-rays immediately after the surgery. A sort of before and after, if you like. Yes, I'm very pleased.'

'When can I go home?' *Pair of them talking as if I wasn't here.*

Mr Armstrong looked towards Frank, a smile playing around his mouth. 'Well, not just yet, Frank. I told you, the physios will take a look at you. We have to discuss the care you'll need at home and you should be considering ways to adapt your house ...'

'That's the first time you mentioned that, about adapting my house ...'

Mr Armstrong glanced at Nina. 'Nothing drastic, Frank, just a few things to make your life easier. The physios will talk to you about, oh, I don't know, grab handles in the bathroom or a second banister. It might not be necessary, let's see how you get on, shall we?' He glanced at his watch. 'I'll be back tomorrow, Frank. Nice meeting you, Mrs Jones.'

In silence Frank and Nina watched as Mr Armstrong walked the length of the ward before disappearing through the swing doors.

Nina put Sebastian down; he immediately grabbed hold of the catheter tube and yanked hard.

'Ow, little tyke, stop that!'

Nina brought out a small packet of biscuits and, after offering one to Sebastian, she smiled at Frank. 'Well, that's good news isn't it? What a nice man, I expect you feel you can trust him, don't you, Frank?'

Frank watched Sebastian eat the biscuit, crumbs scattering on the floor.

'Yes, I suppose so. He's a doctor isn't he? If he wasn't any good he wouldn't be doing operations, would he?'

Nina bent down, brushing up the scattered biscuit crumbs. Her head was at exactly the same height as that of the nurse earlier on.

That's it, get a good look at my bloody pee.

She straightened up. 'I'm glad that you're feeling OK,

Frank. We've all been very worried about you; we came home early, we really were that bothered.'

'No need for that, you shouldn't have done that on my account.'

She smiled at him. 'Only a couple more days left and none of us would have enjoyed the holiday knowing you were in hospital.' She glanced around the ward, 'I'll get a vase from somewhere and then I'll be heading off. I don't want to tire you, just needed to see that you were OK.'

Sebastian was pushing the curtains back and forth, his small fingers making stabbing movements towards the butterflies. Nina hesitated for a second then she walked off quickly.

Frank watched the toddler pushing at the curtain fabric; the clumsy boots on the legs of the butterflies jerked up and down, like puppets answering the pull on their strings.

'Nice little chap, your grandson, is he?' The patient in the bed opposite Frank called out.

At first Frank shook his head, then he cleared his throat. 'Yes, that's right.'

'Couldn't leave either of my grandkids playing like that, they'd wreck the place.'

Nina came back into the ward, both hands holding a chipped pottery vase. She walked steadily towards Frank, her fingers glistened with water.

Frank watched in silence as she arranged the gaudy dahlias, snapping off leaves and ruffling the petals with her hands. She placed the vase on the locker. 'There, looks more cheerful for you.'

She bent down to pick Sebastian up but his hands were clutching at folds of the curtain material. 'Come on, little man, let go.' She prised his hands away and planted a kiss on his nose.

'Would you like me to bring in anything for you, Frank? Some books, magazines perhaps?'

'No, I won't be here long enough to read books but thank you for the flowers, you meant well.' He gave her a brief smile.

For a second Nina hesitated as if she wanted to say something more but instead she chewed at her lip. 'OK, we'll be off then. If you think of anything, just get someone to ring me. Bye, Frank.' She jiggled Sebastian around until he was on her hip and then she walked back down the ward. Frank and the man opposite watched her go.

'Nice,' the man said. Frank nodded. He wished he'd asked Nina to bring him some fruit, he'd have enjoyed a crisp apple.

JONATHAN

I didn't know where I was when I woke up. First of all I
thought I was still in France in the tent. I put my hand out,
checking to see if Sebastian was in the sleeping bag next to
mine but my hand didn't touch him. It just waggled around in
the air. That's when I realised where I was, in my bunk bed, in
Dad's flat.

I could hear his voice, he was on the phone, must have
woken me up.

'He's still asleep … quite late when we got back … yeah,
OK, talk to you later, bye.'

Must have been Mum he was talking to.

It was dark in the bedroom, the curtains are very thick and
I could hear rain lashing against the windows. Dad chose the
curtains when he decorated the room for me. He thought I'd
like *Star Wars*, I used to like that when I was younger. He
didn't mind when I put posters up. I thought it was great, it
was my room and I could choose what I wanted in it. That's
what Dad said to me all the time, 'This room's for you, no one
else will stay here.'

I've got some clothes here, pyjamas, jumpers, stuff like
that. I thought I'd like it always to be my room, to stay the
same, no one messing it about, putting my things away,
clearing up. But every time I come now it feels like some sort
of museum. It sounds mad but it sometimes feels as if I've
died and Dad has left the things in here, not moving them, to

keep everything like I left it.

When Mum and I went to Haworth ages ago, before Sebastian was born, we saw where the Bronte sisters lived. Mum's always banging on about their books and we had a trip up there to see their house. It was OK, nothing special. Mum loved it but it was weird to see where people had lived, where they'd left their shoes, their books. Mum was practically whispering the whole time she and I were there. 'Look at those tiny shoes and that's where Charlotte used to sit when she did her writing.' That's what it feels like here, in this room. As if I'd died and Dad doesn't want to change a thing. It's beginning to give me the creeps.

'Jon? Are you awake yet?' Dad was calling me and I got out of bed.

He was in the kitchen drinking coffee and, in the few seconds before he saw me, his face looked crumpled, like an unmade bed. When I stood in front of him, he sat up and smiled: all the lines around his nose and mouth disappeared, they were smoothed out.

'No milk I'm afraid, but I've got bread. That was your mum on the phone.'

'Is she OK? Was everything all right when she got home, the house?'

'Mm, yes I think so.'

I moved around the kitchen getting myself some toast and finding a pot of jam. Last time I stayed overnight, the jam had the most disgusting green mould. At least he'd bought new jam. I was the first one to use it.

Dad put his mug down, 'Your mum wants to go into the hospital first thing. I said we'd go mid-morning, give us time to check Grandad's house, OK with you?'

I could only nod. I had a mouthful of toast and strawberry jam.

I'd never been into Grandad's house before without him being there, it felt very strange. I even put my hand up to ring the doorbell until Dad reminded me that Grandad wasn't there.

It didn't feel right, the two of us going into each room

checking the windows and doors. Dad said that the neighbours had done a good job on the back door.

'Bet that's the first thing the old man asks about,' he said.

The kitchen looked different, I wasn't sure why. It looked as if it was waiting, waiting for Grandad to come home I suppose. I looked at his calendar, every date had something written next to it. For yesterday he'd written: *Feed hanging baskets.* On the day that we were supposed to be coming back from France, he'd written *J home today.*

Everything looked OK to me and Dad asked me to check upstairs when he went to look at the garden. I didn't want to do that but I couldn't tell Dad, he'd think I was being stupid. Going into Grandad's bedroom, well I knew he wouldn't like that; it didn't seem right. I went up the stairs and I watched Dad from the landing window. He was staring at the flowers, pushing his fingers into the hanging baskets, he couldn't see me.

I put my hand on the bedroom door, it was open. I hadn't been in that room since before Grandma died and it felt wrong that I was going in there without asking Grandad first.

I *knew* Dad was outside, I *knew* Grandad was in hospital but still I tiptoed in, hoping the floorboards didn't creak, hoping no one would hear me. There was a funny smell in the room. Not the smell Mum says is in my room, *eau de rancid socks* she calls it. It wasn't like that, it was a musty smell, an old smell.

I checked the windows first, they were all closed. I pulled on the handles and they were fine. I didn't want to touch any of Grandad's things. I was really bothered that he'd notice if something had been moved, but something happened, I couldn't help myself: I opened the wardrobe door. It's a huge thing, dark brown wood with funny handles. They clunked a bit when I touched them and I froze until I remembered Dad was in the garden and, anyway, he'd asked me to check the bedroom.

When the wardrobe door was open, I could see Grandad's shirts and jackets hanging up neatly. I touched his blazer, the shoulders felt soft, empty. Shoe boxes were stacked on the floor of the wardrobe. Grandad's writing was on each one: *Black lace ups, brown suede brogues.*

If someone had told me that they kept their shoes in boxes with hand written labels on them, I'd tell them to get a life, I'd laugh and call them sad. But instead I felt like crying, crying for Grandad. Why? Because he kept his shoes in boxes?

'Jon? Everything all right up there?'

I shut the wardrobe door slowly, trying not to make any noise.

'Yeah, everything's fine. I'm coming down.'

When I got downstairs, Dad was standing by the front door and we locked up, double checking every bolt and went back to the car.

We didn't say much going to the hospital and it was only when we got to the entrance that I thought we should have brought something for Grandad. 'Some fruit or a magazine or something.'

'It's too late now and anyway your grandad would tell me I was wasting my money.' Dad touched me on the shoulder. 'Let me know if I get like him when I'm his age, OK?'

We didn't say anything else until we got to Grandad's ward. As we pushed open the doors, Dad said he wanted to talk to the nurse and he told me to go and see Grandad.

I knew Mum had been in, I could tell by the flowers on Grandad's locker. She often gets it right, no one else would have thought to bring him a bunch that size. They were really big. All the other flowers in the ward looked tiny compared to the ones Grandad had.

He had his eyes shut when I got to his bed. I wasn't even sure he was breathing and I bent down, closer.

'Don't kiss me, lad, I don't know where you've been.'

I did kiss him, though, seemed silly not to.

He opened his eyes and smiled at me.

'How are you feeling, Grandad?' He looked a bit better than he did before although someone else had done his pyjamas up, they were buttoned up wrong. I didn't tell him.

'Not too bad,' Grandad gave me a quick smile. 'I'd rather be home than here. Where's your dad?'

'Talking to the nurse.'

He frowned, 'What about? Your mother did that too, talking to all sorts of people about me.' He shook his head. 'Have you been to the house? Is it OK? Anything broken…?'

'No, everything's fine. Dad and I checked all of it, it's fine.' I sat on the edge of the bed. I was trying hard not to sit on the tubes and things Grandad had, they were everywhere.

'The garden? Did you check the garden?'

He was getting upset, his fingers were plucking at the sheet. 'The baskets need watering every day.'

'Dad checked it, Grandad. We both checked everything.'

He lifted his head again and stared right at me, 'What about the door? The back door? What about that, eh?'

I looked over towards Dad. He was standing next to the nurse, she was smiling at him. I wanted to shout, *Don't start chatting up the nurses, come here, talk to Grandad.*

I edged a bit closer, 'Everything's fine. We've just come from there. Honest, it's all OK. Don't you want to know about the holiday, about France?'

Grandad put his head back on the pillow. I could see the wiry white bristles on his chin. I thought that someone who kept his shoes in labelled boxes wouldn't still have bristles on his chin at 11 o'clock in the morning. Then I felt Dad's hand on my shoulder and he leant over and gave Grandad a kiss on his forehead.

'Hello, Dad how are you?'

Dad settled down on the chair and he picked up Grandad's hand, the one that had been plucking at the sheet and he held it, cradling it in his big hands. 'They tell me you're doing really well and there's a chance that you can get up tomorrow. See how you manage walking a few steps.'

'Hmmm, why can't they tell me? Talking about me all the time. They must think I'm ga-ga.'

Dad kept hold of Grandad's hand. 'Not at all, it's not like that, don't be daft.'

Grandad snatched his hand away, 'So now I'm daft.'

Dad burrowed into his pocket and brought out a handful of change and gave it to me. 'You were right, Jon, we should have brought some newspapers, magazines or something. Can you find the shop, buy a paper?'

I got the message: *Clear off, let me sort this out.*

I found the area where the shops were and I bought newspapers and a gardening magazine. Nothing much else to buy so I got a Crunchie bar for me and some of those white chocolate buttons that Sebastian likes, Dad won't mind. There were loads of people in dressing gowns wandering about: patients with tubes and bags attached to them. Glad I don't have to stay in hospital.

I didn't know what else to do so I went back up to the ward. Dad was sitting on the bed this time, his head very close to Grandad's. Neither of them saw me until I put the papers on the bed.

Dad hadn't seen me coming and he jumped. Grandad had both his arms folded across his chest and he was glaring at Dad. The bristles on his chin seemed to be sticking out, like a porcupine.

Dad stood up and fumbled around in the locker until he found Grandad's glasses; he put them on the pile of newspapers. 'We'll be off now, Dad, don't want to tire you. Think about what I've said, all we want is what's best for you.'

We both gave Grandad a hug then Dad practically marched to the doors. As we walked away, I kept waving to Grandad but he didn't see me, he'd closed his eyes.

I almost had to run to keep up with Dad. 'What's the matter, what did the nurse say?' He wouldn't answer, just shook his head and pounded down the corridors, me chasing after him.

When we reached the car, he kicked the front tyre. 'Shit, shit.'

'What's the matter, Dad? What did the nurse say?'

He unlocked the car and we got in and just sat there staring at the windscreen. Dad took a deep breath and said, 'Your grandad's got advanced osteoporosis, not to mention osteoarthritis and a broken hip.'

That sounded pretty bad. 'What does osteo ... what does it mean?'

'The nurse said that he'll need a lot of care, a lot of help and there are an awful lot of changes to be made.'

'Won't the hip mend, will he be all right?'

Dad looked at me for the first time since we left Grandad. 'Oh yes, the hip will mend, probably be the strongest part of him, now it's been replaced. But the rest of him is falling apart. Poor old sod, this might kill him.'

I don't know why but the shoe boxes came into my head. All the boxes, neatly stacked up, ready for Grandad to wear them again. 'What d'you mean, kill him?'

Dad turned the ignition on, 'The illness won't kill him but the changes in his life might.'

As we drove home, Dad explained to me what the nurse had said: Grandad's osteo-wotsit was so bad that any fall he had could mean that his bones would break and they wouldn't heal. The nurse had told Dad about the things Grandad would need: grab rails, stair lifts, a new shower instead of a bath. All sorts of things to help him.

'Bottom line, Jon, it sounds as if he'll have to move – a bungalow preferably or a warden-controlled place. But either way, he'll need a lot of care. Oh God!' He thumped the steering wheel.

I felt we should be whispering, this was so serious. 'Have you told Grandad?'

Dad gave a horrible laugh. 'Yeah, went down like a lead balloon. He said all the things you'd expect him to say.' He put on a funny voice, trying to sound like Grandad. '*Stuff and nonsense, plenty of life left in me yet. You're not putting me in any special home. Bugger off.*'

We were nearly home and Dad drove the car into my road. 'I'll need to talk to the surgeon apparently but the nurse said they deal with this all the time. There are all sorts of things we can do, a whole range of agencies that might help. She made me feel quite ashamed, ashamed because I didn't know how bad his condition was. But I didn't know, did you?'

We were outside my house and Dad looked at me. I shook

my head then I remembered Grandad getting stuck in our old garden chair. I remembered how I had to pull him up. I'd thought it was because he was old, but it wasn't, it was because he was ill. I felt ashamed then.

I got my stuff, cases and rucksacks out of the car. Dad said he wouldn't come in, 'Got to get to work, all sorts of things to sort out. I'll ring you tonight, OK?'

He drove off even before I got to the front door.

I could hardly open the door, something was behind it. I kept pushing and yelling, 'Mum, Mum, what's going on?'

The door suddenly opened and I almost fell in. There was all this junk in the hall and halfway up the stairs. A big cardboard box full of books, another one with clothes in and all sorts of plants were lined up on the stair treads.

'What are you doing?'

Mum stood in the doorway of the front room. She looked very hot, curls were stuck to her face and I saw tiny rivers of sweat running down her neck. They looked like snail trails.

'Give me a hand, Jon,' she said before going into the front room. When I followed her she was trying to push one of the big armchairs across the room into the bay window. It's a huge chair and it took both of us pushing and shoving before we moved it. Mum stood with her hands on her hips, 'Looks all right there, doesn't it?'

'Why have you moved everything? What's going on?'

'For your grandad, we'll have to put a bed in here. He can't go back to his house, well not for a while.'

'But he's in hospital, why are you doing it now? We've only just come back from holiday. He'll be there for ages ...'

She looked at me for a second; it was as if she was working something out, adding things up or rehearsing something she wanted to say.

Suddenly she smiled at me, 'Right! You're right. Come in the kitchen with me. I want to talk to you.'

The kitchen looked as if a bomb had gone off. Clothes were everywhere, T-shirts, shorts, Sebastian's stuff, Mum's knickers, everything piled up in front of the washing machine. Boxes of stuff we'd bought in France were huddled on every surface. Even I thought it looked messy.

Mum cleared a space on the table and she grabbed a packet of biscuits and got mugs out, all without saying another word.

When the kettle started to boil, Mum nodded at me. 'Sit down, Jon, there's a few things I need to say and we can do it now while Sebastian is asleep.'

I'd sort of forgotten about him and then I remembered the chocolate buttons. I put them on the table and Mum smiled when she saw them. 'Who bought these? You or your dad?'

'I did, only with Dad's money when he was talking to Grandad.'

Mum took a deep breath, 'Has your dad said anything to you about what's wrong with your grandad? Do you know what the problem is?'

I nodded, 'Something about osteo, osteo …'

'Osteoporosis and osteoarthritis. Literally the bones become porous, that's osteoporosis and chronic inflammation of the joints, that's osteoarthritis. It's potentially very serious. Your Grandad must have been in a lot of pain for a long time.'

I didn't like to think about that. 'But why are you moving everything, I don't understand.'

Mum put a hand on my arm. 'The holiday made me do a lot of thinking, Jon, about what I was doing, with my job, with you two boys, about my men!' She pulled a face and took a biscuit. 'I feel so different right now, full of energy. I've got lots of thoughts running through my head, all sorts of ideas about what I want to do.'

Suddenly I remembered the word Gareth had used when he talked about Mum, he'd called her flaky. 'But what about Grandad? What has all that got to do with Grandad?' She wasn't making any sense to me at all.

Mum looked right at me, really staring into my eyes. It was uncomfortable and I tried to look away but she put her other hand up and held my chin. I couldn't move.

'It's not likely that your grandad can go back home for some time, maybe he can never go home. His house will need huge alterations, expensive alterations and his whole life will have to change and I think that it would be best if he came here. He'll need time to get used to the possibility that he might not be able to go home and he'll need help. I can give him that help.' She put her hand down and then she whispered. 'I promised Nancy I'd help him.'

Grandma.

Mum had tears in her eyes and this time it was my turn to touch her. 'Mum, all that stuff you said, about Grandma wanting to leave Grandad, to come here and live with us, what was that all about?'

Mum wiped her eyes with the back of her hand and looked towards the window for a moment. It had started raining and the panes of glass seemed to be wobbling. She took a deep sigh then sat back in her chair. 'When your grandparents got married, Nancy was young, barely in her twenties. You've seen pictures of her when she was young. She was beautiful, she was clever and her head was full of the things she wanted to do. She moved with your grandad into his parents' old house, your great-grandparents' home and she began her married life with the ghosts of her dead in-laws watching her every move.'

As Mum spoke, I knew there was no one else in the kitchen with us: Sebastian was fast asleep upstairs, Dad had gone to work and Grandad was in hospital. I knew all that but it really felt as if Grandma was with us. As if she was moving about, clearing things up, sorting out clothes, putting all our holiday stuff away. I thought I could hear the sound of her slippers on the floor or the rustle of her skirt as she moved around. I had to concentrate really hard on what Mum was saying.

'Your great-grandparents were very cold people; they should never have got married, at least not to each other and they had no idea how to bring up their son, Frank. He was a very repressed young lad and he grew up into a repressed man. Do you know what that means, Jon, repressed?'

I nodded, I didn't really, I could guess but I didn't want Mum to stop talking.

'When he met Nancy your grandad didn't have a clue, not one, about what a good marriage was. He'd been brought up on silences and closed doors, on point scoring between his mum and dad. Your grandmother told me so much about Frank's early years. They were so sad, they must have been awful for him.'

Mum turned to look at the windows; we watched the rain lashing down.

'Your grandmother said to me once that it took a lot of energy trying to fight the ghosts. She said she'd rush through the house opening windows and doors hoping to blow away all the anger that she felt was left inside.' Mum looked at me for a second then she put her head in her hands and closed her eyes. She began telling me about Grandad's early life; she told me about a terrible picnic he'd had once, she told me about how he wasn't supposed to talk during mealtimes, about his mum and dad not speaking to each other for months; the way they slept in separate rooms. As she spoke Mum kept her eyes closed and I wondered if she was trying to *see* Grandma in her head.

'Your grandma made the mistake so many of us make, we feel that our love, our influence, will change the other person, make them more like the people we are, turn them into someone different.'

It was really weird: Mum was speaking softly, the washing machine was thundering away, the rain was lashing down and yet I could hear every single word she said.

'Nancy thought that when your dad was born, she could show Frank how things could be different, how they would make such good parents, their home would be open, no closed doors, no sulking silences, nothing to upset a child. She told me that she thought in some way she could filter her beliefs into Frank, pour her own feelings into him, something like a blood transfusion, she said.'

Mum opened her eyes and looked at me. 'At first it was fine, your grandad loved your dad and he did all he could to ensure that his childhood was a happy one. They had holidays, always in this country; they spent time together, day trips out in the car; everything was normal, as it should be. But Nancy said to me during all that time it felt as if she was walking on

284

something that had been buried. She found herself watching your grandad, waiting for something to go wrong. It was after your dad left home to go to University that things changed.'

'What do you mean? How did things change?' I was trying to picture Grandad and Grandma as young; I'd seen photos of them wearing old-fashioned clothes so I knew what they used to look like, but all I could see was their white hair, their glasses, their *oldness*.

Mum shook her head as if she was trying to shake something from her hair. 'Your grandma thought that with Chris leaving, that would give them new opportunities, new things to try. She desperately wanted to travel but your grandad wouldn't hear of it. He'd been against foreign travel when your dad was small. Such a narrow-minded attitude he had; he'd tell Nancy that if anything went wrong, if any of them fell ill, he'd never trust foreign doctors. She bided her time, she felt that, as time went on, she'd wear him down, make him change. But he didn't, he wouldn't. It wasn't only the travel, he hated it when Nancy wanted to take a few classes at the adult education centre. He kept asking her why she wanted to do something new. She enrolled at a few classes, pottery, French, English literature and every time she came home, she said it felt as if she'd left all her new-found knowledge in the porch. Frank froze her out, refusing even to discuss where she'd been. Not once did she bring anybody home, anyone from her classes. She said she didn't want to subject them to Frank's coldness.' Mum sniffed noisily and wiped her eyes with the back of her hand. 'She broke my heart when she told me all this. She was a natural learner, she took to everything that she was taught. She'd practise her French on me, telling me that sooner or later Frank would change his mind. He never did.'

She looked at me then as if she was waiting for me to say something. I didn't know what to say.

'Did you know that she took a GCSE in French?' she asked me.

I shook my head but I had a picture in my mind of Grandma sitting an exam. She'd have sat at the front and she'd have bought a new pen just for the exam. I knew she'd have done that.

Mum smiled, it was as if she knew what I was thinking, as if she was smiling at Grandma. 'When she got the results Frank wanted to know where she was going to hang her certificate. He said something about knocking holes in the walls. In the end she gave it to me.'

Mum shifted in her chair, 'Do you remember the way your grandma was with other people? How they'd smile at her in the street, how she'd chat to just about anyone she met? We could be in the library or a supermarket and someone would come up just to chat? Do you remember that, Jon?'

I nodded, 'I remember, it used to embarrass me sometimes.'

Mum laughed, 'It used to embarrass your dad and your grandad, but not me.' She looked away again, 'The thing that hurt her the most was Frank's attitude to other people. It was as if he had nothing left over. He'd used everything up for your dad and Grandma.'

The picture of Grandad lying in the hospital bed flashed into my head. 'And me, he's all right with me.'

Mum nodded, 'Yes he is. He loves you but he thinks he needs to look after you as, in his opinion, I can't. The whole row, the ill-feeling between your grandad and me is due to the fact that Nancy used to confide in me. He was jealous, it's as simple as that.'

I remembered the days when Grandma came to see us, the times she took the bus because she said Grandad was using the car. I remembered how Mum and Grandma used to finish each others' sentences and the books they'd talk about for hours sitting here in the kitchen drinking tea.

Mum got up and she pushed her hands through her hair, 'Don't allow anything I've said to change what you feel about your grandparents. Your grandma was one of the best people I've ever known. Your grandfather loved your grandmother and they both loved you. That really is all that matters, right?'

I nodded.

Mum was silent, she seemed to be looking over my

286

shoulder, as if she was trying to see if Grandma was with us. I felt the hairs on the back of my neck tingle.

We stayed in the kitchen for a bit longer, just talking about Grandma, the things she used to do. We finished off the whole packet of biscuits between us. We only stopped when Sebastian woke up.

It took ages sorting out the house. I still wasn't sure why Mum had to do the front room straight away. I mean we don't know what Grandad's going to do. She kept on saying stupid stuff like, 'I feel like a tube of sherbet, fizzing about. Come on, let's do it!'

So we did, we got the front room ready for Grandad. We got the spare bed that's been in my room for ages down the stairs. We even made the bed. When it was all done Mum closed the door in case Sebastian got in there and she said that we didn't need to go in there again until Grandad came home. I can't see that happening.

FRANK

No wonder the NHS is skint. Easy to see where the money goes. It's as hot in here as the tropical gardens Nancy used to like.

Frank sat in the chair by the side of the bed. He'd read the papers twice. Meryl Jefferies had been in the night before with two paperbacks. 'All about the SAS. My Peter says they're brilliant.' Frank asked the nurse to put them in his locker at the back, underneath his clean clothes.

The patient in the bed opposite had stopped all his attempts to talk to Frank and merely nodded towards him when they woke up each morning.

No loss, silly bugger can only talk about football. Knows sod all about gardening.

Everyone said they were pleased with his progress, the physiotherapists said it all the time. 'You're doing really well, Mr Jones.' They walked behind him as he shuffled up and down the ward. 'Well done, you've made tremendous progress.' Frank felt like a child who'd just grasped the rudiments of toilet training. Eight days he'd been in hospital. *Eight bloody days.*

Time dragged for Frank, each day felt heavy, slow. The other patients stayed in the television lounge; he could hear their laughter, uneven bursts of noise from the TV. Frank sat on his own, either in bed or sitting in the vinyl chair reading over and over the same article in his newspaper. The only part of the day that Frank looked forward to was the visiting hour. Chris came in most days although he was spending a lot of time on a new project. 'Up and down the motorway,' he told Frank.

To be fair Nina came in every day bringing in clean clothes, fresh fruit and once she brought in bags of camomile tea. *Camomile – bloody weed.*

Best of all, though, was seeing Jonathan. He brought his photos in and, perched on the side of Frank's bed, he'd explained where each one was taken. Frank was moved by the effort Jonathan had taken. He was a good lad. The second time he came in with his mother, he'd brought in a big balloon, shiny silver and he'd tied the end of it to Frank's bed. Before long Frank's bed looked like all the others: a bowl of fruit, fresh flowers, cards and the balloon moving lazily in the warm air.

Frank sighed, the surgeon had told him what was wrong, how the osteoporosis and arthritis would affect him, what precautions he must take in the future and what it would all mean to his life.

'But I'll be all right, won't I? I mean, this arthritis, it won't kill me, will it?'

Mr Armstrong had been on his way home, he wore jeans and a faded blue polo shirt. He peered over the top of his glasses. 'Frank, arthritis won't kill you and neither, on its own, will osteoporosis but a fall might. Your bones stand a good chance of fracturing if you fall and it's the fall that causes the problems.'

'But I'm a careful man, take things slowly, I never fall, I'm a ...' Frank stared at the surgeon, 'steady man.'

'I'm sure you are but even those of us who take things steadily fall. Frank, I can't force you to do anything, all I can do is suggest, make a few recommendations. The rest is up to you.'

Frank watched as Mr Armstrong had walked away. *Huh, professional man like that, you'd think he could afford a decent suit.* He'd eased back into bed and thought about what Mr Armstrong had said, what it would mean. His garden, he was moved to tears by the worry over his garden. Chris had checked on it, that fussy Meryl woman promised him she'd watered it. Nina and Jonathan had done the same, but it *wasn't* the same.

Nina came in holding a carrier bag; she was on her own. She bent down as if to kiss Frank, he moved his head and asked, 'Where's Jonathan? Not coming in today?'

Nina straightened up, giving him a brief smile. 'No, he's gone off to play football with some boys from school. He'll be in tomorrow though; he sends you his love.'

'And that baby of yours? What have you done with him, then?'

'A neighbour is keeping an eye on him, he's fine.'

She was standing by the side of the bed and she opened the carrier bag, tipping its contents on to the bed.

Frank looked at the Walkman lying on his bed, a packet of batteries and various CDs and gardening magazines.

Nina picked up the Walkman, 'I thought about what I'd miss most if I had to stay in hospital and it would be that I couldn't listen to my favourite programmes or my music. If the CDs are no good, I'll take them home.'

Frank nodded, 'No, they'll be fine and thank you. More use to me than those damn silly books Meryl Jefferies brought in. SAS – the woman's mad!'

Nina settled into a chair and, speaking softly, she asked 'Frank, have you thought any more about coming to live with us, me and Jonathan? I know it's not what you want to do but talking it over with Chris, well, it does seem to be the best solution.'

Frank looked at her, he stared as if she'd been away for a long time and he needed to check if there had been any changes to her face. Taking a deep breath he said, 'I have thought about it, thought about it a lot and, thank you, I'll come and stay.' His tone was gracious and he nodded when Nina said, 'I'm delighted, Frank. We'll take very good care of you.'

'I will be going home eventually, mind. Living with you

290

will only be a temporary thing. You understand that?'

JONATHAN

Grandad's been living in our front room for ages. He came out of hospital in August and now it's almost Christmas.

When he first came home he had to walk with one of those Zimmer things but now he can manage with just one stick. He's not going back to his own house. I thought he'd shit a brick when Dad said that to him. Dad told him that he couldn't go back. 'It's not feasible,' he kept saying to Grandad. Grandad told him to stop talking like an architect. Dad said he couldn't help that, he was one. They had a massive row but in the end Grandad said OK, he understood.

At first when Grandad arrived, Dad would come here almost every day and he circled around Grandad. It was just like watching those big birds we saw in France, those buzzards. They used to fly around for ages, watching for tiny field mice or baby rabbits. Dad's no buzzard but he watched Grandad, waiting to get close, to talk to him.

Dad and Mum were drinking wine one night and I think they'd forgotten that I was in the living room watching TV. I knew they were talking seriously, they kept shushing each other. I turned the telly down and crept towards the door so I could hear better. Dad said 'I still find it hard to believe that Mum would have dared to leave Dad and what's even more peculiar is that she'd stay here, with you.'

Mum was smiling, I could hear it in her voice, 'Well, that's what she wanted.'

'But it would have crucified Dad, it really would have destroyed him.' Dad's voice rose and Mum told him to be quiet.

'She wasn't doing it to hurt him, she simply wanted to do something before it was too late. Before she got too old. She'd no intention of staying here with me for ever, just until she got herself sorted out. She'd thought of going back to work, she'd thought of working with children. She had all sorts of plans, ideas. She talked of all sorts of things, she even thought of writing books for children. She didn't do any of them, she found her lump and that put paid to it all.'

Dad sighed, 'It won't do any good telling Dad, there'd be no point.'

Mum spoke softly, 'I had no intention of telling him.'

Grandad's changed, I mean *really* changed. Some big changes, some little changes. For a start, Mum's not the best cook in the world but she tried very hard, bringing Grandad bowls of his favourite soup, buying different things for his tea. But one day she forgot the soup and just gave him some cheese and salad. I thought he'd go mad but all he said was, 'Probably time for a change.' Unreal.

In the new year Grandad'll go and live in a new bungalow. They've built six of them just across the park, near the primary school. He'll have his own garden, just a tiny one but he can still grow flowers and put his hanging baskets up. And he doesn't have to sell his car, there's a garage too.

We go to his old house every week. I thought he'd hate that, just visiting where he used to live but he's fine about it. He tells me to check the windows and doors and he wanders around the garden. I can hear him, the *thump* as he puts his stick down on the path. He says he can give a lot of plants to the people that live next door, the Jefferies. 'Easy ones, ones they can't kill,' he told me. We've taken some pots home though, they were Grandma's and Mum said she'd like to have them in our garden.

Mum's going to start her new course soon. She says it can all wait until Grandad's settled. She still works in the attic and, first of all, when Grandad moved in, she started to wear trousers and blouses, old clothes that I hadn't seen her wearing for ages. That didn't last and she's back wearing her flip-flops and floaty skirts.

Dad's going to move too, his company are setting up a new office in Telford and he's buying a big flat up there. He says I can stay in the school holidays and help him choose things to go in my room.

Sebastian's just the same. The first time that the district nurse came to see Grandad, Sebastian gave her his potty. She looked a bit surprised and Mum realised why when she saw what was in it. He'd managed to crap in it for the first time.

I think I'd like to be an architect. Dad says the money's good but I don't think I want to end up in Telford. Gareth's coming to stay soon. His mum and dad say they'll bring him over to see me and have a meal with Mum and me. I guess Alice will be with them too.

I still talk to Grandma. I told her when I got an A for my fountain project and I told her why it felt as if she'd moved in with Grandad, staying with him in our front room.

Sometimes when the house is full – Grandad's sitting in the garden, telling Mum how to prune the roses, Sebastian's asleep upstairs and Dad's just arrived for a cup of coffee – Mum looks at me and says, 'We're all here, we're all doing fine, we're just missing Nancy.'

For more information about Accent Press and
to order books online please visit:

www.accentpress.co.uk